BLOODROOT

This Large Print Book carries the
Seal of Approval of N.A.V.H.

BLOODROOT

BILL LOEHFELM

THORNDIKE PRESS

A part of Gale, Cengage Learning

GALE
CENGAGE Learning·

Detroit • New York • San Francisco • New Haven, Conn • Waterville, Maine • London

GALE
CENGAGE Learning™

LIBRARY OF CONGRESS CATALOGING-IN-PUBLICATION DATA

Loehfelm, Bill.
    Bloodroot / by Bill Loehfelm.
      p. cm. — (Thorndike Press large print crime scene)
    ISBN-13: 978-1-4104-2343-6 (alk. paper)
    ISBN-10: 1-4104-2343-3 (alk. paper)
    1. Brothers—Fiction. 2. Large type books. I. Title.
  PS3612.O36B57 2010
  813'.6—dc22   2009041285

Published in 2010 by arrangement with G. P. Putnam's Sons, a member of Penguin Group (USA) Inc.

For my brothers

I taste like the dreams of mad children.
— ANONYMOUS GRAFFITI ON AN
ABANDONED STATEN ISLAND HOSPITAL

ONE

My kid brother swore to me that he could stop his heart.

The morning he said it we sat in my room, cross-legged and face-to-face, practicing for a first-aid test. We were Cub Scouts, me a Bear and Danny, only a year younger than me, was a Wolf at my heels. I was teaching him how to find the jugular, teaching him about arteries and veins and taking someone's pulse.

As I reached for his throat, Danny's heart pounded so hard that I could watch his pulse throb in his neck, could count his heartbeats without touching him. More out of wonder than instruction, I pressed my fingertips to his throat, marveling at the power surging beneath his skin. It comforted me that something so strong and steady lived inside my brother. My heart didn't beat like that. Mine beat quiet, like it didn't want to be found.

He'd learned to still his heart, Danny said, his voice humming against my fingertips, in another life. Special doctors had taught him. He made me swear I believed him and I told him I did. This happened a lot between us. Danny was always telling me things I had to swear I believed. Usually dark things, odd things. Secretly, I blamed his nightmares, the terrible dreams that he woke from screaming. I was never quite sure if playing along helped or hurt but showing faith in him always seemed the right thing to do. He was my brother, my only brother, after all.

I just accepted whatever Danny gave me, whether it was truth, lies, or some combination. Letting Danny be who and whatever he wanted was the best way to hang on to him. That's what I told myself for a long time.

We were inseparable as boys, even as teenagers. Both of us always on the lookout for trouble, though for different reasons. Danny wanted to get into it. I wanted to stay out of it. Danny had a lot more success than I did. Seeing trouble coming never did me a lick of good if Danny was involved. Nothing was worth letting him feel alone. Because that's what he always was in his dreams. Alone.

Then in our twenties the worst trouble we'd ever faced came hurtling down the tracks at us like a freight train. In the end, it broke us apart. It was my fault. I stepped aside only to watch from a safe distance as the Heroin Express blew Danny away.

People tell me letting Danny go was the right decision and I pretend to believe them. I play along with the idea that I let him go when, in reality, he left me. In my heart, I know I should've dragged him from the tracks, or if I couldn't do that, stepped in front of the train. Would it have changed how things turned out? Would it have kept us together? Probably not, but I'll never know because I didn't try hard enough. True, he ran from me. But I could've done a better job of chasing him. I'm his older brother. It was my job to catch him. I know in my head that chasing him onto the tracks would've only destroyed the both of us, but my heart tells me different.

My heart, when it comes to regret, beats as strong as my brother's.

The pieces of him only got smaller over time. My phone calls went unreturned. When I could pin him down, we'd set up meetings somewhere in the city but most of the time he wouldn't show. He refused to tell me where he lived. His cell phone got lost or disconnected and so I lingered at any bar he had named during our brief, stammering conversations. I left messages for him with bartenders and waitresses all across Staten Island, Brooklyn, and Manhattan. They got sick of talking to me and I never got any closer.

Two

Three years ago, I awoke on my thirtieth birthday with no idea where Danny was, if he was alive or dead. I hadn't seen or heard from him in weeks. Hitting a new decade felt like having a door slam closed behind me, leaving Danny on one side and me on the other, neither of us with a key.

Late that afternoon, I sat alone in the dim kitchen of my Staten Island apartment, twirling limp spaghetti on my fork and curling my toes into the dirty linoleum of the kitchen floor. A hot meal at the kitchen table without the television on, with napkins and silverware and liquid from a glass, was my latest attempt to feel civilized. After five years as a college history instructor, I had a career, not just a job. I was now in my thirties and an adult. I wanted to give myself something private to look forward to, other than reading and masturbation.

My evenings had started following the

same pattern: from work to couch to mattress, the final two-thirds of the journey strobe-lit by five hundred flickering TV channels. My birthday was shaping up no different. I had done cake and candles with my folks the night before, afraid to tell them I didn't have big plans for the day itself with friends or a girl. But I didn't have any of that: plans, friends, or a girl. Still, there had to be *something* I hadn't done a billion times. Drinking beer wasn't it. Neither was TV. I'd graded all my students' essays and done my lesson plans. I wanted to do something different, something fun, but I had no ideas.

Defeated, I slid the dead mass of pasta into the trash. I put my face in my hands. Only ninety minutes after getting home from work, on my birthday, I was utterly stupefied with boredom. Then the phone rang.

"It's Danny. What're you doin' tonight?" His voice was hoarse and ragged. He breathed heavily into the phone while he waited for my answer. "Uh, happy birthday, Kevin."

"Thanks," I said. "Long time. Where have you been? You okay?"

"I'm in the neighborhood," Danny said. "I'll be right over to pick you up. Meet me outside in ten. I'll just pull up and you can jump in. We'll go out. For your birthday."

He hung up before I could say anything.

Staring at the phone, I realized he hadn't answered my questions. He rarely ever did. This was our relationship as adults: he came and went and I waited until he came back around again, sometimes clean, sometimes high. I never told him no, never said I'd had enough. Our folks had turned their backs on him some time ago. Tough love, they called it. They recommended I try it, for my sake more than Danny's. I did, but it never stuck. He was my brother. I couldn't get the love out of the way and get a firm grip on the tough part. And Danny knew it.

I reached into the fridge for that beer, telling myself its context had changed. I had cause for a celebration. I'd reached a new beginning, a new year. And no matter how long he ignored me, Danny's return always made me forget the old hurts. He'd been gone even longer than usual this time. Maybe he hadn't been getting high these past few weeks. Maybe this was one of the clean times. Maybe he had changed for good. I could hope, at least. Danny was what I had wished for the night before, as I blew out the candles on my cake.

I carried my beer and a fresh cigarette into

the bedroom. I stripped off my wrinkled work clothes and grabbed my new David Wright jersey, a birthday present to myself, and a clean pair of jeans from the closet. Sitting on the edge of the mattress, I tied on my cracked and battered Docs. I needed a new pair, but the old boots fit so well and felt so comfortable I couldn't bear to part with them. As I buttoned up the jersey in front of the mirror, an invisible finger tapped at my brain, drawing my attention back to Danny's phone call.

There'd been something missing from Danny's voice. It had none of the usual embarrassment when he finally called after another disappearing act. None of the sheepishness I always heard when he called to ask me a favor, one that usually involved the last of my cash. There was no shame in him this time. Why was that? Because he was coming to deliver good news? I tried to focus on the fact that *he* was doing *me* a favor that night. Figured it made us close enough to even for me to ignore what his voice sounded like over a cheap phone. I waited for him on the stoop.

When Danny's blue '84 Escort turned the corner I walked to the curb. He did stop the car, in the middle of the street. Leaning across the front seat, he threw open the pas-

16

senger door. He pulled hard on the steering wheel to right himself. Bottles clinked at my feet as I stepped into the car. Bottles of Nestea Iced Tea. Half a dozen of them, all empty.

"Thirsty?" I asked.

Danny didn't answer. He grinned at me, sweeping sweaty clumps of hair off his pimpled forehead. His ocean blue eyes quivered in their sockets beneath his raised black eyebrows, not focused on me but merely pointed at me.

"How about this," I said. "I got a new Weber. Let's hit the store around the corner, grab a couple steaks, and fire up the grill. Just take it easy and hang out at my place for the night."

After a long moment Danny turned away and without saying a word lurched the car back into motion. I pulled on my seat belt. I wished I'd thought of the steaks while we were on the phone. The idea might've had a chance if I'd gotten Danny out of the car. I shouldn't have agreed to meet him out front. Typically, I was having all my best ideas about handling my brother after we were already doing what he wanted. So I did what I always do, I kept my mouth shut and went along for the ride.

We rambled down Richmond Terrace, rolling lazily through stop signs and braking late for red lights. I nestled down in the seat, arms crossed over my chest. While we idled at a crowded traffic light Danny fished a tiny roach out of his ashtray and lit it up, pinching the paper and embers to his lips. It didn't seem there was enough of anything to even ignite, never mind smoke, but Danny sucked hard. A thin wisp of smoke curled up between his forefinger and thumb. I wouldn't have minded a hit or two but it looked like an awful lot of effort and so little was left the roach would've disintegrated into ashes in the passing. In fact it soon did, Danny absentmindedly wiping the detritus on his jeans.

"Why don't we grab a beer?" I asked. "You talk to anybody else tonight? Anybody going down to the Red Lion?"

Danny's eyes darted around in the car mirrors. I had made a mistake. I had asked too many questions at once. Didn't matter that they weren't very important, or that they were yes or no questions. Or that we'd been drinking at the Red Lion Tavern since we were sixteen.

"What? Where? Okay. No. I don't know. We could call some people, I guess, maybe. You could. You talk to anybody today? Anybody?" He scratched at the inside of his right elbow. "Anybody call you, like, after I did?"

I looked at him across the car. The random fragments of concentration Danny struggled to string together were focused on navigating. He was concentrating so hard, in fact, I was sure our destination was already lost to him.

"Before we hit the bar," I said, "do me a favor and stop by a cash machine."

"Um, okay," he said, his head bobbing up and down. "Wait, no. I mean, I got money. Hey, it's your birthday, forget cash." He wanted to look at me but couldn't pull his eyes off the road. "I got someplace I gotta go first. Sorry, I forgot to tell you."

We rolled to a stop at a red light. He was sweating like crazy now, the armpits and collar of his white T-shirt stained and soaked. He laughed suddenly.

"It'll just take a minute. You won't mind." He grabbed me hard by the shoulder. "Yeah! Then we'll go get that beer." He dragged the back of his hand across his mouth. "Yeah, then we'll play some fuckin' goddamn darts." The light turned green. "God, I love darts. You're pretty good, aren't you? Aren't you on a team or something?"

"Nah," I said. "Not anymore. They only play on weeknights."

He nodded slowly. "School nights. You talk to the 'rents lately?"

"Dad and I went to the Met game a couple weeks ago." I glanced at Danny. "They won." I rubbed my hand over the 5 on my chest. "Got myself a new jersey."

My brother stared straight ahead at nothing. My mouth went dry and I licked my lips. We had the green light but didn't move. The driver behind us leaned hard on his horn. Danny's eyelids fluttered.

"Hey, Danny, let's get going," I said. "Light's green."

"Fuck," he said, snapping awake. We lurched through the intersection. Without warning, he double-parked outside a deli, the engine running. "I'll be right back, wait here. Move the car if you have to."

I smoked a cigarette and watched the traffic in the rearview mirror. One car got stuck behind us, the driver waving his arms wildly till he could slip over into the other lane. I leaned over and hit the horn. I could see Danny in the store, shifting his weight from one foot to the other, stuck at the end of a slow-moving line. I thought about sliding into the driver's seat and making the block but I couldn't be sure Danny would figure out where I'd gone. I considered rooting around the car and figuring out what had

Danny sweating like a marathon runner. I decided against that, though. I already knew the answer. If I didn't find any evidence, I could continue telling myself that I was wrong.

I could tell myself that we weren't going to loop around back toward my house and swing through the Park Hill projects for another score, that we weren't going to end up standing around under the East River Bridge, or sitting on a park bench by some broken-down Sunset Park basketball court in Brooklyn. I could continue to tell myself that Danny's "errand" didn't include any of these places, or any of the things that came with them. I wouldn't have to admit that he'd sounded different on the phone because he'd gotten worse, not better.

Finally, he bounced out of the door with a brown bag in his hands and trotted to the car, turning his head wildly from side to side like a bank robber. He handed me the bag and settled in behind the wheel, muttering to himself. In the bag were four glass bottles of Nestea Iced Tea. We hung a wide right onto Forest Avenue.

"One of those is for you," he said.

I handed him a bottle and took one for myself. He drained half of his in one gulp, dragging his hand across his mouth and sighing when he finished. He squeezed the bottle between his legs.

"Drink up," he said. "That's good shit. The fucking BEST! God, I'm fucking dehydrated lately."

His eyelids fluttered again and I knew the stop at the deli wasn't the errand Danny had in mind. We turned onto Victory Boulevard, where the traffic thinned and streetlights sputtered to life above us. I watched the storefronts and houses give way to the trees of Willowbrook Park.

I touched my knuckles to the cold window and squinted, trying to see through the wall of shadowy trees and into the park. "Shit," I said. "Long time."

Danny said nothing, his eyes focused on the road.

Twenty years earlier, when Danny's new first-aid merit badge still gleamed on his belt, our Cub Scout pack took its first "camping trip" in Willowbrook.

On a Friday after School, with six fathers keeping careful watch, the pack hiked to the cabins in the middle of the park. I would never have guessed that park, or any park on Staten Island, ran deep enough to hide us from the sight of buildings and the sounds of traffic, to let us feel like we had escaped from the rest of the island, but Willowbrook did.

Tall, thin trees knocked bare for the winter and packed tight as if for warmth crowded the narrow trail, sealing us off from the outside world. We'd been studying the American Revolution at school and as we marched I imagined us as George Washington's soldiers on our way to ambush the Redcoats. I kept careful watch through the thicket of gray trunks for any sign of the enemy. Danny declared himself an Indian scout, slipped a broken branch up his sleeve, and announced he'd be taking scalps.

By the time we reached the cabins, the sun had almost set. I couldn't believe that only hours before we'd all been gathered in the mall parking lot, our nervous mothers zipping up our stiff winter coats.

For dinner, we made hot dogs and s'mores in a woodstove fire, telling ghost stories by lantern-light as the marshmallows burned and the chocolate melted. We complained through it all, about the hike, the dark, the cold, too cool to admit we were enjoying ourselves. That we were actually having an adventure while safely nestled deep in the heart of Staten Island.

Hours after we went to bed, Timmy Mahoney's dad scared the shit out of Danny and me when he rapped on the ice-misted window by our bunks, one arm hidden inside his coat, the other cradling an ax. Our screaming woke the whole pack. We all piled on Mr. Mahoney when he came through the door, laughing. Danny took Mahoney's scalp and fell peacefully asleep long before I did.

A foot of white, powdery snow covered the ground when we woke up. Danny and I hiked for what felt like miles, yesterday's fantasies gone from our minds. We'd discovered something real, animal tracks in the snow, and we followed them all afternoon, right to where they ended at the foot of a tall, gray oak in a patch of wet, black dirt, ragged-edged with pink snow. We stood over the stain, watching each other breathing in white puffs. Whatever we were stalking, something else had found it first.

After a few morbid moments Danny said in a whisper that perhaps the animal we followed had been the hunter and not the hunted after all. I was happy to believe him. We tucked our *Field Guides to Animal Tracks* back into our parkas and retraced our own tracks back to the cabin.

Now, so much older and as far apart as that snowy cabin and the dead end of those tracks, my brother and I traced the edge of the park in Danny's car, sucking dead leaves off the shoulder and pinwheeling them over the double-yellow line unwinding behind us. Danny tossed an empty bottle onto the floor at my feet. I flicked my cigarette butt out the window as we turned onto Todt Hill Road.

Danny's car struggled up the narrow, twisting lane. The wide sidewalks of Victory Boulevard disappeared. Old oaks lined the sides of the street, bulging against dented guardrails at the sharpest turns. High above, the twisted boughs stretched over the road, enclosing us. As we neared the top of Todt Hill the mansions appeared, the newer homes set right up against the road and the older ones hidden far back in the trees. Todt Hill was the only seriously, filthy *rich* neighborhood on the island, a tight, exclusive community of politicians, athletes, Mafiosi, and various combinations of the three. At the top of the hill Danny pulled over onto a shallow patch of shoulder. I wondered why we had stopped. I'd figured he needed to take a leak after all that tea but he hadn't moved. He stared at me across the car like he couldn't remember who I was.

"So," I said.

"I gotta do something real quick," Danny

said. "Then we'll hit the bar."

He fell across my lap and popped open the glove compartment. It was nearly empty: on top of the car registration sat an unopened pack of rolling papers and a hard case for eyeglasses. Danny grabbed the case, slammed shut the glove box and lurched upright in his seat. Leaning forward, he held the case in his lap with one hand and reached under his seat with the other. He produced a short length of yellowing rubber tube. I tried looking anywhere but at him, watching half a dozen caterers in a driveway a few houses up the road. They were unloading covered silver trays from a van. A skinny guy in white coveralls hopped out of the van clutching a huge bouquet of foil balloons emblazoned with birthday cakes, teddy bears, and a number I couldn't read.

"How nice, a sweet sixteen," Danny said, not at all cynical but like a neighbor who had noticed the party while taking in the mail. "You gonna head out to Shea again this season?"

"Probably in a couple weeks." I lit a cigarette, the flame from the lighter trembling at its tip. "I could get three tickets next time." I waited. Nothing. "Maybe not the best seats, but pretty good."

Danny chuckled. "Ah, what's the point?

All they do is lose in the end. Been losin' my whole life, yours, too. Pay all those tolls, pay for parking, ticket prices go up, beer prices go up, for what? Bunch of fucking losers." He looked me up and down. "That's a sweet jersey, though."

"They're the hometown team," I said. "I've been pulling for them my whole life. I don't know how not to."

I watched him. He had the case open in his lap, a bent and blackened spoon on his thigh. He stuck the tubing between his teeth. A hypodermic needle and several tiny bundles of foil waited inside the case. With deft, insectile movements Danny opened one of the bundles and sat it in the bowl of the spoon. He tied off the tubing around his biceps, pulling it tight with one end in his mouth. I watched his fist open and close, open and close, a beating heart straining to inflate his flattened veins.

I suppose I could've said something then. Made some bold statement about how if he wanted to stick a needle in his arm he could do it without me. About how I wouldn't be complicit in his suicide by degrees. About how he could shoot fucking heroin on his own fucking time. But where was that righteousness when I got in the car? When I agreed to meet him outside my house? I knew he was high and what he was high on when I hung up the phone. I dragged on my cigarette and blew the smoke out my nose. Righteousness. Even that was bullshit. What I was feeling was fear. Stomach-burning, palm-dampening fear.

I'd seen Danny high more times than I could remember, more often than I was willing to admit. I'd just never seen him do it, do *this* before. It terrified me, plain and simple. The whole, cheap ritual. The sudden efficiency of his small, careful movements, as if he were threading needles, after sitting beside him while he could barely drive. The hiss of the heroin as it percolated in the spoon, the heavy odor of incense that filled the car. The way he flicked the body of the needle like a soap opera doctor, the way he held it before his face like a priest raising the chalice at Mass.

When he rested his arm on his thigh I saw the ragged black scabs, pink with infection around the edges, dotting the inside of his elbow. Danny slid the needle into a vein. He pushed down the plunger, sucked in his breath through his teeth. I turned away and I drew on my cigarette, watching our blurry reflections in the filthy window of the car.

Danny shuddered once and released a long sigh, packing up his works and stashing them under his seat. He reached for the brown bag at my feet. He uncapped the bottle of tea, lifted it to his mouth and drank it down. Sighing again, he went still. Then he rolled down his window and vomited the entire bottle of tea all over the outside of his car. He cranked the window back up and dragged the back of his hand across his mouth.

"Damn," he said. "That really shouldn't still happen as often as it does." He reached for another bottle but didn't open it. "Shit dehydrates me. You mind driving for a while?"

We switched places. Danny waved to the caterers as we drove past. In the rearview mirror I watched them watch us as we crested the hill. It was only then that other fears, fears I should've felt back on the shoulder, came to mind. Cops. Jail. Explaining to my department chair what I was doing in a car full of narcotics, with a brother full of narcotics, in the island's most exclusive neighborhood.

I could see myself in his office, trying to tell him with a straight face, "Well, Dean Whitestone, sir, I was the designated driver." I laughed at that as Danny scanned through stations on the radio. It was funny because it was true. I was the designated driver. That was why Danny had called me in the first place. So he could still get around when he got too high to drive.

When Danny switched off the radio and told me he had an appointment, one he had to keep before we got that beer, I laughed again. Errands and appointments. I was the chauffeur all right. Happy fucking birthday. At the foot of Todt Hill we headed south.

Right before the intersection of Amboy and Richmond, Danny directed us into the Waldbaum's parking lot. More tea, I figured. Or maybe, hopefully, something for his breath. I turned to park in front of the store but Danny pointed off to the side.

Half a dozen teenaged boys, all sporting buzz cuts and baggy clothes, milled around by the train tracks behind the store. One of them eased out of the pack, walked over, and leaned against Danny's side of the car. He waited, staring at me while Danny rolled the window down.

"Who's he?" the boy asked. A bejeweled watch, way too large for his skinny arm, dangled from his wrist.

"My brother," Danny said. "He's good."

I stared straight ahead, my hands at ten and two on the steering wheel, like a cop and not a drug dealer was leaning in the window. The other boys shuffled their feet

30

and watched the car. I wanted to say something cool and cynical, but I kept my mouth shut. I wanted a cigarette but I didn't want to reach inside my jacket. I seethed at being frozen by the stare of a kid too young to enroll at the college where I teach.

"Dust," Danny said, holding a hundred-dollar bill between his fingers.

The boy took the bill and dropped something into the car.

"All I got right now, I'll bring more to the party," the boy said. "Word's out." He smiled. Perfect teeth. "Every motherfucker in the city's been through here for this shit."

Danny nodded. "Best shit in the city. By far. No doubt."

Best shit in the city. Sold by fourteen-year-olds stalking a busy parking lot in my parents' neighborhood. The same parents nagging me to move out of the "bad neighborhood" I lived in. I wasn't offended or frightened. None of these kids was gonna mug my mother when she went grocery shopping. It was beneath them. Shit, she was probably safer with them around. I just felt stupid. Stupid because when we turned into the parking lot I figured they were sneaking cigarettes before sneaking into the R-rated movie across the street. Stupid because they had me pegged for lost and afraid the instant they saw me behind the wheel. Stupid because I was still trying not to believe they were what they were — miniature drug dealers wearing five-hundred-dollar watches who had no interest in merit badges, camping trips, or baseball teams.

Another boy, a carbon copy of the first, approached the car. Danny slipped out of his seat and the new boy climbed without a word into the back of the car.

"See ya at Al's house," Danny said, returning to the passenger seat.

The first boy nodded and backed away, snapping his gum, pulling the brim of his ball cap low over his eyes. When he raised his hands to his cap, his watch slid halfway to his elbow.

Danny turned to me. "You should come to this party, Kev. Al would bust his ass seeing you there."

"Al who?"

"Fucking Al Bruno, bro," Danny said. "From high school."

"You still hang with him?" I asked. "I thought he went to jail."

"Now and then," Danny said, shrugging. He laughed. "Now and then we hang out. Now and then he goes to jail. Anyways, he's out right now. His folks moved to Florida, left him in that big house by himself. Still throws good parties. He likes the company." Danny turned around. "Tommy, this is my brother, Kevin."

Tommy leaned forward. "You know Al, Mr. Driver-Man?"

"I did," I said. I started the car. "Long time ago."

"That's funny," Tommy said, settling again into the backseat. "You don't seem like the type."

Danny chuckled. "Like the man said, it was a long time ago." He slapped my shoulder with the back of his hand. "Whadda you say we roll?"

I cut a tight U-turn and pulled back onto Amboy Road, heading north at Danny's suggestion. In the rearview, I watched Tommy roll a joint in his lap. Danny handed back the package and Tommy sprinkled the joint with angel dust. He finished his roll with a lick and flourish and passed the joint forward. Danny took it and tucked it behind his ear.

"I could use a beer," I said.

Danny rolled his eyes at the backseat. When I shrugged, he did it again. I finally got it. Our passenger was too young to get into the bar.

"Tommy lives by you, on the way to the

33

Red Lion," Danny said. "Mind givin' him a ride home?"

I almost laughed. My apartment was twice as far away as the bar. "No problem."

"Get on the expressway, it's quicker," Tommy said, leaning forward between us, his hands between his knees. "My mom goes apeshit if I'm not there when she gets home from work. We gonna smoke that shit?" he asked Danny, "or you just gonna wear it all night?"

Danny pulled the joint from behind his ear and stuck it in his mouth. He lit up and took a deep drag, cracking open the window as he held the smoke. He released a long, slow exhale. We left a thin trail of smoke rising behind us into the glow of the streetlights as we ascended the entrance ramp.

Leaning heavy on the gas pedal, I forced the car up to sixty-five, a shade over the limit. We still moved slower than the three lanes of traffic zipping by on our left. Danny handed the joint over his shoulder. Tommy pinched it between his forefinger and his thumb but instead of smoking it, he reached it over my right shoulder.

"G'head, Wheelman," he said, "it's all you."

I shook my head. "No thanks, I gotta drive. I need to make it an early night, anyway." Like I needed a full set of excuses to not smoke angel dust with this kid. Tommy snorted in disbelief and reached the joint farther forward.

Danny snatched the joint with a giggle, drew on it again and passed it back to Tommy.

"Dude here is a responsible ah-dhult," Danny said, the streetlights strobing his grinning face as he spoke. "Got a real job and everything."

I glanced at Danny, praying he wasn't going to tell this kid what I did for a living. He patted my shoulder and nodded at me, as if to tell me he knew what I was thinking and that my dirty little secret was safe with him.

"You still seeing that girl?" Danny asked me.

"Kelsey? I never was."

"Was that her name? The one you met at the Dock?"

"Andrea?" I said. "Shit, I told you, I haven't talked to her in months."

"What happened, man? I thought she was into you."

"I thought so, too," I said. "But she disappeared. Stood me up once, stopped returning my calls."

"Shame," Danny said. "She was pretty

fucking hot."

"You tap it, at least?" Tommy asked.

" 'Scuse me?" I said.

Tommy leaned forward. "You know, tap it, hit it, bang it, nail it?"

Danny laughed into his fist.

"No, I didn't," I said, immediately hating myself for even answering.

Tommy laughed. "And you wonder why she bailed on you." He laughed again. "You got her number?"

I snapped around in my seat, surprised to find Tommy's face only inches from mine. "Somebody know you, Slick?"

"What's this guy's problem?" Tommy asked, talking to Danny but looking at me. "I'm just asking a question here." He turned to Danny. "Where'd you pick up this jerk-off?"

Danny twisted in his seat until he was nose to nose with Tommy. "I fucking told you, he's my brother. Lay the fuck off." He held the joint under Tommy's eye. "You want this or not?"

Tommy took the joint and settled into the backseat.

Danny rolled his head, cracking his neck. "Wait a minute. Then who's fuckin' Kelsey?"

"Prob'ly not Wheelman," Tommy chirped.

I ignored the joke. "Kelsey's that girl from work."

"Doesn't ring a bell," Danny said. "You're dating her?"

"No, but I know I told you about her," I said. "She's the new early European teacher."

"What's wrong with American girls?" Tommy asked.

Danny laughed again. "Jesus Christ. Just smoke your shit, tough guy."

I decided to drop the subject. I had no real point to make. Kelsey was just a co-worker; we weren't dating. And even if we were, Danny wouldn't remember it anyway.

In the rearview, I saw Tommy gazing out the window, the joint burning in one hand, shadowy smoke curling slowly from his nostrils. I wondered where the hell Danny had picked him up. He put the joint to his lips again. He had already forgotten all about me. A pair of headlights grew large in the rearview and I watched an old yellow Camaro whip around us to the left and thunder away, its taillights a pair of red eyes fading into the darkness. Silently, Tommy passed the joint forward again. When Danny didn't take it, Tommy nudged his shoulder. One at a time Danny's eyelids popped open. He studied the joint for a long moment, as if trying to remember what it was. He took it and held it to his lips. The ember brightened and lit his face. I glanced down at the speedometer. I could hear the crackle of the burning paper as Danny inhaled again.

It was then that the unmistakable ruby red flash of a police cruiser filled the car. My palms went wet on the wheel. My mouth filled with the taste of pennies. We were a mile from my house. One more exit. In the mirrors, the lights were blinding. Blinking at the spots dancing before my eyes, I lifted my foot off the pedal and tried to refocus on the road. The cop hit his sirens, swung out to our left and blew past us. I coughed out more air than I thought my lungs could hold. The Camaro.

"Good Christ!" Danny screamed, lurching forward in his seat. "I love this country!" He pounded the dashboard with his fist. "God bless America! Everyone in this car is guilty of at least one drug-related felony and he's nailing someone for fucking *speeding*. I love this FUCKING country."

He laughed like the Mad Hatter, leaning out the window as we passed the cop car pulled over on the shoulder with the Camaro sitting in front of him. Danny fell back in his seat, his hair wild from the wind. "That pig just missed the biggest bust of his career. So much for detective." He fell forward. "Where's my fuckin' tea?"

I lit a cigarette. I asked Danny for a bottle of tea. I needed something, anything, to wash the taste of fear from my mouth. I felt like I'd been puking bleach. Danny was right. The moment that cop landed on our bumper, badged, armed, and full of justice, we were transformed from three bored guys in a shitty blue Escort into a carful of felons. Under those awful misery lights, a blank, empty Tuesday night became ten years in jail — hard penance for the common sin of boredom. I knew my future was what I had felt burn up and flush through my stomach, flush through my seat and pour out along the highway, a trail of ashes blowing over the asphalt. But as quickly as we had been incinerated in those lights, maybe even before the panic had finished fully gutting me, harmless anonymity washed over us and the empty night again unfolded its wings.

When Danny had yelled out the window at the cop, part of me wanted to put my foot in his ass and push him the rest of the way out. But another part of me hummed with the same thrill, the charge of having gotten away with it all, of narrow escape, of having the end of everything pass me by, even if it was never after me to begin with.

But like the panic, the thrill didn't last.

We eased off the expressway at the Richmond Terrace exit, my exit, the last one. My eyes burned from the pot smoke and from the exhausting, post-adrenaline crash. Tommy suddenly remembered our destination and spouted out directions. We dropped him in front of his house, a small, gray-shingled place with a long front walk. A dog barked inside the house when he swung open the front gate.

Danny said something to me about playing darts, about the party at Al's. I ignored him, just piloting the car through the narrow streets of my neighborhood. Danny eventually went silent, scratching his fingernails at the inside of his elbows. It was only when we settled to a stop in front of my house that Danny realized where I was taking us. He looked at me as I unfastened my seat belt.

"Fuck Al Bruno, huh?" he asked.

"I'm beat. I gotta get up early. I go to Al's, I'll be there all night."

Danny and I got out of the car and we crossed paths in the headlights. He shook my hand. His eyes danced. He wasn't twitching yet, but I could feel the itch building in him through his palm.

"All right, man," he said. "Happy birthday.

It was good to fucking see you again. We oughta hang again soon. Maybe catch a game."

I backed away from him toward the curb. "Yeah, it was cool."

He nodded at me. "I'll call you."

I started to say something, maybe please, or maybe don't, but Danny was sliding into his car, in his mind already parked on the first dark street he could find. Standing on my stoop, I watched him get situated in the car. He gave a last wave, pulled away from the curb, made a wide turn around the corner, and was gone.

THREE

I spent the next three years after that night trying to lock the door between us. I didn't see or hear from Danny at all during that time. I didn't try to forget him; that was impossible. But I tried to stop hoping, on my birthday and on his, at Christmastime, anytime I saw a little blue car drive by, that he would walk out of the ether and back into my life. I tried convincing myself that those hours in the car were the last we'd ever spend together and that somehow, some way, we'd had a simple, good time. That it was a normal and amicable parting.

We were like brothers, I told myself, who lived in different countries, separated only by busy lives and thousands of miles. But Danny haunted me. I should've known that he would. I'd always believed his lies more easily than I believed my own.

During the years he was gone, rumors about him trickled under my door like the shadows of passersby. I heard he was clean, and I tried not to hope. I heard that he was alive but rotting from the inside out in a Brooklyn shooting gallery. I heard more than once that he'd died: suicide, murder, OD. When I heard these things, I tried not to despair. When I visited our parents, I told them nothing. I refused to believe anything about him. I couldn't picture any scenario the rumors described. I had a hard time, in fact, picturing him any way at all. I couldn't see his life beyond that night in the car.

In my imagination, Danny's life seemed to stop after his car turned the corner. I hoped it was a failure on my part to let go of him and not that, in my heart somewhere, I knew he had no future. I felt as if that Escort had dropped off the edge of the Earth. Or maybe I just felt Danny had left my life like he had come into it that night, high, lonely, and desperate, lost in some eternal present where the night never ended and tomorrow never came. It seemed, in the depths of his addiction, that the never-ending night was what he both wanted and feared the most.

Then, one warm October night, three years and six months after I last saw him, I walked out of that same apartment building and there he stood on the sidewalk. He seemed shocked to see me. We were both shocked.

He pointed at the intercom beside me. "There are no names. I couldn't remember which apartment was yours."

"Three years," I said. "It's a long time to remember your brother's address. You also forgot the phone number. Mom and Dad's, too?"

He looked so different from the last time I'd seen him. No longer bloated and pimpled from heroin, no longer pale from the nocturnal, nomadic existence it commanded, he looked to me like he always should have. Like a six-foot, deep-chested, wide-shouldered version of the tough, funny, Irish kid I knew when we were boys. He looked like a fit and sturdy young man. Clean and well fed, rested, happy.

Danny wore a black suit jacket over a dark green T-shirt, a new pair of jeans and black motorcycle boots. Gone was the white T-shirt stained with blood, vomit, and iced tea. Gone were the dirty jeans with the black scorch marks from his spoons. His brown hair was no longer sweaty and filthy, clinging in clumps to his forehead. It was cut short and clean, parted in the middle and gelled at the sides. His blue eyes were clear. He looked healthier than I had ever seen him.

My relief at seeing him alive and breathing nearly knocked me on my ass. Seeing him looking that good made me ecstatic. I wanted to leap down the stairs and crush him in a hug, but I held back. I couldn't make it too easy for him. Easy had never done Danny any good, and I wanted to hang on to my pride for a few more seconds. I looked up and down the block, but there was no sign of the Escort.

He looked up the stairs at me from his spot on the sidewalk. "I owe you a beer."

It took me a minute to recall what he was referring to; I was surprised he remembered anything about that night. "You owe me more than that."

"I know, Kev," Danny said. He opened his arms. "That's what I'm here to talk about. I got a lot to make up for. I'm back and I'm staying this time."

"I've heard that before," I said. "It's gonna be a long walk home."

Danny stood his ground, arms still spread. "Then let's get started. You lead." I didn't move; my brother didn't, either. He swallowed hard. "Say the word and I'm outta here. Believe me, I wouldn't blame you."

"Three years is a long goddamn time," I said.

"Would it do any good," Danny asked, "to make it longer?"

I took a deep breath. He had a point. I could keep talking, I figured, or I could do the right thing. I walked down the stairs and into his arms. Fuck pride. And history. This was my brother back from the dead. He had always been my breaking point. Even as kids, he asked and I gave. That's just how it was. Maybe he had changed over the past three years. I hadn't.

He squeezed me hard, lifted me a few inches off the ground. "You are the fucking man. Thank you. I mean it, Kev. I'm off the shit and back for good."

I stepped back after he released me. "I can see that you're clean. As for the rest of it, let's start with that beer and go from there."

"Good enough for me," Danny said, waving his hand in the air. "I won't even ask you to drive."

Headlights popped on down the street. The car, a black late-model Charger with deeply tinted windows, stopped in front of us. It gleamed and purred, immaculate, under the streetlight. Silently, the driver's-side window rolled down. I stepped to the car.

"You remember Al Bruno," Danny said.

"From back in the day."

I did, though he'd lost quite a bit of his hair. What remained was cut short, revealing a prominent widow's peak. In the blue lights of the dashboard, in his black clothes, Al looked vaguely vampiric. He stuck out his hand across his chest, not turning to look at me.

"How you been, Kev?" he asked, nearly crushing my hand when he shook it. Al had been hitting the weights, either at the gym or at the jailhouse.

"Can't complain. I'm still teaching, over at the college."

"Noble," Al said, sliding a medallion back and forth along the gold chain around his neck.

"What're you doing these days?" I asked. Parole? Probation? Hardly anything noble, I figured. Definitely not community service.

Al turned to look at me. "Little of this, little of that. I got a few things workin'."

Those few things working probably wore pricey watches and hung around supermarket parking lots. Danny's choice of companions wasn't doing much for my faith in him.

Danny slapped me on the back. "New, different things," he said. "Right, Al?"

"You gotta change with the times," Al said.

"Okay then, this is cool and all," Danny said, "but wouldn't it be more fun over a beer?"

"Danny," I said, "talk to me a minute." I took a few steps away from the car. Danny stayed put. "Over here."

"I know what you're gonna say," Danny said, "and I don't blame you. But it's all good. Al and I went through rehab together. The old days are behind us, Kev."

Al said nothing, just took a toothpick from behind his ear and put it in his mouth, his same old junior gangster act.

Danny opened the back door for me. "Hop in. One beer. Let me pay you back that much."

I got in the car and Danny climbed in the passenger seat. Al rolled up his window and pulled the car into the street, spinning his tires on the pavement, kicking up a screech and a cloud of smoke as if he needed to announce his departure to the block.

Squeezing between the front seats, I asked Danny where he'd been the past three years. He held up his hand, telling me it was not the time for questions. I thought maybe he didn't want Al hearing what he told me. Maybe he couldn't hear me over Kid Rock. But he smiled as he watched the island fly by out the window and I thought maybe he was just enjoying the reunion. He and I in a car again, heading out after dark, this time with a chance to make things right. I had to admit, I liked the feeling, too.

Al eased the Charger up to the curb outside the Red Lion, the emerald neon of the bar's Budweiser shamrock washing over the car's gleaming black hood, gutter gravel crunching under the fat tires. He kept the engine running. Danny turned in his seat.

"I mean, this was the original plan, right?"

"Works for me," I said.

We hadn't even discussed where we were going; Danny had no doubt planned the whole thing. Danny and I climbed out, careful not to catch the door on the high curb. Al stayed in the front seat, his cell phone open in his right hand, the neon striping his lap. He was reading a text message, brows knit, bottom lip puffed out.

"Al, you coming in?" I asked, walking around the front of the car to his window.

He snapped shut the phone, thinking hard about whatever he'd read. "Nah. I got a girl I gotta go see. I'll catch up."

"Thanks for the ride," I said.

Al put the car into drive, nearly running over my feet as he pulled away. Danny stood outside the pub.

"Used to be," I said, walking over to him, "you couldn't shut that kid up."

"That girl's got him on a short leash," Danny said. "Anyway, Al never could hold more than one idea in his head at a time. A girl takes up all the room he has. How about that beer?"

He grabbed the brass door handle and pulled. Blurry conversations muddled under Shane McGowan's singing drifted past us and over the street. "I've been looking forward to this for a long time."

I threw a soft elbow into Danny's midsection as I passed him. He pretended it hurt.

Inside, the voices and the music got louder. Flushed, heavy-lidded faces rotated in our direction, their mouths still talking in the other direction. Danny pointed out a booth in a back corner, then went to the bar for drinks. I slipped through several sets of hard shoulders and dropped into the booth, sliding into the corner. Waiting for Danny, I picked at the old cigarette burns in the green plastic of the bench and watched the door, hoping our folks would walk in. It was a foolish thought, founded on nothing. I'd been here with Dad a couple times, but Danny had never been with us. Dad and I had talked about him here, though. Maybe that was it.

What was the rush? If Danny really was on the mend, we'd have our reunion eventually. If Danny had kicked junk for good, there was no longer a time bomb ticking underneath our family. Then I thought of our mother. The bomb ticked on, just with someone else holding it now. And there was no defusing Alzheimer's; it didn't matter what wire you clipped. There was no kicking it, either.

Danny set a draft Guinness in front of me and sat on the other side of the booth. All he'd gotten for himself was a tall club soda with lime. I decided to hold back on the news about Mom, at least for the night. I didn't want Danny and me starting over with the taste of bad news in our mouths.

"Totally clean and sober?" I asked.

"I haven't done heroin in over a year," he said. "Nothing else, either, no weed, no pills, no coke, no nothing."

I turned the pint glass round and round on the table. I should've asked for a Coke. "I'm waiting for it to settle."

"Go ahead," Danny said. "No worries."

"You sure? I don't want to fuck anything up."

"Nobody can fuck me up but me," Danny said. He sucked down half his soda water. "I have a few drinks now and then, but nothing more than that." He tilted back the glass, sliding some ice into his mouth. "I'm not supposed to, technically, but considering where I've been, I figure I'm doing pretty well."

I drank my beer, licking the foam off my top lip. "Where *have* you been?"

"No place that matters, but lots of places, I guess," Danny said. "Nowhere I wanna go back to."

"How'd you get back here then?" I asked. "From wherever you were."

"I got a ride," Danny said.

"C'mon, Danny, not to my house, not *here* here. You know what I mean."

"I got a ride." He stabbed at the ice in his glass with his straw. "Ambulance."

I sat and waited, my stomach going sour, my beer getting warmer by the minute.

"I died in Manhattan," Danny said. "That was the beginning of the end, so to speak."

I leaned back against the bench. My hands fell into my lap, nearly pulling the Guinness into it with them. "You died? In Manhattan?"

This is it, I thought. This is when the worms burst out of Danny's eyes and the alarm goes off and I wake up sprawled across the mattress at home, exhausted, depressed, and defeated before the day even started.

"So you're dead," I said. "And none of this is really happening."

"What?" Danny reached for my Guinness, sniffing it, sipping it, then handing it back to me. "You find an old stash of mine or something? No, I'm not dead."

Danny rocked his head from shoulder to shoulder, assembling the story.

"In Manhattan," Danny said. "About a year after I last saw you, I died under the East River Bridge. OD. Got brought back in the ER."

"What the fuck were you doing under the bridge?"

"Living, I think," Danny said. "I'd been there awhile; I don't know how long. A week? Maybe more." He ate more ice. "It's a big junkie hangout over there. It's where I ended up. Junkies are like carnival freaks. Or cops. Or crooks. We prefer our own kind. Anyway, one night my appetite got too big for my heart. So my heart stopped. Or maybe I got a bad shot. Either way, the result was the same."

"How'd you get outta there?"

"Some guy with a stolen cell called nine-one-one. Then he threw the cell in the river and split." He grinned, shaking his head.

"But not before they took my stash, my works, my wallet, and my shoes. That's how the EMTs found me, anyway. Stone dead and stripped clean. I suppose I coulda lost my wallet and shoes long before then."

Danny stretched his arms across the back of the bench and puffed out his chest, watching a pair of giggling, whispering girls walk by. He was breathing hard, as if telling the story took the wind out of him. In the dim light of the bar, I couldn't read his eyes.

"Bumps in the bathroom," he said. "I remember it well."

I did, too. The two of us jammed into a filthy stall in another bar. Another life.

My hands went sweaty. "Jesus fucking Christ, Danny."

"Not where I was," he said. "I didn't see Him, no host of angels, no blinding light, nothing. The EMTs brought me back but they lost me again as they loaded me off. I got brought back for good in the emergency room." He fished the lime from his glass and popped it in his mouth, chewing it without so much as a wince. "I remember noticing I was sitting in piss and pigeon shit while I stuck the needle in, then *bam,* these thick glasses and this big nose right in my face. I don't know who was more surprised when my eyes popped open, me or the doc.

I puked all over both of us.

"That's about all I remember, his goofy fucking face. That and this weird snap in my spine, like a running dog hitting the end of his leash." He shrugged. "Then I wondered where my stash was and when I could shoot up again."

"Did you?"

"I never got the chance. I spent some time in ICU and then got moved to the detox ward. I can't remember how long I was anywhere. It beat detoxing at the folks' house, but it still wasn't no picnic. Better drugs and worse food."

"But you went back. To the heroin."

"Yeah, I went back. Not to the bridge, thank God, but to the drugs, yeah. I felt so fucking good when I got out of the hospital. What better to do than get high? So I did a few snorts with an ambulance driver three blocks from the emergency room. God bless America, huh? I didn't pick up a needle again for six months. Dying was a fresh start. I was back at the beginning and could do it right this time."

"You gotta be kidding me," I said. "You died twice in one night and all you thought was that you'd figured out heroin?"

"I came back from the dead twice, is how I looked at it. Bit of an ego trip. Look, I'm a junkie, that's how we think. I'm not sayin' it makes any sense."

He tapped his empty glass on the tabletop. He wouldn't look at me.

"I'm sorry I jumped your shit," I said. "It's just that the logic is hard to follow. In fact, the whole story is a lot to take."

"No shit," Danny said. "Listen, if I was bullshitting you, wouldn't I come up with something a little more glamorous? Sit through one NA meeting and you'll hear ten stories a lot more far-out than mine."

I thought about it. Who was I to call bullshit on Danny's story? The conversation had certainly moved beyond the realm of my expertise. And what did it matter whether or not he'd told the whole truth? That Danny lived and breathed in front of me, physically healthier than I had ever seen him, was more important than how he'd gotten there.

"Okay," I said. "So you went to rehab."

"I did."

He still wouldn't look at me; he just stared down through his empty glass, through the table, focusing on something only he could see.

"So rehab worked," I said. "Finally."

"Seems like it," Danny said. "Who knows what was different this time? I got busted copping from an undercover in Sunset Park. I gave up a guy selling guns and got rehab instead of jail."

"Good for you," I said.

"Maybe. Anyway, I never bought that Higher Power shit they put on you in those places, especially not after dying, and those meetings are one long misery trip, but I met some people I liked in there. Guys that reminded me of you. They made quitting seem worth it." He reached for my half-empty glass. "Let me get us a fresh round." Halfway to the bar, he turned around and came back. "Thanks for listening, for being here. And if anybody has a right to jump my shit, it's you."

He didn't wait for me to respond; he just headed back to the bar. It was just as well. I don't know what I would've said. I was grateful for the break in the conversation. Danny returned holding a Guinness in each hand.

"This cool with you?" he asked, sitting.

"If you say you're good, I believe you."

We touched glasses and, moving in unison, drank, settled our pints carefully onto their coasters. I knew Danny had only told me a tiny portion of the past three years, but I'd heard enough to get the point. I knew the stuff that mattered.

"So have you talked to Mom and Dad?" I asked.

"No," Danny said. "I wanted to reach out to you first."

"Makes sense, I guess. You and I parted on better terms."

"We didn't part on any terms," Danny said. "I disappeared." He wrapped his hands around his glass. "I'd love to say it wasn't on purpose, but in a way it was. And it wasn't anything righteous like saving you from my sins. You just didn't fit into my life at the time, such as it was. No, that's not even true. I didn't need you again for anything after that night, so I forgot about you."

I sat back in the booth, hanging my head, picking again at the burned plastic and pouting like a little kid who'd got his feelings hurt. I couldn't help it. And it wasn't even like Danny was telling me anything I hadn't figured out a long time ago. But his words still stung. Didn't need me for anything? Maybe if he'd stuck with me he wouldn't have ended up under that bridge, or sweating it out in an interrogation room. But I'd hardly looked for him, either; I could've tried harder.

"Look, this is important," Danny said. "Disappearing was a shitty thing to do, especially to you."

"It was a shitty thing to do to all of us," I said.

"Yeah, but you hung on after Mom and Dad gave up. I owe you. I owe you a lot."

"I'm your brother, Danny. You don't owe me shit."

"Somehow, I knew you'd say that." He pushed his glass aside and leaned over the table. "Sometimes, even now, I dream about that cop car, those red lights. It's never a good dream. I could've ruined your life that night."

"It would've ruined all our lives," I said. "Except for that cop's."

"My life was already ruined," Danny said. "I just didn't know it yet. And Tommy? He didn't last much longer after that. I'm sorry for that night. I'm sorry for it all, for all the bullshit. I'm gonna make it up to you."

"Forget it," I said.

"I'll never forget," Danny said. "I'm gonna pay you back and you can't stop me."

"How're you gonna repay me?" I asked. "You got a time machine?"

Danny leaned farther across the table. "There are some things on the horizon, certain opportunities. The answer has not yet revealed itself, but it will. And I intend to be hypervigilant. We live, after all, in the

Land of Opportunity."

"You could make your peace with Mom and Dad," I said. "I could help pave the way. That's an opportunity that's right in front of us."

Danny leaned back with his hand in the air, just like he'd done in the car. "All in good time. You first."

The bad news about Mom settled on the tip of my tongue.

"Him first what?" Al said, walking up to the table, drink in hand.

"Kids get to bed okay?" Danny asked.

Al nodded.

"You got kids, Al?" I asked.

He snorted, rocking back on his heels. "Me? Rug rats? Fuck that." He sniffed his empty glass. "I need another Crown. You guys?" Danny and I both had half a glass left. We shook him off. "Suit yourselves."

"What's his fuckin' problem?" I asked. "It wasn't that personal a question. You brought it up."

"It's got nothing to do with you," Danny said. "Trouble at work lately."

I pinched my nose. "Well, he oughta be more careful about changing diapers. Even all that cologne can't cover the smell."

Danny leaned out of the booth, checking Al's location, saw he was waiting at the bar.

60

"Let's keep that between us. Al's kinda sensitive about certain things; he fancies himself a bit of a stud. Thanks for not mentioning the hair."

Al finished half his Crown Royal on the way back to us. "This place sucks," he said, not even bothering to sit. "It's a goddamn sausage party. Let's get the fuck outta here."

"Danny and I used to hang out here all the time," I said.

Al raised his eyebrows at me, like I'd asked him a question he couldn't possibly answer.

"Whadda you think, Kev?" Danny asked. "You up for a little more action?"

I checked my watch. "I got school tomorrow, and a stack of papers to grade. I'm behind."

Al snorted and bulled his way toward the door.

"It's not even ten," Danny said. "C'mon. Anywhere you want. The city? Brooklyn?"

"I need to get some sleep," I said, rising from the booth.

Danny grabbed my elbow. "You need to get off this fucking island, is what you need. C'mon, man. We got the run of the capital of the free world. You worried about money? I got plenty for the both of us."

I jerked my elbow back, nailing the guy behind me right in the spine. He spun, his forearm soaked with his cocktail, jabbed two fingers into my chest.

"Yoooo, fucko. I'm standing here."

Apologies caught in my throat but before I could pick one and cough it out Danny appeared between us. The stranger's drink hit the floor. Danny had him by the wrist, bending it back at an awkward angle. Fuck-o's face went white and his eyes started to water.

"All my fault," Danny said, looking past Fucko to his friends. "My bad. Did you know you can make a man wet his pants by bending his wrist just the right way? Should I teach it to you?"

The poor bastard didn't know which question to answer. His friends had backed away from him. He tried blinking away the tears in his eyes.

With his free hand, Danny reached a twenty-dollar bill over the guy's shoulder to one of his friends. "Again, sorry about the drink. Let me get the next two or three. Keep the change."

Danny released the guy and the two of us had a clear path to the door.

Across the street, Al had the car running at the bus stop.

"How bad did you hurt that guy?" I asked as we crossed Forest Avenue.

"He's not *injured* or anything," Danny said. "He'll be fine in the morning."

Danny had overreacted. The confrontation had been one of those accidental moments in a bar that usually went nowhere. But I didn't say anything. I felt too good about it. Without Danny there, I would've slunk away intimidated and embarrassed. Instead, I walked out of the bar with my head up and yet with no real damage done.

Danny pulled open the Charger's back door for me, propped his elbow on it.

"I don't usually do things like that," he said. "But then he put his hands on you . . ."

"No big deal," I said. "Listen, about tonight." I shrugged. "I got a life, you know? Responsibilities. Call me Friday. I'm free all weekend."

"Understood," Danny said. "C'mon, we'll give you a ride home."

FOUR

When we stopped outside my building and I got out of the car Danny got out, too. He walked past me, around the back of the car and into the middle of the street, his frown trained on the corner. He gestured for me to join him out there. I stayed rooted on the sidewalk. A couple of the corner boys noticed him, rocking from side to side for a better look at him, their faces hidden beneath their hoods.

"Those hoppers out there every night?" Danny asked.

"Mostly," I said. "Forget it. It's nothing. I hardly even notice 'em anymore."

And I didn't want them noticing me. These were street corner dealers, armed, arrogant, and angry. A whole different breed from that guy in the bar, a half-buzzed bricklayer who probably hadn't been stepped to for real in fifteen years.

Al leaned his head out the car window,

rolling his toothpick over his teeth. "Problem, D.?"

My knees went weak with relief when Danny walked my way, his head still turned to the corner. The dealers got back to business, satisfied Danny wasn't a cop or a client.

"Cowards, every fucking one of them," Danny said. "Heroin?"

"Who knows? It's nothing. I get more trouble from the neighborhood strays."

We embraced on the sidewalk.

"Let's not make it another three years," Danny said.

"That's up to you, isn't it?" I said.

"Indeed," Danny said. "Friday, then? That's cool?"

"Definitely. Look, Danny, I should maybe stop by the folks' and tell them about this. Just to let them know you're not dead."

"Like they'd care."

"Give 'em a break," I said. "You broke their hearts."

Danny looked down at the sidewalk, scratching his chin. "I know. You're right. Feel them out for me, will ya?"

"Will do," I said.

Danny climbed back into the car and Al drove them away into the night, slowing a little as they turned the corner.

■ ■ ■ ■

Inside my apartment building, I checked my mailbox. Empty. Same as when I walked out the door. I snatched empty beer cans off the apartment stairs on my way up. The lightbulb over the staircase flickered and went out when I hit the landing. I tossed the beer cans out the window and into the yard. In the dark, I climbed the last flight to my floor. I had no trouble finding my front door. It was hardly the first time that light had gone out.

My apartment was almost as dark as the hall. I hadn't left a single light burning. I hated coming home to the dark but I did it to myself all the time. I turned on all the lights in the apartment and got a beer from the fridge. The Budweiser tasted flat and thin after that Guinness. I flipped on the TV, but only made it through five channels before I got bored. I killed the living room lights and opened my balcony doors, the balcony itself about the size of a crooked bookshelf. Still, it beat sitting on the porch like a kid who'd locked himself out of the house.

Not that I ever did anything worth looking at, but I didn't like sitting in plain view of the whole block. Out on the balcony I could watch the nights go by in privacy and solitude. And I liked the idea of being able to see everyone else without them seeing me. I saw more than anybody probably knew.

Though it was long after dark and early October, the night breeze blew warm with the last heat of the extended Indian summer. The air tasted of the dirty harbor and car exhaust, but when I was ankle deep in the black slush of February, I'd remember this night as a free slice of Eden.

I tipped leftover rainwater out of my plastic chair and sat, throwing my feet over the railing, beer in my lap. With my left hand I reached up for the brown leaves of the hard-luck spider plant I'd hung by the door. Right down by the dirt, the leaves stayed green, but the life and the color never got very far. Danny's return to the land of the living inspired a lot of questions in me, but it put to bed the biggest, most important ones. Was he dead? Locked up? Was there any hope? I felt satisfied with the answers I had. Deeply satisfied. But my contentment didn't last.

Two teenaged boys broke off from the crew on the corner and sauntered up the street, shoving each other, yelling taunts at the neighborhood mutts that barked as they passed. One kid popped the other in the chest and darted up an unlit driveway. I lost sight of him. The other watched from the sidewalk, giggling, covering his mouth with his hands. Then I heard the first kid shaking and kicking the gate of a chain-link fence and the high, whiny howling of a dog driven to spasms of anger.

I felt guilty, like I always did when I sat there and did nothing while those same two punks tortured that poor dog. Like I often did after the ritual ended, I sat there wishing for a gun, all different kinds: a pistol, a rifle, a flare, or a speargun. Not to kill anyone, just to drill one of those kids in the thigh, teach him a lesson. I imagined Mrs. Hanson stepping onto the porch one night, cradling a big shotgun. Someone should stick up for that poor dog.

What I really wanted, though, was for Maxie to bust through that gate. Just once. Then we'd see how brave those boys really were, when there was no gate and no lock protecting them from those snapping, snarling jaws. Maxie was old and blind, but I believed in my heart that given the chance, he could still roll with the best of them.

When the porch light came on and the front door flew open, the kids took off down the street. Maxie kept howling. Mrs. Hanson, an eighty-something widow in an orange housecoat, waving a spatula over her head, screamed at the boys from her porch as they wheeled around the far corner. Someone else on the block threatened to *shoot that fucking mutt.* Cursing, Mrs. Hanson went back inside. Moments later, I could hear her in the backyard, singing in Polish to her ancient German shepherd. The howling stopped. Maxie's collar jingled as he followed Mrs. Hanson into the house.

The block stayed quiet after that, the corner boys working car after car without a sound. I sat staring at the numbers above Mrs. Hanson's front door. They commanded my attention more and more these days. 136. Across the island, the same numbers hung over my parents' door.

It shamed me to think it but Mrs. Hanson reminded me of my mother, not where Mom was but where she might be headed. Or maybe it was Maxie and his hopeless striking out at the darkness, his failure to get his teeth into what tortured him. I should've had the nerve to tell Danny. He'd want to know.

Early Alzheimer's, the doctors said, a tragedy but not unheard of. The disease would take its slow, sweet time. We'd have a few more years with her. It was their idea of good news. I could never decide if that was merciful or cruel. Her good days still far outnumbered her bad, but her bad days were awful. She'd wander the house like she still worked at the hospital, scolding my father for taking out his IV tubes and trying to help him from his chair to the bathroom. My father played along, holding his breath for the day she wouldn't come back to him. Who knew what he'd do then?

Staring at the shining skyline of Manhattan, I wondered where Danny was and what he was doing at that moment. It had nothing to do with the family. Probably holding court in some fancy uptown club I'd never heard of and would never see, shaking the ice in his club soda. It'd be just like Danny, making soda water look cooler than any fancy martini, leaving everyone else embarrassed at ordering something as mundane as a fifteen-dollar cocktail. He was probably surrounded by the cool friends he'd made before his conscience prodded him into coming to look for me. Weren't apologies part of those twelve-step programs addicts went into?

I leaned my elbows on the railing. That was a shitty way to think about him. He should have a chance to prove his sincerity about being family again. What did I have to lose? And if his return really was all about the apology, well then, that was the least I could do for him. Maybe that big talk about a big night out had been just that — talk. He could be home sleeping right now. I didn't think so, though. One of those distant lights probably shone right on him. I wondered again where he was and what he was doing.

And where would he go home to after his big night ended? I had a feeling he wasn't back on the island. But I didn't know for sure because I hadn't asked. Where did he live? What did he do? Was he dating anyone? He hadn't offered any of that information. I watched a twinkling ferry cross the harbor on its way to Manhattan. Probably the eleven o'clock boat. I had to get up at six A.M. I poured the rest of my beer into the spider plant and went back inside.

On the kitchen table, my students' essays on the American Revolution sat piled as high as they were when I'd left, the grading gremlins no-shows yet again. I cracked open a Cherry Coke and got to work. I could make it through Thursday on five hours' sleep. I'd done it plenty of times before. I got through a paper and a half before calling it a night.

■ ■ ■ ■

Thursday evening, my father answered his front door in slacks and an undershirt. Though in his early sixties, he had a good four to five inches on me when he stood up straight, which was most of the time. Tufts of gray hair swirled on his bare, bony shoulders. Like a weight lifter's, the thick veins in his long, powerful arms stood out against his ropy muscles. Those muscles and a modest pension were what remained of a long career of heavy lifting.

He didn't open the screen door right away. Though it was fading, the daylight made him squint, the setting sun pouring over my shoulder and into his eyes.

"Whadda you doin' here?" he asked. "I'm outta money."

"Been hanging around the OTB again, have you?"

My father laughed and pushed open the screen door. "That was my brother, doofus. To think you're a college professor. You cracked like your mother?"

I walked into the house and my father closed the doors behind us.

"You know I hate jokes like that, about Mom," I said.

"Always the sensitive one," my father said. He squeezed my shoulder. "I worry about you, boy." He clicked off the TV on his way to his massive armchair, his throne. "You know for a fact she'd be doing it to me, if things were the other way around."

He tossed the remote on the table between his chair and my mother's, a smaller, newer version of his.

He was right about Mom's sense of humor, but it didn't make me feel any better about the jokes. I sat on the couch across the room. The rising dust tickled my nose. "And I'm not a professor, Dad. I don't have a Ph.D."

"Whatever," Dad said, waving a hand as if a bad smell had entered the room. "Who cares what a bunch of eggheads think? Teaching college makes you a professor. A piece of paper don't make you, or not make you, nothin'."

"If I had that piece of paper," I said, "you'd have to call me 'doctor.'"

"Like your grandfather, the sainted Dr. O'Malley, the prince of Park Slope? Ah, what the hell for?" He leaned forward, elbows on his knees, shaking a finger at me. "Only piece of paper I ever got was a paycheck, but I got one every week for over forty years. Let's see if you last that long."

73

I remembered them together, my mother's father and my father. Grandpa liked my father, a lot, I think. Dr. O'Malley just never quite adjusted to his only daughter, after years of piano, ballet, and expensive private school, marrying the son of immigrant Irish tavern owners. It had been my father's double shifts at the bar and then on the docks that paid her way through nursing school, though.

"How's Ma?" I asked. "She feeling any better?"

"I read the paper this morning," my father said. "If there's a cure, it didn't make the morning edition."

"Dad, c'mon."

"I hear it in your voice, son. She isn't getting any better, she'll only get worse. You and I both know that."

I got up from the couch. "Where is she? Out back in the garden?"

"She's in Atlantic City," my father said.

"You're kidding me, right? You still let her take those trips? I thought we talked about that."

"We did," my father said. "And like I told you then, you have no say. She likes those trips. It's only for the day. She goes by charter bus, with her friends. The church always sends a couple nurses to keep an eye."

"You think that's a good idea?" I asked.

"The nurses? Can't hurt." He smiled. "I always thought nurses were okay."

"Dad, that's not what I mean. Mom's not well. She's unpredictable. You know that."

"You're goddamn right I do. I live with it every day." My father looked up at me, one eye half closed, elbows on his knees. "She's sick, but she ain't dead. She worked hard her whole life and if she wants to play the slots all day with her friends, I'll drive her to the bus and slip forty in her purse every goddamn time." He stood, crossing the room to me. "And next time you talk to me like a child, I'll drag you out back by the ear and bust open your melon like goddamn Fourth of July."

"Understood," I said, dropping my head to conceal a smile.

My father had bruised his knuckles a few times in his life, but he'd never lifted a hand to family. As a pediatric nurse my mother had seen more abused children than she cared to remember. My father had too much respect for her to ever bring even a hint of such a thing into our house. Absurd physical threats were how he let Danny and me know we'd crossed a line. At least in the house, Danny and I had always respected that line. Even though we harbored no fear of violence, we also had no curiosity about the other side.

"Thank you for sparing my melon," I said. I eased up to the edge of the couch, looked up at my father. "I'm not here to talk about Mom, anyway. I've got some other news."

My father beamed. "You met a girl." He clapped his hands. "Please tell me you got her pregnant. Your mother and I are dying for grandkids." His face went grim at his own words.

"How about a son?"

My father only looked confused.

"Dad," I said. "Danny's back."

Anger reddened his face to the tips of his ears. He folded his hands over his belt buckle, spread his feet. The muscles of one shoulder twitched. This is what he must have looked like, I thought, guarding the door of his father's bar. I wondered if he knew that wrist trick that Danny had pulled at the Red Lion. I questioned the wisdom of leading my dad to news of his junkie son through a conversation about his sick wife.

"What does that mean?" he asked. "What you just said."

I swallowed hard. "He stopped by the apartment yesterday. Out of the blue."

"Just like that kid to do that. How much did he burn you for? You didn't let him in your house, did you?"

"He's different now," I said. "You should see him. He looks great. Like a new man."

"New man," my father said. "Please. He's my son and I love him but he's the sneakiest bastard I ever met."

"He wasn't high," I said. "He hasn't been high in over a year."

"Then where has that boy been?" Dad said, teeth clenched. "Does he know about his mother? Did he even ask?"

"Of course he did," I lied.

"Wha'd he say when you told him?"

"I didn't tell him," I said. "I . . . I didn't know if he was ready yet. I thought maybe you'd want to tell him about it, or we could tell him together."

My father slid his hands into his pockets, relaxing his shoulders. He stood over me like when I was a kid — when he wasn't angry with me, he was just so disappointed.

"Look at you, boy. One day back in your life and you're lying through your teeth for him. Just like always. When're you gonna learn?"

"He's my brother," I said. "Your brother wasn't such a saint, either."

"Johnny had his faults, rest his soul. Spent

too much time with the wrong people. Right from when we were kids, even, running around with those Southside Boys. But Johnny never stole from his family. Never once. He never turned his back on us like your brother did when there was nothing left to take. My brother wasn't a filthy junkie, like my son."

I wanted to stand, to face my father toe-to-toe and defend my brother. I stayed in my seat. Danny's case for redemption seemed even shakier in the face of my father's wrath. I was the one who taught it for a living, but my father held history closer to his heart than I did.

"He's different this time," I mumbled. "He deserves a second chance."

"A *second* chance? I've lost count of that boy's chances." My father sat down heavily in his chair. "He gets no more from me."

Danny didn't need any more chances from him, anyway. My mother had an endless supply. With my father safely seated across the room, I finally got up. I'd done my duty. I shouldn't have come. Or I should have given Danny more time to prove himself. "So I shouldn't bring him by."

"Don't," my father said. His face relented, just a little bit. "Not yet. Maybe soon. Your mother would never forgive us if she missed

a chance to see him, whatever state he's in."
He stared down into his palms, thinking.
"But if you bring Danny by, you better be
sure he's sticking around this time, Kevin.
She can't take another one of his disappearing acts. If you're not sure, keep him away
from her."

"We're getting together tomorrow night,"
I said. "I'll let him know about Mom. He'll
come see her, on his best behavior. I promise."

"Forget what he says," my father warned
me. "Figure out what he's after. This is on
you, Kevin. This time, if he breaks her heart
again, I'm holding you responsible." He
tilted his head back against the chair, staring at the ceiling. "Now go. I need some
time to forget this conversation before your
mother gets home."

I didn't know what else to do so I headed
for the door.

"Wait," Dad said. He met me at the door.

"I know how you feel, Kevin," he said. "I
really do. It's not like I don't miss Daniel,
the way he used to be, at least. You were
quite a pair, you two. Joy of your mother's
life." He slipped his arm across my shoulders and kissed my cheek. I could feel his
breath in my ear. "Be a good brother, Kevin,
but be careful. Be very, very careful. I don't

like seeing you get hurt, either. The Danny we knew went away a long time ago."

FIVE

That Friday afternoon, my workweek ended with a call from Dean Whitestone's secretary. The dean needed to see me. Now.

Whitestone kept me waiting outside his office for half an hour while he did nothing, I was sure, but stare out the window. As dean of a struggling department at an underfinanced city college of little to no reputation, Whitestone treated his teachers in keeping with his milieu. Like field hands, basically. He conducted himself as if he were dean of Harvard Law. At his own expense, he'd outfitted his office with an enormous teak desk and matching bookshelves. He had a penchant for European vacations, often taken sans wife and stepchildren. Research trips, he called them, though no one could figure out what got researched beyond pricey hotels. He hadn't taught in years and what little he published concerned a little-known corner of Staten

81

Island: the history and possible futures of the abandoned Bloodroot Children's Hospital. He'd even started some kind of activist group called the Friends of Bloodroot. Some crap about turning the old hospital into a medical museum.

He'd been on me and everyone else in the department to join. Or at least write checks to support the group. Most everyone else in the history department had done one, the other, or both. Besides me, the only remaining holdout was Kelsey Reyes, the closest thing I had to a friend in the department. The big guns in admin were not happy about Friends of Bloodroot, I'd heard. The old hospital sat in Willowbrook Park, not far from our own beloved Richmond College and admin wanted that land for new off-campus dorms.

When his secretary finally sent me in to see him, Whitestone was waiting for me behind his desk, his hands folded in his lap.

In his oversized black leather office chair, Dean Alvin Whitestone looked like an elf trying on Santa's chair for size. Barely over five feet tall, he had spindly legs that dropped from almost obscenely wide hips, into which collapsed a round, bulging chest. All of that crowned by a bald, ovoid head. He reminded me, more than anything else,

82

of a walking thumb. A walking thumb in Coke-bottle glasses.

"Close the door," Whitestone said. "Take a seat."

I did as I was told.

"Eight." He dipped his chin at a pile of papers on his desk. "That's how many student complaints I've gotten about you this semester."

"I thought you said it was six," I said.

"It was, last week. This week, it's up to eight."

"So I got two more?" I asked.

Whitestone slid his glasses to the tip of his nose. "Are you sure history is your calling? Your math skills are astounding. You assured me, you promised me there wouldn't be *any* more, yet here before me are indeed more complaints."

"Am I safe in assuming it's more of the same?"

"Despite the popular clichés," Whitestone said, smiling, "you are safe in that assumption. You are nothing if not consistent in your shortcomings."

"I'm catching up on my grading," I said. "I'm almost there. Those'll be the last two."

"These students," Whitestone said. "They deserve to have their work returned to them in a timely manner. And to have proper attention paid to that work when their instructor evaluates it. Maybe if you spent your office hours focusing on your work and not consorting with Ms. Reyes, you'd make better progress."

I threw my hands in the air. "But the students' work *sucks*." I swallowed hard. Twice. "I said that out loud, didn't I?"

"Perhaps their teacher is failing to provide a proper example."

I set my hands on my knees, took a deep breath. Whitestone was a dick, but that didn't make what he said any less true. "Perhaps." But he was wrong about Kelsey and I wanted him to know it, for her sake if not mine. "Ms. Reyes and I are coworkers. We talk teaching, compare notes." Whitestone grunted. I soldiered on. "We have very similar schedules, so we see each other a lot. Here at work, I mean. We don't socialize."

My boss stared at me. I wished, not for the first time, that Kelsey and I did have a thing going, not that I'd ever tried, just to piss off Whitestone. I'd heard from her personally that Whitestone had put the moves on her himself. Until Kelsey made it clear that she wouldn't settle the matter through the usual channels and charges, but that resolution would come in the parking lot, delivered in the form of a Louisville Slugger. I smiled, despite myself. Kelsey Reyes was good people.

Whitestone, frowning at my smile, lifted the pile of papers, brought it into his lap. Licking his fingertip every time he turned a page, he silently read the complaints. When he was done, he looked up at me. "What happened to you, Kevin?"

"When?"

"You're not the teacher you used to be. Inspired. Dedicated. There has to be a reason." He tossed the papers on his desk, a few slid off onto the floor. I left them there. Whitestone shook his head. "These are the strangest complaints. They all start out defending you. *I love Mr. Curran's class,* they say, *his class is awesome, he knows everything about the Revolution.* It's a lovefest, until the inevitable 'but.' *But I don't know my grades, but I'm still waiting for three papers.*" Whitestone chuckled. "Half of them ask me to help you. Like maybe you need a tutor. As if you're the struggling student and they're the frustrated teacher. Strange, don't you think?"

"The kids have always loved my class," I said. "I get more write-in requests than any other teacher, three-to-one."

"I guess our quandary is this, then,"

85

Whitestone said, straightening his tie. I noticed his hands were badly scarred. "Why don't *you* love your class anymore?"

I waited to speak, measuring my answer. He'd never gone this far with me. Our meetings had always ended at the insult and reprimand stage. He'd asked a legitimate question. The students' work often did suck, but hadn't it always? Why was it so burdensome now? In truth, the tedium had gotten to me. The kids never changed. They always made the same mistakes on their assignments, whined the same complaints when I corrected them. I could tell within the first week of the semester which students would pass and which would fail, who would excel and who would struggle. The whole gig had gotten so easy, so predictable, that it had become nearly unendurable.

As for me, I'd been teaching the same class the same way for eight years. The past never changed, so why should I? As a student I'd always figured that when a subject got easy it meant I had it mastered. I'd applied the same logic to teaching. But I realized, sitting there, Dean Whitestone waiting patiently for my answers to his quiz, that as a student another subject, another challenge was always coming at me. Now that I was the teacher, my test was to provide my own challenges. And I had failed.

I taught history but had started, a couple of years ago, living in a perpetual present, where I knew everything that was going to happen next. Like watching a movie for the tenth time, only my movie bored me to tears. I kept watching it because it was the only one I had. I thought of Danny. His return was the first surprise I'd gotten since the birthday phone call three years ago. And his resurfacing certainly put a new actor, one with a gift for improvisation, on my screen.

Whitestone coughed into his fist. I had to throw him something.

"I do love the classroom," I said. "I love seeing the lights come on in their eyes when they see something new, or in a new way." It was trite, but it was true. "That never gets old."

"Ah." Whitestone leaned back in his chair. "The dropping of the veil. There is nothing like it."

"It's just . . . the past couple of semesters," I said, though the atrophy had started longer ago, "I can't find the energy for the other stuff. Am I burned out? Already?"

"A little singed, maybe," Whitestone said, "but not burned out. This happens to all of us, especially as we approach the ten-year mark. Our subject can't be our sole inspiration, Kevin. We need outside interests. I have some of my own. And we need the aid of our compatriots in bleak times. Certainly a scholar of the Continental Army knows this." A smirk flashed, then vanished. "Perhaps if you spent more time with the rest of the department, became more involved. Certainly the Revolution is fascinating, but there are endless compelling subjects in American history. Some right here on Staten Island." He shrugged. "My latest endeavor, for instance."

"Bloodroot," I said. I leaned back in my chair, nodding. I felt like the new kid at boarding school. If you'd just try harder to make some friends . . . why don't you join my chess club? So that was the inspiration for Whitestone's sudden attack of sensitivity. Nagging me to join his group had failed and he had turned to seduction. I thought of Whitestone's scarred hands. *Join me, Luke. Know the power of the dark side.*

"Those lost children from Bloodroot deserve a champion," Whitestone said. "When the atrocities they suffered saw the light of day in the late seventies, care of the orphaned and the disabled there and everywhere else in this country changed forever and for the better. The changes were, dare I say it, revolutionary. Their sacrifices, though unwitting, deserve commemoration."

It was quite a speech. I was almost moved. I knew the stories, too, about how kids left at Bloodroot from the forties through the seventies lived little better than the inmates of concentration camps. My family had been part of that story. Grandpa O'Malley had played a huge role in shuttering the place and disgracing the doctor in charge. But that wasn't the reason I was getting the hard sell. Whitestone surely knew about what my grandfather had done, but he didn't know I was Dr. O'Malley's grandson. It was the kids at Richmond that Whitestone wanted. The students, complaints and all, loved me. If I joined the Friends of Bloodroot, kids would start signing up the next day. Admin didn't much care what their teachers wanted, but the kids who paid tuition? That was another story. I could be a hell of a recruiting tool for him.

"I've got to catch up on my grading," I said, standing, "before I can take on anything else."

"Before you go," Whitestone said, "pick up those papers for me."

I bent and gathered the fallen complaint forms.

"I understand your workload," Whitestone said. "But I don't know how long I can carry someone unwilling to show true commitment to the department."

"Duly noted," I said, handing the papers across the desk. "I'll get caught up. No more complaints. I promise."

Whitestone reached for the papers but snapped his arm back when he saw me staring at his scarred hand. "Childhood accident," he said. "You're dismissed, Curran."

About twenty minutes after I got home from campus, I heard Al's Charger rumbling outside the apartment building. I buzzed Danny in when the doorbell rang. I would've preferred a call first as I was staring into the fridge, wearing only my boxers, strap-T, and dress shirt when Danny knocked on the door. I let the fridge door swing closed and answered as I was.

Looking sharp again, I thought. Another fifty-dollar T-shirt, midnight blue, under another black suit jacket that probably cost more than everything I owned put together. He had a diamond in his ear now, replacing the dull silver hoop he'd worn for years.

"Nice outfit," Danny said. "The look works for you."

"You'd think it's the tie that kills me," I said, passing through the living room toward my bedroom. "But it's the pants. I fucking hate dress pants."

In the bedroom, I dropped the boxers, pulled on some jeans. I opened my wallet. Payday wasn't till next Friday. Forty bucks had to last me a week. Like they did every time I counted my cash, thoughts of a second job jumped into my head. The idea made me want to throw the bedroom lamp out the window. I didn't know where Danny wanted to go that night but it didn't much matter. I couldn't even afford the movies. I sat on the bed, gazing into my closet, thinking again about Danny's clothes.

He wasn't flashy, but I wondered how he financed the upgrade. Maybe his wardrobe caught my attention because three years ago he dressed one step up from homeless. It's not like I knew the first thing about fashion. The clothes probably weren't half as expensive as I thought. But that didn't explain where Danny got his money.

Most of my clothes that weren't for work were either grad school leftovers or bought at the thrift store around the corner. Maybe that's what got to me: maybe I was just jealous. I tossed my wallet on the bed. Forget the cash to go anywhere cool that night.

Even if I did have it, I certainly didn't have the clothes.

Wearing my ratty jeans and the same wrinkled dress shirt, I walked into the kitchen, where Danny was drinking one of my last Cherry Cokes and peering into the freezer.

"Four Cherry Cokes, two pounds of coffee, and a huge box of Oreos." He turned to me, looking concerned. "Have you even been to a grocery store since I last saw you? You certainly haven't gained any weight."

"Like I want this grief," I said, opening the balcony doors.

Danny joined me outside. "You realize you've got a Weber grill in your living room."

I sat in the chair. Danny leaned against the railing, his back to the street. The way that railing was bent and rusted, I'd never had the nerve. Danny didn't seem to care. He threw a glance at the corner. It wasn't half as busy in the daylight.

"If I leave the grill outside," I said, "there's not enough room to sit. The smoke just blows back into the house anyway. I don't remember why I bought it in the first place."

"It is a great view," Danny said, looking over at Manhattan.

"It's a quiet place to sit and think," I said. Right then, the couple living two houses down burst out of their front door. The woman screamed from the porch steps as the man, beer bottle in hand, stomped away from her and toward his car.

"Yeah, peaceful and serene," Danny said as the screaming continued, now in Spanish.

Before he got in the car, the man turned, yelled something in Italian, and threw the beer bottle. It smashed on the step at the woman's feet, spraying her bare ankles with glass. She laughed and flipped him off as he drove away. She spat on the cracked walkway before running back into the house. Maxie howled in his yard.

"Tony and Maria," I said. "He must've started his bender early. Or maybe he got fired again. They usually don't get really cranked up until Sunday afternoon."

"Tony and Maria?" Danny asked. "You're not serious."

"Not entirely," I said. "That's what I call them. I don't know who they are. Unless they really are named *Puta* and *Cabron*."

"Please tell me they don't have kids, at least," Danny said.

"She had one," I said. "The city took it away not long after Tony moved in. I heard she's pregnant again — with Tony's brother's kid. I think that's what they're always

fighting about. Four years in this neighborhood, I've picked up some Spanish. And
Italian. And Polish. It's very multicultural
here."

"Fucking savages," Danny said, scowling
at Tony and Maria's house. "That kid'll
never know nothing but pain. And turn out
just like them."

"Maybe, maybe not," I said. "She's young,
maybe this time it'll be different, whoever
the father is."

"Bullshit," Danny said. "That dog across
the street? He probably got his balls cut off
before he was three months old. But those
animals two doors down can crank out as
many kids as they want and no one says
boo." He took a deep breath. "Whatever you
say, Kev. Maybe it will be different."

"Look at you," I said. "You got your shit
together. I mean, look at those fancy threads
you got there."

Danny pretended to dust his lapels. "Yeah,
I look all right these days. You, however. You
still got your bum's eye for clothes."

"My clothes money goes into my work
wardrobe," I said. "I gotta look professional.
I can't get my clothes . . . wherever it is you
get yours." I was getting worked up, desperate to cover the fact that I bought about
two new shirts a year. And that the only

time I got new dress pants or ties was Christmas and my birthday, when our parents bought them for me.

"You remember high school," I said. "We always knew who was wearing the same stained-up shirts and ties. Image is more important in teaching than you might think. It's called the subjective curriculum."

"Hey, I was just breaking balls," Danny said. "I'm sure it is important. You know better than me. What I remember from school? How Mrs. Fallenti's nipples always poked through her sweater. That's what I remember about teachers' clothes."

"Those rumors that Al fucked her when you two were seniors," I said, "are they true?"

"You can ask him yourself," Danny said. "He's picking us up in ten minutes."

I looked myself over, hands in the air, my cheeks burning. The bedroom lamp was doomed.

"Look, about going out tonight," I said. "I thought on Wednesday night that I get paid today, but it's not until next week. Maybe we can hang out here, get a movie or something."

"Fuck that," Danny said. "You know how much TV I watched in rehab? I hate TV. You oughta throw yours in the street. I got the tab tonight."

"You don't have to do that," I said.

"I know. I'm doing it anyway." He leaned over me, smiling but jabbing his thumb hard into his chest. "I got the tab tonight." It sounded almost like a threat. "Don't worry about money, your clothes, nothin'. You're with me tonight."

Six

Al drove us over the Verrazano and into Brooklyn. To my surprise, we got off the highway before the Manhattan bridges.

The sun setting, we cruised through Park Slope, my mother's old neighborhood, slowing for schoolkids still in uniform playing football in streets lined with SUVs. We slid by the regal brownstones, the sun an orange fireball in their windows, and we drifted through the shadows of expansive oaks and elms, acorns and itchy-balls crunching under the tires.

Al dropped us off on Flatbush Avenue, along the edge of Prospect Park, outside a restaurant called Santoro's. As he had on Wednesday night, he declined to join us, even offering the same excuse.

"He must have a girl in each borough," I said as Al drove away. I was glad to see him go. "Nice racket you've got, though, him driving you around."

"I kick in for gas and tolls," Danny said, turning in a circle on the sidewalk. "I still can't believe what they've done with this neighborhood. I'm glad Grandpa passed before he could see what happened to it."

An Irish pub nestled into one corner, Guinness and Harp signs glowing in the small windows. A trio of guys in suits with guilty looks on their faces stood smoking around an empty flowerpot. They didn't speak to one another. On the opposite corner glowed a Starbucks doing brisk business. Men and women in business attire shouldered open the glass doors, each with a paper or plastic cup in one hand and a BlackBerry or cell phone in the other. Inside, a laptop on every table. Salons and boutiques occupied the rest of the block, most of them closed for the evening, their high-dollar, faux-bohemian offerings spotlighted in the wide, immaculate shop windows.

"Fucking yuppies," Danny said. "All they talk about is how much they love the neighborhood and then they completely fucking ruin it. Who drinks coffee through a fucking *straw?* Watch, Kev, your neighborhood'll be next."

"And then they cry about how great it used to be," I said. "Like they didn't grow up in Connecticut."

"See?" Danny said. "You and me? We still think alike. And we're not entirely alone." He gestured toward the Irish place. "Shanahan's remains true to the game, bad food, three-dollar pints, no dogs small enough to fit in a handbag, but even he's had to make compromises. He finally told his bartenders to start making specialty martinis, though he lets them charge fifteen bucks a pop. Three weeks ago, he got free wireless."

Danny grabbed the brass handle of Santoro's oak door and yanked it open. "This place, too, is still cool. A true sanctuary. Same owner for forty years."

A bald old man, thick salt-and-pepper mustache twitching under his nose, greeted us on the other side of the door. He wore an immaculate white apron over a shirt and tie. He kissed Danny on both checks, vigorously shaking my hand as Danny introduced us. His name was Gino Bavasi. "Ciao, ciao," he said, over and over.

To my surprise, Gino and Danny exchanged pleasantries in Italian as we took our table in the back. Gino handed us menus. Moments later, he brought out a pitcher of ice water and filled our glasses. He waddled back to the host stand.

I opened my menu and scanned the prices.

The forty in my pocket might cover a few olives. I remembered what Danny had said about the tab and closed the menu.

"Gino knows you pretty well," I said. "You working here?"

"I live upstairs," Danny said. "On my own, I can barely afford to walk down the street in this neighborhood anymore, but I do a lot of work for Bavasi, and sometimes for the guy that owns this building, a few other people. I manage the POS, the sound system, security. I'm in here a lot."

Bavasi took our orders. Three tuxedoed waiters idled in the bus station. I wondered how it was that the boss waited on our table. Danny ordered for both of us without even a glance at me. I didn't mind. The menu was mostly in Italian anyway. I eased back, water in one hand and my other arm stretched along the back of the bench, trying to look like I ate in places like Santoro's all the time.

"So that's what you're doing these days, for work?" I asked. "Sound?"

"Some," Danny said. "Video mostly."

"No more recording studios?"

"Nothing there for me but sweeping up. I burned too many bridges getting high. I'm doing private systems, now. It was tough for a while, catching up on the new technology, but Bavasi's old tech took me under his wing. Al set it up, after I got outta rehab."

I was shocked and a little ashamed of how relieved I was at Danny's answers to my questions. They explained a lot. "So there's decent money in this?"

"When Bavasi's other guy retired," Danny said, "I took over all his accounts. It's pretty profitable, making sure the yuppies can hear their Norah Jones in every room in the house. Making sure they can hear precious Toby's every breath from his thousand-dollar crib. Setting up their multimedia entertainment systems. I can charge a fortune to show up at the condo and follow the owner's manual. They're proud to get overcharged for it. I think in their heads, techs are the new servant class."

Bavasi brought over a bottle of red wine, poured us each a glass.

"So you work for Al?" I asked.

"No, I work for me," Danny said. "Like every man should. Al throws me a job every now and then, some things we do together. Bavasi's my main source; he knows everyone in this neighborhood. It's strictly word of mouth." Danny reached into his jacket pocket. "But I do have these."

He handed me a business card.

"Impressive," I said, taking the card. There

was a laughing devil in one corner and a weeping angel in the other. I read the card aloud. "Far Beyond Technology. I like the name. Good play on words."

"You get it?" Danny asked. "The joke in the company name?"

"Of course," I said. "It's technology beyond what your clients are used to, you know? And having your own company, that's far beyond where you were personally a few years ago. I like the name. I like it a lot."

Danny smiled at me, benevolent and amused, his eyes a little sad. It was the look you give a kid who believes his dog died because God wanted it that way.

"I love you, man," he finally said. "I envy your mind. I always have." Danny studied his reflection in his gleaming silver knife. "I wish I thought more like you, Kevin. When I came up with the name, I was thinking in terms of beyond the grave."

"Morbid, bro," I said. "As usual."

Danny shook his index finger at me. "But true." He stood. "We got time before the food gets here." He grabbed his wine. "Come upstairs. I'll give you a tour of the empire. Explain a little more."

Outside, only a few feet to the right of Santoro's, Danny unlocked a windowless metal door, first by punching a code into a keypad, then by turning three different keys in three separate locks. He led us up a brightly lit, narrow staircase carpeted in a deep maroon.

His front door opened into a high-ceilinged room with white walls and a gleaming blond wood floor. To our left was a small kitchen area, the walls and floor tiled in chessboard black and white. Stainless steel appliances shone like surgeons' equipment atop the granite counters. In the wall to our right a huge black pocket door sealed off Danny's bedroom. Seven cherubs carved in a panel of blood-red wood writhed in wicked, twisted contortions over the doorway.

"Something else, isn't it?" Danny said. "It was here when I moved in."

"I can't tell if they're fucking or fighting," I said. "It's disturbing."

Danny laughed. "That's what I love about it. I can't tell if that's agony or ecstasy on their faces, if they're in Heaven or Hell. Betcha they can't tell, either."

"Maybe they're in between," I said, "trying to get one way or the other."

I walked farther into the room, toward what I took to be Danny's workstation, a sprawling, patchwork construction of desks and shelves covered with monitors, hard drives, and an assortment of devices I didn't recognize. Danny followed me, hovering over my left shoulder. The whirring and blinking hardware, no doubt expensive and complicated, impressed me. But it was the enormous painting hanging over the work-station that had caught my eye. It had to be ten feet tall. Twice, maybe three times the size of the original. I stood beneath it, awed and repulsed.

"Saturn," I said. "Devouring his young. Goya."

"I paid a fortune for it," Danny said. "Gave the artist, this girl I ran with for a while, a nice bonus, compensation for the two weeks of nightmares that painting gave her. It's funny. She dumped me right after she finished the painting."

I stared up into the inhuman, crazed blue eyes of a naked, muscle-roped wild man, his white hair flying, a small, headless figure clutched in his withered fist. The cannibal god's chin dripped with blood, the blood of his own children.

"It's monstrous," I said. "Why would you want *that* watching over you?"

"It reminds me not to be afraid," Danny said. "Fear. That's why Saturn murdered his own children. Fear of the future. Fear of the unknown. Frightened people are capable of awful things. Believe me, I know. I used to be one of those people. I'm not anymore. He's not watching me. I'm watching him. Caught in the act."

"I thought the problem with fear," I said, "was what it kept you from doing."

"A common misconception," Danny said. "A guy like bin Laden? Everyone thinks hatred motivates people like that. Or that he's so courageous because he takes on the American Zeus. But that's all bullshit. Bin Laden's just another wannabe god hiding in a mountain cave.

"I don't care what he says on those tapes. He murders because he's afraid, of the future, of worlds and people he'll never understand and never be part of. We call them terrorists because they cause terror, but it oughta be because that's all they feel. The War on Terror? It should be the War *of* Terror. It's about who feels it more, them or us." He sat in his black leather office chair, turning in it to face me. "So there it is." He raised his hand. "Sorry for the lecture. As you can imagine, there's no talking to Al about this stuff. He's not much of a thinker. And I spend most of my time either with him or alone."

"No apology necessary. You wanna come

guest lecture in my class?" I said, touching one of the hard drives. Its warm metal shell vibrated under my fingertips. "All this gear, all these ideas. Is this when you tell me you work for the CIA? That you're really fighting the War of Terror?"

"Nonsense," he said, turning in his chair. "The feds don't pay nearly enough."

Danny tapped his mouse and six different monitors flickered to life. "Stereos and baby monitors isn't all I do," Danny said. "Some of my work is more . . . complex."

All the images looked live. Two I recognized: the sidewalk in front of Santoro's and the hallway leading up to the apartment. The four others captured people's apartments, the screens blinking back and forth from living rooms to kitchens to bedrooms. On three of the screens nothing much happened. A baby slept in a crib, an older couple watched TV, a woman read in an easy chair, holding a glass of cold white wine. I could see the beads of condensation on the glass. Sudden motion on another screen caught my eye. I stared, trying to believe what I was seeing. The scene was shot in profile.

A naked woman, about forty or so, her bottle-blond hair tied back in a ponytail, perched on the edge of a bed giving a nude, standing man a vigorous blow job. Her enormous, obviously fake breasts quivered as her entire upper body pistoned up and down. The recipient of her efforts stood with his buttocks clenched and his fists pressed hard into his fleshy hips like Superman atop a skyscraper.

My brother's fucking with me, I thought. He's called up some Internet porn site as a joke. But the scene looked awful real.

"You want sound?" Danny asked, wiggling his fingers above the keyboard. "A close-up of those tits?"

I forced my eyes away from the screen. "No thanks. What is this? Who are these people?"

"I'll tell you who that woman isn't," Danny said, tapping his fingertip on the woman's thigh. Her legs needed a shave, but her hero didn't seem to mind. "She is not Superman's wife. She is, in fact, his sister-in-law. Her name is Denise. She's visiting from Red Hook. She and her husband just moved into a new condo of their own out there. They had Park Slope Chad, here, and his wife, Sharon, over to dinner just the other night."

I was deeply confused. "So, you're doing some kind of PI work on the side?" Chad dropped his head, his shoulders and ass started to shake. "Turn this shit off. Please."

"Sure thing," Danny said. "Every episode ends the same, anyway." He tapped some keys and the couple disappeared, replaced on the screen by an aerial map of Park Slope. One street featured a blinking red dot. "There's Chad's wife, Sharon. Same place, same time as always."

"Doing what?" I asked. I tried not to care, but part of me was fascinated. "These people, they don't know they're being watched, right?"

"Whadda you think?" Danny rocked back in his chair. "Sharon's pumping iron, in theory, at a women-only gym."

"In theory?"

Danny shrugged. "Rumor has it it's more of a singles club. Private lounges, fancy showers. You get the picture."

"I do." I tilted my chin at the screen. "I'm surprised you don't."

"I haven't figured out whether it's worth anything to me." Danny checked his watch. "Time for steak. We better get back downstairs."

"So wait," I said. "Denise's husband, he hired you to catch her in the act with Chad?"

"Nope." Danny powered down his monitors. "You know where they live? Sharon and Chad? In Grandpa O'Malley's old brownstone."

"You're kidding."

"I shit you not," Danny said. "It's the same building. Tell you what else, when Santoro drops whatever he's got planned on Chad and Sharon and their marriage implodes? I'm gonna snatch that building up. Mom grew up in that place. It oughta be in a respectable family, not with those cretins."

"I thought you couldn't afford to walk the street around here."

Danny stood, patted my shoulder. "I got some things working."

He led me out of the apartment, speaking over his shoulder as we walked down the stairs. "You see what I mean about fear and awful things? Those sad, terrible people? Disgraceful. If they would show some nerve and tell each other how they really felt, what they really wanted, they wouldn't have to shame themselves. They might not lose that beautiful house."

"Maybe that's part of the excitement," I said as we headed down the stairs. "The risk of losing everything, the thrill of breaking the rules, of maybe getting caught."

"Yeah, sure," Danny scoffed. "That's why I became a junkie. For the excitement of losing everything from my shoes to my heartbeat. There's no risk, no thrill in cowardice. If Chad's wife walked in on that blow job, he'd drop a turd right there on the bedroom floor." He opened the door out onto the Brooklyn night. "You wanna really walk the line? Try telling the truth."

Not thirty seconds after we sat back down, a blank-faced waiter arrived at our table, a huge plate in each hand. After setting down the steaks, he refilled our wineglasses, generously overpouring the deep purple pinot noir. My steak, a porterhouse, was enormous and served blood-rare, exactly the way I liked it. It steamed in the center of its bone-white platter in a pool of its own hot blood.

"You gonna eat that?" Danny asked, already chewing. "Or stare at it all night?"

"This thing is a miracle," I said, picking up my knife and fork. "I hate to defile it."

"Then send it back. We'll save it for Al. He's got no problem defiling things."

I set my silverware back down, plucked a warm roll from the basket. It steamed when I broke it open. I set both halves on the edge of my plate. I had to ask. "What was that? Upstairs."

Danny took a big gulp of wine before he

spoke. "Look, I had some help getting back on my feet after rehab. I'm not exactly qualified for straight work, you know?" He waved his knife over the dining room. "Santoro, who owns this place, he's a man of varied interests, business and otherwise. In this neighborhood and beyond. He's a man of considerable . . . influence. Reach. Much of that influence comes through information."

"Which you gather by spying on people," I said. "Jesus, Danny."

"I help a little. Slip in an extra camera here or there on a job, when he asks. Watch who he tells me to watch."

I kneaded my fingertips into my temples. "Danny, this is fucked up. You steal people's secrets."

"What? Nobody's watching you?" Danny said. "Every store, bar, bank, and restaurant has cameras. Every dressing room, tollbooth, gas station, ATM, and half the intersections you drive through. Fucking *Starbucks* is filled with cameras. You probably got them at school. Most of your life is lived in front of a camera, Kev. And do you really know when you're being watched and when you're not? If you ask, will they turn the cameras off for you? And you, you're just goin' about your all-American business.

It's a violation. Illegal search and seizure, that's like, what, amendment two? Three? You taught me that."

"But that's what you do. Watch people that don't know it."

"No, it's not. People who live outside normal society surrender its protection." Danny gulped his wine. The waiter floated over and refilled his glass. "I promise you, everyone I watch is into Santoro for something. I don't waste my time peering into the lives of innocents. I got respect for people."

"That lady? Those old people?"

"They look innocent enough," Danny said, "but not one of them is." He tipped his knife toward me. "Nobody is. That's why they need to be watched." He slid a huge slice of steak into his mouth. Blood ran down his chin. "Besides, the pay is extraordinary. Cash. Tax-free."

"Fuck that," I said. "It's gross and it's gotta be illegal."

"I never said it wasn't either of those things," Danny said. "But after you've been where I have, seen what I've seen, those words don't mean a whole lot anymore. No offense, Kev, but school's out." He tapped the point of his knife on the edge of my plate. "Now eat that glorious steak before it gets cold. You can worry about the ethics of it later."

We walked over to the park after dinner; both of us had eaten too much and we didn't get very far, nor did we talk much. I didn't know what to say. What could I tell Danny about what he was doing that he didn't already know? That Mom and Dad wouldn't like it? That I'd tell? Those threats had never worked before; they wouldn't work now. I considered threatening to not see him again, not until he got away from Santoro, but it would have been empty and Danny would know that as sure as I did.

We sat on a bench, on the street side of the stone wall bordering the park. The street was quiet. I tried shoving aside what Danny had told and shown me, to not let it ruin the evening. If I was going to help him, I had to hang on to him. I threw one arm over the back of the bench and gazed down the road at the columned façade of the public library.

I had good memories of our grandfather taking us there when we were young. We walked over together, the three of us leaving Dad asleep on the couch and Mom and Grandma snapping green beans in the kitchen, Danny and me throwing acorns at each other the whole way. But once we entered the library, the foolishness ceased. Grandpa insisted on reverence, even more than at church. The library was Grandpa's cathedral.

Inside, Danny usually grabbed a random book and snuck off to nap on one of the leather couches. He always woke up with a red blotch on his cheek, like he'd been slapped. I disappeared into the stacks, wandering from shelf to shelf, searching for any book that fed my most recent obsession. In grammar school I began with dinosaurs, then moved to whales then sharks and then on to the ocean herself. In junior high, I turned to Egypt, Rome, Greece and Sparta, the empire of the Moors. To the barbarians whose names rolled off my tongue like an ancient spell: Celts, Gauls, and Visigoths. I absorbed the Inca, the Maya, and the Aztecs. I imagined windswept African deserts, or emerald European valleys, or dark, wet South American rain forests where I surveyed a long-hidden ruin. In high school, I discovered America and it stuck.

The children's section bored me. The librarian arched her eyebrows as my grandfather checked out the adult books on my favorite subjects. I could tell he was proud of me. I had an exploratory mind, he said. As we checked out, Danny stood off to the side, rubbing his red cheek and yawning.

"I miss that library," I said.

"Do you?" Danny asked. "I got so sick of it. The same shit every Sunday, church and the library. I couldn't stand it."

"I miss it," I said. "I loved it in there." I thought about work. I hadn't even read a new book about American history, from a library or anywhere else, in a couple of years. Somewhere along the line, long before Whitestone had gotten on my case, I'd just lost interest.

"Come back over to Brooklyn one day," Danny said. "On a Sunday, even. I'll take you there." He smiled. "I never even notice it and I'm on this street all the time."

"I'd like that, but it's tough getting here without a car," I said. "It takes forever."

"I'll have Al drive you over," Danny said. "We'll get a pizza after." He leaned forward, his eyes trained on his shoe tops. "I'll tell you what, though. I probably slept better in that library than I ever did at home." He looked up at me. "There's something I want to talk to you about. I need help with something."

I braced myself. "Anything."

"You're the only one around that'll understand." He wiped the corners of his mouth with his fingers. "My nightmares are back. They came back soon as I cleaned up again."

I blew out a long breath I hadn't known I was holding, running my fingers through my hair. Danny's constant nightmares had plagued him his whole life. As a child, he could go hardly two weeks without one. At least in my mind, the dreams played a big part in his turning to drugs. They were the only answer. It was his best solution, to sleep while he was awake. Sleep through the night was about the only thing I could do that Danny couldn't.

When the nightmares came, he awoke sweating, gasping, and falling out of bed. They'd leave him jumping at the slightest sound and afraid of everyone and everything. Nothing Mom and Dad tried, guidance counselors, talking to friendly doctors, sleeping pills, nothing helped him. The only thing that settled him was talking through them with me.

I never asked him questions, never wanted him to feel crazy or guilty for something so obviously beyond his control. Our talks never stopped the dreams from coming, but they helped get him through the day after. I wished I could do more, but was pleased to help even a little bit.

Sitting with him on that bench, I again felt guilty for leaving him alone for those three years. In my brain, I knew it was stupid. He had walked away from me. When his heart stopped, he was living under a bridge. How would I have ever found him? But the thoughts in my brain did nothing for the cold hole in my gut. I reached for the only answer I had, pushing aside my worries about his career in voyeurism.

"Tell me," I said. "The most recent one." I stood and stretched. "Tell it to me walking. Like we used to. We'll go back to Santoro's. Pretend we're walking back to Grandpa's after the library."

Turning, Danny peered into the dark woods behind us, as if making sure there was no one, or nothing, behind us to overhear.

"Trust me," I said.

"Not where anyone can see us," Danny said, walking toward the park entrance.

Danny started his story as we passed under a stone bridge, where it was so dark I could only hear his breathing and his footsteps.

"A hospital," he said. "A hospital and children but not a normal hospital. No recovery rooms, no beds, no nurses' desks, or gift shops, or elevators even."

"Same as always."

"Pretty much. The white walls, the tile floors, the rusty stains from the leaking water pipes. The stains, they run from the ceiling to the floor and they're wet and red and spidery, like veins." He looked up into the shadowy leaves over our heads. "And the water is always running. I can hear it gurgling and hissing in the pipes." He spread his hands. "And there's one door. A huge, puke-green metal door, huge like for a giant. With one barred window, way up high, a yellow light glowing behind it. That's the window the doctors watch us through.

"But now, sometimes," Danny said, "and this is what's different, now I can see something through the window. A nose with big, black-rimmed glasses on it. I can see the glasses but not the eyes. And the door-knob turns and clicks, like they're making sure it's locked.

"There are children in the room with me. A big white room full of children. Filthy children, young — five, six, seven years old. They're everywhere, moaning and crying."

"Fucking awful," I said. Danny didn't hear me.

We passed under a light pole and I saw his eyes had glazed over. His jaw had gone slack. He was back in that room and he hadn't taken me with him.

"We're all really sick. Drenched in sweat, wearing dirty, ragged hospital gowns. Their breath is horrible, like dead fish. Some have no arms, some have no legs. On some of them, their arms and legs are switched. Their eyes are dead. Like they're zombies. Sometimes they'll take one eye out and show it to me. Sometimes I'm one of them and I can take my own eyes out. But I can still see.

"This last dream was the most different. That's what really scares me about it. I'm still me but an adult this time. I'm lying on the floor at the foot of the big door. I feel the cool air coming from underneath it. I can see the yellow light. From the other side of the door, I can hear the scratching of a sharp pencil on paper, murmuring voices.

"I'm trying to get up, but I have no legs, none of us have any legs. The sick children, they're all coming for me across the floor. Dragging themselves by their hands. I can hear the skin of their stubs squeaking on the tile. It's the only sound. The squeaking, and the water running through the pipes.

"And then, suddenly, I'm standing. But now I've got no arms. And then they're all around me, the crippled children, drooling, their mouths opening and closing but not making any sound, like these pink, slimy . . . *things* that crawled up from a cave. They're reaching up for me, clutching at my legs, trying to pull me down. I can feel the doctors watching us through the window, but I know that door is never going to open. What's happening is exactly what they want to happen."

"Jesus," I said, terrified. Danny seemed so much better, how could the dreams be getting worse? "How does it end?"

"It never ends," Danny said. "I just wake up. But sooner or later, I know they're going to get me. The babies, the doctors — one of them is going to get me and that's the night I'll never wake up. I know it's crazy to think that way, but that's how it feels. Down into my bones."

We walked along in the dark. My brother's eyes darted over the shadows on either side of us, electrified with terror, as if at any moment a tiny, dirty hand might emerge from the bushes, a bloodshot child's eye rocking in its palm. I couldn't think of a damn thing to say. I knew that if our places were switched, I'd never have cleaned up. I'd stay high forever.

Our family had never uncovered the root of Danny's dreams. That was why we never could make them go away. True, our family had a history with hospitals. Our mother was a nurse, our grandfather chief surgeon of Methodist Hospital, where both of us were born. I'd always thought, if anything, that knowing hospitals should make Danny less afraid. He knew doctors as wealthy, gentle men who drank scotch and smoked pipes while watching golf on television.

As a little kid, I'd been to the emergency room once, when I was five, maybe six. I'd fallen so hard on a patch of ice that a bump the size of a peach rose on my head. My folks had me checked for a concussion. I couldn't recall Danny's reaction to the hospital, which was weird. I remembered a lot about that accident, the smell of my mother's snow-damp wool coat when she picked me up off the sidewalk, the blast of dry heat as we entered the emergency room, even the dull, hollowish sound my head had made hitting the ice. In fact, I couldn't remember Danny there at all, but he must've been. There's no place my folks could have put him. Regardless, that one crisis hardly seemed enough to traumatize a kid for life. Danny himself had been an indestructible child. He hadn't been in a hospital since he was born, at least until his heart failed. I couldn't remember him ever being sick.

"I don't know what to tell you," I finally said. "I don't know a thing about dreams. And I don't remember you even being sick much, never mind in a hospital. But still, I could be wrong. Maybe you're getting better and that's why the dreams are changing. Maybe they just need to get a little worse before they go away."

"I doubt it," Danny said. "And I'm not willing to risk it. You think I'm crazy?"

"No, Danny. I don't. Everyone has nightmares. As real as they feel, try to remember that they're not."

We came out of the park right by the library. Yellow spotlights shone up from its steps, glinting off the brass of the heavy doors and the building's tall, gold-leafed columns.

"Suddenly," Danny said, "I don't feel so much like going back there. Ever."

"Me either," I said, backing away from the building, my hand on my stomach. Danny's story had made me ill. I hoped that nightmares weren't contagious. "I don't read like I used to, anyway."

Walking back toward Santoro's, Danny glanced once over his shoulder at the library. I patted Danny on the back and quickened our pace. We could see Al waiting for us outside the restaurant, pacing in the gas-light.

"I've got some ideas," Danny said, "for getting rid of those dreams. That's where I'm gonna need your help."

Before I could ask Danny what he was thinking, Al caught sight of us and stormed in our direction yelling Danny's name, reaching us as we made the last block back to Santoro's.

"Where the fuck have you been?" Al asked Danny. Al held up his cell phone, clutched in his fist. "I been tryin' to reach you for half a fuckin' hour. We got a job. An *emergency* job."

"I had dinner with my brother and we took a walk over to the park," Danny said, pushing past Al. "I turned the phone off."

"Off? You turned it off?" Al said, trotting up beside us. "You can't turn it off. That's rule number fucking one."

"Don't yell at me," Danny said. "I haven't seen Kevin forever. I didn't want us interrupted."

"I didn't know you were on call," I said to Danny. "I didn't know you did that."

"In a manner of speaking," Danny said.

Al froze, staring at me as if I'd materialized out of thin air. He said nothing to me, turning to Danny instead. "What're we

123

gonna do with him?"

"How big is the job?" Danny asked.

"Medium to big," Al said. "And very fucking urgent."

Danny studied Al and then refocused on me. "So it can't wait?"

"We should be there already," Al said, his voice wavering. "We gotta be done before our guy gets off." He sounded afraid, like a good kid desperate to beat curfew. I got the feeling that whatever had gone wrong, Al had screwed it up. Al tilted his head in my direction. "I know this isn't how you wanted to do it, Dan. We could put him in a cab."

"I'll wait in the car or whatever," I said. "Just drop me off after. I'm off tomorrow. I don't have anywhere to be."

Al threw his toothpick down and immediately replaced it with another. He looked over at the Charger. "If we hurry, maybe we could drop him off."

Danny opened his mouth to speak, looking like he was about to agree. Then his words caught and his expression changed. "Could we use an extra set of hands?"

"Of course," Al said. "I've even got enough tools, but is now really the fucking time?"

"We can trust him," Danny said.

Al raised his hands in the air. "It's not that. You vouch for him, that's gospel for me. You know that, Dan."

"I don't need vouching for," I said. "I'm waiting in the car, right?"

Mr. Bavasi walked out of the restaurant, wiping his hands on his apron. I don't know what he thought he had on his hands; the apron stayed pristine. He gestured for Danny to approach him. "You boys got a call about a job."

"I understand," Danny said.

"There was a second call," Bavasi said.

Al went ashen. "He called back? He called *twice?*"

Bavasi glanced at Al, then turned back to Danny. "I told him you were already gone. Why are you still standing here, making a liar out of me to Mr. Santoro?"

Danny and Al both turned to me. Somehow, just by being there, I was fucking up their plans. They had something important to do, I realized, that they didn't want me to see. Something requiring tools. Before I could say anything, Bavasi sensed the heart of the problem.

"Kevin, let your brother do his work. Stay here with me. I've got a crème brûlée left. We'll have a cognac and dessert, like civilized men. I can tell you stories about the old Park Slope. Mr. S. and I, we knew your grandfather from back when he was running the hospital. He and your grandmother, they ate with us all the time." He smiled. "Pride of the neighborhood they were. I bet there's lots about them you don't know."

Danny considered it. He seized me by the arm. "I'm sorry about all this," he said, though to me or Al or Bavasi I wasn't sure. I hated being apologized for.

"Thanks, Mr. B.," Danny said, "but he'll come with us."

"You're sure?" Bavasi asked.

"It had to happen sooner or later," Danny said. "Why drag it out?"

I jerked my arm free from Danny's grip, liking the whole situation less and less.

"Forget it," I said. "I love crème brûlée. After, I'll take the L into the city and catch the boat." Danny reached for my arm, but I backed away. "I can find my own way home, thanks."

I wanted to shove him and remind him that though it was only a year, I was still the older brother. But all the cryptic talk had set my brain racing. I was desperate to know what Danny had gotten into; he might need my help getting out of it. Maybe dragging me along was asking for that help without tipping off Al and Bavasi. Maybe Danny wanted me to see exactly what he was doing. He had showed me the stuff in his apartment. I'd go with him, if it helped him, but he had to know that I had limits. I grabbed Danny by the arm, pulled him off to the side.

"Look, I'm not judging what you do," I said, keeping my voice low, "but that doesn't mean I want to be part of it. Not spying on people, peeking through their windows or whatever and digging up their secrets."

Danny slipped his arm across my shoulders. "I understand, but it's nothing like what you saw upstairs. This is a totally different thing."

"Danny, you better be sure," Bavasi said from behind us.

"I've been thinking about it for a long time," Danny called back to him. "You know that."

"The old man is making me nervous," I said.

"I told you before," Bavasi said, "there's no way back for him after this. Remember that."

I looked at Danny. "That doesn't help."

"Forget him," Danny said. "I need you with me."

He pulled open the back door of the Charger, but climbed into the front seat. He'd left the other door open for me. He looked up at me, waiting. Al hit the horn, impatient. Danny stayed calm, waiting. I could feel Bavasi standing behind us, watching. Getting into the car seemed like the quickest solution for everyone.

"It's just a thing I have to do," Danny said. "Nobody's gonna get in any trouble."

"Sure," I said, climbing into the backseat, slamming the door behind me.

We cruised across the Verrazano, the red-and-white lights of its blue-gray towers and spans reflected on the black, rolling waters of the Narrows below us. As we passed through the tollbooth on the Staten Island side my bravery waned and I suddenly hoped for an unspoken change of plans. I wanted Al to take me home. Danny could just tell me everything tomorrow, in the safety of the light of day. But we stayed on the expressway and headed south into the heart of the island, leaving my neighborhood behind.

"Where are we going, Danny?" I asked.

"How much further?" Danny asked Al.

"Three minutes," Al said.

Bullshit. There was no driving to anywhere on Staten Island in three minutes. "Stop ignoring me, Danny. Answer my question. Where are we going?"

"Take it easy," Danny said. "We're good. All of us."

Al left the expressway at Victory Boulevard and headed east. We wound our way through a maze of side streets and then pulled into the woods onto a dirt road I hadn't even seen coming. More like a trail, it was barely wide enough for the car. Al swore as branches scraped the sides of the Charger. He had killed his headlights and drove by the glow of his parking lights. I stopped asking questions. Nobody would answer.

Danny rapped his knuckles on the window beside him, staring out into the darkness. "I told you I didn't want to come here anymore."

Al hunched over the wheel, his eyes focused on the next few feet of dirt trail visible in front of the car. "I know. That's why I did it myself Wednesday night."

"You shouldn't have put 'em here," Danny said.

"This is a good spot," Al said. "Always has been. I'm not the only one that uses it, you know."

"It's banned territory now," Danny said. "What's wrong with you? You bucked a direct order. The dump, the Meadowlands, the East River, that's where we're supposed to go." I could barely see him in the front seat, but his voice gave away his growing agitation. "Anywhere but here. You got lazy and now we gotta bail you out."

"I hadda do it quick," Al said. "You hadda hang with your brother. I don't like using the dump, after the Towers went there. I told Bavasi that. And I didn't have time to drive all over the eastern seaboard lookin' for a place that met with your fuckin' approval."

"I'm not the one you gotta worry about," Danny said.

The branches, bare and dead, closed around the front of the car, scraping the windshield like bony fingers. Al stopped the car, threw it in park and cut the engine. The lights went out. We were swallowed in darkness and silence.

"Hey, I'm sorry," Al said. "If I'd known we'd have to come back for them, I never would've put them here in the first place."

"Come back where?" I asked. "Put what here?"

Danny opened his door and the dome light came on, illuminating both their faces as they stared at me, two men about to give bad news that it pained them to deliver. Al reached up and switched off the dome light.

"I am not getting out of this car until I get some answers," I said.

"I hate this fucking place," Danny said.

He and Al got out of the car, slamming their doors in unison. I crossed my arms and stayed put in my seat. I heard them arguing outside in heated whispers. My door flew open and fists clutched my shirt, dragging me across the seat and out the door. I fought but it was no use. Al yanked me out of the car and threw me down in the bushes.

"Take it fuckin' easy," I heard Danny say. "He's my brother."

"Then get him in fucking line," Al said. "I'm outta patience. You promised me he could handle himself."

"He can," Danny said. "I just didn't plan on going this far this soon."

"Then you shoulda left him in fuckin' Brooklyn."

"Handle what?" I said, getting up, brushing dirt and leaves off my clothes. I'd torn a sleeve. One less work shirt.

"Enough bullshitting," Al said, and he opened the trunk.

He unloaded a pick and two shovels, leaning them against the bumper. A black plastic tarp lined the trunk. I started to shake. Beads of sweat popped out on my forehead.

"You gotta be fucking kidding me," I said.

There was a long silence.

"I'm sorry," Danny said. "But it's better this way in the long run."

SEVEN

Carrying the tools, we made our way by the glow of a penlight on Al's keychain.

"Jesus," Danny said, stopping to free a thorny branch caught in his jacket. "You know what this jacket cost me? Nice flashlight, limp dick. I should've brought my iPod. We'd have more light."

"Fuck off, Curran," Al said. "You want someone seein' us out here?"

"Nobody could see us in these woods no matter what we carry," Danny said.

"That's what somebody says," Al said, "right before they get caught."

I walked in silence behind them, a shovel over each shoulder, trying to imagine what we'd be digging up — money, or guns, or maybe even a stash of drugs. But I couldn't forget Al and Danny talking about "them" or how that word called to mind the strange excuses Al had made at the bar a few nights ago, how he talked about putting people to bed. I kept my gaze trained on Danny's dark form in front of me. That's your brother, I kept telling myself. You can't get him out of it if you don't know what he's gotten into. You wouldn't be here with this shovel, I told myself, if you'd done your job and stood between Danny and the needle like a big brother is supposed to.

After what seemed like a good half-mile, we finally broke into a clearing. Al and Danny set down their tools and stood on either side of me, picking sticks and dead leaves from their clothes.

We'd arrived at the edge of a lumpy field, the whole thing overgrown with monkey grass and tall dandelions. I swore I heard rats rustling around in the weeds. The half-moon hovered atop the black trees in the distance, casting everything in a faint, pearly glow. Tiny, swirling shadows darted across the stars. Bats.

Across the field loomed the shadowy ruins of a large, abandoned building. The windows were either boarded or shattered. The bell tower had fallen, now a pile of rubble among many other strewn over the grounds. Despite the damage, the building still resembled what it had claimed to be: a hospital. I turned to Danny and Al.

"I know this place," I said. "This is fucking Bloodroot."

"No shit," Danny said, staring at the building. He chuckled under his breath. "I wondered if you'd remember."

I looked down at my feet. "Oh, shit." I started dancing around on the tips of my toes, looking for a clean place to put my feet. "Danny, fuck, Danny, we're standing in the graveyard."

The graveyard where the doctors buried the children who died under their care. The children no one claimed. Dozens of them.

Al was already striding purposefully across the field, his penlight focused on the ground. He looked back at us. "Tell your ghost stories later, kids. We got work to do."

I threw down my shovel. "All right, fuck this. You had your fun, Danny. Nice joke. C'mon, Al, you can quit playing around. You scared me, all right. Ha, ha. Now let's go."

I expected Al to walk back to us, shoulders shaking and head hanging as he laughed. I knew Danny had told him when suggesting the prank about how when we were kids, Danny used to lead me through the woods of Willowbrook Park to the Bloodroot children's asylum.

Danny and I would exit the woods and hide behind the low stone and mortar wall encircling the graveyard. From there, we tried to glimpse the resident freaks. Danny would yelp that he'd seen someone in a window, naked and deformed, staring blankly through the glass, but by the time I found the right window, the vision had always disappeared. When Danny bored of this game, he introduced another, more exciting competition. Without warning, he'd leap the wall and sprint across the graveyard, tap the nearest marker and run back to our hiding place. We dared each other to see who could run deepest among the graves and touch the marker standing the farthest away. Danny always won.

Once, I thought I had him. An older brother can only take so much ribbing from his younger, and in a fit of daring I not only touched the farthest marker but circled the graveyard twice before tearing back to the wall and tumbling over it to land right on top of Danny. Not only had I thought him beaten, I thought I'd added a new level of danger to the game, an act that was almost exclusively Danny's purview. Instead of laughing or congratulating me, Danny just stared me down, anger boiling in his eyes.

He leaped over the wall and ran across the graveyard toward the crooked plywood cross I had touched. He reached it, plucked it from the ground without breaking stride and circled back for the wall. Shocked, I stood openmouthed as he ran to me, laughing so hard he could barely breathe and holding the cross in front of him like a relay runner's baton. On my side of the wall, I backed away, hands in the air. I knew instinctively what he wanted. My role in the game, as always, was to repair the damage he had done. I was to run back and replant the cross. I wanted no part of it.

Panting, Danny stood on the other side of the wall, holding the cross over it. He was sweating, clumps of his black hair sticking to his forehead. He waved the cross in the air before me, as if he was playing with a pet and the moving object would incite me. All I did was back away toward the woods. Danny didn't say a word, but the anger reignited his eyes. With savage blows, he smashed the cross on the wall. Splinters sprayed everywhere, landing on our clothes and in our hair. I jumped around in circles, swatting at the splinters as if Danny had dumped a box of spiders over my head. Danny laughed. I didn't say a word to him all the way back through the woods.

From then on, when our folks took us to Willowbrook Park, I refused to follow Danny into the trees. Instead, I went fishing for perch and bluegills in the weedy pond while my folks shared a beer or two at a picnic table. I figured Danny went back to the graveyard. He's only eleven, I told myself as I watched my bobber dip and jiggle in the water, how much trouble could he really get into? But I was afraid to ask what he did there by himself. Not afraid enough, though, to go looking for him.

Now, here we were, standing in the grave-yard again. It had taken a lot of years, but he had maneuvered me back here. To one of the few places where I had told him no. Well, this night could be like that afternoon. I wouldn't take what he was trying to hand me, not the cross, not the shovel, or anything that came with it.

I tried to push past Danny and go back to the car but he grabbed me hard by the arm and pulled me close to him.

"This isn't a joke, Kevin," he said. "Get your head outta your ass."

Before I could answer, Al's shovel broke open the earth, the scratchy ring of the blade biting the dirt silencing every cricket in the field, freezing whatever crawled around in the weeds. Al dug for several long seconds as Danny and I glared at each other. The strokes of Al's shovel sounded in my ears like the chimes of a clock. Danny's eyes begged a promise from me like they did when we were little: *I need you with me on this. Don't tell Mom and Dad.* I took a deep breath. The scent of freshly turned soil filled my nose.

"There's no way I can be involved in this," I said. "There's just no fucking way."

"You're here," Danny said. "You already are involved."

"I'm not doing it," I said. "I'm not digging up these kids' graves. It's sickness. Maybe I can't stop you, but I'm not doing it."

Danny released my arm. "Christ, we're not digging up these kids. What kind of monster do you think I am?"

Al threw down his shovel and stormed over. "What the fuck? I could use some help over there." He turned on me. "And this fuck, you told me he'd be cool." Al spoke to Danny but poked me in the shoulder as he did it.

Danny smacked Al's arm away. "Watch yourself, this is my fucking brother you're talking to. He's just in shock. He thought we were digging up the kids."

Al spat at his feet. "What the fuck for? What the fuck I want with a bunch of dead retards? That's gross. He always think the worst of people, your brother?"

Danny bent down and picked up my shovel. He handed it to me. "Al, he's good, I swear."

"Totally," I said. "I'm good."

Al looked back and forth between us like we were kids he'd caught in a lie and he was too exasperated to argue. "Break it down for him," he said to Danny. "Then get over there and help me."

Danny watched Al until he went back to digging and then turned to me.

"Remember the other night in the bar," Danny said, "when Al talked about putting the kids to bed?"

I nodded.

"That was a figure of speech, kind of," Danny said.

"We're digging up bodies," I said. "Bodies Al buried out here the other night."

"Yes," Danny said.

"Christ Almighty," I said, wiping my hand down my face. "Just tell me, Danny, tell me they aren't really kids."

"Fuck, no. You think I'd be involved in that kind of work?"

I didn't know what to think. "Who are they?"

"Don't worry, they had it coming."

"Al killed them?"

"I'd say the odds on that are seventy-thirty

against," Danny said. "Al's a loyal, obedient soldier but in case you hadn't noticed, he's kind of a moron. He does mostly disposal work."

"And you ended up in this how?" I asked.

"I owed Al a favor," Danny said, looking over at Al. "It's a long story. Look, I wanted to ease you into this, that's why I showed you my apartment, took you to the park, but I couldn't find the right words. Then, well, circumstance conspired against us. You gotta tough this out. I'll help you through the aftermath. But if Al thinks you're weak on this, it puts both of us in danger."

Too dumbfounded to speak, all I could do was nod. Twelve hours earlier I was lecturing about *Common Sense* in class. Now, I was digging up murdered people for the Mafia, or the Devil, or whoever. With my brother. What the fuck?

"Lead the way," I said.

Danny held two bandannas in his hands. He poured cologne into them. "Take one. Wrap it over your mouth and nose."

I did as he said. The cologne made my eyes water.

"It's better than what we're about to smell," Danny said. He handed me a pair of black gloves. "You can have mine."

I pulled on the gloves and followed Danny

across the graveyard, toward the sound of Al's shovel tearing at the ground.

I only puked twice.

When Danny's shovel blade pierced dirt, tarp, and flesh and cracked a bone, I threw up Santoro's glorious steak into my bandanna and down the front of my shirt. Al laughed, joking about popping my cherry as I retched on my knees. Danny rubbed my back, gave me a piece of gum and a cigarette. I hadn't smoked in two years but I took the cigarette gladly. I had the smell of myself to contend with now, not just the bodies. I smoked the entire thing without removing it from my mouth, afraid to touch anything with my hands.

I retched again when Danny and Al heaved the second body onto the ground at my feet and the head rolled away from the corpse, leaving a glistening trail in the grass like a slug. Al apologized as he darted after the head. He grabbed it by the hair and the face stretched like putty.

"What's the fucking point of that?" Danny asked. "If you're gonna bury the head and the body together. Defeats the whole fucking purpose."

"I buried 'em like I got 'em," Al said, clearly embarrassed.

We carried the bodies back to the car one at a time, Al at one end and Danny and me at the other, mud and gore sloshing around inside the tarp. We managed not to drop the loose head.

At the car, Danny and I heaved the dead into the trunk. Al arranged them so they fit better. After I tossed in my puke-stained shirt and bandanna, Al slammed the trunk closed. We washed our hands and faces with water from a plastic gallon jug Al had in he car. Danny stripped off his T-shirt and gave it to me. Al walked around the other side of the car to take a leak. Danny and I leaned against the hood, me wearing his T-shirt, him there in a wife-beater and a black suit jacket. His cuffs glistened in the moonlight. He didn't seem to notice. Ladies and gentlemen, the Curran brothers. Just another night out on the town. I took another smoke from my brother.

"How you doin'?" he asked.

"I'm completely fucking numb," I said. "So I'm either in shock or an emotionless, soul-dead sociopath."

"I'd put the odds at ninety-ten in favor of the former," Danny said.

"I think I hate you for this," I said. "I think I'm unbelievably pissed off."

"We're almost done," Danny said. "Then

we can sort this out between us."

"Sort this out? Jesus, Danny. It's not like you stole my Halloween candy."

Danny handed me a bottle from inside his jacket. I drank the whiskey down until my eyes watered. The liquor tore my empty, sick insides to shreds. But I held it down. Al had climbed into the car. He had the stereo turned on low.

"I am done," I said. "I'll fucking walk home from here if Al won't take me back."

"You don't want to go home," Danny said. "You think you do. You think you want to go home, drink all the beer in the house, crawl into bed and pretend this never happened. But it did. You need to be with us when it hits you. And it'll hit you tonight. The last place you want to be is alone."

"Maybe that's true," I said. "But I won't want to be around you and Al."

"Who else is there?" Danny asked. "Who else knows what you went through tonight?"

I spat on the ground. I took a deep breath. The smell of the dead and their graves clung to me. "Tell me we're not on film."

"You think I'm out of my mind?" Danny said, chuckling. "I don't record anything *I* do."

"Let's get this fucking over with," I said. "Get in the car."

Danny didn't argue. I climbed into the backseat and slammed the door closed behind me. I thought Al might gripe about it but he just threw the car in reverse and backed us out along the trail. We didn't hit a single tree on the way out. I knew that Al's talent for reversing down a dark and narrow trail came from an abundance of practice.

When we made the asphalt, Al swung the car around. "Double-check our clearance for the dump," he said, leaning on the gas.

Danny pulled his cell from his jacket. "I'm thinking about a table for two . . . Okay. No problem." He turned to Al. "As long as we get there within the hour. That's when his replacement comes on."

"Good, good," Al said. "We'll be in and out before he even gets off."

As it was for everyone else who lived on Staten Island, the dump was a regular part of my life. I passed it going to the mall, the movie theater, and the bowling alley. On any trip from the southern end of the island to the north, the dump was impossible to avoid. But despite having grown up with the dump, I had never been inside it.

A few times when we were kids my father drove out there to toss old furniture or a broken-down appliance. My mother had never let us go. As kids, we thought mountains of trash translated into acres of undiscovered mysteries. The dump reminded me of the ancient ruins I read about at the library. Danny just wanted to get dirty. But Mom wouldn't see it our way; she couldn't stomach her sons being that close to so much filth. Every kid heard the rumors about the Mob stashing bodies out at Fresh Kills. We all secretly dreamed of discovering one, like finding a fossil, and of being a player in the drama that followed. The find would imbue us with a neighborhood notoriety we both craved and feared. It felt like a gyp to me then, being deprived of my shot at stardom.

Now, as Al turned off the service road and into the entrance to the dump, I couldn't believe that me, my kid brother, and one of our high school pals were about to bury our own gruesome treasure. I was fulfilling one childhood dream that would've best been left forgotten.

The Charger's tires crushed random bits of glass and plastic as Al slowed under the choleric lights of the guard booth. He rolled down the window and a damp stench wafted into the car. I gagged and wished for a cologne-soaked bandanna. Al and Danny didn't flinch. Danny lit a cigarette and passed it back to me. I took it gratefully. The guard scrawled on something with a pen. He handed Al a yellow ticket that Al placed on his dash.

"Just in case you pass someone on your way out or back," the guard said. "Not likely, though." He leaned forward, trying to get a better look at me. "Who's the third?"

"Nobody. Forget you ever saw any of us," Al said. "Same as always."

Danny leaned across the car, pointing over the guard's head — with a .45. "That fucking camera off?"

The guard raised his hands. "Of course. Whadda you think, I'm stupid? You wanna come in and look?"

Danny cocked the hammer. "You want me to?"

Al handed the guard an envelope. Danny tucked the gun into his waistband at the small of his back. The guard stuck the envelope in his pocket and leaned out the window to give directions.

"Stay away from hills three and four, they're bein' worked on. Keep to one and two up front here. And the ones way in the back? That's where the Towers are." The guard crossed himself and closed his window against the stink.

"We need a new guy out here," Danny said. "That one scares too easy."

"Maybe it was the gun?" Al said. "Just sayin'."

"Cops have guns," Danny said. "They keep them close when they ask questions."

"We do the dump guy," Al said, "where we gonna take the body?" He laughed. "That's like ironical, right? Like one of those Chinese puzzles."

Danny crossed his arms and sank down in his seat. Al drove on, his window still rolled down.

In the distance, hills three and four glowed under towers of fluorescent lights. In the shadows at the edge of the light trucks and tractors crawled over the hill like giant insects with enormous, bright white eyes. Their black exhaust rose like clouds of ink, disappearing as it drifted out of the light.

"This place is supposed to be closed," I said. "What're they doing out there?"

"Leveling if off," Danny said. "And cleaning out all the chemicals and biohazard shit that never shoulda been here to begin with." He turned in his seat to look at me. "One day this is gonna be a park, with a golf course and a nature preserve and a wind farm. At least that's what the city says."

"Yeah, right," I said. "And I'm gonna be pope."

For the first time, Al laughed at one of my jokes. "When you're pope, Kev, can I have some of the forty virgins you get?" He bounced in his seat, thrilled with his own wit. "You can keep the hat."

"You got it, Al," I said. "So, Danny, the guard recognized everyone but me. You've been here before."

Danny turned in his seat. "No, I have never been here before in my life. And neither have you, and neither has Al." He turned to Al, who slammed on the brakes at the foot of a massive, seeping mountain of trash. "Relax, he's still learning. He'll get it."

Al said nothing as he climbed out of the car. Danny and I followed. Standing there amid acres and decades of garbage, about to add two dead bodies to the pile, all I felt was ashamed of embarrassing my brother. And sick from the stench that engulfed us. I could feel it settling into my pores like humidity.

Al stood back from the open trunk as Danny and I lifted out the first body. I held the feet and Danny the shoulders. We rocked him three times and tossed him onto the pile, just like my father and I used to do when we threw Danny in the pool, only the body didn't go nearly as far as Danny used to. It hit the pile like a bag of wet phone books. I wiped my hands on my jeans, glad I couldn't see what came off in the dark. Danny and Al handled the next body. It landed right beside the first.

Danny and I passed the whiskey bottle back and forth as Al tore open the tarps, exposing the bodies. Holding his breath, he stuck out his hand. Danny passed him a bottle of lighter fluid.

"Anybody see you buy that?" Danny asked.

"Jesus Christ. I stole it off my neighbor's porch, okay?"

Al doused the corpses and stepped back, tossing the empty bottle high into the darkness. Danny pulled his lighter from his pocket. I felt his hand on my chest.

"Step back," he said. He licked his finger and held it aloft, gauging the wind. There didn't seem to be any.

"Your brother?" Al said to me. "He likes this part the best. The fire."

"We should be okay," Danny said, "but be careful not to get the smoke on you. And for godsakes don't breathe it in."

He handed me the lighter.

"I don't want it," I said, raising my hands.

150

"I've done enough."

"You have to take it," Danny said. "It's important."

"What?" I asked. "Digging up corpses and hauling them around isn't enough to pass the audition?"

"Calm down," Danny said, stepping closer to me. "You're making Al nervous. Tonight isn't some tryout, that's your imagination running wild. Tonight's just tough timing." He grabbed my right hand, pressed the lighter into my palm. "It only takes a second. Do it. For me."

My fingers closed around the Zippo. But I just stood there holding it, staring at my fist. Sweat beaded on my forehead. Suddenly, I wanted to run, even more than I had in the graveyard. But there was nowhere to go. Acres of darkness and wasteland surrounded me.

"Let 'er rip," Al said. He didn't sound nervous.

I stood there.

"Go ahead," Danny said quietly. "Do it and we can bail, get back to civilization."

"Won't somebody see the fire?" I asked. "Won't they ask questions?"

"It doesn't matter," Danny said. "There are spontaneous fires all over this place every night, chemicals, methane pockets, poison bird shit. It's all just garbage. No-body even wastes their time putting them out."

I licked my lips, tasting rot on my tongue. Danny's eyes twitched at the corners. His hand reached behind his back. Al had moved out of my line of sight. At least in the movies, this was when the hero heard the click of the hammer. I didn't feel like a fuckin' hero and I didn't hear anything but the growling of the distant machines. No footsteps, no breathing, nothing. The stench swallowing us had even subsumed Al's cologne.

It dawned on me that Al would have no problem leaving me here as body number three. Maybe Al wasn't as dumb as I thought. He'd fooled his third corpse into coming out here under its own power. He worked with Danny, seemed to follow his lead, but it was Bavasi and Santoro who scared him. I didn't know what, if anything, Danny could do to protect me. I watched Danny's eyes, trying to find Al through their motion. But all Danny's eyes did was plead with me.

Danny was right. It didn't matter. Those bodies were nothing but empty shells. I wasn't hurting anyone. If I didn't burn them, Al or Danny would and maybe burn me with them. What had Danny told me in the car? None of us had ever been here, ever in our lives. Anything that happened here couldn't be our doing. We were never here. What choice did I have but to believe him? Any chance to get out of this had passed me by long before Danny handed me that lighter. The lighter. I looked down at it, sitting, silver, innocent, and cool, in my palm. It was an expensive Zippo. What a waste. I pushed back the hood with my thumb, ignited the flame, watched it burn for a long moment, and tossed it onto a dead man's chest.

He went up fast, low blue flames running frantic only briefly before igniting into leaping golden waves.

I backed away until Al and Danny's dark forms merged into one black shadow before the fire. The trash around the bodies began to burn. The stench hit me like a kick to the back of my knees. I thought it might make me blind. I forgot not to breathe. I spit up a mouthful of bile and whiskey, wiping my mouth on my arm. What the fuck had I done?

The shadow broke in two as Al headed for the car. Danny waited for me by the fire. The fire gurgled and spat, feeding. The heat made me squint. It ruffled Danny's hair.

"I need to know," I said. "Who were they? What did they do?"

He threw his arm over my shoulder, walking me away from the car. He nearly pulled me down as he stumbled over something. I looked down. The head. We had dropped it again. Danny grabbed it by the hair. This time I didn't look at the face. Al started the Charger.

"Remember how I told you," Danny said, the head hanging from his fist, "how I took over for Santoro's other tech guy?" He held up the head. "*This* is Santoro's other guy." Danny tossed the head into the fire. "He talked too much. Mostly to that other guy next to him."

I doubled over, dry heaving.

"I know you can keep secrets, Kevin," Danny said, rubbing my back. "I remember it well."

"Let's roll," Al yelled, gunning the engine.

EIGHT

On the ride back to Brooklyn, Danny and
Al abandoned me to my thoughts and the
last few swigs from the whiskey bottle. I
drank it all, hoping in vain the alcohol
would put me to sleep. Alcohol was how
you treated open wounds, right? Hadn't
Grandpa taught us that? And I felt
wounded, all right. The Continental Army,
all they'd had for bullet and bayonet wounds
was bad rum. If cheap liquor was good
enough for George Washington, it was good
enough for me.

As we crossed over the Verrazano, I curled
up tight against the door, my forehead resting on the cool glass of the window. I stared
straight down at the white lines passing
underneath us. I thought about opening the
door and falling out. I saw myself bouncing
once off the pavement and dropping over
the side, tumbling down through the night
and splashing into the cold, deep Narrows.

But that bastard Al had power locks on all his doors.

As a boy, I had loved crossing the Verrazano, the mammoth, sky-blue arc of steel and asphalt stretching from the northern end of Staten Island to the eastern edge of Brooklyn, its wide roadway hanging on heavy cables over the water. The Verrazano spanned the space where the Colonials and the Redcoats had fought the Battle of Brooklyn. I used to look down from the car and picture the British warships sailing from the coast of Staten Island and into the cannon fire from the Colonial forts dug deep into the Brooklyn soil.

On those Sunday drives, after we passed through the tollbooth, the road would rise onto the bridge and Staten Island would shrink away behind us, the world opening wide in the dirty windshield of our Dodge Dart. The gleaming silver spires of Manhattan spiked the sky on my left, the limitless slate expanse of the mythic Atlantic unfurled on my right. In front of us waited Brooklyn, sunlight washing over a thousand different hues of brick and brown and gray. A place of parks and pizza joints, of museums and libraries. The home of my grandfather's fireplace and my grandmother's grand piano. Of Easter egg hunts and twenty-foot

Christmas trees. Staten Island only seemed to me a place still in search of a king, kneeling before the silver crown of Manhattan.

Riding over the water with Danny and Al, I felt like one of Washington's naïve, terrified soldiers staring down the British fleet: overwhelmed, outgunned, caught in the current of forces far beyond my control or comprehension. Like one of those poor, dumb farmers, I'd marched into a world far more brutal than the one I thought I saw from my porch, a world inhabited by people far more dirty and dangerous than me. I worried that even if I survived my stint in Santoro's army, I'd already started leaving important pieces of me on the battlefield.

Far below me, the ruby and white lights of the bridge shimmered, reflected on the hard black face of the Narrows. The steel cables rushed by like the bars of a cage, of a jail cell. Every time oncoming headlights swept through the car I sank deeper into the backseat, hiding from the eyes of the drivers. The dark void over southern Manhattan choked on stars. Brooklyn still revealed herself shadowy and seductive before us, her white lights clustered like jewels against her Indian red flesh. But as we cruised down the highway and off the bridge the lamp-lit road stretched out like a bruised blue vein under papery, yellow skin.

Taking me to that graveyard, Danny had put me through something that should've driven us apart for good. But I knew it would only draw us closer. He knew it, too. It was why he'd insisted I go. Secrets, no matter how terrible, can bind as strong as blood.

Al opened his cell phone, projecting an eerie blue glow. The light faded when Al moved the phone to his ear, waiting for an answer to his call. I closed my eyes.

"It's done," he said. "We just crossed the water."

There was a pause as the person on the other end spoke.

"Three," Al said. Another pause. "Aw man, now you tell me that? No, of course I'm not complaining, it's just —" Al snapped his phone shut and tossed it on the dash. "Motherfucker hung up on me. Fuck." He slapped Danny on the arm. "Three-way split. Did you know about this?"

Danny shook his head, rubbing his eyes. He'd been asleep.

Three, Al had said. *Three-way split.* I wondered how close I had really come to Al's answer being *two* instead of *three.* I wondered again, had I failed, what my brother would have done. Would he have let

Al shoot me down like a deserter? A meaningless question, I told myself. I hadn't
failed and I had saved Danny from having
to make that choice. For once in my life, I'd
gotten to him before the needle did.

Bavasi watched us carefully as we climbed
from the car and walked toward the restaurant, slouched and plodding like zombies,
the only noise on the street the buzzing of
the streetlights. He pulled open the door
and turned his head to double-check the
empty street as the three of us filed into the
restaurant.

In the lobby, Danny and Al took off their
shoes and socks, so I did the same. Bavasi
locked the door behind us. Instead of
frightening me, the heavy shot of the bolt
hitting home was a comfort. I was safe from
the gaze of strangers.

Bavasi had the lights turned down, the
wall lamps painting the restaurant in a
warm, golden glow. The room smelled of
buttery garlic and sharp pepper and fine
coffee. We followed Bavasi to the booth
where Danny and I had eaten steaks that
same evening. As I slid across the rich
leather, the memory of that meal drifted far
back in my mind, floating ethereal among
recollections I had of Danny and me from

159

long ago, reading not at all like the newly minted memory that it really was.

A crystal decanter sat at center table surrounded by four shot glasses. A lone coffee bean sat in the bottom of each glass. Bavasi removed the decanter's top and poured a shot of foggy, syrupy liquid for each of us. It smelled like burning licorice. Bavasi lifted his glass. We all did the same. *Salud,* he said quietly, and we all drank. The liquor coated my mouth and throat with a warm, simmering heat that was unlike the sharp, electric tang of the whiskey I'd drunk before. My whole head and throat felt purged and clean. The vomit, the dump, the smoke, they were all scorched away. I wanted a few minutes to recover but our host poured another round. He toasted again, we swallowed, and I reached for the pack of cigarettes my brother had thrown on the table. Bavasi capped the decanter and walked away from the table.

I stuck out my hand to Danny for a lighter but he just shrugged at me.

"That Zippo I gave you was the only one I had on me."

I looked to Al. He shook his head.

Bavasi returned to the table and set down a pitcher of ice water and three glasses. He slid a glass ashtray, a pack of matches from some other restaurant in it, across the table to me.

Danny sighed as I lit up. "If you get back in the habit because of me, I'm gonna feel really guilty."

I exhaled a long cloud of smoke and shook out the match. The alcohol was making things distant and fuzzy. "Don't worry about me. I'm a grown man. Besides, I'm the oldest, you can't tell me what to do."

After pouring us each a glass of water, Bavasi leaned on the table, his weight heavy on his palms. Like my father, thick veins roped his hands and forearms. There was plenty of room in the booth, but he showed no desire to sit.

"Gentlemen," he said, "I know you wouldn't be here accepting my hospitality if the work wasn't done" — turning to Al — "and done right this time, so I congratulate you. I know you're anxious to get clean. Everything is ready for you in the locker room. Leave your clothes by the back door, as usual." He turned to me. "Kevin, you are the new man here so I'm sure you're the most eager to get started. Why don't you go first while I review the night's events with my *paisans* here?"

I knew a polite dismissal when I heard one and got up from the table. The colonel wanted a moment with his senior officers. Bavasi rested a hand on my shoulder. His grip was firm.

"Through the kitchen to the right," he said. "Take your time. There's no hurry now."

Through a heavy door marked STAFF I found a long row of tall, narrow lockers. Three shower stalls stood off to my right, clean towels stacked by each one. Hanging from the nearest locker was a fresh set of clothes: dark pants, a long-sleeved, deep green T-shirt, a black suit jacket. Inside the locker waited new underwear, socks, and a brand-new pair of black leather shoes. At first, I thought I'd found Danny's stuff but everything was in my size, all of it too small for him. There was even a fresh stick of deodorant and a new razor. A goddamn toothbrush. A few lockers away hung new clothes for Danny and Al.

Listening for anyone coming through the door, I walked the lockers, peeking through the vents. I jiggled a couple of the latches but they were all locked. Through the narrow vents, I couldn't see anything other than white clothes I took to be chefs' jackets and waiters' coats. Did Bavasi's regular employees know what went on here late at night? Were they part of it? When they came into work tomorrow would there be any sign of us? I couldn't see Bavasi letting that happen. He probably knew everything I was and wasn't doing at that moment just from the sounds he didn't hear.

I headed back up the aisle to my own locker and undressed, leaving my old clothes in a pile on the cold concrete floor. The room felt plenty warm, telling me the goose bumps on my naked flesh weren't from being cold. I was afraid of being alone, and afraid of walking back into the restaurant not having done what I was told. Was Santoro out there, waiting to meet me?

Who had Santoro really had in mind when he built this room? Was it for Bavasi's cooks and waiters and bartenders, or was it for their other, more specialized employees? Who hid behind whom? Where had it all started? I couldn't even conjure a face for Santoro. All I saw when I thought of him was a pair of long, long arms. I reimagined Bavasi at twenty, thirty, a backroom butcher for some neighborhood meat shop in Italian Brooklyn — his thick, hairy forearms coated in the blood of his work, his white apron splattered with crimson gore as he stood at the butcher's block. Santoro walking in, eyeing the blood, offering his hand and asking for a favor.

The shower smelled of bleach and disinfectant. Waiting for the water to warm, I ran my fingertips along the cool white tile. Was this what a gas chamber was like? Did anyone use gas anymore? I stepped under the steaming water, washed those questions from my mind. Surely what we had done, gruesome as it was, didn't warrant that kind of punishment. But it was a crime. A serious crime that covered others. Like murder, for instance. I was a criminal now. A felon. Guilty of aiding and abetting, accessory after the fact, and probably plenty more charges I couldn't name. I studied my hands. They looked the same as they had that afternoon, back when they were just a teacher's hands.

I unwrapped the soap and lathered up, scrubbing every nook and cranny. Bowing my head I let the water pound my shoulders. Through half-open eyes I watched the suds and water pool at my feet before it ran down the drain. How many people had washed the filth of the dead off their skin in that shower? My brother had. I lathered and rinsed again.

If things went bad for Danny, I'd have a lot more than student complaints on my permanent record. I had to keep him close, figure out a way for both of us to break free of Santoro's orbit, though I had no clue how and when I would do that. One major complication was that Danny seemed happy where he was. Good luck getting him to do something he didn't want to. Another problem was the fact that crossing Danny's superiors was a quick way to make us both dead. Even I, minor player that I was, could see that. I was washing off the proof in their shower.

I turned off the water and stood there dripping, staring at my hands again. What did any of it matter to me? I'd never be here again. The graveyard, the dump, Santoro's, "putting the kids to bed" — this wasn't my world. I was a teacher. I taught American history for Richmond City College in Staten Island, New York. I lived in a crappy apartment in a forgotten neighborhood in a minor borough of a major city where I graded papers, reread the same old textbooks and lesson plans, jerked off, and watched TV. Sometimes I varied the order, but not often.

I sat on my balcony and watched my neighbors throw their despair all over each other between drug deals. Sometimes I went out to a bar down by the water. I had nothing to do with this world. I was only visiting this other place, like going to a museum or a movie. Those bodies would've burned with or without me. Right at that moment, some other poor schmuck was probably sinking into the swamps of Jersey. And the world kept right on turning. What I'd done that night didn't matter to anyone, and no one would ever know. I lived on scraps and needed new clothes, but I wasn't a foot soldier fighting for a place in history in any general's rebel army. I wasn't even a footnote in Santoro's story.

I took a few minutes to smell my skin everywhere I could reach with my nose. Nothing but skin and soap. Everything else had gone down the drain. I was clean.

Millions of people across the city smelled like I did. I was just another one of the freshly washed masses. Nothing of the night clung to me, not even under my nails.

I toweled off and dressed in my new clothes, happy to have them. They made me feel that much further away from the graveyard and the dump. I wiped the fog off a mirror over the sinks. I looked pretty good, not much the worse for wear considering the night I'd had. I checked the whites of my eyes, like what we'd done would leave traces. There was nothing to hide in them. I stepped back from the mirror. I would walk into the dining room looking a lot like my brother, wearing his uniform.

I left my old clothes in a pile by the back door, like Bavasi had said.

Bavasi, Danny, and Al were laughing when I walked into the room.

"That's fucking disgusting," Al said, rising from the booth, jamming half a breadstick into his mouth. "Kevin, there better be hot water left." He walked into the kitchen. I took his seat at the table.

Bavasi poured another shot and walked away from the table, wiping his hands on his apron. I protested when Danny slid the glass toward me.

"Sip this one," he said. "There's nothing better after a hot shower."

I left the glass on the table.

Danny sipped his own shot. "Okay, I've got one more slice of advice for you. Easy to follow, but important. As we leave, which we will do right after I get cleaned up, Bavasi will hand you an envelope. In it will be cash. Not enough to retire on, but probably more than you've ever seen. Put it in your jacket pocket. Don't protest, don't even thank him, just put it away. Remember the guard at the dump? Do it like him. Count it when you get home." I started to say something, but Danny cut me off. "If you have moral troubles over the money, throw it in the trash, give it to a bum on the corner. Nobody will ever ask you about it. Just take it when Bavasi offers it. And, yes, you get to keep the clothes." He pulled back the lapels of his jacket. "Obviously."

"I think I can handle all that," I said. "Listen, Al said something about a three-way split in the car. I'm taking a cut of his money, aren't I?"

"And mine," Danny said, sinking back into the plush leather of the booth, seeming to grow larger as he did so. "But don't worry about it. Al defied an order. He's lucky it's only his pay and not his throat that's getting cut."

Danny leaned his head back and closed his eyes, putting his feet up on the bench, a man comfortable and at home. I realized, suddenly, I was witnessing something I had rarely ever seen: my brother still and at rest. I enjoyed it, regardless of the circumstances. Like with heroin, there'd be no forcing or tricking or fooling Danny into leaving Santoro behind. Danny had to make that decision for himself. What I had to do was be there when the moment came and give my brother a push in the right direction.

"Now, finish your sambuca, big brother,"

Danny said. "You don't wanna hurt Bava-si's feelings."

First sunlight stained the eastern sky when Danny and Al dropped me off at my apartment. I tossed Santoro's envelope on the coffee table, ashamed to open it. I would keep that money. What that said about me I would worry about later.

Holding a beer I didn't want, hoping the sambuca wouldn't wear off before I went to bed, I watched the rest of the sunrise from my balcony. I smoked half the pack of cigarettes Danny had bought for me on the way home, reaching over my head to bury the butts in the spider plant.

I'd never seen my street at sunrise. As the burning orange light crept along the cracked sidewalks and the weedy front yards, I noticed things I'd never seen before. Across the street, a mailbox hung askew on one nail, white envelopes scattered beneath it on the porch. In the window of the house next door, someone had taped up an American flag cut from a newspaper. Underneath the flag a photo peeled away from the glass: a daughter lost in the Towers, a son serving in Iraq or Afghanistan. Another house down, the morning light glinted off the brown glass of beer bottles piled high in a recycling bin that hadn't been to the curb in weeks. Someone had broken into a car, pebbles of broken glass glinting like diamonds in the street. In a week the diamonds would be pulverized to dust under passing tires.

The streams of morning light merged into a flood, setting the windows of the ramshackle homes on my block ablaze with reflected sunshine. The weathered houses, crooked on wasted plots and afire with borrowed light, reminded me of lonely old women all in a row, their unlucky faces hidden behind drugstore sunglasses and turned toward the sun while they waited on the Atlantic City bus. Something rustled around behind those big window-eyes, fighting to recall how to come to life. But with each passing day it got harder to remember. And so the morning fires went out and a million minor distractions instead filled the day — noisy and empty of promise — just like all the days before it. Each day another dull coin offered in worship of a stingy spinning wheel. Each day the pocket that much closer to empty.

I could take a lighter and gasoline to the whole damn block and the flames would be thirty feet high before anyone noticed. Most of my neighbors would die in their sleep. I wondered who would miss them. Mass arson. Would that be criminal enough to make me ashamed of myself? Because, despite what I had done, sitting in the morning sun with a buzz and an envelope of cash, I felt no shame at all.

Mrs. Hanson's back door squeaked as she let Maxie out into the yard. He ran in circles in pools of light, barking like mad. Maybe catching up on whatever he missed overnight. I could picture him sleeping the night through curled at the foot of his mistress's bed, keeping a list of all the things — squirrels, cats, rats, and bats, thugs and thieves — he heard in the night. Or maybe he was giving the day fair warning. *It's a new day,* I could hear him saying. *Today is gonna be different around here. Today, I'm tellin' all you motherfuckers I ain't taking no mess.* I had more respect for that broken old mutt than I had for any of the people on my block. I wondered if that was an indictment of them or me. I gave up on my plans to burn everything down. I couldn't do that to Maxie.

Finally, the dramatic colors of sunrise gave way to the pale, blank daylight. I rose from my seat and went to the railing. "Go ahead, Maxie," I yelled. "Go ahead." The dog let loose a long howl. My howl died in my throat and some other dog in some other yard answered in my place. Mrs. Hanson called her dog in for breakfast. I went inside and passed out on the couch, destroyed by exhaustion.

At some point during the day, I must've moved to my bed because that's where I woke up at sundown. In the bathroom, I avoided the mirror. I took off my clothes and staggered into the kitchen for a bowl of cereal. As I ate, I stared at the pile of essays on the kitchen table. I tried to forget the stack of money on my coffee table. I left the cereal bowl in the sink and went back to bed, where I stayed until Sunday morning. I only got up then because of the doorbell. I knew it was Danny.

"You look like ass," he said when I opened the door. "Why is it every time I come over you're in your underwear?" He held up a brown paper bag as he walked into the apartment. "I brought bagels."

He set up shop in the kitchen, pushing aside my essays. "Remember how Mom and Dad used to take us for bagels after Mass at Saint Brendan's? Then we'd get cold cuts for lunch at Pastorelli's. Ain't that New York in a nutshell?"

He'd thought of everything: hot coffee, butter, cream cheese, a Sunday *Times.* The way he chattered reminded me of our mother. She did the same thing when she fed us, anxious to capitalize on the attention attracted by the food. He smiled at me, buttering an onion bagel. "Jets are on in half an hour."

I tossed my essays on the counter, reaching for a coffee as I sat. Danny snatched away the cup I grabbed and handed me the other.

"You don't want mine," he said. "It's loaded with low-fat milk. And a little hazelnut creamer. All those years shooting heroin and I still drink my coffee like a pussy."

I pulled the plastic top off my cup. Black as tar. Danny dumped about ten sugar packets out of the paper bag. "Enough to make the spoon stand up, right?"

I nodded, smiling, tearing open one packet after another. It was a line I'd beaten to death when we were teenagers, after I was blown away by *True Romance* and wanted to be Christian Slater. That movie may have started me drinking coffee in the first place. Danny sat across the table from me. I wanted to reach out and tousle his hair. I ached again for the years his addiction had cost us.

"I thought they taught you to drink coffee like a man in rehab. You want a straw?"

"I never did take to that part of the program," he said. "And fuck you and your straw very much, by the way."

"So, you drink, you don't go to meetings," I said, "you do other things I'm pretty sure aren't in the twelve steps. What parts of the program did you take to, exactly?"

"Aren't we a ray of fucking sunshine this morning." He raised a finger, a hunk of bagel inflating his cheek. "I got the 'heroin is real bad for you' part. And that the people around it are as poisonous as the drug." He shook his head, reaching for his coffee. "I don't want to be poisonous anymore."

"So Al isn't into any of that stuff?" I asked. "Santoro, either?"

"Al doesn't deal, if that's what you're asking," Danny said, layering butter on his second bagel. "And he doesn't use. I don't think he ever did. Back in the day, he just liked throwing parties in that giant house, playing the big shot and getting his Gatsby on. He doesn't even do that anymore. I know that for a fact."

"And Santoro?"

"He's partial to real estate, contracting, shit like that. Couldn't say for sure, but drugs seem dirty for him."

"Not like murder," I said, picking at the rim of my coffee cup.

Danny set down his bagel, reaching out for a napkin. He wiped his hands and mouth, crumpled the napkin into his fist. "You give away that money yet?"

I stared at him across the table.

"Didn't think so," Danny said. "Far as I know, Santoro's never killed a man in his life."

"He gives the orders," I said. "Like bin Laden. Are you going to tell me that prick's not a murderer?"

"Are you calling yourself Al Qaeda, Professor?" Danny asked. "You did follow orders like a good soldier."

Danny pushed up from the table and walked into the living room. He picked up the remote and turned on the TV, raising the volume way too high. I left my bagel half-eaten, grabbed my coffee and joined him on the couch.

"You think the three of us will ever watch another game together?" Danny asked

"Me, you, and bin Laden? Probably not. I hear he's more into horses and soccer."

"No, asshole," Danny said. "Me, you, and Dad."

I took a deep breath. "If the Jets make the Super Bowl, maybe."

"So pretty much never," Danny said. His shoulders slumped. "It's un-American, fathers and sons not watching football together. It's borderline criminal."

"How'd you meet him?" I asked.

"Dad? Well, Kevin, when a man and a woman really love each other —"

"You're fucking killing me."

Danny muted the TV, tossed the remote on the coffee table. "I can't tell you anything about Santoro that's gonna make you feel better, Kevin. I'm sorry. I've never met him, never even seen him, and I don't want to. All I can tell you is he's got reach, big reach, and there's not a cop or criminal that doesn't know his name. And I owe him everything I have." He stood, picked up the envelope of cash and ran his thumb along the bills. "No offense to Mom and Dad, but I'm better protected and better taken care of now than I've ever been in my life." He laid the money on the table. "And now you are, too."

Sitting before me on the edge of the coffee table, Danny reached out and palmed the back of my neck. Our knees connected. "This is who I am now, Kevin. I'm not evil. I'm not a hit man, or a drug dealer, or a terrorist. And I am off the shit. I swear it."

I lowered my eyes. Danny's fingertips pressed into the base of my skull.

"Why're you doing this to me?" I asked.

"Look at me," Danny said.

I did, seeing nothing but those haunted blue eyes.

"You wanna know things?" Danny asked. "I sucked dick in doorways for heroin, Kev. Married guys, cops, and, yeah, teachers. I robbed dope from a guy with a broken bottle in his throat. Who knows, I might've put it there. I stole everything I could get my hands on from our folks, used you till you almost went down with me. I killed a fucking kid and ditched the body. After what I've seen and where I've been you think *illegal* means anything to me? It's like that night in the car three years ago. We're all guilty, Kev. The only difference is some of us get caught and some of us don't."

I jumped up from the couch. "Wait, wait, wait. You *killed* someone?"

Danny rubbed his palms into his eyes. "Yes, I did. By accident. With a needle." He looked at me, his shoulders hunched, fingers splayed open on his thighs. "Remember that punk Tommy? He died in my arms, OD. I was the one that tied him off, that shot him up. Al, it happened at one of his parties, the last one, he helped me hide the body out at Bloodroot, right before he ditched me at the clinic. Tommy stayed hid and I got clean."

177

"The favor you owed," I said.

"You got it," Danny said. "I get outta rehab, Al puts me up at his place, asks me to help *him* help a guy named Santoro, says there's work to keep me off the street. I'm gonna say no? Because it might be a little shady? Might be, God forbid, illegal?" He raised his hands, gazing around my apartment like he couldn't remember how he got there. "And now here we are. It's not like I planned it. At least we're in it together."

He stood, hands out in front of him with his fingers curled. He stared at his hands like they held a crystal ball. "And I see the beauty of it, this new life I have. I see opportunity. It's coming." He looked up at me. "Al and I are more than even by now, but I got a lot to make up for, to you, to Mom and Dad, and Santoro's the way. I just need a leap of faith, a little brotherly love. Like the leap I took coming back to you."

NINE

We watched the football game. We talked no more about the big opportunity Danny saw coming our way. Danny yelled and screamed at the TV with the ups and downs of the game, absorbed in it. I sat beside him on the couch, vaguely aware of him and sick with the images he'd jammed into my head like, well, like a broken bottle. Had I heard anything about Tommy's disappearance, what was it, about a year and a half ago? Maybe read something in the paper? I remembered nothing. Worse, I felt no sympathy for him; he'd come to the end he'd been headed for when I met him.

Had Danny left himself out of Tommy's story my only response would've been some sarcastic joke. If anything, unfair as it was, I wasn't anything but mad at Tommy. Like it was his fault, the goddamn lightweight, my brother had crossed paths with the mysterious and seductive Santoro.

Danny left not long after the Jets had taken their usual Sunday beating, me mute and nodding at his promise to call and check up on me later in the week.

I wasted most of the evening reading the Sunday *Times* cover to cover. In the book review section I saw a new Jefferson biography I wanted to read, maybe use for class. I wondered if the department would cough up the thirty-five bucks. Then I remembered the envelope from Santoro. Before I went into the living room, I grabbed a cigarette from the porch and lit it, carrying Danny's leftover coffee to the couch for an ashtray. I'd thrown out all my real ashtrays when I'd quit. I counted the money.

Five thousand dollars. *Fifty* hundred-dollar bills. Same as what I got paid for each class I taught, five months' work. Only this was cash, Ben Franklin's honored visage, fifty times over, tax-free. And for one night.

The rest of the year's rent with money left over. Food from a real grocery store, not that dirty bodega around the corner. A cab to and from work instead of the bus. Fuck that, a used car? I squeezed the bills in my fist. The insurance might break me; I'd have to be careful. Or make more money. It was an option. The money gave me choices. Instantly. A lot more than I had when I got home from work last Friday afternoon, a few crumpled Washingtons and a torn Lincoln in my wallet. What I had now was options.

I also had the option of finding the local police station and telling them everything I'd seen and heard over the weekend. I could leave Danny out of the story. Or tell them I'd come in on his behalf. It was a ridiculous thought, stupid and uninspired. Something people only ever did in the movies and even then it hardly ever worked out. Only a fictional conscience could be that strong, or that naïve. I'd never even told my folks about Danny stealing the paperboy money from the junk drawer in the kitchen. I was really going to turn him over to the cops? What would they do anyway?

Santoro couldn't be who he was without having taken care of the cops a long time ago. No. He'd never be touched. Not him, not Bavasi. Danny and I would take the fall, or worse, if Santoro got ahold of us. What was done was done. There was no going back. Meanwhile, I held in my hand five thousand dollars that nobody knew I had.

Leaving the money on the couch, I turned off the living room light and peeked out the balcony doors, checking the block for any windows that gave a view into mine. I didn't see a single one. I told myself I was being careful, not paranoid. Maybe if I lived in a decent neighborhood I'd be worrying too much. But I didn't. I could though, if I did a few more jobs with Danny. I could get away from that bullshit on the corner. What if there was more innocuous work? It wouldn't pay as well, but I could live with that.

God, what was I thinking?

Maybe at the dump I'd breathed some of that poison smoke Danny had told me to avoid. Maybe I'd stood too close to the fire.

I grabbed up the money and headed for the bedroom. In the dark, I stuffed the bills under the mattress. Enough gangster fantasies. I had real work to do, real responsibilities. I grabbed my book bag and hurried into the kitchen. I collected my student essays and stuffed them into the bag. I called a cab and found my keys. But before I went downstairs to wait, I went back into the bedroom. I dug the hundreds out from under my mattress and, rolling them up, packed them deep into the toe of an old shoe. Forty-nine of them. One I stuffed into my pocket. And then, before I locked up the apartment, I ran back inside for one more bill.

■ ■ ■ ■

On campus, I waved to the security guard as I unlocked the front door of the history building. He was used to seeing me on weekends and in the evenings, when I liked campus the best. Some students hung around, but not many and none of them mine. Even better, most of the other teachers were gone.

I hit the mailroom first. An essay sat curled in my box. Fishing a pen from my bag, I scrawled *late* across the top. I hadn't gotten through enough of the pile to even notice I'd been missing one. For a moment, it seemed unfair to penalize the student when I hadn't noticed until Sunday night her paper was late. It wasn't like she'd held up my progress. Still, rules were rules. Most of my students were freshmen. I had to teach them deadlines were serious business in college, even if I filed their grades late.

The spare, cold office I shared with five other instructors looked like we'd all bolted out the door for a fire drill; none of us was anywhere near organized. Except for Kelsey. Her desk always looked ready for summer vacation. It was her voice that scared me out of my skin as I unpacked at my desk. A dozen essays flew into the air.

"Jesus Christmas," I said, student papers fluttering to the floor around my feet. "You scared the heart out of me."

She shouldn't have. She liked working at the same times that I did. In fact, sharing the department office with her on Sunday nights was the closest thing I had to a regular social life. I hadn't even realized I was feeling so jumpy.

Kelsey leaned in the doorway, her hands jammed in the pockets of her faded jeans. Under her corduroy suit jacket, complete with leather patches at the elbows, she wore a Man United jersey. She'd wrapped her russet hair in a braid that reached the small of her back.

"Getting ready for midterms?" she asked.

I stood, tossing the papers on my desk. "Midterms? I'm still trying to get through their first set of essays so I can get on with grading the second set." I sifted through the debris on my desk, searching for a copy of my syllabus. "When the hell are midterms?"

"Two weeks," Kelsey said.

I breathed a sigh of relief. "That's forever. You had me nervous there for a minute."

"Seems you were already nervous. You feeling okay?" She frowned at me. "You don't look so good."

My hands shook and my face burned like she'd caught me holding that dead guy's get-away head, not a stack of student essays. Like she knew everything I'd done that weekend. Impossible. There was nothing to know. As far as Kelsey was concerned, I hadn't done anything that weekend. Nothing.

"There's fresh coffee brewing in the lounge," Kelsey said. "I made enough for both of us, but maybe you shouldn't have any."

"I haven't had enough," I said, rubbing my hands together. I felt my face contort into an ugly fake smile. "That's the problem."

"I'll get us some, then." She smiled and backed out of the doorway.

I listened to her combat boots echo on the tile of the empty hall, convinced for a moment that she was calling the cops or the fellas in the white coats. Well, nothing I could do about it now. Let the Fates decide. I cleared some space on my desk and sat down to work. Maybe if I looked sane and innocent when they broke down the door . . .

When other teachers were around, Kelsey and I talked shop: grades, lesson plans, our favorite student excuses. On Sunday nights when it was just the two of us, we talked family. I listened a lot and said little about her dead mother, her crazy father, and her still vibrant wish that she hadn't been an only child. She asked for story after story about Danny and me as kids. I told her every adventure I could recall, except for the graveyard stories. She had her favorites and I told them often.

Kelsey listened as I wrestled out loud with having a brother and then losing him, only to find and then lose him again. Outside my family, Kelsey was the only one who knew the bad parts. She went a lot easier on me about it than I did, or my folks, for that matter. My mother, before she got sick, wouldn't talk about Danny at all. It only made her cry. After the diagnosis, she started talking about him again. Sometimes on her bad days she talked *to* him, confusing him with one of her old pediatric patients, apologizing to an invisible boy Danny about painful shots and mean doctors. After that started, my father couldn't discuss Danny without flying into a rage. When it came to my brother, Kelsey was all I had. I hid that from her as best as I could.

I couldn't be bothered with the rest of the office: TAs so frazzled by graduate work and second and third jobs they could hardly assemble a sentence, recent MAs yet to shed the protective pretentiousness they'd cultivated in graduate school. Kelsey and I were the office exceptions. I was in my eighth year as an instructor. Kelsey had come on three years ago, taking the job at Richmond so she could be close to her ailing mother after a couple of years of teaching high school out west. She had a degree from some Buddhist/hippie college in Nevada and it was her mother's cancer that had ruined her plans to quit teaching and join the Peace Corps. But her mother died six months after Kelsey had returned to Staten Island and yet here she still was. Her sticking around made me wary of her.

Since we were friendly pretty much with only each other, most of the office, like Whitestone, pegged us for a couple. I didn't mind. She was certainly pretty enough: high Iroquois cheekbones dusted with freckles, hazel eyes flecked with gray, a small, sly smile. Taut, muscled legs. And something about her rough-and-tumble tree-hugger/ thrift-store Ivy League look turned me on. But I'd never made a move. The tepidness of my cross-office lust really had nothing to do with her, and at times I felt weirdly compelled to tell her that. It was all me. Most of my life most of my desires had been vague. Getting naked with Kelsey was no exception.

She perched on the edge of my desk, handing me my coffee. "Extra sugar," she said. "Just how you like it."

Kelsey reached into her jacket and produced a white envelope. "I want to show you something. I got in."

"Got into what?"

"Not what," she said, "but where. I got into a Ph.D. program in Chicago."

She handed me the letter. I stared down at the paper but didn't read it. "I didn't even know you'd applied."

"I didn't tell anyone. I was going to need this job next fall if I didn't make it in anywhere. I got the letter on Friday; I've been carrying it around all weekend. You're the only person I've told."

"I'm honored," I said.

She laughed. "Don't be. You're the first person I ran into that would care. But I *was* hoping you'd be here tonight."

She held out her hand for the letter but I didn't return it. I looked back and forth between her and the paper. It took me a moment to put a name on what I was feeling: disappointment. And not for her.

"So?" she asked. "Whadda you think?"

Kelsey beamed like she'd been asked to

the senior prom by the star quarterback. Like she couldn't believe something this good had happened to her. She'd gone after the spot, deserved it, but to her it felt like dumb luck. I was happy for her, and proud of her — an emotion that surprised me. And I would be sad to see her go. I hoped her quarterback wouldn't turn out to be an asshole.

"I think Chicago's fucking cold," I said, handing her the letter. "I'm a little . . . confused. What happened to the Peace Corps? Or that other thing? What was it, Teach for America? You've been all about that 'save the world' stuff since I met you."

"Chicago has one of the best history programs in the country, you know," Kelsey said. "And I plan to go, but I'm not iron-clad married to the idea. It's a hell of an accomplishment just to get in."

She sighed and walked away from me, tossing the letter on her desk. She kept her back to me, staying quiet for a long moment. I guess I'd meant to hit a nerve. I wasn't just disappointed she was leaving; I was angry, too. But I hadn't meant to hit that nerve that hard.

"You ever wonder why I'm still here?" Kelsey asked.

I shrugged, raising my hands. "The exorbitant salary and scintillating professional camaraderie?"

"Can you be serious, please?" Her chair squeaked when she sat, elbows on her knees, hands hanging limp between them. "I should've known you'd give me shit for this. I'm a sellout, I admit it."

"Sorry." I mimicked her posture. "I'm just surprised. You were so gung-ho." We stared at each other across the office. I shifted my weight in my chair; it was busted and leaned to the left. "Okay, when you say 'here,' do you mean the island or the job?"

"Both," she said.

"Yeah, I wondered," I said, lying.

I already knew the answer. It was the same reason everyone else in the department with big or even medium-sized plans, including me, lingered. Staten Island was boring as hell, fourteen miles long, and had the gravitational pull of Jupiter.

"For a year and a half," Kelsey said, "I've been trying to work up the nerve to fill out those apps, the Peace Corp, Teach for America, Americorps. I've got Lonely Planet books on half of Africa, South America, Eastern Europe. Hell, I even looked into getting on a Greenpeace boat at one point." She raised her hands in the air. "Don't shoot! Save the Whales!"

She didn't laugh so neither did I. "So what happened?"

She rubbed her palms on her cheeks, her eyes everywhere but on me. "I lost my nerve, or the heart, or both. I don't wanna do that shit anymore. I don't see the point."

"So you don't want to go live in some hut in Djibouti for three years," I said, "scarfing down malaria pills and telling people not to shit in their own drinking water. That's nothing to beat yourself up over, Kel. In fact, it puts you firmly in the sensible majority."

"I know," Kelsey said. "That's what I don't like about it." Her shoulders slumped. "My old classmates would be so disappointed."

Right, I thought, like they're all balancing on a mountaintop and holding the lotus position, energizing their auras or whatever. But running down her fellow karma college alum for the flat-screen-watching, SUV-driving suburbanites they probably were didn't seem like the best way to cheer her up.

With her embarrassed slouch and her pursed-lips pout, she reminded me of another kind of teenager. One who's finally realized they're not going to Mars, or selling out the Garden, or replacing Derek Jeter at short and can't believe both that it won't happen and that they thought somewhere inside that it really might. I wondered what had hurt Kelsey more, the death of the dream or the loss of faith that killed it.

Me, I never had that moment, but I saw it in my students all the time.

"So the Third World isn't your gig," I said. "It's no big deal. It just means your time, your next opportunity, is elsewhere. The world's a big place and it needs all the help it can get. Be patient. Isn't that what Buddha always says?"

"Is that what *you* tell *yourself?*" she asked. "That you're being patient. You're the same as me. You don't belong here, either."

Her question got my back up, but there wasn't even a whiff of sarcasm in it. I wasn't sure what to think. Was she offering me a compliment or asking how not to end up like me?

"We're not talking about me," I said. "And besides, I'm different than you. I never gave a shit about Djibouti to begin with. So I have no problems with lowered expectations." I rolled my chair closer to her. "Kelsey, really. Give yourself a break."

"You know, I almost called you," Kelsey said. "To celebrate with me on Friday night."

"I would've liked that," I said. "A lot. But I would've missed the party anyway. I was out."

"Wasn't much of a party," she said.

Her prom-girl energy had dried up and blown away. Nice fuckin' job, Curran. What was it they said about true failures, that they resent others their success? That was why Lee was late to Trenton in 1776; he thought he should've had Washington's job. I should've played along. Wasn't that one of the things I did best? It's what I always did with Danny. Who really cared what I really felt? I took a deep breath.

"I'm happy for you. I am. How often do people get what they want? Even if they do have to adjust their ideas a little bit. Washington built this country on tactical retreat, knowing what fights to pick and which ones he couldn't win."

"Thanks, Kevin. I'm happy for me, too. I just have to accept that the Ph.D. is my important battle right now." She stood and walked along the wall, moving away from me, trailing her fingertips on the cold concrete blocks. "I will miss this place, I guess. The whole institutional underdog-proletariat vibe of it."

"That's such an elitist, doctoral-student thing to say," I said.

"See? Maybe I am headed where I really belong." She laughed, rocking back on her heels. "I don't feel like working. Let's get outta here. I'll let you buy me a drink."

I turned to my desk, pressing my hand to my belly to keep it from doing somersaults. Now who was ninth-grade nervous? I threw my musket down and ran for cover.

"I'd love to," I said, "but I can't. I didn't get a single thing done over the weekend. I was busy the whole time. I've got all these papers to grade."

Big mistake, the "busy weekend" excuse. Kelsey would think I was lying. I hadn't had a busy weekend since she'd joined the department and she knew it. And considering what had taken up my time that weekend, I was in no position to defend myself.

"Ouch," Kelsey said. "Who knew all it took was an invitation from me to turn the department procrastinator into a workhorse."

"It's not like that," I said. "Look, maybe . . ."

"Maybe another time? Don't make it worse and give me that line." She tapped her watch. Her feelings weren't as hurt as I'd thought.

"Remember, the clock is now ticking," she said. "I won't be around forever."

She grabbed her bag off her desk and headed out the door, easing it closed behind her. I heard the latch click into place. I dug my red pen out of my bag and picked up the first paper on the pile, trying to put Kelsey out of my mind. I didn't have much luck.

If I'd shown a hint of courage and charged the field of battle months ago, maybe Kelsey'd be my girlfriend now. Maybe that would've changed how this weekend went. What if Kelsey had called me on Friday? What if she'd gotten to me before Danny had? I might never have ended up in Santoro's restaurant and in that graveyard. I wouldn't have those moments in my personal history, on my permanent record, now.

But it wouldn't have changed the big things. She'd still be leaving and Danny would still be back and working for Santoro. There's no way she would've chosen me over Chicago, no way I would've chosen her over Danny. If it hadn't happened last Friday, I would've ended up in Danny's plans one way or another. No, I'd been smart, not scared about Kelsey. All I'd really missed was getting gut shot and dumped for Chicago. Kelsey was as good as gone. In a way, we'd been brilliant, and broke up first. The worst was already over.

I caught up to her as she was backing her car out of her parking space. Shocked to see me but smiling, she rolled down the window. She waited for me to catch my breath.

"I'll be damned," I said, "if I let you ruin my bad reputation around here."

"Buy me two drinks," Kelsey said, "and I'll help you make it worse. Get in the car."

I did. She patted my knee as I pulled on the seat belt. "Let's go to the Red Spot," she said. "I want to go someplace that has some history."

"Good Lord, is that place still open?"

"Believe it or not. Besides, it has a courtyard. We can smoke. I feel like smoking a whole pack." She had that bright-eyed schoolgirl look again. "Let's show up for work in some real pain tomorrow."

"I quit smoking," I said.

"The hell you did. I smelled it on you soon as I walked into the office."

"Okay then," I said. "Guilty as charged."

I ordered us drinks, double Ketel and soda for her, double Maker's and water for me while she got us two packs of cigarettes from the machine. There was no one else in the place. The bartender, a forty-year-old guy with a nose ring and a dyed-black Mohawk that paused at a bald spot, slid a couple packs of matches across the bar with my change.

The Spot had opened to great fanfare in the late eighties, a seedy rock club for those of us too broke for the Limelight and too uncool for CBGB's. I spent many a night waiting to get in, Danny chattering at my side while he skillfully applied eyeliner, unable to decide if I was too cool or not cool enough to belong. To me, the Red Spot wasn't much different from the coke-den dance clubs that surrounded it. It was another place to play dress-up, get served underage, and get all fucked up on cheap draft beer, bad bourbon, and shitty cocaine, only with better music.

But Danny loved the place, the dim red lights, the Day-Glo paint-splattered walls, the thundering music — they played everything from the Cure to the Cramps to the Crüe, all at ear-splitting volume. He loved standing at the bar, striking up conversations with every thin, white Nikki Sixx and Wendy O. Williams wannabe that pushed up next to us for drinks. He was fearless. He seemed, even at only seventeen, in his element. He could be anyone, anything: a singer, a painter, a fugitive, a thief, whatever got him what he wanted. More than a few of the girls lifted their vinyl skirts for him in the bathroom. He looked discreetly away while I got hand-jobs under the bar. He borrowed a lot of money from me that neither of us drank and he never paid back. It wasn't until a couple years later, when it was far too late, that I finally admitted to myself that the Spot was where Danny learned to lean over a mirror without seeing himself. I knew the needles had come not long after.

As Kelsey and I walked through the bar, heading for the courtyard, I saw that the Red Spot had aged about as well as Nikki Sixx had, or, for that matter, about as well as I had. The red lights remained but the neon explosions had faded to weak stains. Twenty years of staples from band posters scarred every wall. Hip-hop songs that even I could tell were dated pulsed from the speakers at a volume low enough to talk over. I couldn't believe I'd once let my brother paint my fingernails black for this place.

"We have our choice of seats," Kelsey said. She picked a table next to the fence. We sat underneath a stencil of the Ramones logo, over which someone had scrawled F.T.W. in white spray paint. Kelsey relaxed in her seat, smiling at the artwork adorning the fence.

She lifted her drink. "After these, I'm gonna buy us a pitcher of the nastiest beer they got."

"Good idea," I said. "See if the bartender'll put some DK's on and we can do shots of well bourbon from plastic cups."

"Deal," Kelsey said. She leaned across the table. "But first, Kev, there's something I want to ask you. You ditched it back in the office, but I need an answer. It may be a little personal, but it's important to me."

"Shoot."

"Well, why do you keep teaching at Richmond if you hate it so much?"

I sat back in shock. "Who says I hate teaching, or teaching there? Did Whitestone put you up to this?"

"That creep? Are you kidding?" She sipped her cocktail, wincing at the vodka's bite. "I'm here because I want to be. Because there's no good reason we didn't go out for drinks a long time ago."

"You're right," I said. "I'm sorry."

"Listen, when we talk about work, you always come off like someone who's been at it for twenty years. You sound bitter, about the kids, about admin."

"Oh, come on," I said. "We all complain. It's a teacher's prerogative. It's just a part of the job I have a real talent for. It's a frustrating profession. You know that. Give it some time, it'll start happening to you."

"That's what I'm worried about," Kelsey said. "Listening to you was one of the things that drove me to apply for the Ph.D."

I crossed my arms. "I'm not sure how to take that. It's hardly a compliment."

"How come you've never moved on to something better? You were top of your class at NYU. You had your pick of doctoral programs, yet here you are years later. Still teaching at a community college. What's that about?"

"I was sick of school," I said. "I blew my wad on my master's. Besides, these kids need decent teachers more than the spoiled brats at Harvard and Princeton do."

"If you're so dedicated," Kelsey said, "then why are you always on the edge of getting canned?"

"I am not."

"How was your meeting on Friday?"

"Let's say I'm not counting on a raise," I said.

"I heard the stories about you when I got to Richmond. Everyone thought you'd be gone in a semester, soon as you chose the fattest fellowship. Now, everyone wonders how you keep your job. You won't get anything done on time — for the kids or for admin. You won't show for department meetings. Whitestone hates you."

"So I'm a loser jerk then for sticking with the job they gave me? I'm the best classroom teacher in the department, present company included. Maybe that's why I'm still there. And Whitestone only hates me 'cause I won't pimp for his stupid Friends of Bloodroot group."

"I won't, either," Kelsey said, "but no one ever calls the office looking for me." She edged her chair closer to mine. "What happened to your drive, your ambition? Where'd you lose it?"

"I never had any," I said. "If I had any ambition, I'd be on Wall Street grading stocks instead of essays written by kids who think Canada's a state." I wanted her to laugh, but she didn't. "And who knows? Richmond might be a better place to be soon. I'll get my shit together and everyone will forget the past. They're doing work all over the campus. We got that new science building. There's the plans to go more residential with new dorms, attract more students from off the island."

"I haven't heard anything about the history department," Kelsey said.

"Not yet," I said. "But we're probably on the list. You know Whitestone'll make sure of that. That's probably why he started that Bloodroot museum bullshit to begin with, to make sure he gets his cut of the state money coming in." I shook the ice in my plastic cup. "Speaking of getting one's due, you owe us a pitcher."

"Don't change the subject," Kelsey said. "It's bullshit that you never had any ambition. I know different. What happened?"

"That's a good question." I slouched in my chair. She really wanted an answer. This isn't Whitestone breaking your balls, I thought. This is someone you like trying to care about your life.

"Right around when I had five years in," I said, "about three years ago, I guess I started cruising. I stopped paying attention. It got so easy to keep doing the same things over and over. And then the road tipped downhill and I picked up speed." I looked at her. "I never knew inertia could have momentum. Probably why I'm not a physicist." I leaned forward. "You know, I never realized it, but when Danny disappeared for good, that's about when things started going south for me. Weird."

Kelsey blinked at me, as if trying to bring my face into better focus. I couldn't tell if she was trying to see me, or picturing her life if she didn't go to Chicago. But she didn't look away and I was thankful for that. Did she see a difference in me, after only a few days with Danny back in my life? Did I feel different? Once the initial rush of the adventure and the money had worn off, I'd felt nothing but bad for the two days after the graveyard, but sitting at the Red Spot with Kelsey, I had to admit that I felt pretty good, optimistic.

Looking at her pretty face, I wished she could tell me my future. Did she see herself in it? Why would she? Kelsey had already said she was all but gone. That letter, her ticket off the island, was in her pocket as we sat there making up for lost time with cigarettes and bad booze. And what about Danny? He and I had no chance of staying together if I abandoned him to his night work, if I walked away from the important thing, our reunion, because of the crazy shit I'd seen and done Friday night. I'd vowed a thousand times that I'd do anything to get my brother back. I had to be willing to find out what "anything" really meant.

If I was going to hang on to Kelsey and Danny, I couldn't treat them like I did my job. I had to stay focused. Be creative. I had to shake off my lame, lazy existence and take some risks. Maybe this past weekend, without me even realizing it, the process had already started.

"It's never too late," Kelsey said, standing, "to start paying attention again. Objects right in front of you may be closer than they appear." She slung her purse over her shoulder. "Okay, you're off the hook. We're supposed to be celebrating. We'll have fun when I get back."

I dug into my pocket for some cash.

She waved me off. "I got this."

I held out a twenty. "Let me get the shots. Forget the well shit, get us some decent bourbon, even if it does come in plastic shot glasses. I'm too old for the rotgut." I pulled out another twenty. "Tip big and ask him to change the music."

She took one twenty from me, eyebrows raised. I jammed the other back in my pocket.

"Dead Kennedys?" she asked.

"Or Black Flag. Or Social D. At least some Kiss or some Clash."

I turned in my seat to watch Kelsey walk away. Over her shoulder, she glanced back and caught me looking at her. She stopped walking. I didn't look away. I ran my eyes over her head-to-toe as she watched. I'd never let her see me do that before. The doorway was dim, but I saw her grin before she entered the bar.

She carried a first-rate body under those secondhand clothes. I'd known this for three years, though I'd done fuck-all about it. Kelsey knew I knew it. She was one of the least vain people I'd ever met, but she knew what she had. I got the feeling she was gonna give me a shot at *really* making up for lost time. That would be just like me, hooking up with a girl on her way out the door.

Kelsey set the shots and the pitcher down on the table. "All he's got for music is satellite radio. I talked him into some early alternative station."

The steady kick drum thump and ragged, shining guitar riff of the Cult's "Rain" tumbled from the speakers over the empty courtyard. "This'll do just fine," I said.

We downed our shots. She poured each of us a beer while we recovered from the burn. I lit her cigarette, her cheeks flushed in the match light.

Kelsey leaned back, stretching her legs under the table. She sat so close to me now that her thigh rested against mine. I could feel the warmth of it through my jeans.

"I thought this place was the coolest," she said. "I had a different color vinyl skirt for every day of the week."

"I'm gonna pretend you didn't say that."

"Oh please," Kelsey said. "And where did you hang out?"

"Here," I said, laughing. "A lot. Like everyone else our age who couldn't dance."

"I knew it. God, I had a whole gang of virgin sluts from Sacred Heart I ran with back then," Kelsey said. "We partied here every weekend. We'd prance around like strippers and then giggle like idiots the moment a boy tried to talk to any of us. I heard some real sex, drugs, and rock 'n' roll shit went on but I never even kissed anyone here. I was such a wuss back then."

"Most of us were like that," I said. "There was always a lot more posing than there was danger. We all wanted to be in the glow, as long as someone else was doing the real dirty work." Someone else, I thought. Someone like Danny. "What the fuck, right? It was fun."

It was then I felt her hand on my cheek. She turned my face to hers and kissed me.

"There," she said, her mouth just far enough from mine for us to speak. "I finally got my kiss at the Red Spot."

I closed the distance and we kissed again.

"You were probably cute as shit back in the day," Kelsey said, pressing her forehead against mine. "I wish I'd seen that, you and your badass rocker crew."

"You probably did," I said. "Though it was usually just me and my brother."

"You guys really did everything together, didn't you?" Kelsey said.

"Yeah, back then I couldn't imagine life without him. Never even thought about it." I leaned back in my chair. "Before the drugs came along." And then it hit me, like a revelation, that Danny wasn't gone anymore.

"You really miss him," Kelsey said.

"I did. I used to." I leaned forward, put my hands on her knees. "But listen to this. He's back." I couldn't believe how good it felt to say that. Joy, excitement, relief, everything missing from telling my father, they all welled up inside me like a ten-foot wave. It was all so pure. Even the darkness of the weekend couldn't stain it. I felt, for a few moments anyway, that the weekend was just another bad memory that Danny and I would soon forget. The last bad adventure.

Kelsey covered my hands with hers. "Kevin, that's wonderful. Where's he been?"

"That's a long story," I said. I didn't care to tell it. It didn't matter. "But he seems a lot better off than the last time I saw him."

"He's clean?"

"Looks like it," I said. "I mean, you never know for sure or for how long, but he seems

207

real good so far."

"That must've been so great, hanging out with him again. I'm so happy for you. What did you guys do?"

"Dinner, drinks," I said. "Nothing major."

"I'll bet it was special anyway."

"You could say that," I said with a smile.

"And I thought *I* had news worth celebrating," Kelsey said. She stood and chugged her beer. Looking down at me, she straddled my thighs. My heart started pounding. She settled down into my lap, wiggling her hips. My hands on the small of her back, breathing in her skin, I moved my mouth over her throat. Searching until I felt her clean, strong pulse on my tongue, pumping away through her veins.

"Come home with me," she said, her hands in my hair.

"What? You don't wanna do it in the bathroom?" I said into her shoulder. "Like in the good ol' days?"

"Forget this teenage shit," she said, her hips rocking. "You really wanna dry hump out here all night when you could have the real thing? You spend the night with me, you might even get to work on time tomorrow."

"Forget work," I said, grabbing her braid,

winding it around my forearm. "Forget to-morrow."

TEN

Monday evening, the cab dropped me in the middle of my street. Al's black Charger was docked in front of my building, taking up three parking spaces. Al sat on the stoop, staring off into some random slice of sky from behind a pair of dark aviator glasses. A decent impression of a man deep in thought. I wasn't fooled. And no way was this a social call. He cracked his knuckles and rolled a toothpick over his teeth.

I slung my bag over my shoulder, paid the driver, and headed Al's way, holding my head down, pretending I hadn't noticed him. He stood as I approached, jamming his hands into the pockets of his leather jacket. I feigned surprise as I hopped the curb.

"What's up, Al?"

"Cute," Al said. "But not my type."

"The cabdriver?"

Al unleashed a loud, fake laugh. "You're

almost as quick as your brother. Between the two of you, I'm gonna get a complex." He removed the toothpick, touched it to the tip of my nose, and put it back in his mouth. "Not the cabdriver, smart guy. The professor lady you went out with last night. What's her name? Kelsey? The one with the apartment on Van Buren. I'm talking about her."

"For fuck's sake." I dropped my bag and turned away. "You've been following me? What the hell for? Where's Danny? Does he even know you're here?"

"Don't get your shit crossed up," Al said, "and go thinking I take orders from Danny. Your brother's busy. Don't worry about him."

"Kelsey's got nothing to do with the weekend. And she doesn't know a thing about it, if that's what you're here for. Leave her alone."

"Relax, loverboy," Al said. "Nobody's going after your girl." He set his hand on my shoulder. "Long as she stays ignorant, bang her till your dick falls off for all I care. You did hit it, right? Tell me you at least sealed the deal."

"That's none of your business."

"You're right," Al said. "I really don't give a fuck. I'm just trying to be friendly here."

He sat back down on the stoop, patting the concrete. "C'mere, sit down, have a smoke with me."

"No thanks."

"Suit yourself," Al said, lighting up. He eased back on his elbows, blocking my path up the stairs. "How long you worked at that college?"

"Like it's any of your business," I said. "I'm going up to my apartment. Move out of the way."

"If you invited me upstairs, you could relax a bit, change clothes, have a beer."

"No way," I said. "You shouldn't get your shit crossed up, either. Just because you and me had a few beers in high school doesn't mean I'm gonna take any bullshit from you." I put my foot on the bottom step. "Quit following me and get off my stoop. I'm tired. I had a long day at work."

"When you get irritated," Al said, "I can see the family resemblance. Your brother's got a temper, too." Al looked down at my foot, grinning. He didn't move. "I could give a fuck about high school. You and I are going to have a conversation whether you like it or not." He kicked my foot off the step. "I got all day."

I crossed my arms, turned in a circle on the sidewalk. Kelsey had left me feeling better than I had in forever but Al's visit had killed that buzz. I felt almost as hollowed out as I had on Saturday. I hated him for it.

"Quit dancing around like a fag," Al said, "and sit."

I did, on the bottom step, wondering if Al's main function in this world was as an impediment, a block of granite that other people broke against. He reminded me of a bully I knew from grammar school. Caving in would only encourage him. I wanted nothing to do with Al, but what else was I going to do? Kick him in the balls and run away? "Just tell me what you want."

"That's more like it," Al said. "So it's been in the papers that your college wants to build new dorms. Over on the old Bloodroot property. Seems everything's ready to go, except for one problem. Your boss. You catch the way I'm drifting with this?"

"I don't have anything to do with the dorms or the museum. I'm low-level faculty. A name on a schedule and a paycheck." I bummed a smoke from him. "There's nothing I can tell you or Santoro or anyone else that they can't find out for themselves."

"I thought maybe you had some inside scoop," Al said. "That Friends of Bloodroot group did start in your department. Tell me about them. That Whitestone guy, your boss, tell me about him."

"I don't know anything about him," I said. "The group's a bunch of tenured old farts and some kiss-ass instructors. A few biddies who like getting their name in the *Advance* throw lunches and write checks for him."

Al raised his eyebrows. "Is Kelsey in the group?"

"No," I said. "She isn't. And I still don't see what this has to do with you following me around."

"That's a different thing. Bavasi wanted me to keep an eye on you," Al said. "Just for a coupla days. Because of this weekend. Things like that, they can make people squirrelly."

"I'm fine with this weekend. I'm not telling another living soul about it. You think I want people knowing what I did? I'd just as soon forget it." I scratched my fingernail at the faded gang sign spray-painted on the concrete. "Not a word to Bavasi about Kelsey, understand?"

"Or what, tough guy?" Al said. "He's gonna ask and I'm gonna tell."

"It's none of his business."

"You took his money," Al said.

"I wasn't helping him, or you," I said. "I was helping Danny. I wasn't joining up for anything. Santoro can't buy my life."

214

"He might disagree with you there."

Something clicked in my brain. "Construction," I said. "Danny said Santoro's into construction. He's hooked up to build those dorms."

Al tossed his chewed toothpick in the street, pulled a fresh one from behind his ear and stuck it in his mouth. He said nothing.

"Al, forget about Kelsey, as a favor to me. She's not even staying in town much longer."

"Then get it while you can," Al said. He stood and stretched, looking again at his empty slice of sky. "Think about this. Is now really the time to drag someone new into your life? You live small; keep it that way. We may have more work to do. You may put her in a bad position. A lot worse than any of the ones you put her in last night."

"Fuck you, Al. Don't come by my place again."

He laughed again, this time for real. "Whatever. Talk to Danny. Spend the rest of that cash and see how you feel. Ditch Kelsey and spend it on hookers. That usually works for me. Maybe I can find you one that likes soccer jerseys."

I ran at him, shoving him against his car.

"Whoa there, tough guy," he said, chuckling, raising his hands in the air in mock surrender. "What'll the neighbors think?"

I stepped back, now furious at myself as well as at him. All I'd needed to do was laugh him off, ignore his gangland-enforcer act. I'd just shown him I wasn't that tough a nut to crack. What would Santoro think of that information?

Al dusted off his jacket, got in his car, and drove away. Across the street, Maxie barked in his yard. I picked up my schoolbag and stormed inside.

After a long shower, I grabbed a Coke and went out on the porch, trying to figure out who made me angriest. I settled on myself. I had no reason to be mad at Danny. He hadn't put Al on me, and Al was only following orders. I was the one who'd lost control.

The sun was going down, streetlights popping on like sleepy eyes fluttering to half-awake. In the distance, a ferry bulging with commuters steamed across the bay, heading home from Manhattan trailing a boiling green and gray wake, the fading sunlight glinting off its windows.

People from the neighborhood trudged up my street toward the bus stop, most of them hoping to catch up to that same boat for a ride into the city. They counted change, fiddled with clip-on IDs, stared at cheap watches that beat in strict allegiance with the stern, merciless time clocks waiting on the other side of the water. Few people worked days in my neighborhood. Janitors, night watchmen, all-night discount-store cashiers, tow-truck drivers, judging by the uniforms. The bus stop crowd, anonymous in blue and gray and khaki, looking like so many cheap wine bottles wrapped in paper bags, formed a sad counterweight to the bustling, bouncing, blinged-out dealers on the other corner. A cop car rolled by, pretending to pay attention.

I thought of my father, of the night shifts he pulled at the dockside warehouses, of the weeks on end that he left for work when the other kids' dads came home. I remembered Danny and me running amok through the house with our exhausted mother snapping at our heels. We were so devoid of mercy for her adult worries and aches. I wondered if even then my mother was getting sick, tiny tendrils of her brain curling in on themselves like burning hairs. Had I missed my father in my sleep?

Like our father, Danny had become a creature of the night, first as a junkie and now as whatever it was he called himself. I doubted my father saw the irony that I did. Was that all Danny had really done, follow his father out into the night? I knew Robert Curran hated the choices his youngest son had made. If he only knew, I thought.

It was Monday evening, turning fast into Monday night. I was supposed to be, at that very moment, with my parents. I went inside and checked the phone; they hadn't called. Normally, I couldn't run ten minutes late without hearing from them. Dinner was an hour ago. What were the chances my folks had forgotten? Nonexistent. My insides chilled over. My mother was having a bad day, an awful day, maybe her worst yet. That had to be it.

I called a cab and ran downstairs to wait, horrific images — her lost, her bloody, her screaming — gliding like ghouls across my mind. I stood at the curb, bouncing on my heels, my arms crossed, twisting my bottom lip between my finger and thumb. What had my mother done that my father would allow me to stay away from her?

From the day of her diagnosis, there was only one reaction to her disease my father would not tolerate. Shame. He would not be ashamed of his wife, he said. And he would not allow me, he said, to be ashamed of my mother. He would not cancel visits if she turned unwell. I would not slip away out the door if she took a bad turn in front of me, leaving her asking later where I had gone. My father made no blushing apologies, offered no explanations or excuses to the neighbors. As best as he could, he let her be who she was and tried to fear neither who she was becoming nor who she was no longer.

I tried my best to emulate him and rise to the challenge. I spent as much time with them as I could stand, which was much less than I truly had at my disposal. When I could I went with them to the doctors. I set my hand on his forearm when my father clenched his fists at their insistence he consider a nursing home. *Maybe not yet, but soon, Mr. Curran.* I nodded in agreement as he told each doctor the same thing. *I will not send my wife who I love away from me.* Unlike so many other people that I knew, perhaps even unlike me, family was a simple thing to my father. You stayed together. Always.

For the most part, I failed to follow my father's example. I did the best I could to hide it from him. To hide my panic when Mom disappeared in front of us, in the middle of a meal or a conversation. To hide the fact that I became deeply afraid, not only for her but of her. I tried to conceal the shame I felt at my own fear, at the shame that soaked my bones when I let that fear feed me lies that I mumbled over the telephone, lies claiming I was too busy or too tired to keep an appointed visit. As my mother got worse, though, my father only got stronger.

He endured her memory lapses and her confusion. He took the blame when he could, admitting to misplacing things that she'd lost years ago, or claiming to have forgotten right in step with her where and when they got married. He played along when she awoke from an evening nap and staggered out of the bedroom in her night-gown, her hair wild as Medusa's, chastising him for being an unruly patient. It had happened once when I was there. That night she spoke to me as if I was her father, upbraiding me for smuggling beer for the patients into the hospital. Such a terrible thing for the chief surgeon to do. Sometimes she just paced, wringing her hands, wondering aloud how to save Danny from the doctors.

The only time I'd seen the cracks in my father was the night she stood out in the backyard, as if it were twenty years ago, calling Danny and me in for dinner. He said nothing, sitting in his chair, trembling every time her voice called out our names. I begged him to bring her inside, to throw her over his shoulder if he had to. He finally spoke when I threatened to do it myself, accusing him again of passing off selfish denial as strength in the face of anguish.

"She's calling for her boys," he said, his voice a thick, quiet rasp. "It's what a mother does." He glared at me, baring his teeth, showing me the fearsome countenance of a wise man losing his patience with a fool. "I deny nothing. That doesn't mean I have to deny your mother her freedom, or her nature."

That night, for the first time, I wondered what hurt him more: that she was going away or that he couldn't follow. If a way to stay with her existed, he would have found it. My father's loyalty was without mercy.

My father met me at the front door, barefoot, wearing sweatpants and a white strap T-shirt that desperately needed a wash. He looked drawn and pale in the porch light, his thin, gray hair greasy and matted. Instead of letting me into the house, he stepped outside, pulling the door closed behind him.

"Is she okay?" I asked.

221

"She had a bad morning," he said, "and afternoon."

"Where is she now?"

"Asleep. I got her to take something."

I wiped my hand down my mouth, looking away from my father, desperate for a cigarette, suddenly aware that I'd brought a pack. But I didn't go for them; I didn't want the old man knowing I'd started again. I should've let my folks alone for the night. I felt foolish for the panic that had brought me there.

"Come on in, anyway," my father said, opening the door. "You came all this way. Let's at least have a drink."

My mother wasn't in bed when we walked in. She was at the dining room table, setting out a plate of cookies and three glasses of milk. My father and I said nothing, sitting on either side of her, facing each other. She'd cut her hair; it was all but gone, short as a boy's. It was shocking but cute, stripping years off her face.

"Kevin, I wish you'd call," she said, sitting, "if you're going to be this late. I'm always happy to see you, no matter the time, but you missed dinner."

"The boy can feed himself, Eileen," my father said. "Don't you worry about it."

He gave a slight shake of the head, telling

me that there hadn't been any dinner to miss. He sat hunched over, but electricity crackled in his eyes; he was on his guard, protecting my mother or me or both of us from something. I decided not to ask my mom about her day.

"I'll call next time," I said, reaching for a cookie. Oreos. Danny's favorite. "Your hair looks great. I like the new look. Pretty radical, Dad, don't you think?"

My mother said nothing. She moved her hand to touch her head but her fingers hovered in the air, a slight tremble in them. Suddenly sheepish, her eyes darted from the tabletop to my father's face and back again. He took her hand and gently lowered it to the table where he laced his fingers with hers.

My father shot a glare across the table that could've peeled the paint off the wall. I didn't get it. I'd gone for harmless conversation. That was the cue, right? Plus, not only was what I said complimentary, it was true.

Then my mother stood at her seat, reaching for the cookie plate, her head coming into the hanging lamp's full light. Patches of color, multiple colors, stood out against her dark hair. Neon colors, muted but distinct in the direct light: blue, pink, purple. Stupidly, I thought of the Day-Glo-splattered walls of the Red Spot. I stared at her and she felt it.

"I'm sorry, Kevin. I'm tired," Mom said, holding the cookie plate in both hands at her waist, her face masked in politeness as if I were a salesman at the door. The colors stained her fingertips. "We thought you weren't coming so I took a pill, to sleep, not long before you got here. I think it's working. I have to go to bed."

"Sure, Ma," I said. "No problem."

I wanted to apologize, for noticing, for staring, for even being born. I wanted to convince her I didn't need or even want to know what happened to her hair. I needed her to know she was my mother and I just wanted some time with her but she had already disappeared into the dark kitchen. I got up from my chair, intending to follow her.

"Sit," my father said, and I did. "It ain't her job to stop you from feeling stupid. So sit there and feel stupid." He slouched in his chair, crumbling his cookie in his hand, the corners of his mouth twitching. "Boy, couldn't you cook your own damn dinner for one night?"

"Dad, you can't pick up the damn phone?"

I stood and this time didn't sit when told.

I walked out the front door.

But I only got as far as the front yard, where I stood wishing I'd left my mother to my father's capable hands where she belonged. I tried to remember the distance to the nearest train station, bereft now of even the nerve to go back inside and call a cab.

"Give us a smoke," my father said, stepping outside.

"I quit, Dad, a while ago," I said, staring down at the brick patio. "You know that."

"You got the Devil's own stink on ya, son," my father said. "Quit dickin' around. Your brother's the only decent liar in this family."

"I guess that's a good thing," I said, equally relieved at being discovered and at being able to smoke. I lit a cigarette for each of us.

Dad took a long drag and breathed out a billowing cloud of smoke, scattering the moths and mosquitoes hovering around the porch light over his head. He tapped his ashes in the weedy, overgrown flower boxes beside the front door. He'd built them from old railroad ties when I was six. I'd helped, handing him the nails as he worked. Where had Danny been? We always both helped Dad with his projects. I couldn't remember.

"I'm having a hell of a time keeping up,"

Dad said, tilting his chin at the weeds. "Though she don't notice so much anymore." He stared down at the cigarette between his thick pink knuckles. "First one in thirty years."

"Don't be too hard on yourself, Dad. These are difficult times."

"Girl across the street?" my father said. "The pretty blonde? The one your mother wanted you to date?"

"I remember. Sasha something-or-other."

"Right, her," my father said. "The Russian. Anyway, the other day she comes home from work or wherever with her hair dyed bright pink." My father chuckled. "Looks fucking great. Who'd a thunk it, right? Freakin' pink hair. Since I find this remarkable, I ask your mother if she can believe that pink hair can look decent on a person, never mind good. I'm just makin' conversation, small talk, like we do every day. Just shit around the neighborhood. She just kinda shrugs at me, you know, like it's nothin'.

"Well, today I gotta go down the union office, right? Pension and insurance bullshit, for the doctor bills. I come home and your mother's in the bathroom bawlin', going at her head with the scissors. Her hair is like six different colors and she's desperately tryin' to chop it all off before I see it. It's everywhere, in the sink, on the floor, in the bathtub. Blood on the scissors, in her hair. The bathroom walls still look like someone puked Magic Marker all over the place. I don't even know where she got the shit. Seems Sasha gave your mother an inspiration, but she couldn't decide on a color."

My father stared for a long time at his cigarette, watching the ash accumulate as the ember burned, a thin trail of smoke spiraling toward the porch light. His face sagged again, as if child's fingers pinched his cheeks, pulling them down toward his jaw. His slate eyes danced, an old argument renewed behind them. "Maybe it wasn't Sasha, maybe it was something I said."

He brought the cigarette to his lips, the long ash falling on his T-shirt. "Who knows, right?" He laughed, though it came out as a raspy croak. "You shoulda seen me with the phone book, trying to find a goddamn hairdresser that does emergency work. Then tryin' to get her into the car . . . I'd just got her settled when you showed up."

He glanced at me, then looked over at the flower boxes. I said nothing. Trying to talk him out of his guilt was pointless. In that way we were alike. He'd never gotten far trying to talk me out of mine over Danny.

Besides, he wasn't asking for my counsel, just that I listen. My mother had her trips to Atlantic City. I realized for the first time that since the onset of my mother's illness, my dad had become the shut-in. I wondered how I could get him out of that dim little house for a ball game or maybe just coffee or a cocktail. Why hadn't I thought of this before? After today, getting him out of the house would only be that much harder.

When my mother opened the front door, busting the both of us cold with our cigarettes at our lips, I don't know who jumped higher, me or my father. We tucked our smokes behind our backs, wispy evidence in the air all around us.

My mother shook her head. "You two. Can't you at least do that around the corner, where your father won't see you?"

She gave us the same sad, benevolent smile Danny and I used to get when caught with our hands in the Oreos, literally or figuratively. The same smile Danny had lately taken to giving me. "Come in and brush your teeth when you're done."

"Okay, Ma," I said. "Sorry."

She closed the door. My father had turned away from me. He walked the length of the brick path that split the lawn and like an old pro flicked his cigarette halfway across the street, the burning ember and the dead filter arcing through the air in opposite directions.

"You see now," he said when he got back to me, "why I'm so careful about your brother. One dumb comment about some girl's haircut and she falls apart. There's no telling these days. Who knows what fireworks will go off in her head if she sees him?" He set his hands on his hips, shaking his head at the front door of his home. "I wouldn't want to be us, though, if she finds out he's around and we didn't tell her."

"Don't worry," I said. "I'll take care of it." The confidence in my voice surprised me. It made no impression on my dad.

He opened the door. There was no sound from inside the house. "I'll call you a cab. I'd give you ride, but . . ." He pulled some cash from his pocket.

"I understand," I said, closing his hand over the wrinkled bills. "I'm okay, money-wise."

"That's a first." My father held out his hand. "Gimme a couple more a those coffin nails then, High-Roller. I might want 'em with my evening whiskey, long as your mother stays in bed."

I passed my dad the smokes. He nodded as he shut the door, locking the dead bolt and turning off the porch light while I stood there. I walked to the curb to wait for my ride, wondering if trying to get Danny back into the family was even worth it. We'd have to tell a lot of lies.

It'd be a lot more difficult watching Danny lie about his living than it had been watching him lie about breaking into the liquor cabinet. And that was if I got Danny and my father back on speaking terms. If I remained a go-between, I'd end up lying, too, about Danny's life, the same as when Danny was a junkie. Only it wasn't just Danny anymore with things to hide.

It probably wasn't yet ten, but the homes on my parents' block sat dark behind their post-and-rail fences and manicured lawns. Low-slung, brick ranch houses just like the one I grew up in formed two neat lines like train tracks or the double-yellow of the highway. The flickering blue glow of televisions misted through living room curtains. There wasn't a sound: no insects, no traffic, no dogs barking or kids crying. The whole block had shut down for the night, everything and everyone put away, turned off, and locked up.

I had a hard time believing that the crazy drama my father had described could happen on a street like this. The one I lived on now? That was a different story. Chaos played out on my street every other day, only with more profanity and less privacy.

But then again, this quiet block had hatched my brother, the junkie. And his other brother, the teacher. Both of them now doing things no one would believe. That kid Tommy, the block we left him on three years ago could've been this one. So could the block where Al used to live. Tommy could've been any one of the kids Danny and I had grown up with.

People like Tommy, like the dealers, thieves, and miscreants who haunted my neighborhood, people like my crazy neighbors Tony and Maria, like Al, they didn't necessarily start life in the world they ended up living in, or dying in. Who from history had? Hitler had started out as a painter, bin Laden a rich man's son with every advantage in the world. There wasn't a garden growing the lost and the criminal in one flower box and the quiet and the good in another, the Fates overseeing the whole project with seeds in one hand and a scythe in the other. Considering how I'd spent the past few days, the world felt more like a weed-choked, garbage-strewn lot. Instead of beautiful women at a spinning wheel, deaf, dumb, and blind luck decided who got rained on and who got pissed on, who flowered and who seeped poison and who withered in the dark.

My brother and I sprang from the same ground, from the same set of roots but how differently we'd grown and how strangely we'd re-entwined. Would we ever be disentangled? Would one of us have to be cut down for the other to finally flourish? Even if I had a choice, what did I want?

My cab slid to a stop at the curb. Climbing in, taking a last look around the block, I felt grotesque. Like I was black-winged and leaving brimstone fumes floating above the asphalt, mingling with the cab's exhaust.

Once upon a time, I was the good son.

ELEVEN

I called Danny as soon as I got home. He answered on the first ring.

"I've been waiting for this call," he said. "I didn't know a thing about Al tailing you."

"You knew," I said. "Maybe it wasn't your idea, but you knew."

"No," Danny said. "I didn't."

"You could've given me a heads-up," I said. "It would've helped."

"How? What would you have done different?"

"Keep him away from me," I said. "Talk to Al, talk to Santoro, do what you have to do, but I want him off my ass."

"I don't talk to Santoro," Danny said, "and I don't question his orders." He paused. I could hear him breathing through the phone. "I was hoping you'd roll with the punches here, that you'd trust me. That said, I can't blame you for not trusting me. This isn't something we can do over the phone. There are things you need to see for yourself. Meet me at Willowbrook Park, by the cemetery, at ten."

"You're kidding me, right? I'm not moving any more bodies. You've got Al for that."

"No bodies," Danny said. "No Al. This is something between you and me."

"Then come over," I said. "We'll split a six and talk, like real brothers. Like we should've been doing all along."

"You have no idea," Danny said, "how much I wish we could do it that way. But we can't."

"You tell me why not," I said. "The truth."

"Meet me in the park," Danny said, "and you'll see why not. At the graveyard, I'll tell you everything you want to know, and maybe a few things you don't, but should. See you there." He hung up without waiting for my answer; we both knew I'd show.

I sat on the couch, spreading out the week's lesson plans on the coffee table. Valley Forge. The same plans I'd used for the past three years. I could recite them from memory. Maybe that was why they couldn't hold my attention. My eyes kept wandering to the fuzzy green numbers of the cable box. I stayed on the couch until 8:47. Then I walked to the liquor store around the corner for a pack of cigarettes and a small bottle of

Bacardi.

At nine sharp, I lit a Camel, made a weak rum and Coke, and emptied my schoolbag. I set aside what I needed for work and emptied everything else out of the bag: every dried-out pen, every nub of chalk, every crumpled department memo, my expired faculty ID. Fifty-three cents in chalk-dusty coins. I couldn't recall the last time I'd cleaned out that bag. If I ever had, I hoped it hadn't been that long ago. I hadn't accumulated much of worth or use during my time in the halls of academia. The pile made for one sad time capsule of wasted effort. I gathered up the detritus of my career in two hands and dumped it in the trash.

I grabbed my flashlight from the cabinet and packed it in the bag. It'd be smart to bring a weapon, too. I found my lone steak knife among the kitchen utensils in the sink, rinsed it off, and stuck it into my boot — promptly pushing it through my sock and slicing a thin gash in my ankle. Gritting my teeth, I tossed the knife back in the sink. I dumped some rum on a piece of paper towel and stuffed it through the hole in my sock, limped in circles till my red badge of courage stopped bleeding. I added more rum to my Coke.

In the junk drawer I found a hammer. I tried stashing that in my jacket pocket, but the head fell hard against my ribs. It was more stable upside down but that way it just tangled in my pocket and then I couldn't get it out, not without taking off my jacket. Instead of the hammer, I put the bottle of rum in my jacket. I dropped the hammer into my book bag, cracking the lens on the flashlight. Fortunately, after a few good shakes, the bulb lit up. It would have to do. I set it gently into the bag. Was I ready? I was pathetic, that's what I was. But I was also out of time. I called a cab, slung the bag over my shoulder, and, keys in hand, headed for the door.

The phone rang as I locked up. Kelsey. Had to be. Isn't that always the way? I'd have to think of something to tell her when I saw her at work. I let it ring.

I had the cabbie drop me off at a twenty-four-hour deli a few blocks from Willow-brook. I waited until the cab drove out of sight, lit a cigarette, and hustled over to the park.

The street was pitch dark, no sidewalk, no streetlights. I stuck close to the guardrail, my fingers trailing along the rough, cool metal. Up ahead, floodlights bathed the park entrance in a white cloud. Without thinking, I walked right into the light, where anyone could've seen me, and turned up the gravel path, stepping over the heavy chain that kept the cars out after dark. Swearing at myself, I scurried out of the light, thankful no one drove by while I was making a show of trespassing. I decided to wait until I hit the woods before breaking out the flashlight. A wall of shadow against the starry night sky, the trees weren't hard to find. Off to my left, I spied the softball backstop silhouetted against the night sky. A sharp right at first base would lead me to the trail through the woods to the cemetery.

Wary of picnic tables and trash cans, of forgotten soccer balls and softball bats, I made my way across the park, holding my bag against my hip. I shivered in the chilly nighttime breeze, my nose running. October was remembering herself. My boots made no sound on the wet grass. Swallowed by the surrounding dark, I felt invisible, like less than a ghost. I liked the feeling a lot. Tension I didn't even know I carried seeped out of my shoulders. I felt free. Then I remembered Al.

When I reached the edge of the woods, where the trail began, I looked behind me. All I could see was the light at the entrance.

Everything between me and there was darkness. No sign of Al. I held my breath, listening for the Charger. Nothing. No sound at all. No animals in the woods, no insects. Winter was on its way. Everything was shutting down. Instinctively, I put up my jacket collar. I slid the bottle out of my pocket. As I unscrewed the cap a moan, or maybe the echo of one, drifted from deep in the woods. I drank two long swallows and strained to hear. The moan echoed again, deeper this time. It might have been a name.

Holding the lip of the bottle to my mouth, breathing in the sharp, burnt-sugar scent of the rum, I waited — listening to the building orgasm of a woman somewhere off in the dark. I waited till she was done, put all the other places I could've been right then out of my mind, and stepped into the trees.

The trail was slow going. I wasn't a Scout anymore, wasn't a kid. I'd lost my field guides and compass long ago. I didn't have Indian Scout Danny leading the way, charging ahead unafraid of fallen branches and hidden holes, oblivious to the welts and scratches on his hands and forearms. I was too old to be unconcerned with my next step.

Thirty yards deep the trees closed behind me and I turned on the flashlight. I held it at my hip in one hand, reaching the other out to clear away the thorny undergrowth crowding my path. Rotting leaves stuck to my soles at every step, raising the scent of wet, clean earth. It smelled like the cemetery had when we first turned the dirt, before we unleashed the stink of the carcasses. Soft, blurry moths bumbled through the beam of my flashlight. Harder, shinier things scuttled out of the light. I was afraid to breathe too loud. Compared to my younger self, I was an old man, hunched and shuffling.

Just as I started to worry I'd picked the wrong trail, or that there was no trail left, I saw stars through the tree branches ahead of me. Right as I was about to emerge from the trees into the graveyard, I tripped, tumbled through a bush and landed on my face in the clearing. My flashlight bounced out of my hand and rolled to the foot of the stone wall, where it caught Danny's feet in its glow.

He hopped down and picked up the flashlight, turning it off as he walked toward me. I was on my feet and dusting myself off when he reached me. I took the light from him and put it back in my bag.

Danny lit a cigarette and handed it to me. "You all right?"

My elbow had slammed hard on a stone

and throbbed like hell. I felt like the rum bottle had bruised my ribs. Thankfully, it hadn't broken. Bruised was okay, but this was not a place I wanted to be bleeding. "I'm fine. What the hell are we doing out here?"

"It's a long story," Danny said. He turned away from me and walked back to the wall. He leaned forward on it, his weight on his palms. The moon hung high over him, a pale eye trained on his shadow.

"I'm ready to hear it." I stayed where I was, bending my arm, working the pain out of my elbow. "I'm not cool with this, these people you've got me mixed up with."

"Al and I work together and I guess we're friends," Danny said, "but I don't have any control over him. He doesn't take his orders from me. I don't always know what his orders are. Everything comes from Santoro." Danny climbed over the wall and turned to face me. "Whose name you can never say over the phone again. We can never discuss his business over the phone."

"No problem," I said. "I'd just as soon never have anything to do with him again."

"Maybe someday soon that'll be possible," Danny said, walking away from me across the graveyard. "But not right now."

I climbed the wall and caught him. Together, we walked over the long cold graves of dead children, the tall grass whispering at our steps. All the sad, plywood grave markers were long gone. Looking around, there was no telling what lay buried beneath our feet. But Danny and I knew.

"Santoro needs you," Danny said. "Or he's decided he needs you, pretty much the same thing either way."

"To get him information about the school?" I asked. "C'mon, he can do better than me. There's got to be someone higher up he can buy off."

"This is true," Danny said. "Most of that's already taken care of. That state construction money's at his fingertips. There's just one glitch where a buy-off might not be the answer. Trust issues. Santoro's hoping you can help us figure an approach."

"Would that glitch be my boss?" I asked. "Whitestone?"

"I was hoping you could help me, too," Danny said. He stopped walking, looking up. We'd reached the grounds of the old children's hospital. "Santoro's future plans are not the only reason we're here."

As we passed the tumbledown, smashed-up bell tower, the lush graveyard grass stopped cold at the buckled asphalt of the parking lot. The whole building sagged as if sat upon by a giant. Broken glass cracked beneath our feet. We kicked aside fallen bricks. Graffiti-stained boards covered the first-floor windows. Above, as high as anyone could throw a brick, all the other windows had been smashed out. I could smell the mold and the stale char of old fires. Two-by-fours formed pale *X*'s across the front door.

Danny climbed the fractured marble steps. His foot shot through a space in the two-by-fours, kicking the front door. It fell straight back like a drunk, slamming to the floor with a sound like a gunshot. I yelped, about leaping out of my boots. Danny ducked through the door and into the darkness.

"Stop!" I shouted, running to the foot of the steps. Danny's shape was all but lost in the darkness. "What are you doing?"

"I need you," Danny said, "to come in here with me."

"You're outta your mind," I said. "Come back out here."

Danny's face glowed in the flame of his lighter then disappeared again. I watched the marigold tip of his cigarette brighten, bathing his fingertips in yellow light. I heard him exhale. He disappeared again, nothing remaining but the smell of smoke and an orange ember hovering in the dark.

"What're you afraid of?" he asked. "I'm right here."

I opened my mouth to speak but nothing came out. I wasn't sure how to answer. Every kid on Staten Island heard the horror stories about Bloodroot. In grammar school, it was a place and a fate the meaner parents used to threaten their unruly kids with. If you didn't straighten up and fly right, you'd get shipped off to Bloodroot — where they knew what to do with bad children. What the demon staff of that place really knew about handling bad kids we were afraid to ponder. New York called it a hospital because it was full of children, but Bloodroot was an asylum if there ever was one.

After New York State shut it down, when we were in junior high, its reputation only grew worse. We heard the true crazies never left, that they were locked in and left to subsist on rats and birds and toilet water and, in the worst of the stories, each other. We heard that teenagers, those vampiric greasy-haired mysteries we glimpsed haunting our neighborhoods, took it over. As if all the kids that should've been sent to Bloodroot ended up there anyway. Rumors flew about evil doings after dark. Murders, rapes, and devil worship. It seemed that every cat or dog that ran away from home got sacrificed to Satan out there. There were stories of the same happening to runaway children. Even the cops were afraid of the place.

"You want to know what everything's about," Danny called to me, "then you need to come in here with me. You need to see it."

I walked up the steps and ducked under the boards. I felt Danny's hand on my shoulder as I stood.

"Give me the flashlight," he said. I did.

Danny shone the beam over the grimy chessboard floor. Muddy footprints, human and otherwise, ranged in every direction. Rats scurried away from the light, rattling empty beer cans, swarming over a battered, broken wheelchair in their haste for the darkness. The whole room stank of rot and mold. It was like standing inside an abandoned crypt. I was afraid to look up. A dirty film crawled over my skin. I told myself it was only my imagination.

"Okay, I'm in here," I said. "It's fucking gross. It shouldn't be a museum. I agree. One hundred percent. I'll tell Whitestone. Can we go now?"

Danny guided the beam over the cracked, water-stained walls. One wall was tiled with giant mosaics. Looming human figures, twenty feet tall, their blank faces and long-fingered hands jaundiced by moisture and time. A nurse in an old blue uniform, her hand on a blind child's shoulder. A white-coated doctor stooping, his stethoscope pressed against the heart of a legless child in a wheelchair. Danny moved the light. Another wall, old photos ruined in their warped frames, the faces they memorialized consumed by rot. To our left, an old sofa long ago set afire slumped blackened and broken against one wall. To our right ran a long, warped wooden counter. That, too, was burned in places, smashed in others. At the outer edge of the light hovered the first few steps of a marble staircase.

"This was reception and processing," Danny said, heading for the stairs. "Coming in was the only time a kid saw this room. The only kids that left this place went out the back door. Wrapped in a sheet." He stopped at the wheelchair, fingered a thick leather restraint on one of the arms. "This is what it was like in here." He turned the light on the giant doctor. "Not like that."

He started up the stairs, his hand releasing clouds of dust as it ran along the railing. I followed, my hands in my pockets.

"In high school, sometimes when I cut class," Danny said, "I came here. Exploring.

I wanted to see what was left, I guess, after all that time we spent looking through the windows. Few years later, after I figured some things out and I got real bad with the needle, I used to shoot up here. Always had the place to myself."

We passed the first floor and continued ascending.

"Nothing happened there," Danny said. "Storage, mostly. A staff lounge. They didn't want people downstairs hearing anything."

"Hearing what?"

"Oh, you know. Crying children. Yelling nurses and attendants. Screams."

We made the third-floor landing. There was no tile here, just flat, smooth, colorless concrete. The floor, the walls, the ceiling — like a cell block.

"This is where most of the action was," Danny said. "Here on the third floor." He kicked at the bottom edge of a fallen metal door. "The walls are thicker. And the doors. You can't even tell this level is here from the outside. There aren't any windows. There was no stop for it on the elevator."

Danny passed through the doorway and into the hall. I caught him by the elbow.

"How do you know this stuff? What're we doing here?" I asked. "It's not because I'm a history teacher."

Danny stared down the hallway, the beam of the flashlight pooling at our feet. "No, it's not." He turned to me. "You ever wonder about the history you don't know? All the things that happened, that people did, all the lives that came and went with no one stopping to notice? Not the General Washingtons that you love so much, but the poor bastards that dragged the cannons through the mud. There were hundreds of them, right?"

"Thousands," I said. "I don't know, Danny. I feel sometimes my curiosity for what came before us, the big people and the small, died a long time ago. One of those guys in the mud, that's what I feel like these days. All I can see is the next step in front of me."

"A lot more gets by us than we ever notice, doesn't it?" he asked.

"Yeah, Danny," I said. "I guess it does."

"And yet we can never get away from it. The past. No matter how small we try to make it. No matter how much we tell ourselves it doesn't count. Even if we do forget something, for a while, it still comes back from wherever we buried it. The past doesn't stay in our memory, it gets in our bones, our blood. It stays."

"Danny," I whispered. "I need to know

why we're here. I need to know now."

He turned to me. "This place. This is where I'm from."

"What're you talking about?"

"I wasn't born your brother," Danny said. "I came to you from here."

"Bullshit, you're imagining things," I said. "It's the nightmares. You know you've always had them. I mean, c'mon, you're better now, but you've cost yourself some brain cells over the years."

Danny walked away from me, down the dark corridor. He stopped and shone the flashlight through the small window in a big metal door. I ran up beside him.

"Let's get outta here," I said. "We can talk about this someplace else."

"This was one of the laboratories," Danny said.

I looked through the window. Instead of concrete, everything was tiled. The tile was cracked and molded over in green, brown, and black now but, in its day, easier to clean than even concrete. I realized only neglect and abandonment had brought any color to this place. In the past it had been a two-color world: white and red. Tile and blood. In the center of the room stood a long, metal examination table. In the flashlight beam, through the rust and corrosion, some of the steel still gleamed.

"Dr. Calvin's *office,* they called it," Danny said, "but a lab is what it was. It's where we got our shots, among other things." He pointed the light down the hall, shining it on one metal door after another. "Calvin was the only doctor I knew by name. Knowing it didn't help any."

Danny led us back to the stairs. As we climbed, skipping the fourth floor, I wondered if the drugs had damaged my brother more than I ever knew. The places he'd been, the things he'd seen, the shooting galleries and crack dens, the emergency rooms, the psych wards, the junkies, dealers, hookers, paramedics, cops, and doctors, the needles and spoons and guns and handcuffs — they'd gotten confused in his brain. To make sense of it all, he'd put them together and built this haunted house. One roost for all his demons. Maybe that somehow made his memories bearable for him.

But then there was Dr. Calvin. I'd heard that name from my mother in the midst of one of her fits. Someone she used to work with, I'd figured. An old boss. But where would Danny have heard that name?

We left the staircase at the fifth floor, the top floor.

"Boys' residential floor," Danny said.

"Girls lived on the fourth."

We walked slowly down the hall and into an ammonia stench that made me gag.

"Jesus," I said, fighting for breath and searching my bag for my cigarettes. "What the hell is that?"

"Bat shit," Danny said, unaffected by the stink. "They live in the attic and the roof. Hundreds of them, maybe thousands. Take shallow breaths. You'll get used to it."

We passed door after door, these smaller than the ones downstairs, without any windows into the rooms. The doors wilted in their frames, bent and weakened. Nailed into each door was a rusty metal number, just like the apartment doors in my building. I touched the number nine, my apartment number, and rust flaked off on my fingertips. Glued under the number was a small ceramic clown. Missing one hand, it clutched broken balloons in the other. Still, this clown had held up better than half the building. I rubbed at the filth on its smiling face with my thumb and the door creaked. I jumped back and hustled after Danny, who had stopped before a door at the end of the hall.

"This was my room," Danny said, pushing the door open. "Me and six other boys."

I walked up behind him. Room fifteen.

His clown had both hands but no head. No balloons, either. Over Danny's shoulder, I peered into the room. It was about the size of a walk-in closet. Tile walls, tile floor. Chessboard black and white. Like the asylum lobby, like the kitchen in Danny's apartment. Huge, thick water pipes ran across the low ceiling. No way seven children of any age or size fit in that room. There wasn't room for more than three beds. There was no toilet, no heater. I saw no fixtures where either might have been. One window set higher than any child's reach and guarded with thin iron bars stared out at the world. One concrete eye to watch the moon.

"Danny," I said, "your room was next to mine, in our parents' house."

"They didn't even give us beds," Danny said. "Just filthy blankets that they washed once a month. We had fleas, like dogs. One kid couldn't even scratch himself. He had no hands."

"We each had our own bed in our own room," I said. "The same one, with the ship's wheel for a headboard. Remember?"

"What do *you* remember, Kev?" Danny asked. "About us at five, six. We're less than a year apart. Shouldn't you remember *something?*"

I searched: the two of us Christmas morning under the tree, or out in the backyard under Mom's watchful eye while she tended her garden, or getting dragged off to church in our Easter best. I could see the two of us at eight, ten, twelve years old walking back and forth to school, playing Wiffle ball in the street, but back before that was only me. No Danny in the emergency room after I'd hit the ice, no Danny building flower boxes with me and Dad. There were places he wasn't and should have been so I tried putting him there.

Danny came into the pictures and flickered back out, a snowflake that wouldn't stick. I squinted my mind's eye and tried to focus on specific things, his eyes, his hands, the sound of baby talk and crying, but I came up empty. In every memory he should have inhabited, Danny floated beyond the edges of my vision, inches out of the frame. I could feel him out there but I couldn't pin him down, couldn't get a grip on him. He was like a lost name dancing on the tip of my tongue.

"You're asking about a time," I said, "when I was . . . when we were very young."

"But you remember other things, I bet," Danny said. "Birthday parties, preschool, trips to the park, moving to Staten Island.

Where am I? I'm not *there* because I was *here*."

I was surprised, in fact, how far back I could remember. Details from when I couldn't have been more than four or five. The stink of baby goats at a petting zoo, the rye-bread smell of the crackers I fed them. The blue and white blanket I carried everywhere. Red cowboy boots I always wanted to wear to church. God, I had pitched such a tantrum the day we left Brooklyn to move across that big, scary bridge. I screamed myself hoarse. All kinds of things popped up. But not Danny.

"I mean, yeah, there's some shit," I said, "but it's all vague. Bits and pieces. I was . . . we were so young. One day it was me, Mom, and Dad in Brooklyn, and then it was the four of us on Staten Island. One day you're just . . ."

"I'm just there," Danny said. "Out of the blue. All of a sudden. You can't remember me in the Brooklyn house at all, can you? Shouldn't I be there? I would've been five when we . . . when you moved."

Couldn't be. Danny couldn't be right. Then I thought of Mom. Talking to Danny like a baby patient, talking about Dr. Calvin, pacing the living room carpet wondering how to bring Danny home. I covered my

253

mouth with my hands. Everything blurred and my knees went watery. Holy shit.

"It took me months to put it together," Danny said. "In here, walking the halls, my own nightmares in front of my face like some old ghost town movie set. Maybe 'cause I was so fucking high." He walked to the window. "It clicked for real when I took a good look out this window."

I stood beside him and looked out. There was nothing to see but the night sky and a rolling, empty field beneath it.

"This place takes its name from that field," Danny said. "Bloodroot Valley. Every spring that field goes white with bloodroot flowers. I've only seen it a couple of times. The blooms don't last but I know it happens."

I swallowed hard. "Mom's garden. That's when we knew spring was here, when the bloodroots bloomed."

"This is where she got them," Danny said. "And this is where she got me. She worked here; I fucking *know* it. How do you think Grandpa knew so much about Calvin and what went on here? He had an informant. He had photos, for chrissakes. You think that would've been allowed here?" He chuckled. "Mom fucking stole me from here."

I believed. I remembered enough for that. My mother suddenly quitting nursing not long after the move to Staten Island, when that was the reason we'd moved there to begin with. That she got a new job at a big children's hospital. At least that was what I'd always been told. But no one had ever said which one. Had Grandpa sent her here? Made our mother his own spy in the enemy camp?

"Imagine finding out," Danny said, "your worst nightmares are actually your memories."

"I never knew. No one ever told me." I pulled the rum out of my jacket and took several long swallows. "This is un-fucking-believable."

I offered Danny the bottle. He waved it off.

"That doesn't make it go away," he said. "Believe me, I know."

"Why? Why are you telling me all this, after all these years?"

"Those people at your school," Danny said, "they want to build a memorial here, for all the kids that never made it out. Restore this place, give tours. Make it a museum. Show off the antique exam tables and the old-fashioned wheelchairs. How sick is that? It was a living hell, a mad

255

scientist's laboratory where they gave kids diseases as experiments. Made us into pincushions before I ever even heard the word *heroin*.

"This fuckin' place needs to be ground into dust. I need that to happen. Santoro can make it happen, if we help him." Danny gripped the bars over the window. "Can't you see the symmetry here, Kev? It's fate. It's irresistible. Me, after all these years, coming back to destroy this place. There's millions at stake here, Kev. Millions. And we can get us a slice. A big one. All of us, you, me, Mom and Dad can get taken care of for life by bringing this place down. It's perfect. It's justice. This place that made me a monster is gonna free me from every shitty thing I've ever done because of the needle." He turned to me, his eyes shining in the moonlight. "You gotta help me. One last time. So I can sleep through the night without a head full of chemicals. Help me finish what Mom and Grandpa started. Let's make Dad proud."

How could I say no? True blood or not, he was my brother. We'd lived too long that way for it ever to be different. That was one thing all our secrets would never change.

"Sometimes I still come up here to this room," Danny said, turning back to the window. "Early, early in the morning. Instead of getting high I watch the bats come home. Count them like they were stars."

Twelve

At noon, I sat on a bench outside the history building, two cold slices of foil-wrapped pizza in my lap and two warm Cokes at my feet. The young elms and birches behind me rustled in the breeze, their shadows playing over the concrete at my feet. Nearby, two squirrels sat on their hind legs, eyeing me sideways, their eager paws fidgeting at their chests.

I watched Kelsey stride my way, her arms swinging freely, a big brown paper sack in one hand. Thankfully, she'd brought something of her own. On my way out to the bench, I'd realized I should've had something delivered for us, since I'd made the invitation. Unfortunately, that realization came early enough for me to feel guilty about it but too late to do anything other than be willing to give up a slice. Maybe we'd save the crusts for the squirrels. I knew that's what they were hoping for.

When Kelsey got close, the squirrels darted away, scrambling up the same tree, where I knew they'd watch us, eager to snatch up whatever we left behind. I wondered what or who else watched us. I scanned the campus for Al, half-expecting to spy him propped up against a building, hidden behind an upside-down newspaper. The comical imagining did me no good. I didn't trust Al. I couldn't shake the feeling that in his eyes I wasn't a welcome addition to the family. I wished Kelsey and I had planned to eat inside. Or that I'd been smart enough that morning to kill whatever it was we'd started between us.

She surprised me with a kiss on the cheek. Pulling off her jacket, she sat close to me. She wore a purple short-sleeved soccer jersey with a red and green crest I didn't recognize over her right breast. She had gracefully muscled arms, something I'd failed to notice in the dark the other night.

"What's the good word?" she asked.

"Paranoia," I said.

"Ah, don't worry," she said. "Everybody thinks we've been doing it all along anyway. Maybe the word for the day should be 'self-fulfilling prophecy'?" She noticed me checking her out and tapped her index finger on the crest. "Portugal. Europe's first great navigators. They invented the compass."

"If you say so."

"Wow. You're in a mood," Kelsey said, unpacking a plastic container from the paper sack. "Did your eleven o'clock go that bad?" She handed me the container. It was heavy and warm.

"No, it went fine," I said. "I'm sorry. I've been sitting here thinking thoughts I'd rather avoid."

Out of the sack she produced a paper bowl and two plastic forks. She took the container back from me and peeled off the lid. The hot, tangy scent of lasagna, rising on steam, made my mouth water.

"If you're gonna dump me," Kelsey said, "which would be a record, by the way, we only did it two days ago, can you wait until tomorrow? I did cook for you, kind of." She shoved half the lasagna into the bowl, stuck a fork in it, and handed it to me. "And I'd like some company tonight."

I opened both Cokes and gave her one. "I think that can be arranged."

"If it's not too much trouble," Kelsey said. "So eat. You need to keep up your strength."

I happily shoved huge forkfuls of sauce and beef and pasta and cheese down my throat. Thoughts of another night with her thrilled and relaxed me at the same time.

As appealing as the sex was, I really craved the sanctuary she offered, a dark, warm place away from everything else. It wasn't a perfect secret but I wasn't going to let that blunt my enthusiasm. Al could sit outside all night if he wanted. We'd draw the shades and shut him out. It felt real good having something to look forward to.

"I need to ask you something personal," I said when we finished eating.

"Yes, I'm on the pill," Kelsey said. "And as long as you've been tested recently, we can forgo the condom this time."

I laughed. "Appreciated, but that's not what I was going to ask."

"Do you realize," Kelsey said, "that I've directed every attempt you've made at conversation back to sex?"

"You don't love my mind," I said. "I can live with that. Neither do I most of the time."

"You were good to me at the Red Spot," she said. "I owe you one. What's the question?"

"When your mother was dying," I said, "how far would you have gone to save her?"

Kelsey took her time answering. She first packed up the remains of our lunch, everything going back into the paper bag. "Odd question. How about you give me a cigarette?"

Instinctively, I reached into my pocket and there they were. It was strange. I couldn't remember picking them up that morning before I left the apartment. After a couple of drags, she started talking.

"You know, I thought about that a lot before she died. I had way too much time to think. I prayed for a while to trade places with her, but then did I really want her at my bedside watching me die? I would've blown my brains out before I let that happen. Or at least slunk off somewhere where she wouldn't know what was happening, like dogs and elephants do."

"Did you ever wish she'd done that? That she'd left you out of it?"

"God, no. It was the hardest thing I've ever done, spending those last few weeks with her. Half the time I felt like a vulture, just sitting around waiting on death. But there's nothing worse than suffering alone. I couldn't let anyone I loved endure that. She would've forgiven me for not being there, but I never would've forgiven myself."

"So you can suffer alone," I said, "but it's cruel for anyone else to do so. Contradictory, isn't it?"

"I can do that," Kelsey said, "for I contain

multitudes." She smiled. "It's part of my charm."

"Say there was a cure," I said, "but for some reason you couldn't get it by ordinary means, like you couldn't afford it or it was illegal or whatever. What would you have done?"

"That's easy. I'd have done anything. Lie, steal, con, sell my body."

"Kill someone? Would you do that?"

Kelsey slid down the bench, stretching her long legs, folding her arms across her chest. "That's a tough one." She released a long sigh. "No. I'm lying. It's easy. Yes, I would've killed someone to save her life, especially with her suffering like that. I'd put myself at the top of the list. No doubt. Anyone that says they'd do otherwise is a liar."

She sat up suddenly, leaned close to me. "What did you do, Kevin? What are you trying to justify? This is hardly conversational foreplay." She blinked at me, backing away, an idea flickering across her face. "Your brother's in trouble, isn't he? That's why he came looking for you."

Feeling caught and exposed, I looked away, struggling for what to say next. I should've known Kelsey would make the leap to Danny. That she was so sharp was a big reason I liked her. Maybe I'd wanted her to make that connection, to get me somewhere I couldn't on my own. Still, I had to be careful.

"He's not in trouble," I said. "He's doing great, actually. Now. It's just . . . I know there are things he did while out on the streets, things he did to survive, that I might be struggling with. Where do I stand if, say, Danny's history puts me, technically, at cross-purposes with the law? Like, because of things I knew."

"Your brother was a criminal," Kelsey said.

I stared at her. She did get to the point a lot better than I did, I thought, even if the past tense didn't apply to Danny. Or to me, for that matter. "Well, he's not a serial killer or anything like that. He's just a former junkie."

"Are there cops at your door?" Kelsey asked. "Is he a threat to you or your family?"

"No," I said. "It's not like that. I'm talking about the past."

"You're his brother," Kelsey said, "like I'm my mom's daughter." She paused, took a deep breath. "That shit's forever." Kelsey put her hands on her thighs and set her shoulders. "There are, and I believe this to my core, higher laws than the few, sad ones mankind has devised. I'm not going to get all Jesus on you; God is a whole different conversation. So let's call them blood laws. Blood as in family. When blood laws and human law contradict, blood laws rule."

She'd given me the answer I wanted. I didn't know why I couldn't just accept it. "Is there anything that absolves you from these so-called blood laws?"

"Nothing," Kelsey said. Her voice had bite. "Not in a serious situation, certainly not in a life-or-death situation like the one with my mom." She relaxed. "Okay, so it can affect whether or not you come over for Christmas, or something like that. But you get my point." She leaned close to me, her hand gripping my thigh. "I will tell you this. If I had a chance to get my mother back, like the chance you have with Danny, there's nothing I wouldn't do to keep her. And I mean *nothing*."

She stood, staring into the trees for a long moment before looking down at me. "Kevin, whatever is happening with you and Danny, I don't need to know. It's between you and him. I'm here if you need help, and if you want to keep it private, that's cool, too." She bent and grabbed her bag. "You'll do the right thing; I got faith in you. You're kind of a slacker, but you're a good man."

265

She nodded at the history building. "Now let's go. Duty calls."

I stared up at her. I hadn't been called a good man in a long time, hadn't felt like one in even longer, but I did right then. I glanced at my watch. "What? I don't have class for another ninety minutes."

"Yeah, but Whitestone's press conference started five minutes ago."

"Aw, fuck." I'd actually read that memo. You couldn't miss it. The announcement for the latest Friends of Bloodroot event was plastered all over the office and I'd managed to space out on it anyway. Every teacher in the department had to attend, per direct orders of the dean. And he'd be enough of a prick to take attendance.

Kelsey and I slipped through the double doors of the conference room and stood with our backs against the wall. A few heads in the standing-room-only crowd turned at our entrance. The crowd of about fifty seemed to be mostly history teachers and yawning students I figured had been offered extra credit for attending. Up front against the wall leaned a few bored-looking reporters and photographers. Whitestone, who spoke into a microphone at a podium in front of the room, never broke stride. On the screen behind him hovered a large projection of an artist's sketch of the new museum. I had a feeling that was as far as the planning process had gone.

"And so," Whitestone was saying, "though the sacrifices of those children were unwitting, they deserve commemoration. Justice needs to be done. Their tiny, forgotten souls demand it. Those children need a champion, and that's why I've called you all here today. To publicly acknowledge, praise, and thank Ms. Ida Horace, the first recipient of the Friends of Bloodroot Children's Champion Award." Applause began. "Ida, stand up for us, please."

"I think I'm gonna be sick," I whispered. Kelsey, thinking I was kidding, shushed me and slapped my arm.

Whitestone approached a pint-sized, blue-haired lady in the front row who couldn't have been a day over ninety. Ida looked like she hadn't left the house since the Eisenhower presidency. Stooped with age, she reached only to Whitestone's shoulder. He slipped his arm around her, turning Ida toward the cameras, and smiled big enough for the both of them. I waited for him to present her with a plaque or certificate, some token of appreciation, but the photo op comprised the entirety of Ida's award.

After kissing her powdered cheek, Whitestone helped Ida resettle into her wheelchair, then strode back to the podium.

"Thanks to Ms. Horace's generous five-figure donation," Whitestone said, "the Friends of Bloodroot, who I am proud to represent here today as their founder, can continue their work on behalf of the brave, forgotten children whose suffering effected revolutionary change in the history of this island, this city, and, in fact, all of these United States."

More applause. Whitestone spent several moments nodding, as if agreeing again and again with the greatness of his own words. All I could think about was Danny's revelation to me the night before. What the dean was doing was sick. Worse, I felt like he knew it and he didn't care. I wanted to choke him right then and there. Let's see him smile through that for the cameras. He was only in it for himself; I was sure of it. All Ida's check would do was send him to Europe for another research trip. Whitestone was no better than Dr. Calvin in his using those kids, using my brother, to feed his own ego. Why couldn't these other jokers see through him like I could? Because they didn't know what Danny and I knew, that those lost kids didn't need a fucking museum; what they needed was payback. To give their souls, my brother's soul, some rest.

I leaned my shoulder into Kelsey's. She turned to me.

"One thing a lifetime of studying history has taught me," I said, "is that those selling themselves as the most high and mighty have the lowest and foulest things to hide." I raised my chin at Whitestone, now glad-handing in the front of the room. "That guy isn't just creepy. He's dangerous. Well, pride cometh before the fall. I gotta go." I squeezed her hand. "Tonight?"

Kelsey gazed up at me. "Stay out of his way. He'll run out of steam eventually."

"Tonight?" I asked again.

"My place. Eight," Kelsey said.

After work, I went to my parents' house for dinner. My father had called the office to tell me my mother spent all afternoon in the kitchen making her special lasagna. He begged me to help him eat it. Though they'd been only two for a long time, my mother had never stopped cooking for four. How my parents stayed whippet-thin mystified me. I told my father I'd be happy to do him this favor. For an Irishwoman, my mother made a hell of a lasagna.

269

Once we got settled around the dinner table, me sitting opposite Mom and my father next to her, it only took me four bites to screw up.

"Ma," I said, "this is even better than Kelsey's." I kept eating, head down, hoping my comment had slipped by unnoticed. It hadn't.

"Kelsey who?" my mother asked, a flicker of fear in her eyes. I knew she worried Kelsey was a name she'd known but forgotten.

My father sensed it, too, and jumped right in. "Yeah, Professor. Kelsey who? I've never heard you mention no Kelsey."

"She's a friend of mine from work," I said. "We had lunch together this after — , last week, rather, and she brought homemade lasagna."

"That's nice, boy," my father said, "but get to the point. She a 'just a friend' friend or a 'friend with benefits' friend?"

I dropped my fork and glared at him, blood rushing to my cheeks. "Jesus, Dad."

My mother slapped the back of his huge hand. "Robert W. Curran."

"What? We're adults here," my father said, wide-eyed, clutching his injured hand to his chest. He'd always excelled at playing the misunderstood innocent suffering under my mother's iron thumb. My mother tried not to laugh at him. She failed. They traded sly glances. I was watching my parents flirt. I dropped my eyes to my plate.

As parents, my folks were an inseparable team. Even Danny had struggled to play them against each other. But that night I realized for the first time that they had never hidden being a romantic couple, too. That they were the best of friends. I finally started to grasp how deeply and hard my father's heart must be breaking. I knew he held his rosary every night praying for one thing. A little more time with his beautiful girl.

My eyes watered. I missed Danny like crazy. I was furious with him, too. What the hell was he doing in Brooklyn, staring at those screens, the monster Saturn staring down at him? What was he so afraid of? I had to get him back here, no matter what it took, before the nightmares dragged him under again, and before Mom got too far away for any of us, even Dad, to reach her.

My mother covered my father's hand with hers. "You're awful quiet over there, Kevin. Forgive this silly man. I know you forget what a Neanderthal he is; you don't live with it every day like I do." She smiled at him and then at me. "Please do tell us about Kelsey. I promise your father will behave."

My father left one hand under his wife's and resumed loading lasagna into his mouth with the other. I was relieved he used a fork.

"Kelsey and I work together at the college," I said. "She's in my department. It's nothing serious. We've just recently started hanging out away from work. I like her, she's cool. Smart, intense." I decided to skip the part about her leaving town. "We're getting together tonight, in fact."

"That's excellent news," my mother said. "If the chance comes along, I'd love to meet her."

"She Irish?" my father asked, his mouth full. He was being extra slovenly for my mother's entertainment.

"Her last name is Reyes," I said, "so probably not one hundred percent."

Mom splayed her fingers on the tabletop. "It doesn't matter. Besides, the Currans are black Irish, which means there's probably some Spanish in you anyway. Right, Robert?"

My father grunted, tossing his crumpled napkin onto his empty plate.

"Well, I'm pleased as punch for you, Kevin," Mom said. "Let us know how it goes." She rose to clear the table. My father touched her forearm. He stood and started gathering the plates himself. She sat back down, glaring up at him. "I'm not an invalid."

"I know, Eileen," Dad said. "You cooked all day. Fair play to you. Talk to your son. I'll do the dishes and make us a round of whiskeys."

"Come sit by me," Mom said, patting the back of the chair my father had just left. "I'm very happy to hear about that girl."

"Kelsey," I said.

"I know that," my mother said, hurt. "You just told me her name a few minutes ago." She feigned a grin. "I'm not that far gone just yet."

"I'm sorry," I said, feeling awful. Not for the first time in my life, I wished I'd inherited my father's charm. "We get along well, I think it helps we knew each other already, but let's not get ahead of ourselves."

"How could anyone not get along with you?" Mom said. "I just . . . I want to see you with someone who loves you. And I want to know her, too. While I still can."

"Don't say things like that," I said.

"Why? Because they hurt? Because they're true? I made that mistake with your brother, looking the other way. Let's not you and I make it. Don't be afraid of me, Kevin. Please." She reached out and touched my cheek. "You're a handsome, smart, wonderful boy but you were never very brave."

I groaned, clutching at my chest with both hands, a sad attempt to imitate my father. Mom didn't laugh, maybe because my feelings really were hurt. And she was right. I thought of Danny walking the halls of Bloodroot, and of Kelsey gripping my thigh on the park bench. I had to toughen up, as my father would say. My time to be brave had arrived.

"The two of you," she said, shaking her head. "Danny running headlong into everything, you running away. It's no wonder you lost each other. You seem so lost to me sometimes, too, Kevin. Adrift. Like your father was when I met him. This life is hard and full of surprises. You need a partner, an ally. You can't drift though life up among the clouds, waiting for wherever the wind takes you. You'll miss too much. You need a compass, Kevin. I don't want both my babies lost in the world."

She looked over her shoulder at my father, who stood at the sink, washing the dishes and whistling "Whiskey in the Jar."

"What would happen to me now if I didn't have your father?" she said. "Crazy as he is, he has always been true. This Kelsey may be your compass; she may not. But be brave enough to find out."

"I will. I promise to be brave," I said. "If you promise me the same, right now."

"I'll do the best I can," Mom said. "I know we've never talked much about it." She scratched at a stain in the tablecloth. "There's a lot we've never talked enough about." She looked back up at me. "And now I'm forgetting what a lot of those things were. It's a terrible disease, but I'm facing it as best I can."

I reached out and took her hands. "I know you are, and one day soon we'll sit and talk about it. Tonight, though, there's something else." I squeezed her hands. "I know about Danny."

"What about Danny?"

"I know where he came from," I said. "How he got here. How come you never told me?"

My mother snapped around in her chair. "Robert! Come in here, please."

Dad rushed into the room, wiping his hands on a dishrag. "What? What'd I do?" He jerked his thumb over his shoulder. "It ain't broke, just chipped it a little. I swear."

"It wasn't Dad," I said. "It was Danny. He's back. He turned up at my house a few days ago."

Mom whirled back around. "What do you mean turned up? How is he?" Her eyes

275

darted back and forth between my father and me, betrayal burning in them. "Bobby, you knew about this?" She covered her heart with her hand. "Danny. My God." Blood rose to her cheeks. "Where is he? Why hasn't he come to see me?"

My father put his hands on her shoulders. "That's my fault. Kevin told me right away but I wanted to make sure Danny wasn't pulling the same old act. I didn't want him putting you through that again."

"It's only been a couple of days, Ma," I said, leaning across the table. "I had the same concerns Dad did."

Mom shook her head. "All the time you men have lived with me and what do you know? Nothing. He's my *boy*, for chrissakes. That's all that matters." She stared me down. "Tell me about my son."

"He's good," I said. "Clean for over a year. Living in Park Slope. He's got his own business installing home electronics and computers."

"All this before he comes to see his mother?" Mom said, pressing her palms to her cheeks. "I'm so relieved he's doing so well. He's never been clean that long."

A line of sweat had gathered along her hairline. She didn't know what to feel, the poor woman. She was overjoyed that Danny

276

was alive and well, outraged that she was the last to know. I watched the emotions battle it out across her face, wanting to rewind the evening back to when we first sat down. My father brought her a glass of ice water from the kitchen. She sipped it and then looked up at him.

"I thought you were making whiskeys," she said.

"Coming right up," Dad said, grateful for an excuse to bail.

Mom held her glass but didn't drink again. She rubbed at the fog on the side with her thumb. She hadn't answered my questions.

"Did Danny tell me the truth?" I asked.

"It depends on what he told you," Mom said.

"He told me you worked at Bloodroot," I said. "That you brought him home from there."

Mom slumped in her chair as if exhausted, staring away from me.

Dad placed three glasses of whiskey and water on the table. He sat at the other side of my mother, across the table from me. "What's going on?" he asked.

Mom turned to him. "Danny told Kevin we got him from Bloodroot."

My father lowered his untasted glass from

his lips. "The asylum? That's ridiculous." The ice rattled against the glass as his hands shook. He couldn't look at me. "It's all lies. It's more of your brother's crazy bullshit. Another one of his crazy excuses for becoming a junkie."

"Bobby," my mother said. "Calm down."

"I have to give him points for originality on this one," my father said. "You see, Eileen? You see why I thought twice about letting that boy come back around?"

Mom straightened in her seat, gathering her strength for my father's sake. Her jaw was tight and she wouldn't look at either of us. "I know. I understand. It's okay."

I drank half my whiskey down, shifting in my seat with discomfort. It wasn't the tension that unnerved me but the intimacy between my parents as they struggled to protect each other from my brother, the great burden of their lives. I'd caused the moment, but it still felt like something that should have no witness, that should exist only between them. I racked my brain for a graceful exit, checking the clock on the wall. Could I go to Kelsey's early? No, I wouldn't run. I'd promised my mother I'd be brave.

My father finally turned to me. "Yes, your brother is adopted." He drank. "We never told you because it never mattered. The minute we carried him through that door, he was our boy, our blood. So now you know. What's the big deal?"

"Then where did he come from?" I asked. "Really?"

"Back when I was a nurse at Methodist," Mom said, "when we still lived in Brooklyn, a cop brought him into the emergency room —"

"Ei, why go into detail?" my father asked. "Kevin knows the important parts. None of that matters now. Right, Kev? The past is best forgotten."

My father's fierce eyes warned me, his history teacher son, not to contradict him. I struggled to make up my mind whose story I would believe, my folks' or my brother's. I decided the choice could wait. Right then, I just had to decide whose version of the truth I'd *say* I believed. I gave my parents another chance to be more convincing than my brother.

"So what about the nightmares?" I asked. "They make perfect sense if what Danny said is true. He told me the doctors there tested vaccines on the kids, hepatitis vaccines. Malaria, measles. Kids died, six, eight at a time, from the mistakes. He said most of the kids had severe deformities or retardation and they were just abandoned there, like Bloodroot was a junkyard."

My father leaned across the table, a forced calm on his face. "Do any of those things describe Danny? Those things about Bloodroot are true. It all came out in the papers and on TV. It's public record. You can look it up."

"I did," I said.

My father choked down something angry. "That doesn't mean Danny's *from* there. What it means is that he could've found out about it, heard about it anywhere."

"Danny mentioned a doctor by name," I said.

"Calvin," my mother said. "The doctor in charge was named Calvin."

My head snapped around. I'd almost forgotten she was there. I studied her for signs that she recalled speaking that name herself. I saw nothing. I turned to my father. His face had gone pale. He remembered. "That's him," I said.

"Kevin, listen to me," my mother said, crossing her forearms on the table. She scratched lightly at the inside of her elbows, watching her fingers as if they moved of their own accord. "I worked with children a long time. What happened at Bloodroot was an atrocity." She looked up at me. "But these stories Danny tells? It's just his own confused explanation for his problems."

"Ma, he gave me a *tour*," I said. "Level by level. He showed me his *room*. He knew things that happened, details."

"Calvin was a monster," my mother said, blood rising to her cheeks. "He was a disgusting man. He devoured children in the name of progress, as he called it. My father, your grandfather, I'm proud to say, was instrumental in exposing Calvin's sickness to the world and putting an end to it. But Calvin never preyed on your brother. Danny has never been able to let go of what scares him, so he's never been able to let go of the stories."

"Then what about Grandpa?" I asked my mother. "Bloodroot was a horror show for years and no one knew. If you didn't tell him, how did he find out?"

"People knew," Mom said, "but until my father came along, they looked the other way."

"Your grandfather was a strong man," Dad said. "And he had powerful friends in the hospital and around the neighborhood."

Mom glanced at my father and then at me. "Kevin, listen to me. No one loves Danny as much as I do, but he has terrible problems. He has awful fears and so he needs terrible stories to make sense of them.

It's something children do. They're afraid of the dark so that means there's a monster under the bed. Nobody wants to be afraid of just the dark, of nothing."

"So you're telling me Calvin's a bogey-man that Danny's latched onto," I said, "and that's all it's about."

Danny's horrid painting of Saturn flashed across my mind. I put my face in my hands. My faith in Danny was wavering and it felt like a terrible betrayal. I didn't know what to think. He had been so convincing, so calm and sure. But he'd been that way before and been full of shit.

"When he told me," I said, "his story made so much sense."

My mother reached across the table and took my hand. "Of course it made sense," she said. "That's the whole point of self-deception, to make things that we can't understand, things that we wish weren't true, explainable."

"I don't know what to think," I said. "I feel kind of sick. Why does he always do this to me?"

"Don't be too hard on Danny," my father said, surprising me, since he'd always been tougher on my brother than any of us. "By now, he probably believes every lie he's told you."

"So what is it, then," I asked, "that he's so afraid of?"

"I wish we knew," my mother said. "It's not like he could tell us. He was barely five years old when he came to us."

"In the arms of the cop that found his mother's corpse," my father added. "Needle still in her arm."

"So you adopted him from the hospital?" I asked. Something didn't sound right to me. "Is that even legal?"

My parents traded glances.

"Your grandfather had a lot of influence," my father said, "at the hospital and beyond."

He sounded to me like Danny talking about Santoro.

"And things were different then," Mom said. "The cop that brought Danny in knew your grandfather from around the neighborhood. Knew all the work he had done for children." She smiled. "It was because of my father that I got into pediatrics in the first place." She leaned across the table, gripping my forearm. "Who'd take better care of that poor baby than your father and me? The state? The city? The same people that turned a blind eye to Bloodroot?"

My father covered the hand my mother had locked on my arm, massaging her fingers until she released me.

"A lot of Danny's troubles belong to your father and me," Mom said. "I was naïve. I thought we could make everything he'd seen as a baby go away. We knew he'd been damaged but we didn't think he'd come so close to being destroyed. I don't know what more we could've done, but we should've done something."

Dizzy, I stayed glued to my seat trying to piece together everything I'd heard. And I'd thought I was the one who'd come to the table with shocking news. All these explanations only made my family more confusing to me than ever. All those years it had seemed such a tragedy that my brother became a junkie. In reality, he had already outlived both his odds and his origin. He seemed a miracle to me.

"Eileen," my father said. "We saved that boy's life. Everything good he's got is because of us."

His voice was desolate, the voice of a man who knows what he's saying will never be believed but who's powerless to stop speaking. He watched her, a stricken look on his face. There was a need in him, a weakness that I'd never seen before. My mother said nothing to him, finally too exhausted, I thought, to offer even insincere consolation.

I couldn't leave my dad out there alone,

so I asked a stupid question. "So Danny's birth mother was a junkie?"

His gaze was so fixed on my mother that it took him a full minute to answer.

"Yeah, far as we know." He turned to me, looking surprised to see me sitting at his table. "Explains a lot, doesn't it?"

My mother picked up her drink and walked away from the table, over to the living room window. She stared into the backyard, the light going out of it with the setting sun. I wondered what she saw out there.

I went to her, leaving my father at the table. We needed a change of subject. I'd heard more than I'd ever put together into the truth. And I'd heard nothing that would change my plans with Danny, for the family or for other things. It was what he believed that drove him, so it was what he believed that mattered. There was no reason to keep stumbling through the brambles and weeds of the past.

"Mom?" I asked. "What're you looking at?"

"The garden," she said. "At my bloodroot patch. Though it's not much to look at this time of year."

I slipped my arm across her shoulders. She stiffened, but she didn't move away.

Even through her blouse, she was cold to the touch. I could smell traces of whiskey on her breath. Our breathing made one cloud on the window. She tapped the window with her fingernail, in a slow rhythm, as if counting.

Tick . . . tick . . . tick.

"I planted that garden as soon as we moved in," Mom said. "In honor of Danny's coming home. It's like him. It always comes back."

THIRTEEN

Not long before midnight, I walked barefoot across the cool hardwood of Kelsey's living room and stretched out on her overstuffed, dark espresso sofa. Her apartment, like her body, put mine to shame. After her mother died, Kelsey had told me, she'd sold the house she grew up in for a solid profit. Letting it go was tough but even then Kelsey knew she wasn't planning to stay on Staten Island.

A fair chunk of the money went into furnishing and adorning the apartment. The sofa, two matching easy chairs, a modest flat-screen TV, a long low coffee table that seemed hand carved from a piece of the Amazon or darkest Africa. Soft light emanated from tall brass lamps standing at attention in the corners. A huge bed wide as it was long anchored the bedroom, leaving room for little else. We'd yet to make use of the arcing wooden headboard, but I was looking forward to it.

The apartment, not much larger than but in every other way different from mine, was fitted out for comfort and quiet, an island on an island. This place alone seemed reason enough to stay in town. My apartment was a place to live; Kelsey's was a place to have a life. As long as our rendezvous continued, if I had my way, they would happen here.

She walked out of the kitchen carrying a jelly glass of ice water for each of us and wearing a red satin scrap of a robe that she hadn't bothered to tie. She handed me my glass, sitting on the coffee table in front of me, sweat, mine and hers, shining on her collarbone.

"This place is amazing," I said. "You wanna come over and do mine next?"

"I just did yours," she said. "Rather well, if I do say so myself."

"Oh," I said, raising my eyebrows at her. "That you did."

She sipped her water. "You let me loose with a few grand and leave me alone for a week and I'll see what I can do." She slid a ceramic coaster to her hip and set down her glass. "When do I get to see your place? I'm curious about the inner sanctum of Kevin Curran."

"Inner sanctum," I repeated, scoffing. Her choice of words made me think more of Danny's place than of mine. "Ever been inside a shooting gallery? My place is a little cleaner. I have electricity, though I steal my cable from the downstairs neighbors. Otherwise, it's about the same deal." I shrugged. "I have a nice porch. Well, let me clarify. I have a shitty, crooked-ass porch with a great view of the city."

"Why is that?" Kelsey asked.

"Well, my block points right at Manhattan."

"No, retard, why live somewhere so depressing?" She gestured around her living room. "This place was nothing special when I got here. My landlord's no prince and he was no help getting the place fixed up."

"I'm not much of a fixer-upper," I said.

"Neither was I," she said. "But I learned, basic shit anyway."

"That puts you ahead of me," I said. "You should've seen me the last time I picked up a hammer." I sat up, drank down half my water. "I don't know why but ever since I got there I've felt like I'd be moving out any day. The place didn't seem worth any kind of commitment. Like you said, I was going places."

She cocked her head at me, dipping her

chin. "How long have you lived in this place that you're always getting ready to leave?" She pulled closed her robe with both hands.

"Five years," I said. "Why?"

"No reason," Kelsey said, standing. She tied her robe, walked to the kitchen window and peeked through the blinds. "There's this big black car coming and going at odd hours, always parking across the street. It was out there when you got here. It's still out there four hours later." She turned to me. "Nobody on this block can afford a ride like that."

My throat dried up and I reached for my water. "I didn't notice it."

She turned, gave me a rueful smile over her shoulder. "Of course not. You're not a woman living alone."

I walked over to her, slipping my arms over her hips and wrapping them across her belly, letting my chin drop onto her shoulder so I could look over it. Out in the street, just outside a circle of streetlight, sat the Charger.

"Anybody approached you?" I asked. "You getting weird phone calls? Knocks on the door?"

She shook her head. "No, nothing like that. Nothing but that car."

"Have you told anyone else in the building about it?"

"I left a note for the girl upstairs. And I told the cop downstairs, this old guy named Waters. He helped a girl that used to live across the hall last year with her ex."

"What'd he do?"

"I don't know," Kelsey said. "But whatever it was, it worked." She turned in my arms, leaning back against the windowsill. "He can't do anything for me officially, but he said he'd keep an eye out. Told me to get the plate if I could."

"You had any luck with that?" I thought about heading out there myself, decided against it. What if Kelsey could tell from watching us that Al and I knew each other?

"I can't read it from up here," she said. "And I don't want to go out there." She shuddered. "I know it's probably nothing, but something about it gives me the creeps."

I held her closer to me so she couldn't see my face. "Yeah, me too."

I waited until Kelsey fell asleep before I took her cordless phone into the bathroom to call Danny. I hung up on his voice mail twice, calling back each time. I realized he might not answer because he didn't recognize the number. I didn't know what I'd do if Kelsey found me in the can with her phone; I just hoped I didn't get caught. The third time I left a message telling him who it was and that I'd keep calling until I got him. He answered the fourth call. "Yo."

"I need to talk to Al," I said.

"Don't know the guy," Danny said. "Who's this?"

I squeezed my temples in my hand. Danny and his phone paranoia. "Allison, the Italian girl who overloads on perfume all the time."

"Oh, her."

"She and I *really* need to talk," I said. "Just me and her."

"Why don't you leave a message with me? I'll deliver it."

"It's personal."

A long moment passed before Danny spoke again. "So it's like that."

"Yeah," I said. "It's like that."

"That's a tough request. I'll see what I can do. Can I call you back at this number?"

"No," I said. "No one can call me here, tonight or any other time. And I'm not accepting any visitors, either. I'll call you back in the morning."

I hung up and sat on the closed toilet for a few minutes, listening hard for any sound in the apartment or out on the street. I looked out the window. The car was still there.

Back in the bedroom, I saw Kelsey hadn't stirred. I sat at the foot of the bed watching her breathe. Don't, Kelsey, I thought, please don't be too smart for your own good. Just keep your head down and your mouth shut until you reach Chicago. I'm not smart enough to keep myself out of trouble, never mind the both of us.

The next morning, as Kelsey and I crossed campus on our way to the office, I spied Danny sitting on the bench where Kelsey and I had shared lunch a day earlier. He watched us walk by from behind mirrored shades. Kelsey and I passed close enough for me to see our tiny, distorted forms cross Danny's lenses. I fell a step behind her and nodded at Danny as I walked by him.

After my first class, I went back outside. Danny was waiting. No surprise. I stopped to light a cigarette a few feet away.

"The student union," I said. "Other side of campus. I don't want her seeing you." I walked away.

Danny showed up at the student union a few minutes after me. We got coffee and took a table outside.

"Let a guy in on the dark side," Danny

said, easing into his chair, "next thing you know he thinks he's Jason Bourne."

"Where's Al?" I asked.

"I love you, bro," Danny said. "But for a teacher you're a hell of a slow fucking learner." His face smiled at me beneath his shades, but there was a warning in his voice.

"The issue seemed more urgent at the time than it probably was," I said. "But Al was outside Kelsey's house for hours. She says he's there even when I'm not."

"I understand that's unnerving," Danny said. He folded his arms on the table and leaned across. "But you, me, other people at our level, we don't make demands, especially out of panic. It's not how things are done."

"How about your better half getting made? By the mark, no less," I said. "A mark who's got a den mother cop for a neighbor. Is that how things are done?"

"Again with the spy shit," Danny said. "Try to relax. I'll look into it."

"Kelsey has nothing to do with any of this," I said. "She's completely apart from it."

"No she's not. Because you brought her into it." Danny held up his hand, his forefinger and thumb less than half an inch apart. "Now, for her the distance is always this

slight. Look at where you were a week ago."
He moved his fingers even closer together.
"And the distance went like this when you
started spending the night with her. Really,
Kev. Kelsey's been around how long? You
pick *now* to go after her?" He spread his
hands. "She certainly looks like your type,
tomboy on the outside, protecting us weak-
minded men from that inner sex goddess.
Working that stealth hotness that you've
gotta have the soft, easy eye, an eye like
yours, to catch. As your brother I'm thrilled
you finally have someone, but your timing
sucks."

"You want me in on this project with Mr.
S.," I said, "then Kelsey gets left alone."

"She's Al's mark," Danny said. "Look, I'm
not interested, except as your brother. And
I respect your privacy."

I looked around the patio. "At least you
respect someone's."

Danny sat back in his chair. "Was that
really necessary?"

"It is what it is," I said. "I want to help
you, and if anyone else benefits from that,
so be it. But I'm not handing over control
of my life to Bavasi and Santoro. Or to you."

"Nobody's taken control of your life,
Kev," Danny said. "You control everything.
Just do what you promised, just paint your

small anonymous corner of the bigger picture and Santoro and his minions creep back into the shadows."

"Does that include you?" I asked.

"Not unless you want it to," Danny said.

"Of course not," I said. "Though you do test me sometimes."

"Some things never change," Danny said.

"Ever the fucking charmer, you are." I checked my watch, stood. "I gotta get ready for class."

Danny remained in his seat. "I'm gonna finish my coffee here in the sunshine. I don't see it much anymore."

"Listen, I told Mom you were back around," I said. "I told her you were doing well. You need to come see her. She misses you."

My brother smiled up at me. "This isn't an ambush? The old man is wily."

"No, it's not. I cleared it with Dad." I checked the time again. "Mom is sick, Dan. She's got Alzheimer's." I stretched my arm across the table, bending my wrist so he could see my watch. "The clock is ticking."

"Isn't it always?" Danny said. "Alzheimer's? Fuck me." He slipped off his shades and looked away from me, pinching the bridge of his nose. "There is no fucking justice in this world."

"Tell me about it; I'm a history teacher. You need to go see her. Soon."

"I will," Danny said.

"Don't wait too long," I said. "Their number is the same."

Danny said nothing. I watched the muscles of his jaw twitch. I hated dumping this on him without more time to talk, but there wasn't a lot to say. He knew what he had to do. All I could do was offer to help him with it.

"I'll go with you," I said. "Anytime you want."

He held up his fist and I bumped it with my own. "Thanks for telling me, Kev. I'm glad I know."

I stepped closer and leaned over him. "I meant what I said about Kelsey. Leave her alone or I'm out. That's the deal."

Getting back to business seemed to yank Danny back to earth.

"The thing with the cop might give me some traction," Danny said. "No promises."

"Call me later," I said. I squeezed his shoulder. "Don't pass by the history building when you leave. I'll carry on as if I've been heard."

"Affirmative, double-oh-seven," Danny said. There was no joy in the joke.

I couldn't think of anything funny to say,

so I just walked away.

Later that afternoon, I waited for Kelsey on our bench. Campus was quiet, all the undergrads and most of the teachers gone for the evening. A few disheveled night school and graduate students trudged across the grounds, books open in their hands and cell phones glued to their ears. To a one, they were already exhausted from the jobs they worked all day, the kids and homes they tended. I empathized with them. Not too long ago that had been me.

I was younger then, but I pushed myself to the same raw, scratchy-eyed, zombie-stagger state. Three master's classes a semester and an assistantship teaching freshman-level history survey courses. Not to mention the ninety-minute commute back and forth to NYU from my parents' house. I carried my whole life in the bulging pockets of a shoulder bag that was as much a part of me as the color of my eyes.

Searching that same bag for my smokes, I tried to remember the last time I didn't feel exhausted. It didn't make sense. I did less work and had a lot more experience at the work I did do. I had by most accounts an easy life. Yet these last few days running around with either Danny or Kelsey were the only time I'd felt anything like alive in the past couple of years. What did that say about me? Was I that desperate for excitement? That bad at living on my own? I had the feeling that other people, normal people like ones I was watching, didn't make the same choices I did. And only a matter of days ago I considered my life so normal I felt like hanging myself from the shower rod. Of course, those other people didn't have Daniel Curran for a brother.

"Yo," Kelsey yelled, striding out of the history building. "I've been looking all over for you. You said meet you in the office."

"I needed a cigarette," I said, lighting up.

She sat close to me, our legs touching. "You don't look so good." She brushed my hair back off my forehead. "You're kind of pale."

"What do you know about Whitestone?" I asked.

Kelsey leaned back on the bench, narrowed her eyes. She didn't answer my question. The playfulness had left her, wariness in its place, but her fingertips rested on my shoulder.

"I need to talk to him," I said.

"Why?"

"About some things I'm working on." I wet my lips with my tongue. "I might design a class on Bloodroot, see if he'll let me teach it."

"For real?" Kelsey asked. I could tell she didn't doubt my story. She was just shocked at my initiative. "It's bold. Give him what he wants, but on your terms. I like it."

The truth, like bile, rose to the back of my tongue. It was only fair to let her know what I was getting into. It was my fault Al watched her apartment. But I'd already promised Danny she wasn't involved and that she wouldn't be. Could I trust Danny to help me protect her? Did his loyalty extend that far? Even if I could trust Danny, what about Bavasi and by extension Santoro? Bavasi would smell the betrayal of his confidence on my skin, maybe even smell it on Danny if I forced him to keep secrets from his bosses. I knew what happened to the people who didn't keep Santoro's secrets. I didn't want Al or anybody else hauling Kelsey's corpse out to the dump. Mine, either.

But I liked her, more than I should considering both our circumstances, and I didn't want to lie to her any more than I absolutely had to. I took a deep breath. I could do this. I could keep my two lives close but separate. I just had to be careful.

"I don't want to go see him completely

ignorant," I said. "This Friends of Blood-root thing, how serious is he?"

Kelsey's hand slid up the back of my neck. I felt the warm pressure of her thigh against mine. "It's not the museum he cares about. He's just into sticking it to admin."

"What for? He lives like a king up in that office. He hardly ever comes out of it."

"He wanted the liberal arts chair and they gave it to someone else." She grinned. "A woman. A black woman with half the service time that he has." She stretched her arms over her head and laced her fingers, cracking her knuckles. "A black woman who's twice as smart and whose people skills are four times better."

"That's not saying much," I said. "He can't think he'll win, that he'll stop the dorms from happening."

"Who knows? He's already slowed things down," Kelsey said. "He's done a great job working the press. He's got people on the island behind him. It's hard to take up the cause of dead, disabled orphans and not make some friends. It's pretty bulletproof. Don't think he doesn't know that."

"Anybody we know in tight with him?"

"Not that I know of," she said. "Everybody from our department but us signed up for it, but that was just to get him off their backs. They don't actually do anything. He's got a few members from other departments. A couple instructors from the psych department, a full professor from over in biology, a couple from urban sciences. All the profs most disgruntled with the bosses."

"Anybody with any juice?"

Kelsey leaned toward me, one elbow on her knee, her chin on her fist. "Listen to you, Mr. Gangsta-speak." She batted her eyes. "I must say I'm intrigued. First me, now Whitestone and his crew. All of a sudden you're interested in this department?"

"For very different reasons," I said. I smiled. "Selfish reasons."

She waited for me to say something more, her eyes aglow with cheer and curiosity. This was a thing that couples did, share plans, ideas, and thoughts. And there she was, all in for it. We're a couple, that's what her face was telling me. Her face showed the truth, and I knew mine didn't. Something slow and heavy turned over in my gut, like a sleeper turning beneath cool sheets in the dark.

I remembered what my brother had said about the distance while holding that tiny sliver of sunshine between his fingers. I'd just used her for information, that after putting her in the sight lines of dangerous people I knew very little about. In my mind I could see the light between Danny's fingers going out. I'd made a terrible mistake in getting involved with Kelsey, but I knew I'd keep on making it. For so long, I hadn't had the nerve to start with her; now I lacked the strength or desire to stop. But that didn't matter right then. All I had to do was not let the remaining light go out.

The lies were for her protection, I told myself. And temporary. When my work with Danny was done, my lies to Kelsey would be erased. In a short time, it'd be like they never happened. So I went ahead and told them.

"Bloodroot is American history," I said. "The exposé that eventually got it closed had nearly every state in the country re-evaluating their schools and asylums. We're about to make the site a part of campus. Sounds pertinent to an American history class, which happens to be what I teach. I've got half a syllabus worked up already."

Kelsey sat silent for a moment. Suddenly, I was terrified that she hadn't bought any of it. I was on the verge of blurting out the truth when she took my hand.

"I have to tell you, Kev," she said. "That's a pretty aggressive idea. Your own course? Built from the ground up? I'll bet you haven't done something like that in years. I'm impressed. Must feel good."

Her words would have warmed me to the core, maybe for days, if I didn't already feel like an utter shitheel for lying to her. The ease with which I did it sounded a deeper, darker alarm within me.

"Okay. I can't take credit for this resurrection," Kelsey said. "Though I'd like to. Every girl wants to believe she's got the magic garden in her jeans. But I can be happy about it. And I can help." She stood and turned toward the building behind us. "Let's go see if Whitestone's up there right now."

"No." I reached out and snagged her arm — hard enough to almost jerk her back down to the bench. She pulled her arm free and glared at me.

"I should do this on my own," I said. "It's been a while since I showed any initiative around here." Her glare softened. "Thanks, though. Sorry about the arm."

"No problem," she said, setting her hands on her hips, squinting at me. "You sure you're all right? No offense, but you look even worse than when I got out here."

"I'm fine," I said. "Long day."

Kelsey leaned over, inspecting me, her hair falling over one eye. My heart flipped over.

I dropped my eyes and coughed into my hand, trying to hide my face. I wanted her to stuff me in her bag and take me home, take me anywhere, and make me forget everything.

"I am a little out of sorts. I think maybe I'm dehydrated." I patted my pockets, looking for my wallet. Anything not to look at her. I started to stand. "I could use a water or an iced tea or something."

Kelsey grabbed my shoulders and eased me back down. "Sit. Relax." She dug her change purse from her bag. "Don't worry. I got it."

She trotted away toward the history building, leaving me alone on the bench with only the sandpaper scratch of my conscience and the fading evening light for company. I hoped she never came back, that something clicked in her brain and she took off for the airport. I hoped I could pull off this assignment for Santoro without anyone getting hurt. I stared down at the toes of my old, scuffed-up shoes. I had to stop this hoping for what I wanted. I was so out of practice I kept picking the wrong things.

FOURTEEN

His black eyes on fire, Al sat alone in the back booth at the Red Lion when I arrived, a watery, half-finished cocktail in front of him and three empty glasses beside it. His simmering fury told me my conditions had made it at least as far as his ears. Had I gotten him in trouble with Santoro? I tried not to care. I swallowed hard and glanced around the room for Danny. I didn't see him.

I stopped at the bar, ordered a Jack and Coke. I slurped at it while waiting for my change, thinking about the scene in *Star Wars* where Han Solo blows up that alien bounty hunter from under the table. Sweat trickled down both sides of my rib cage. What if I'd made things worse for everyone? Or maybe just for me? I could feel Al's eyes boring into my back. That a sci-fi movie was my only reference for this situation made me horribly aware of how much of a fucking amateur I was at these dangerous, grown-up games. All my life I'd excelled at keeping my mouth shut. Why'd I pick *now* to be brave?

I slid the ones from my change around on the bar. If I stuck a couple in the jukebox, I could kill another few minutes and hope Danny appeared. I looked over at the door. Maybe I should walk back out. What if Al followed me? Caught me alone on the street? In his voice message, Danny had told me to arrive at nine. He hadn't said specifically that he was coming. What if he wasn't? Could Danny have set me up? No way. Never. I didn't really think that; I was just scared. Al was an overpaid, overgrown schoolyard bully. I wasn't gonna let him get to me like he had outside my building.

I picked up my cocktail and walked over to the booth. I opened my mouth to say something as I sat but Al cut me off.

"He'll be here in a little while," Al said.

He shifted in his seat. My stomach cramped up. I told myself to relax. I'd asked for this conference. Danny knew about this meet, had set it up. I'd be okay. Al might not think twice about splitting my skull, I knew that now, but he wouldn't cross Danny like that.

"You got my message?" I asked.

"Are you on crack?" Al spat. "I thought Danny was the crazy brother, but you? You got me rethinking my opinions. What the fuck are you doin' making demands on me? On Mr. S.?"

I reached for my glass. Al's arm shot out across the table, pinning my wrist. He slammed the elbow of his other arm on the table. I searched the room to see if anyone had heard. If they had, they were ignoring it.

"Eyes front, motherfucker," Al said. He pinched the forefinger and thumb of his hand close together; the same gesture Danny had used just that afternoon. I wondered, bizarrely, if Bavasi had taught them that move, like a secret handshake.

"You, shitbird, are a tiny, tiny piece of all this. That means you carry exactly no weight, which means you got exactly nothing to say. Zero. Playin' hero for that frisky cunt you're bangin' is only gonna get people hurt. People that ain't me." Al released my wrist and sat back hard in the booth. His hands settled into his lap. "Follow me, Professor?"

My hand tingled and burned as the blood returned. I curled my fingers as best I could around my glass. I leaned over the table, never taking my eyes from Al's, from his self-satisfied grin. I put all my energy into keeping both my voice and my Jack and Coke from shaking.

"You call Kelsey that name again," I said, "and right before I burn you to death in that fucking short-dick car of yours, I'll feed you your own balls."

Al blinked at me a couple times. Never let it be said I didn't learn something from my old man. Then Al moved. I froze. All the breath fell out of my chest. Al was halfway out of his seat when a hand seized his shoulder, pushing him back down. Danny.

"I only caught the end of that," Danny said, "but something tells me there's trouble in the sandbox."

He smiled as he spoke, but the air around him rippled with menace like heat waves rising off sunbaked asphalt. It frightened me and it was no trick of the light.

"I was just explaining the facts to your brother here," Al said.

"That true?" Danny asked.

He hadn't sat, or even taken his hand from Al's shoulder. I noticed Al had started sweating, spiking the strength of his already powerful cologne.

"More or less," I said.

Danny clapped his hands. Al and I both nearly jumped out of our skin.

"Okay then," Danny said, dropping into the booth next to me. "Who's gonna buy me a drink?"

Al about exploded from his seat. "I got that. Just let me hit the pisser first."

I watched Al make his way to the men's room, wondering if he had really just asked my brother's permission to take a leak. I realized that no matter how hard Al tried to sell it as an equal partnership, the balance of power in their situation had tilted in Danny's favor.

"As long as he doesn't put on any more cologne," Danny said, waving his hand in front of his face. "How'd he take it, about the cop?"

"I thought you told him," I said. "And I thought maybe you'd told our uncle, too. I figured that's why Al was so pissed."

Danny laughed. "Our uncle, you're getting good at this. It's okay, though, save that shit for the phone. I told Al that you wanted to speak privately with him and that Bavasi approved it."

"So Santoro knows about this meeting?" I asked. "You got through that high?"

"Are you kidding? You think Santoro gets involved with this piddly shit? I told Bavasi that the three of us were meeting tonight to map out an attack strategy and that's all."

Danny elbowed me, nodding at Al, who was on his way back from the bar. "I bent the truth a bit in Al's case. He'll be more receptive if he thinks Bavasi's mad at him. But it's best if we work this out among ourselves. The bosses hate drama."

Al set drinks in front of Danny and me and sat down across from us. The volume on his Drakkar had come down a notch, but he was breathing a cloud of bad tequila all over the booth. He'd helped himself to some liquid courage at the bar.

"Two Jack and Cokes," he said. "That cool?"

Danny nodded. Al seemed to relax. I felt relief but also a twinge of disappointment. I wanted Danny to make Al crawl some more.

"Kev," Danny said, "tell Al about the cop."

"What cop?" Al asked, a squeak in his voice I hadn't heard before.

"There's a cop that lives in Kelsey's building," I said. "A detective named Waters. You scared her. She put him on to your car. He's looking for you, asking for the plates."

Danny burst into hysterics and Al actually blushed, deflating in his seat. I could almost hear the air whistling out of him. I looked at one then the other, totally lost. My brother was the first to recover.

"Oooooh, shit," he said, giggling. "Too

much. Al, you have no fucking luck." He drummed his hands on the table. "Let's flip the script. Al, why don't you tell Kevin about the cop?"

"Fuck you, man," Al said, staring straight down. With his thumb, he tore pieces from the wet cocktail napkin under his drink.

"What else did Kelsey tell you about Waters?" Danny asked, clearly reveling in Al's misery.

"That he was older, lived alone," I said. "He keeps an eye out for the single women in the building. He helped out another girl with an ex-boyfriend last year."

Danny's eyebrows danced on his forehead. "Oh, really?"

"This girl sicced Waters on her ex and the guy never came around again. Nobody knows how it went down."

"Not nobody," Danny said, jerking his thumb at Al. I finally caught on.

"No way," I said. "Al? You're the ex?"

"Yes, indeed," Danny said, clapping his hands. "I love this shitty island, there's no getting away with anything." He leaned across the table, calling Al's name in a low, singsong voice. "Tell him, Al. Or I will."

Al shot up in his seat then tilted a bit, looking for the first time like he might be really drunk.

"All right, fuck both you bitches. So Cheri fills this fat cop's head full of lies about me, she's probably bobbin' his knob like she was everyone else in the fuckin' neighborhood, cokehead whore that she is, which, might I add, is why she was the problem to begin with, not me, and gives him my name, tag number, all kinds a shit. He's got nothin' else to do, the no-life-havin' motherfucker, so late one night he pulls me over on the South Shore Expressway. He makes me spread 'em on the trunk and then suckers me with his flashlight when I ain't lookin'. So I'm already all dizzy and when I turn around to even the score he shines that fuckin' light right in my eyes, blindin' me, and so I trip and twist up my ankle real bad and hit the pavement. Then, the pussy-whipped dicklicker that he is, Waters works out on me while I'm down, talking like a tough guy the whole time, when he's really just a no-account sneaker."

"Wow," I said. "That's some story."

"The beauty is in the telling," Danny said. "Some of it's even true."

"In case I forgot to say so," Al said, "fuck you bitches."

"Anyway," Danny said, "the point is, Al, that this cop knows you."

"Fuck him. I don't even drive the same

car anymore."

"Is that what I should tell Bavasi," Danny said, "when I gotta tell him you've been arrested?" He snapped his fingers in Al's face. "Look at me, fool. When Kevin goes to see his girl, you leave them be. In fact, leave Kevin be at all times."

"It ain't up to us," Al said. "Fuck, Kevin here is about the most boring-ass motherfucker I ever met. You think I like following around after Mr. Excitement here? But Bavasi wants Kevin babysat until this is over." Al shrugged. "It ain't our call, D."

"Long as Al leaves Kelsey alone, I'm cool," I said.

"Well, thank fucking Christ," Al said. "That's a load off my fucking mind."

"I want them left alone," Danny said. "Permanent. Let me worry about Bavasi. I got you covered."

Al threw up his hands. "Fine, fine. Just don't fuck me, Danny. I don't want Bavasi asking me for information that I oughta have and don't got. You can't lie to that guy, you know that."

"Trust me," Danny said.

Al scoffed and slid out of his seat. "Trust you? You're a fucking junkie. I'm fuckin' outta here." He staggered away from the table. "Seems you two got everything fig-

314

ured out."

"Hey! Come back here!" I shouted. I tried to push past Danny. He wouldn't budge.

"Forget it," Danny said. "It's not like it ain't true."

"What's gotten into him?"

Danny sighed. "He's already in the doghouse over that shit with the bodies. Now he thinks he's blown another assignment. I know what he's thinking, that the minute you showed up his life hit the shitter."

"Me? All I'm doing is what you asked. Getting me involved was your idea, remember?"

"Hey, forget it," Danny said. "Al's been on borrowed time for a while."

My brother seemed pretty nonchalant about Al's situation. It didn't seem to me that people got demoted in Santoro's organization; they burned up at the dump. Danny plucked his cocktail straw from his drink and stuck it in his mouth.

"What happens when Bavasi asks Al about me," I said, "and Al's got nothing to tell him?"

"Relax. It's not like Al's gotta file a daily report," Danny said. "He says nothing, Bavasi assumes nothing's happening, at least for a while." He sighed, rubbing his hands on his thighs. "Still, it's probably best if we get things moving along. I did tell Bavasi that we're making progress. Am I gonna go back to him with my dick in my hands?"

I swallowed a huge mouthful of Jack and Coke. "Word around the office is that Friends of Bloodroot is nothing serious. Whitestone's fucking with his bosses. There's a position he wanted that he didn't get. He's getting his jollies being a thorn."

"Good news, I guess," Danny said. He stared into his drink. He'd hardly touched it. "If this guy Whitestone was a real crusader, he could be a problem. How do we get him to back off?"

"I don't know," I said. "But, listen, I'm gonna tell Whitestone I'm designing a class on Bloodroot, get on his good side for a change. I'll learn more that way. I know the faculty in the group. I'll get in touch with each of them and see what they know. In a couple of weeks I'll have details. We can go from there."

Danny shook his head. "Santoro's losing his patience." He tossed his straw on the floor. "This bullshit's already held him up almost a year. The longer Whitestone's stupid vanity project hangs around, the more churches and charities and little old ladies start kicking in. We need an angle on the man. Somewhere to squeeze him. You need to work that meeting with him. If you can't get something professional, get something personal."

"Jesus, Danny," I said, raising my hands. "What do you want from me? I don't like where this is going."

"Where'd you think it was gonna go?"

I crossed my arms, sank deeper into the booth. I thought about Ida Horace. "I think the money keeps him going. He got a donation the other day worth at least ten grand. Why not just buy him off?"

"Bribes mean establishing contact," Danny said. "Starting a relationship. We don't know Whitestone from Adam, if he's greedy, if he scares easy. Can Whitestone be trusted to take his slice like a good soldier and keep his mouth shut? Is he smart enough to fool the IRS? You find these things out for us, maybe we can make that move."

While Danny talked, I watched the bartender flip channels on the TV. I didn't need a meeting to know bribing Whitestone would never work. I'd just wanted an easy answer. You couldn't take bribes in front of a camera, at least not the kind of camera that Whitestone liked. And once the payoffs started, he'd never let go. He'd be worse than that guy with the bad hairpiece in *Goodfellas,* always nagging after his money. Which meant Whitestone would come to the same bad end, as well. And it wouldn't be Joe Pesci doing the job; it might be Danny.

All our lives would be a lot easier, though, if Whitestone turned up dead. It was a horrible thought, but I couldn't let it go. "How come no one's just shot him?"

"This ain't the fucking movies, Kev," Danny said. "Bodies are like bribes, they create a connection and lots of opportunities for mistakes. Our buddy Al Bruno's a case in point. Execution is only for the most extreme circumstances. They're never good business." He reached across the table, grabbed my forearm. "And another thing. If I thought this gig involved killing, I'd never have brought you near it. What's gotten into you?"

I set my elbows on the table, put my face in my hands. I couldn't believe I'd asked that question about killing Whitestone. Sure I didn't like him, but Whitestone was a regular guy, with a job and a family and a life. Maybe a dog. I couldn't believe I'd even for a moment wished him dead out loud and maybe just for a second meant it.

Danny flicked his finger against the back

of my hands. I swatted him away. "Get off."

"Don't get twisted over this," Danny said. "Have your meeting. Talk to these other people. Just do it soon and come back to me with —" He stopped, concern bunching the skin of his forehead. "I gotta ask you, who's your source for this 'word around the office'?"

I waited too long to lie. "Nobody. It's just an expression. You know, like 'word on the street.' " I felt my pulse pounding under my ears, a headache coming on. I wanted to be home in my apartment, alone with all the lights out. "I talked to Kelsey."

"Bad, bad, bad," Danny said, dropping his hands hard on the table. That swirl of menace bent the air again. "Tell me what she knows. Everything. This is very, very important."

"She doesn't know anything," I said. "I told her the same story I told you, about the class."

"She bought it?"

"I think so," I said.

Danny put his hand on my shoulder. "You can't *think*. You have to *know*."

"She wants to help me plan the class." I stared into Danny's eyes until my own quivered in my skull. "That's all this is to her. A new class I'm going to teach."

Danny squeezed my shoulder. "Let's bail," he said, standing. "I need a cigarette."

Outside, the October wind kicked up baby twisters of pavement grit, candy wrappers, and dead leaves. Ducking our heads, pulling our jackets tighter across our chests, we lit up. Small clusters of smokers, all guys, gathered in front of the other bars, scratching at the concrete with their shoes like pigeons in a park as they checked us out. Everyone held their shoulders bunched high against the wind, some standing with their beers concealed up their sleeves. They were all strangers with no interest in my brother and me, but I felt watched anyway, like they'd been waiting for us and weren't speaking because they wanted to hear what Danny and I would say. They looked to me like a silent jury.

An old, grungy city bus, insides bright as an operating room, dropped two stooped, waddling passengers at the Shell station across the street. I'd be riding a bus just like it into work the next morning. The thought depressed me. I waited till the bus trundled away before I spoke.

"Look, Danny. I just wanna —"

"Not here," Danny said, tossing a glance at the other smokers.

We made a right off Forest, climbing a hilly street lined with tall old oaks, their roots bursting through the sidewalk, their twisted, leafless branches ashen in the streetlights. Above us, thick black power lines stretched from the light posts to peak-roofed brick houses like the cords of a busted net. Aged sedans slumbered in driveways, abandoned to the elements outside garages stuffed with bad paintings, beaten-down lawn mowers, one-wheeled bikes, and busted bowling trophies. Rusty, padlocked chain-link fences framed every scraggly yard, a BEWARE OF DOG sign hung beside every lock. I didn't hear any barking as we passed house after house. I didn't hear anything but the wind in the trees and the occasional burble of a television. Danny stopped us at a dark corner where the streetlight had burned out.

"You got nothing to worry about," I said.

"Cut Kelsey out of it," Danny said. "This bullshit about the class. Cut her out completely. Tell her you gave up on the idea."

"She'll have no trouble believing me," I said, looking back down the hill, running my fingers through my hair. Man, how was I going to tell her that? Her believing in me, even under false pretenses, had felt so good. I didn't want to go back to the same old

Kevin. "I'm not dumping her. I won't."

"Damn right you're not," Danny said. "In fact, you better keep her happy. Last thing we need is some pissed-off woman riding your shit. I could tell by looking at her, that woman gets scary mean. When're you gonna tell her about the fake class going to hell?"

"Shit, I don't know."

"Tomorrow," Danny said. "Tonight."

"Is she really in that much danger?" I asked.

"Again with her," Danny said, rolling his eyes. "I'm talking about us. You and me, Kev. The family."

"Yeah, I know. It's just . . ." I spread my arms, dropped them to my sides. "She's where my brain goes first these days."

"Not just your brain," Danny said.

"Gimme a break here. You know what I mean."

"Sorry, sorry," Danny said, shaking his palms at me. "Let's talk serious a minute. How much do you like this girl?"

I didn't want to lie to myself or to Danny. Now did not seem like the time. "A lot. More than I thought I would. More than I should, considering the circumstances."

"How well do you *know* her?" Danny asked.

I knew where he was heading. "Not as well

as I should, considering the circumstances."

"Exactly," Danny said. "So here's what you're facing." He held out one hand. "Either you keep spinning lies about what you're doing, each time increasing both the guilt and the chances she catches you, and I know you, you'll fold under questioning." He opened his other hand. "Or you come clean and tell her the truth, which puts her, me, and you in danger."

Dry leaves crunched under Danny's feet as he moved closer to me, setting his hands on my shoulders. My lungs felt a lot like those leaves, parched and frail. Danny's eyes glittered in the fractured light coming through the trees.

"This isn't a game we're playing, Kev. We're not working on our extortion merit badges here. The construction contracts for those dorms are worth fifty million. Santoro's got those contracts and more. Clearing the land, a ten-year maintenance contract for the dorms. All he needs to chow down is that fat little fly Whitestone plucked from the grease so the state'll release the money. We get to be the fingers, hardly even get dirty. For that we get five percent. Two-fifty large to start, split three ways." He shrugged. "Two if Al doesn't make the finish line. That's life-changing money, Kev."

He raised a forefinger. "But here's the punch line. If we fuck it up, Santoro will eat us alive. Us and everyone around us that might've played a part. But . . . but if we do right, we'll be set. And free to spread the wealth."

"I thought this was about destroying Bloodroot," I said. "About you burying the past. Now you tell me it's about money."

"Let me ask you this," Danny said. "If it was just about the money, and it's not, but if it was, would you be in or out?"

"In," I said. I wanted to believe different, but that wasn't the truth. I fumbled through my pockets, searching for my smokes. "God, what does that make me?"

"Not some kind of monster, if that's what you're thinking," Danny said. "It makes you smart. A red-blooded American."

He leaned aside, peering over my shoulder. I turned in time to see curtains fall across a window. "That's the third time," Danny said. "Let's get moving before one of these sinister old biddies calls the cops on us."

I turned back toward Forest Avenue but Danny walked the other way. He pulled keys from his pocket and the parking lights on a black, two-door Saturn flashed at us.

"I'll give you a ride home," Danny said.

"When did you get this?"

"Today," Danny said. He pulled open the driver-side door. "I promise you, no way Kelsey makes *this* car." He shook his head. "Fuckin' Al. He refuses to learn the finer points of our business. Like that it's *bad* when the whole world knows you're a criminal. One day it's gonna cost him."

I climbed in the passenger seat. "It's got that new-car smell. I love that smell. Not that I've ever had a new car."

"That could change real soon." Danny lit a cigarette. "That smell everyone loves? Fucking formaldehyde."

Danny eased the Saturn to the curb outside my apartment. He reached across the car for my arm when I opened the door. I closed it and turned to him, waiting.

"I have an idea," Danny said, tapping his temple. "Something that might speed things up."

"I'm all ears," I said. I lit a cigarette and hung my elbow out the window.

"Can you get *me* into Whitestone's office?"

"I don't like this idea already," I said. "I thought you said no contact with anyone but me."

"Relax," Danny said. "We can bend the

325

rules a wee bit this one time. You can just say yes or no and I'll take it from there."

Cigarette dangling from my lips, I rubbed my hands up and down my thighs. "Tell me what you're thinking."

Danny turned in his seat, framing an imaginary box with his hands. "Okay, listen to this. You get me in. I slip some equipment into his office, his computer, simple shit I've already got at the apartment, and then we kick back and wait. Why hunt him down when we can set a trap? I'll know in a week or two if he's stealing the money and we can confront him with that. He'll fold. Bang, we're paid and done." He brought his hands together, as if in prayer. "Just me and you on this. No Al. No Kelsey. Everyone stays safe and clean."

"Everyone except you and me," I said. "Shit, Danny, you're talking about breaking and entering, just to start with. On city property, no less. I know this is Staten Island but after nine-eleven everything's locked down tight."

"Not everything," Danny said. "That's simply impossible. Besides we're not breaking, we're just entering. You *work* there. You have a *key.* You have perfectly legal twenty-four-hour access to the building."

I was about to answer when a blinding

light hit my eyes. I shaded my face with my hands and watched the patrol car glide up beside us, coming to rest with its driver and Danny inches apart. Danny already had his hands at ten and two on the wheel.

"Passenger," the driver cop said, "put your hands on the dash."

I did as I was told, my cigarette warm on my knuckles as it burned down to the filter.

My eyes sideways, I watched the other cop lean forward. "Everything okay here, gentlemen?"

"It's all good, Officers," Danny said. "I'm dropping my brother off at his apartment."

"That true?" driver cop asked me.

"Absolutely," I said, tilting my head toward my building. "Mine's the one with the balcony."

"Face me, passenger," the cop said. He pursed his lips, nodding. "Right, I know you. I've seen you up there. You're the guy who sits outside all night and never sees anything. What's your name again?"

"Kevin. Kevin Curran."

"It ain't the safest move, Misters Curran," passenger cop said, "to be sitting out here in a new car. Maybe you wanna finish your conversation indoors?"

"You're right," Danny said. "Will do."

The patrol car eased away, both officers

staring straight ahead.

"Good lookin' out," Danny shouted, waving at the cops. "Stupid pigs." He turned to me, chuckling. "Jesus, Kev, how bad has this neighborhood gotten? What was that about, anyway, that cop saying he knows you?"

"Do you *always* have to antagonize them?" I asked, dropping my cigarette butt out the window. It had burned my knuckles. I stuck them in my mouth. "Those cops work the neighborhood. I live in it. We see each other around."

"What else?" Danny asked. "You're afraid to drop a done cigarette out the window in front of them. You're white as a ghost, like you're a fucking criminal or something."

I just stared at him.

"All right," he finally said. "Poor choice of words."

"That drug shit up on the corner," I said. "The cops like to ask me questions. They think because I'm white and I sit outside that I like to take notes on the neighborhood or something."

"That's fucking prejudiced, is what that is." Danny studied me across the car. "And what do you tell them?"

"What do you think? I got nothing against the police and I don't like those gang-bangers out there, either, but I have to live on this block." I jerked my thumb over my shoulder. "Who do you think comes sniffing around right after the cops do?"

Danny turned in his seat, straining to see the corner over his shoulder. He reached for his door handle like he might get out, then decided against it. He turned back to me frowning, his mind working overtime. "So what's the verdict on Whitestone's office?"

"When do you want to go?" I asked.

"Well, I need to get in twice," he said.

"Fuckin' A."

"The first time, he can be there," Danny said. "I just need to get the lay of the land, any security cameras, alarms, shit like that. I'll need a look at his computer. The second time'll need to be at night when no one else is around."

"And how're we supposed to get into his office in the middle of the night?"

"Leave that to me," Danny said. "You think I can't pick a lock?"

I turned to him. I had an idea of my own. "Okay, I'll do this with you. But I have a condition."

Danny swore in mock exasperation. "Again with the demands. What? I gotta buy Kelsey a new TV now? Fine. Done."

"I can get you in tomorrow," I said. "But

after I'm done with work, you gotta go see the folks with me. That's the deal."

Danny puffed out his cheeks, turning away to stare through the windshield. "Tomorrow. I don't know. I'll need to have some gear ready for the first visit. Might take a couple days."

"Bullshit. You just said it was simple shit you had on hand."

Danny glanced at me then looked away again.

"Quid pro quo, Agent Starling," I said.

"You watch too many fucking movies," Danny said.

"No doubt," I said. "This is what it's like to have no life."

The slick, defiant Danny who moments ago had shone on the cops evaporated into the night air. He pretended to debate my demand in his head but the tight skin drawn across the side of his face, the jackrabbit beat of his pulse in his throat, they told me he was scared; he was deeply terrified, in fact.

"Me and you, we'll go together?" Danny said.

"Of course."

"Dad's cool with this?" he asked.

"He will be," I said, "for Mom's sake."

"Get out of the fucking car," Danny said.

I did, walking around to Danny's side of the car. I crouched down to his level, my arms folded atop the door.

"Sorry to be rude but I gotta get home and get started on tomorrow," Danny said.

"For Whitestone or for Mom and Dad?" I asked.

"Both." He nodded to himself. "I'll do what's right."

I stood and patted the roof of the car. "I know you will. Meet me at the campus Starbucks at one."

"Will do," Danny said, looking up at me, his blue eyes soft and young. He smiled. "When do I get to meet Kelsey? You know, as your brother?"

"When I say so," I said. "When all this shit is done."

Danny started the car and I backed away to my stoop. He made half a U-turn then stopped in the middle of the street and called me back to the car. I walked over and leaned in his window.

His eyes were locked on the corner. A black semiautomatic pistol sat in his lap. He picked it up and handed it to me. I figured he wanted to get the gun out of the car so I took it, dropping it into the inside pocket of my jacket. It fell heavy and awkward against my ribs, like the hammer had a few nights ago. I thought of our recent encounter with the police. "Where the fuck was that hiding?"

"Don't worry about it," Danny said. "Take it. In case the wrong people come knocking."

"I don't want it," I said, reaching into my jacket. With both hands, I shoved the gun into his chest.

I took a step back from the car, raising my hands in the air. Thoughts of nosy neighbors watching us pass a weapon back and forth made me nervous. Someone could come walking up the block for the bus stop at any time. What if those cops passed by again just to be dicks? What if the dealers saw us?

"Would you put your fucking hands down?" Danny said. "It looks like I'm fucking mugging you. Calm down." He waved me back to the car with the gun. "C'mere, for chrissakes."

I stepped back to the car and leaned my weight on the door.

"I promise you," Danny said, "no one has ever been shot with this gun. It's brand-new. Never even been used in a crime. Unlike every human being walking the earth, it's totally clean."

"It's not that," I said. "I've never used a gun before."

"Not a problem." Raising the gun, Danny turned it so I could see it better in the streetlights. "Nine-millimeter. Real powerful. One shot should get the job done for you, God forbid. It's fully loaded with one in the chamber. Point it anywhere near the target and you're good. Hammer goes back like so. This is the safety." He thumbed the switch back and forth several times. "On, off, on, off. Got it?"

He handed the nine back to me but this time I wouldn't take it.

"These dealers or whatever," I said, "they don't care about me. I do a hell of a job acting intimidated. They're like the trash or the potholes around here, an occasional pain in the ass but no real danger. It's no big thing. I don't need a gun."

"Take it," Danny said. "For me. I'll feel better."

He rested the gun on my shoulder, looking into my eyes. I wished I'd seen where he'd left the safety set. I took the pistol back and put it in my jacket. It was the only way to end the conversation.

"Just keep it in the house for a couple of days," Danny said. "If it still makes you nervous, I'll take it back." He smiled. "You don't like the gun, we'll go get you a fucking dog." He exhaled hard, fogging his windshield. He rubbed the cloud away with his sleeve, peering again at the corner. "You and me? We're gonna get you the fuck outta here. This neighborhood is infested with fucking criminals."

Danny shifted the car into drive and rolled away up the street, giving the corner boys a long stare as he turned the corner.

I went upstairs, the gun bouncing against my ribs with every step. I'd left my apartment dark again. I started to wonder if I flat-out didn't like it better that way.

Later that night, I sat out on the balcony watching the corner boys, my hands folded over the gun in my lap. I felt foolish carrying it around the apartment but didn't know what else to do with it, afraid it might somehow go off unless I kept close watch. And I kind of liked holding it.

Down on the corner, every few minutes a car slunk up to the curb, idling until a figure stepped out of the shadows. The figure leaned in long enough for the exchange, then rose up flashing whatever hand signs completed the deal. Once in a while a real hard-core fiend came staggering down the street, clutching a bum arm or a dead leg and flashing a gap-toothed grin like he was walking into his office Monday morning and heading for the coffeepot. The dealers took care not to get too close. The smell, I figured.

The junkies were all the same, men and women alike. The drunk back end of some zombie parade. They all had the same stagger, the same smile, the same hands. Crooked fingers of one hand holding out crumpled bills they couldn't surrender fast enough, twitchy fingers of the other hand curling around the invisible vials they longed to hold. It was like they'd rolled off some junkie assembly line: Cocaine Barbie and Heroin Ken, complete with Super Jonesing Junkie Grip. Everything from the Dream House hocked in an alley years ago.

The scene was nothing unprecedented; it happened every night. The only new part of the situation was my interest in it. What limb had gone numb for Danny? Did he smile that desperate, lying smile? How many people had backed away from his stink?

I couldn't let him go back. Ever.

The people I taught about at work: Washington, Jefferson, Hancock, and Hamilton, all the names everyone knows and all the ones lost to history, technically they were all criminals. Every one of them, from the signers of the Declaration to the grunts with rags for shoes, was hangable for treason.

They knew the noose was waiting should they back down. So they did what they had to do, simple as that. And because they won, instead of getting the gallows, they went free, went on to new lives in a new nation.

Danny and I weren't looking to start a revolution, but if I had to become a temporary criminal so my brother could be a permanent ex-junkie, could live free from heroin and not die, I would find a way to survive the aftermath.

I turned away from the corner and stared into the Manhattan skyline, my damp fingers sliding over the cooling metal of the gun. What did I care about people getting high? So what if they bought the drugs on my corner. If it wasn't mine; it'd be another. Danny had found plenty. Had I the right to wish this dirty business on other blocks, other neighborhoods? There were plenty worse of both. My corner was pretty tame by comparison.

Who knew the answer? The whole deal had a chicken-or-the-egg quality to it that smarter, braver, and better-paid men than me and the cops in the patrol car had tried to puzzle through. The dealers would sell anywhere, everywhere, and anything they could as long as the customers kept buying. And the customers lived loyal to the product until death and beyond. If one guy in the whole country was left selling, they'd sniff him out and line up from New York to the Mississippi.

I was on my way to bed when Maxie started barking. That hysterical bark that had one lone inspiration. The chains of his gate rattled and I heard the snickers of teenagers. I looked down at the gun in my hand. There were some things, however, that perhaps no longer needed to be tolerated.

Standing just inside the balcony doors, I raised the gun and squinted down the barrel, sighting on the back of the nearest boy's thigh. The other one kicked the gate again. Maxie went berserk. I lowered the gun. It was damn dark in that driveway and I had never fired a gun in my life. Danny's instructions had been for close range.

I closed the door to my apartment building quietly behind me. My bare feet made no sound on the stoop or the steps. Like I'd seen in the movies, I carried the gun stiff-armed at my side, behind my right thigh. My heart raced and I felt as though I was sitting on my balcony, looking down on someone else who looked like me. What the hell was I doing? Darting across the street, gun in hand, in the middle of the night. Over a blind old dog that wasn't even mine.

337

Doing something.

I stepped up onto the curb and into a cloud of marijuana smoke. I held my breath.

One boy crouched at the gate, crab walking from side to side in front of the small opening between the gate and the fence. Maxie's black nose and tan muzzle darted again and again into the space, long white teeth flashing. He threw himself at the fence then at the gate then at the fence again, his barking loud and close enough to hurt my ears. I focused on the second boy, the closer one. The laughing cheerleader.

I eased up behind him, slipping off the safety as I raised the gun. I pressed that black muzzle hard into the back of his head. It couldn't be this easy.

"Shut the fuck up and don't move," I said.

The boy stilled and raised his hands out to his sides. The other was too involved in torturing that poor dog to notice.

"Tell your buddy to do the same thing."

"You said shut up."

I kicked him hard in the back of the knee. It buckled and he stumbled backward, his skull leaning hard into the gun. My big toe screamed in pain and I really hoped I didn't have to kick him again.

"Do it," I said.

"Dawg, shut up and stand still."

Dawg turned around. "What the fuck?"

It took a minute to compute. When he understood the situation, he took a moment to think about it, factoring my white face into the equation. I cocked the hammer back, like Danny had shown me, to aid Dawg along in his thinking. It helped. Now he had to factor in his friend pissing his pants. Dawg raised his hands in the air.

"I could give a fuck what you do on that corner," I said, "but anyone ever bothers this dog again and you won't see it coming next time." I had no idea what I was saying but it felt good coming out. I'd made my point. "Now get the fuck out of here."

Dawg backed away across the lawn, his hands in the air. I tapped the gun against his friend's head. "Move out, mother-fucker."

The friend started walking, his piss-stained legs wide apart.

"I'll remember your face, motherfucker," Dawg said.

"Good," I answered, hoping to God that he wouldn't. "You better."

I stayed in the driveway far too long, plenty long enough for someone to come racing around the corner and blow my head off. But I had to watch them walk away. I had to savor their defeat; I couldn't help it.

I felt like Motherfucker of the Year. Don't tread on me, indeed. Or on my neighbor's dog.

I almost shot myself in the foot when the porch light came on. Old Lady Hanson leaned out her door.

"Next time, just shoot them and give me the gun," she said. "You think the cops are gonna look twice at an older-than-dirt white lady with two dead drug dealers on her front lawn? Get some sense, young man."

FIFTEEN

The next day, walking into the office after my eleven o'clock class, I found Danny perched on the corner of Kelsey's desk. I froze, my hand on the open door, stunned into paralysis. Kelsey wiggled her fingers at me in a flirty wave, but quickly turned away. The murder in my heart must've been broadcast across my face. If Danny saw it, he didn't react.

"Should I leave?" I asked. "Am I interrupting something?"

Kelsey stood. "Excuse me?"

Danny raised his hand. "It's me Kevin's mad at." He laid his hand over his heart. "I'm early."

I finally unstuck myself from the doorway, flinging my bag onto my desk from across the room. I followed it there and dropped hard into my chair. Kelsey sat back down. Danny didn't move.

"We're going to see Whitestone," Danny said.

"Together?" Kelsey asked.

"You wanna answer that, Danny?" I asked. "Since you seem to know everything."

I knew I shouldn't act so pissed off; there'd be no explaining my tantrum to Kelsey later. But I couldn't help myself, after all the shit he'd given me about bringing her into this — there he was sitting on her desk. The balls on this guy. Then again, I should've expected different?

"This is your office," Danny said. "I'll defer to your authority here."

I leaned forward in my chair, elbows on my knees, contemplating just how much damage to do. Questions flashed across Kelsey's face. Why wasn't I thrilled to see my brother, the way I talked about him? Shouldn't they meet if she and I were going to be together? Kelsey looked like my mother had the other night when I told her about Danny's return. Everyone who spent five minutes in a room with us seemed to end up looking like that. Confused and frustrated.

Danny, on the other hand, stayed perfectly composed, eyebrows high on his head, looking for all the world as though he had *no idea* what the fuss was about, like a bemused and slightly bored owl. I burst out laughing. The fact that our situation was anything but funny only made me laugh harder. I covered my face with my hands until I could gain control of myself. I never could stay mad at my brother. Catching my breath, I slouched in my chair.

Now that I was relaxed the lies flowed forth without a second thought.

"The prison that let Danny out on work release?" I said. "It doesn't have an undergrad program that really turns him on. So he's thinking of enrolling here."

Except for the prison part, it was pretty much the same lie I'd prepared for Whitestone.

Kelsey looked up at Danny. He kept his eyes on mine.

"It's true," he said. "Who wants to major in soap-dropping?"

"With a minor in license plate making," I added.

"You guys are retarded," Kelsey said. "Like short-bus, helmet-wearing retarded."

"Seriously though," I said, "Danny is thinking about getting his degree."

"The history of psychology," Danny said. "Asylums and hospitals and things like that. Kevin said Whitestone will help me get started." He cracked his knuckles. "And maybe help get me admitted. My previous academic record is spotty, to say the least." He smiled. "As a younger man I was big into chemistry."

Kelsey stared at me, more questions simmering on her lips. I knew what they were. Since when did Kevin Curran, one hundred and fifty pounds of departmental deadweight, have any sway with Whitestone? And if he really had it, where did he get it? From Danny's checkbook? Who was I really trying to fool? Whitestone, Danny, or her? But Kelsey had mercy. She didn't say a word. She bent over and pulled a brown bag from her knapsack.

"Sorry, fellas," she said, standing, "I didn't bring enough for three."

Danny hopped down off the desk. "This meeting won't last long. Save that for tomorrow. I'll take us out for lunch."

"Can't," Kelsey said, brown bag swinging at her hip.

She walked to the door and pulled it open. Instead of walking out, she turned to us. I sensed something in the way she looked at Danny and me, something in the way she wrinkled her nose at us. We weren't two separate men to her. For the moment at least we were a single unit. And she wasn't sure she liked it.

"I have class in forty minutes," she said. "And so do you, Kevin." She rolled her eyes toward the ceiling, pumping one leg, clearly deciding if she had any more to say. She did. "Danny, I know you've been gone a long time, but were you really in prison?"

Danny turned and hunched over, pointing at me. "This man? This man right here? He has his whole life been an unrepentant liar."

"I have not," I said.

"A-HA!" Danny yelled. "Caught you again."

Kelsey's nose wrinkled a little more. She looked us up and down, Danny still locked in his finger-pointing crouch. "So this is the Curran Brothers?" she asked.

"Aye, lass," Danny said.

I lifted my palms, as if to show there was nothing up my sleeve. "In their unrepentant glory."

"The act needs some work, fellas," Kelsey said. "Seriously." She walked out the door, the lock clicking into place behind her.

"If she only knew," Danny said. He raised his thumb, turning his pointer into a gun.

"You, motherfucker," I said, "are gonna ruin my life."

"If it wasn't for me, motherfucker," Danny said, "you wouldn't have a life to ruin."

■ ■ ■ ■

We had to climb five flights of stairs to Whitestone's office. No elevator for us. Cameras in every one, Danny said. All the way up, he sang an old Doors tune, ignoring my repeated snapping at him to shut up.

"I'm a spy/In the house of love," Danny sang, poorly, while smoking a cigarette. "I'm a spy/For the Maf-i-a."

I covered his hand with my own when he reached for the doorknob at Whitestone's floor.

"Can't you play this a little cooler?" I asked. "Some of us here aren't experts at this. I'm the one that works here. Shouldn't I go first?" I looked him in the eyes. "Are you high?"

"Define cool," Danny said. "And high."

I growled at him through clenched teeth.

"C'mon, lighten up," Danny said, rubbing out his cigarette on the wall, leaving ugly black streaks of ash. "Just high on life, but thanks for asking. This is the fun part; I'm enjoying myself. You should be, too. No bodies, no guns. No creeping around in the night, no Drakkar." He bumped me away from the door. "Admit it, there's a rush in your veins right now that you don't get

346

spouting off about the Constitution for the thousandth time. Relax, Teach. Enjoy the ride. Some excitement, a little adrenaline. It's one of the job's better perks." He pulled the door open. "I got this."

Whitestone's secretary spotted Danny first, our emergence from the stairwell surprising her. Her head rose high on her goose neck, her arm rose into the air. She snapped her fingers for my brother's attention. "Excuse me, sir. Can I help you?"

I peeked around Danny's back. "Hey, Lucille. This is my brother, Danny. We're looking for Dean Whitestone."

"Oh, it's you," she said. Her arm came down. "He said you might be coming up."

"Yeah, I left a note in his mailbox this morning."

Lucille smiled a cold, mean smile. "I told him I'd believe it when I saw it."

"Believe it, sister," Danny said. "It's the man himself, Sir Kevin Curran, intellectual acrobat, resident genius, Grand Pooh-bah of American History. Ask him anything about the Constitution. *ANYTHING!*"

"There's no smoking anywhere inside a campus building," Lucille said. She turned back to her computer.

Danny dashed to my side when he saw me ready to knock on the door.

"One second," he whispered, digging into his jacket pocket.

He pulled out his keys, gripping what looked like a laser pointer between his thumb and forefinger. A red beam of light passed over the door handle. "Digital impression," Danny whispered. "Got it on eBay. You take the lead here."

I hesitated, afraid of what I was about to unleash.

"Go ahead and knock," Danny said. "We're already halfway there."

I knocked and the dean called us in.

"Dean?" I asked, leaning in the half-open door as if he might not grant entrance if he knew who was knocking. "A few minutes of your time?"

"Of course," Whitestone said, waving us in. "My goodness, Curran. You're actually early." He grinned when he noticed Danny. "There's another chair against the wall there."

Danny grabbed the other chair, aluminum-framed with maroon cushions, and placed it next to the identical one before Whitestone's enormous desk. We sat and folded our hands in our laps simultaneously. I wondered if we weren't overplaying it. Whitestone begged a moment's indulgence, turning to his computer.

I had no doubt he was checking his stock portfolio on the Internet, or maybe booking another trip. He fiddled around at his keyboard for a good ten minutes, to show what a busy man he was, to impress upon us that our audience was a special honor.

"Kevin, won't you introduce me?" he finally asked.

He didn't offer Danny his hand, keeping them hidden in his lap. He had never before called me by my first name.

"Dean Whitestone," I said, "this is my brother, Danny. He's interested in enrolling at Richmond and considering his subject area, I knew he had to meet you."

"What's your preferred area of study, Dan?" Whitestone asked.

"The history of child psychology," Danny said. "Especially treatment of the mentally ill and the severely disabled."

Whitestone turned to me, his eyebrows raised and his bottom lip puffed out to show he was impressed.

I forced my best competition smile. "You can see why I brought him to you."

"Indeed," Whitestone said. "Kevin's given you some background on our Bloodroot project, then?"

"Some," Danny said. "I've also done some research on my own."

Whitestone gave me a sad shake of the head. "Kevin, considering your brother's interests, your reluctance to join the fold only confuses me further."

"Chalk it up to sibling rivalry," Danny said. He laced his fingers and leaned forward in his chair. "I really wanted to hear about it from you, anyway, since you're the authority."

"True," Whitestone said. "I've been involved in the Friends of Bloodroot since the beginning, founding it, in fact."

"Of course the history of the place interests me," Danny said. "I'm already pretty well informed about it. I've done some research. I just wonder what would make such a place worth preserving?"

"A reasonable question," Whitestone said. "To begin, what happened there was unconscionable. No one is denying that or trying to whitewash it. Children being used in unsupervised experiments, living in Holocaust-like conditions. All right under the nose of the greatest city on Earth in the latter half of the twentieth century. Shameful. Worse, Bloodroot was not the only place of its kind. How could such things happen?

"But let's put our emotions aside for a moment and ask another question. Why does Germany give tours of the concentration camps? Why do the Japanese commemorate Hiroshima and Nagasaki? Why do American museums and art galleries have exhibits about slavery and lynching, or address the eradication of Native Americans? Because, as we like to say in our department, those who forget history are doomed to repeat it."

Whitestone leaned forward, his face a perfect mask of sincerity. He breathed heavily through his nose as he spoke. "Bloodroot changed American history. Who knows how many innocent lives were sacrificed in the darkest days of that place? But what came out of it: the oversight, the legislation, the funding — it saved thousands more. As a historian and as a father, I can't let such an important place fade unmentioned into the past."

"It's a sound argument," Danny said, scratching at the inside of his left elbow. "But has anyone thought of the families? Bloodroot was only closed twenty-odd years ago. There are surely families in the city who placed children there. Surely there are survivors of that place? How do they feel about their ugly past being put on public display?"

Whitestone's face lit up with excitement, as if he'd been waiting the entire meeting for that one question. "I have letters from a dozen families supporting the Friends of Bloodroot. Had Kevin attended that press conference, he could have told you as much."

"I went to the last one," I said. "About the award."

Whitestone ignored me. Danny had captured his exclusive attention.

"How involved in this museum is Dr. Calvin?" Danny asked. "Could be redemptive for him."

"I haven't even attempted to find him," Whitestone said. "He hasn't been heard from in over two decades, disappeared without a trace right after the story broke. You can imagine his disgrace at being discovered."

"Is he dead?" Danny asked.

"He very well could be. He'd be rather old by now. At the time of the controversy, there were whispers of suicide, but no body was ever discovered."

"So no one knows for sure, then," Danny said. "It'd be a coup to track him down. He'd certainly have a contribution to make to the conversation."

"I don't know who'd want to hear it," Whitestone said. "He had his chance to explain himself back then and chose instead to make his escape." Whitestone shrugged, holding out his hands. "Dr. Calvin is hardly of any consequence anymore."

"The people who wrote those letters," Danny said, "might feel differently."

"Any of those letters of support from the survivors themselves?" I asked. "That would certainly be powerful stuff in your favor."

Whitestone tossed a commiserating glance at Danny, then looked back at me, pity and impatience dulling his eyes. "Well, Kevin, most anyone at Bloodroot could barely speak their own name, never mind write a letter. It's pretty impossible for any survivors to understand the situation, never mind express approval or objection."

"These families supporting the project," Danny said, "their Bloodroot children are still alive?"

Whitestone shook his head. "No, no children. People as severely damaged as those poor souls usually did not live very long."

"Usually," Danny said. "How hard have you looked?"

I snuck a glance at Danny. I feared that he'd taken on more than he could handle in discussing Bloodroot with someone who felt *very* differently about the place than he did. A single blotch of hot, red blood bloomed behind his ear. The clock had started ticking on his temper. Time to draw the meeting to a close. Hopefully, Danny had learned what he needed to know about Whitestone's office.

"Man, I'm fired up," I said, standing. "I think the three of us can really get into this Bloodroot thing. I'm not going to miss the next board meeting. Dean, you'll be sure to let me know about it?"

Whitestone had sunk back in his chair, tapping his lips with a pen, studying Danny and trying to ascertain, I was sure, exactly how much use Danny could be to him.

"I hate to bring a halt to things," I said, "but I do have a class to teach." I set my hand on Danny's shoulder. He hadn't moved. "Maybe we can get together again another time, set up some introductions over in Psych." I looked down at Whitestone. "Thank you, Dean, for your time."

Without moving his head, Whitestone shifted his eyes away from us and settled them on his bookshelf.

Danny finally stood. I let slip a huge sigh of relief and backed toward the door. Danny didn't move.

"As soon as I'm enrolled," Danny said, "I think we can do a lot together, me, you, and Kevin." He glanced at me then back at the dean. "Don't let Kevin fool you. He knows more than you think. Our grandfather was Dr. Henry O'Malley. You might be familiar with the name."

Whitestone practically leaped over his desk to get to us.

"Kevin, why keep this information a secret? I have such immense respect for Dr. O'Malley; he's practically a hero of mine." He lowered his eyes, licked his lips. "If you'll forgive my immodesty, I sometimes think of myself as your grandfather's heir. That I'm continuing his work on behalf of abused children." The dean paused, folding his hands across his chest, playing for reverence before he spoke again. "We have a prominent display planned for your grandfather at the museum. Perhaps, Kevin, you and your brother could speak at the next FOB meeting. The O'Malley name and reputation, now that would give some weight to our modest organization. I know the *Advance* will send a reporter *and* a photographer." He cuffed me on the shoulder. "No school paper for Dr. Henry O'Malley."

I could practically see the dollar signs in Whitestone's eyes. The old ladies would remember my famous grandfather. His name would be worth its weight in gold at the fundraisers. Gold that would line Whitestone's pockets. I pulled the office door open wide, feeling dirtier than I had at the dump. I desperately needed some air. "I'll put something together," I said.

"Dan?" Whitestone asked. "I hope you'll consent to be part of this, too. Carry on the noble labors of your bloodline."

Danny snatched Whitestone's hand from his side and squeezed it in a firm grip, resting his other hand on the smaller man's shoulder. "Dean Whitestone, I feel like I already am part of it. More than you know." He turned the dean's wrist, eyeing the scars on the back of his hand. "Painful?"

Whitestone pulled his hand away. "Childhood accident."

"Happens to the best of us," Danny said.

Whitestone raised his hands, backing away from us, his yellow-toothed smile oozing across his face. "Enjoy the rest of your day, gentlemen."

Danny and I couldn't get out of the building fast enough, barreling down the stairs and bursting out the building doors like we had the Redcoats' breath on our backs.

"God Almighty," Danny said, shaking off a chill. "I feel like boiling myself. And that's saying something considering the people I know."

"Danny, I told the folks about our conversation that night you gave me the tour. They remember things differently. So I did some research of my own. Grandpa was the public face of the city's medical community during the entire scandal. His name is in every article in every local newspaper, every national story." I took a long drag on my cigarette. "And there's more, Danny. The cops talked to Grandpa about Calvin going missing. A couple of times. That was in the papers, too."

I stopped, waiting for Danny to say something. He stayed quiet.

"There was talk that Calvin didn't disappear very far from home," I said. "His home in Brooklyn. Park Slope, Brooklyn." I dropped my cigarette butt on the ground and crushed it out. "The night you first took me to the restaurant, Bavasi said something to me about him and Santoro knowing Grandpa. The other night, when we were talking about you, Dad talked about Grandpa having powerful friends, not all of them doctors. What's that sound like to you?"

"Ancient history," Danny said, holding his smoke to his mouth and staring down at his shoes. "So Mom and Dad said I was lying to you? About where I came from."

"No, not really," I said, sitting on the bench. "They just think you misremember some things from when you were really young. That you've got a couple things mixed up in your head. They blame the drugs." I stretched my arms across the back of the bench, trying to look casual, like Danny had at the restaurant. "Danny, you think Grandpa really killed someone?"

Danny stood a few feet away from me, his head tilted back, staring through the dead leaves of the trees and into the sky. "You think I'm a liar? You think my drug-addled brain made up all that shit I told you the other night? Maybe you do think I made it up. To trick you into helping me. Same old Danny, right? Only out for himself and fuck everyone else. That's what the folks said, right? That what you're thinking?"

Danny's self-righteousness grated on me. Drug-addled or not, he had to know his history gave cause enough for questioning his true motives. He'd hurt the people closest to him the most, with me at the top of the list. He knew that. He remembered. He'd said so himself.

"That's how it works in history, right?" Danny said. "Whoever's left around gets to decide the truth. Like whether or not Grandpa killed a man who had it coming."

He kicked at the concrete again and again, a kid who'd watched the ice cream truck turn away around the corner. "God, I hope he fucking did it. I wish we could know for sure."

"He did everything he could to put an end to that place," I said. "I'm sure he went as far as he felt was necessary." I stepped up to my brother. "And now we'll go the rest of the way. We'll bring that place down. We'll do it. What's it matter what I think? What I *believe* is I'm into this thing all the way. I promise. That's what matters."

"It matters to me," Danny said, "that you believe me. Mom and Dad can go screw. But you? It matters a lot, Kev. Believe that."

"I've known from the minute I saw you again that you weren't the same old Danny," I said. "And you never will be. Believe *that.*"

Danny stared at me long and hard. He was smart enough to know I hadn't answered his questions, I hadn't told him who or what I believed. All I could think was that I had learned to dance around the truth from the best liar I knew, my own brother.

But I hated seeing Danny like this, his shoulders slumped and his head turned away to hide the sad eyes in his quickly paling face. He looked like a kicked dog aching to be petted. And perfectly willing to be kicked again, if that was what it took to stick around. The sight reminded me too much of Danny the junkie crawling home, drooling on himself, dope sick, lovesick, and helpless.

"What time tonight?" Danny asked.

"The folks? Oh, man. Listen, it's been a long afternoon. If you wanna put it off, that's cool."

"Deal's a deal," he said. "I promised you. No more same old Danny, remember?"

"Seven," I said. "Dinner might be a bit too much. Let's stick to dessert and drinks. Ease everyone into it."

"Still cookies and whiskey?"

"Every time," I said. I glanced at my watch. "I really do have one more class to teach."

"See you at seven, then," Danny said. He started walking away then stopped and turned. "Hey, I'm sorry for fucking with you over Kelsey. I should've let you make the call." He shrugged. "It seemed like a normal brother thing to do, swing by the office and shoot the shit. I should've known better." He raised a finger at me. "She seems first-rate. Don't fuck it up."

"I'll try not to," I said, walking over to him. I didn't mention that it really wasn't up to me. "Listen, tonight'll go fine. I'll make sure of it. And I don't care if you say you came from the moon and Mom and Dad insist it was Mars. You're my brother. That's all that matters. I mean it."

Danny held out his fist and I bumped it with my own.

"Stay away from Whitestone," he said. "I'll handle things from here. When you've been where I have, you can spot the evil ones like their fangs are four feet long. It's a myth they only come out at night."

I asked Danny what he meant but he just shook his head. "Trust me. See you tonight."

Watching Danny go, I worried maybe I *was* getting played: about Bloodroot, about Santoro, Whitestone, Al, some of it, all of it. Maybe even Danny giving up the drugs. Sure as hell wouldn't be the first time I'd been the fool. Could be he didn't even know he was doing it anymore. Maybe the lies and manipulation were only habit now, freeing Danny, really, of ill intent.

Maybe the hell he'd been through had marked my brother in ways neither he nor anyone else could ever undo. Maybe Danny had track marks on his soul. Or maybe Danny had always been a shape-shifter and an acrobat who served only his own shadowy needs. For all its power over Danny, maybe the heroin had been nothing more than a placeholder, an apprenticeship, a black fire in which he forged his heart until he found his true calling as one of Santoro's dark angels.

According to my folks, Danny had been born screaming in need, had breached the world shrieking into the dirty Brooklyn air for what his frantic blood told him he'd die without. Utter selfishness wasn't a choice for Danny. It was the mandate, the prime directive of his blood. Wherever he'd come from, one thing was true. My brother had entered this life alone and already lost. Danny never even *had* the faith or innocence the rest of us get to throw away.

As Danny's silhouette moved away from me, growing smaller, I realized something else. Believing in Danny now wasn't about him. It was about me. I was the one with the choices. And I chose to stand by my brother and get fucked for it every time rather than risk turning my back on him the one time he really, truly needed me. If I got hurt, the only one to blame was myself. Everyone else around me, including Danny, stayed innocent. I knew in making that choice, I was as selfish as Danny. My conscience stayed clean no matter what. But the other option was admitting to myself I couldn't trust my brother. Ever. I didn't want to live in a world where a man couldn't trust his only brother. So I chose not to.

Like so many before me, I rewrote history the way I wanted it to be. There was no one to stop me.

SIXTEEN

After I finished teaching for the day, I bought a cup of coffee and a bottle of fancy water at Starbucks and cabbed it over to Willowbrook Park. Kelsey played soccer one night a week in an "old fart" coed league and she'd invited me to watch. Of course I agreed. This was a thing that couples did and a couple was what I wanted us to be. The future would take care of itself.

The ferocity and the pace of the competition surprised me. I'd expected something akin to beer-league softball — brief episodes of clumsy barreling about on the field, a soccer ball somewhere in the mix, followed by long periods of wheezing, foul-mouthed trash talk and sipping from water bottles full of golden, carbonated liquid. I had expected soccer played the same way boiling packs of eight-year-olds did it, only with beer and cursing. These people played, though, like they had something serious at stake — money, pride, memories of former glories. Something more than which team got stuck buying the pitchers that night.

They ran, they sweated, they knocked one another over often and hard. And they were good. Organized and able. These people had played the game all their lives. Maybe that fact set the stakes. The players needed to prove that despite age and responsibility, there was at least one thing left they did well. Watching the combat, I couldn't remember the last time I'd put that much effort into anything.

Approaching the sideline, I took off my tie and shoved it in my pocket, where I discovered my cigarettes. I thought about lighting one then decided against it. Bad form around people running themselves into the ground. I wasted a few moments sorting through possible excuses for my tardiness to the sideline before I realized Kelsey probably hadn't been standing around waiting on me. She had other things to do.

She wasn't hard to find; I heard her before I saw her. She was clearly the field general for her team. Playing midfield, she worked her teammates, men and women both, from one end of the field to the other. Shouting directions at a full sprint, she led the defense like they were the last of their battalion, fighting for the lives of the women and children. Then, her territory successfully defended, the ball rolling at her feet, Kelsey would turn and unleash the offense, the forwards sprinting downfield like charging cavalry coming over the hill. She held the ball for just moments before she sent it soaring off to land on the shoe tops of a teammate. My girlfriend was the best player on the field. I loved it.

I stood there, my chest swelling with pride, suddenly eager for the players and spectators to know I had come at her invitation, for them to know that she and I were together, a couple. I felt like I'd suddenly found out she was famous.

During a break in play Kelsey finally stopped running. Mud splattered her legs and her shorts. One of her knees bled. Grass fell from her sweaty hair when she shook her head. When she set her hands on her hips and leaned backward, her eyes closed, the lean muscles of her thighs, calves, and arms rose like swells on the surface of the sea. Her stretch pulled her shimmering emerald jersey taut over her breasts and shoulders. The jersey rode up from her waistband, exposing a few sunlit inches of smooth golden belly. Looking at her, I felt dry and brittle. I was made of sticks and ashes; she was sleek and powerful.

"A lioness," a voice beside me said. "Untamable. Even as a young girl, I bet she was a terror."

I turned to see Whitestone, his hand elbow deep in a bag of peanuts. Though the evening was cloudless and warm, he wore thin leather gloves to hide his scars. His bald head and thick glasses reflected the evening's pink and orange light. I couldn't see his eyes. What was he doing at the game? Stalking Kelsey? Surely she wouldn't stand for that.

"There she goes," Whitestone shouted. "On the hunt!"

Kelsey hurtled by us, her cleats churning up ground as she ran a step behind an opposing forward that had broken into empty space. She caught him in time to intercept and trap the pass from the center. I pumped my fist at her success then groaned when she overshot her own upfield pass and turned the ball over.

"Don't worry," Whitestone said. Bits of red peanut skin stuck to his top lip. "She recovers well."

I glared at him, playing angry at the interruptions. It was true that I didn't want to miss a move Kelsey made. But more important, something in the way he spoke about her made the hair stand up on my arms. His voice had the damp, husky undertones of a Peeping Tom talking to himself at the window.

"I'd really just like to watch the game, Dean," I said.

"Oh, I'm not staying. Just passing by. I have other interests across the park."

With a hard slide tackle, Kelsey sent a woman with a bouncer's build flying head over heels. Kelsey popped up and hit a dead sprint with the ball at her feet. She covered ten yards in a blink and booted the ball a good thirty yards upfield. A perfect lead for her team's streaking winger.

Whitestone smacked his lips. "She sure can run. It's her greatest strength. She can run forever. Smart, too. Like she always knows what the other players are thinking. You think you've got her then *poof!* She's gone." He grinned up at me. "But you can see all that for yourself, I guess."

"No disrespect, Dean," I said, "but it's probably best if you don't talk to me about Kelsey. Ever."

"Not difficult," Whitestone said. "Since Miss Reyes is moving half a continent away in what amounts to a matter of weeks, leaving both you and me to our own devices here on wonderful Staten Island." He offered me the remainder of his peanuts. I felt I'd rather stick my hand in the sewer and I almost told him so. "A fascinating young man, that brother of yours. Between Danny and your grandfather, there may yet be a future for you in our department."

He crumpled the peanut bag and dropped it. Then he raised his foot and stomped down on the bag.

"Better make sure that doesn't happen to your nut bag." He raised his chin toward the playing field. "Halftime. Here she comes."

In all the weirdness, I hadn't even heard the whistle. By the time I regained my senses, my boss had waddled too far away for me to respond to this threat, or warning, or tasteless attempt at humor, or whatever that had been. I whirled around when Kelsey called my name.

She jogged toward me, ducking her nose into her armpit and then laughing, a big paper cup in one hand. Her smile died when she got close enough to see my face.

"What did he say to you?" Kelsey asked.

"Nothing." I reached into my coat pocket and pulled out the bottle of water. "I brought this for you."

"Thanks. That's really sweet." She glanced at the cup of Gatorade in her hand. She took the water from me, stuffing the bottle into her back pocket and smiling up at me from under her sweaty bangs. "I'll keep it for after the game, when I can savor it."

"Works for me," I said. "Maximum enjoyment. That's what I'm about."

Over Kelsey's shoulder, I could see her teammates watching us, waiting for her to return to the huddle. She seemed to sense their eyes on her.

"Thanks for coming," Kelsey said. "It means a lot." She rose up on her toes and kissed my cheek. "You enjoying the game?"

"More than you know," I said.

"Good." She kissed me again, this time on the lips. She jogged back to her team.

Watching her go, her cleats kicking up dirt as she ran, clapping her hands to rally her team, I realized I didn't need Danny to set myself up for a world of hurt.

Kelsey's team lost by one goal, scored not three minutes before the ref's whistle ended the game. Despite her intensity on the field, losing the game had no effect on her. I waited off to the side as she talked and laughed with her teammates as they packed up their gear. Most seemed in a hurry to get home. I took her gym bag from her when she reached me. We walked together toward the parking lot, taking our time.

Grammar and junior high school kids playing soccer and flag football monopolized every other ball field we passed. Their high-voiced shouts melded into a musical cloud of nonsense. Every now and then the rusty-gate shriek of an overenthusiastic mother pierced the air and made me cringe, not at the sound but for the sake of the poor child on the receiving end. For the most part, though, the adults just stalked the sidelines, arms crossed against their chests, their watchful gazes trained as intently on the coaches as they were on their kids.

The fathers wore their dark, rumpled suits, the sleeves of their watch-arms rolled to the elbow. The mothers hovered on tiptoe, eyes flitting between the child on the field and the other cherubs gamboling at their feet. The mothers clutched jackets, sweatshirts, hats, blankets, and water bottles in their arms. Everyone looked so much the same that there was no telling which father went with which mother. I wondered how often the wrong husband, wife, or child was brought home and if any effort got put into finding the right one, if in fact the difference was ever noted.

"Not for me," Kelsey said. "You?"

"What's that?"

"Kids. No thanks. I have no interest." She paused. "You?"

"Kids? Are you serious?" I said. "I can't even manage to buy myself a bed." I thought about the immortal spider plant on my porch. "I can't see myself as a father. I have a hard enough time with one brother."

"Interesting cat, your brother," Kelsey said. "It was good to meet him."

"Yuck."

"What? Please. Relax. I only date one man per gene pool, thanks."

"That's not what I was thinking," I said. "Whitestone said almost exactly the same thing about him." I waited while Kelsey bent to loosen the laces on her cleats. "That guy creeps me out. He makes you feel like you're standing there naked."

"Tell me about it," Kelsey said. She held out her shoes to me. So I carried those, too. "I have no problem being naked but I really insist on deciding the audience for myself."

"He come to your games often?" I asked.

"Yes and no," Kelsey said. "I see him at nearly every game, but he never sticks around. I think one of his sons plays pretty regular on one of the other fields. That's always where I see him when I leave. Over by the kids."

We reached the parking lot. I stopped

walking and set down her bag and spikes. Kelsey stopped beside me.

"Is it just me or did we not just have one of *those* conversations?" I asked, holding my thumb over my shoulder. "Back there, when we talked about kids."

"What kind of conversation is that, pray tell?" Kelsey asked.

"You know, the kind that couples have. Couples thinking about the future."

"It was a meaningless question."

"It *so* was not," I said.

She laughed. "I wish you could see yourself, Kevin. You look like you just figured out I was your long-lost sister. Am I that scary?"

"You're not scary. But you leaving town gets more terrifying by the day."

"Yeah," Kelsey said, looking down at her feet. "Yeah, it does."

She leaned into me. I put my arm around her.

"There's no point denying we've already gone farther than we had planned," she said. "Well, maybe you. I gotta admit, I've wanted this for a while." She ran her fingers through her hair, stared at her dirty hands. "And now here you are and I got these other plans."

"I'm not asking for anything," I said.

"I know," she said. "I know you're not. And I think calling us a couple is an honest assessment. I certainly feel that way." She set her chin on my shoulder, spoke into my ear. "I'm tired and sore and filthy. Can we talk more about this another time?"

"Sure," I said. "Whenever you're ready." I planted a kiss on her hip as I bent to pick up her stuff. "You need to change before we head home? Need anything from the office?"

"Nah," Kelsey said. She stopped on the edge of the gravel parking lot, wiggling her toes inside her socks.

"I'm not carrying you," I said. "You didn't even win."

"You sure you don't want to tell me what Whitestone said?" Kelsey asked.

"It was nothing worth repeating. Just bullshit."

Kelsey squinted one eye at me. "He likes to think he knows things about me."

"I wouldn't trust a word that guy said about you," I said. "Or about anything else, for that matter. Don't worry about him. I don't."

We walked to the car, Kelsey stepping gingerly over the gravel. She took her bag and shoes from me and tossed them in the backseat. She held the passenger door open for me. "Some of the team is meeting up for beers. Why don't we —"

"Oh," I said. "Listen, I got plans."

Kelsey slammed the door. "Okay. I blew off your big relationship conversation and now you're blowing me off. Passive-aggressive much?"

"It's not like that," I said. "I'm due at my folks'. My brother's gonna be there. His first time home since . . . since he's been back." I smiled, touched my forehead to hers. Her skin smelled like fresh dirt and sweat. She had orange Gatorade on her breath. I wanted a taste, but I didn't take it. "Over-react much?"

She leaned into me, applying pressure to where we touched. She set her hands on her hips and narrowed her eyes. "You and me, Curran? When we have our first knockdown-drag-out, it's gonna be straight-up volcanic."

"Looking forward to it," I said. "Imagine what the makeup sex will be like."

"Get in the car," Kelsey said, "before I get us charged with a wide array of embarrassing crimes."

Kelsey pulled the car to the curb in front of my parents' house, right behind Danny's new Saturn. She left the engine running.

Halfway down the block, a shadowy figure stood beneath a tall oak tree, smoking a cigarette. Kelsey saw him, too.

"The man of the hour," she said.

"A nervous wreck, I bet. Poor bastard."

Kelsey set her hand on my knee. "This isn't going to be a glorious, hugs-and-kisses reunion, is it?" she asked. "There's a lot of history here that I don't know."

"One day I'll catch you up," I said. "It's quite a story." I covered her hand with mine but kept my eyes on Danny. He hadn't moved from under the tree, probably expecting me to arrive in a cab.

"I hope I didn't make a big mistake here," I said. "I pushed him into this. Too soon, maybe."

"You worried he won't stick around?"

I'd never told her my mother was sick. Kelsey'd watched her own mother disappear and die. I knew I could trust her, but death was a deep thing to have in common. Until she told me she was sticking around, I didn't want too many bonds that hurt to break. On the other hand, I'd already told her too many lies.

"Our mother is sick," I said. "She's got Alzheimer's. There's no time to be gentle."

"Wow. Jesus, that's brutal," Kelsey said. She set her jaw hard behind her words, as if to lock in any thoughts tempted to follow. "We'll talk." She shoved my shoulder. "But for now, go. You've wasted enough time with me already."

I got out of the car. Danny turned and headed up the street toward us.

"Call me later," Kelsey said.

"I don't know how late this is going to go."

"Call me later," she said. "Doesn't matter what time."

I agreed. She pulled a U-turn in the driveway across the street. I watched the neighbors look up from their TV when Kelsey's headlights hit their window. Without expression, they turned back to the TV when the lights went away. They looked like two tortoises at the zoo peering up from a hunk of lettuce.

"You're late," Danny said, arriving soundlessly at my side.

"Sorry," I said. "Kelsey's soccer game took longer than I thought."

"It's all right," he said. "They win?"

I shook my head. "But she is awesome."

"You talking about soccer or her in general?"

"Both."

"Good news," Danny said. He rubbed his hands together. "Shit. I ain't been this nervous since I thieved a guy's stash in Sunset Park."

SEVENTEEN

My father answered the door. His hair was combed and he wore a clean, ironed, short-sleeved dress shirt. His thick arms strained at the tightly rolled cuffs. He had a cigarette tucked behind his ear. I saw a flash of the trim, fierce man my mother met all those years ago leaning over the pool table in his father's tavern.

Danny stood behind me, and my father looked straight past me over my shoulder, hard into the eyes of his other son.

"The butcher was fresh out of fatted calves," Dad said, stepping into the yard. He let the door close behind him. I thought he might swing on Danny. I hoped I'd be quick enough to sidestep the punch. "Hope you fed yourself tonight."

Dad puffed out his chest, pushing the thrill of seeing his son deep beneath his duty to protect his wife. "I'm talking about your stomach, Daniel. Not your arm."

"I'm good, Pop," Danny said. "Every part of me. It's good to see you."

My father glanced at me. I dropped my gaze and stepped aside. He walked up to Danny.

"If you break her heart again," my father said, "I will kill you for it."

My head snapped up. It was the simplest, plainest threat my father had ever made to either of us. The two of them stared into each other, my father's rage percolating under his skin, Danny, always the superior actor, looking calm and unafraid but wary. I had made a huge mistake. These two men were not ready to be in a room together. They'd probably never be.

"Mom feeling okay?" I asked, forcing my father to break first. Tonight wasn't about either of them, or me. I'd just have to trust in how much the both of them loved my mother.

"Grand," my father said, turning to me. "So excited you'd think the damn pope was comin' over. No monkey business tonight, you mopes. I'm warning you. We better get inside before she bursts."

Mom sat upright in her blue armchair, wearing a faded but pretty dress I had never seen, her face soft and warm in the glow of the lamplight. Her hands rested folded in her lap and her ankles were crossed. She seemed immobilized by the anticipation, as if set in place by a puppeteer, hardly as excited as my father had said. For a panicked moment I worried that while my brother, my father, and I talked outside she had forgotten the three of us. But then the tears rolled forth and I realized why she'd been so still. Joy. She was basking in the sight of her three men walking together through her front door. She wanted to see us so intensely that nothing, not time, not her sickness, could ever take us from her. This was the scene, I realized, she had chosen as the drape over her eyes in her last moments before the final darkness came. So shot through with emotion she was, Mom could only lift her shaking arms as Danny crossed the room.

Danny knelt before her chair, one knee down then the other, his arms reaching around her. Our mother folded herself over him, a bird shielding her young from the storm. She pressed her cheek against the top of his head, her teardrops falling into his hair, her thin, pale arms stretching down his back, fingers spread wide. It was how she'd held him when his nightmares sent him screaming through the house, when years later he lay twisted and drenched, dope sick in his boyhood bed. Not embracing Danny as much as absorbing him, straining to put all of herself between her son and the beast at his heels.

There was no screaming this time, though. There was only the sound of my mother's wet, undulating breaths as her body rose and fell against her son's.

My father had teased Danny about being the prodigal son. It was an old joke, one the black sheep boy of every Catholic family on the island had to endure. It was a story most every family played out, up and down every Staten Island street and far beyond. I saw no reason the Curran family should be different. But then I remembered what had happened to Danny under the East River Bridge. I remembered Danny had stopped his heart, had died, not once but twice. The other families, their prodigal sons quit college, or refused to work in the family store, or knocked up the high school slut their parents had warned them about. What I was seeing, what I had *done* by bringing Danny home, was bigger than any of that bullshit. How many of those families all around us, I wondered, got to live out the story of Lazarus?

I felt my father's hand on my shoulder. The tremor in his grip told me I didn't have to turn to see his tears. Me? I thought of Santoro. Of Whitestone and Bloodroot. Something lit up inside me I had never felt before. A furnace caught fire, pumping a new heat through my blood with every beat of my heart. I hated my nervousness, my hesitation on the stairs outside Whitestone's office. How had I even thought twice about going through with that? How had I ever agonized over telling a few measly, meaningless lies that no one would ever remember? Or about committing worthless, victimless crimes when the scene in front of me was what my family stood to gain? Time together. I understood the things Kelsey had said about her mother, about family, and about blood rules. She was right. At the end of the day, love's the only virtue there is. Everything else, every rule, every law, withered to dust and ashes in comparison.

For the first time in too many years, my family was whole again. If I had any soul left, Santoro could have it, if that was what it took to bury Danny's demons and keep the family together, at least for a little while. There was no hem for my mother to touch, there'd be no savior to lift her shroud and call her forth. But I could save her son.

Mom rose from her chair and we moved the ceremony from the living room to the dining room table. My father put a Chieftains CD on the stereo, set out a round of whiskeys and a plate of Oreos. Danny ate six while no one else ate any. We took our time with our drinks. Mom hardly touched hers, having all she needed seated around her. She was enjoying one of her best days in a long time.

Danny held court, giving my folks a mild, condensed version of his past three years. My folks had lived through the cycles of Danny's addiction many times. There was no point recounting bouts of withdrawal and succumbing to temptation or tales of run-ins with the cops and criminals who worked New York's heroin trade. He omitted his East River Bridge experience. Danny's current circumstances commanded much greater interest from my folks. Keeping Danny where he was trumped how he had arrived there.

He told them about Gino Bavasi and his restaurant, about the lucrative Far Beyond Technology and his apartment near the park. He apologized for waiting a year to return to the family, insisting he needed to know his sobriety would stick before asking anyone else to believe in it. When my mother said the family could've helped him, Danny demurred that the family had done too much for him already. My father didn't disagree with him.

"I couldn't come back asking for anything," Danny said. "Things had to be different. I had to come back offering something."

At this my father sat back in his chair and crossed his arms over his chest. He tossed me a stern glance. We both knew that Danny had mastered the art of asking for one thing by offering something else, something he rarely delivered. I thought for a moment that given the chance, my father would've made a hell of a judge.

In my mother's eyes, Danny the junkie was a victim of people who preyed without mercy on the misfortune and physical weakness of others. In her mind, Danny had been whisked away by vampires who fell on him from the rafters when her back was turned. She was like those mothers perched on the edges of the soccer fields at Willowbrook Park. Harm only came to children because their parents failed to prevent it. It was not part of the natural order of things.

To my father, Danny's addiction signified a weakness of spirit. He may have excused the flaw in light of Danny's origins, but he blamed his son for not overcoming it. Danny had rejected the hard work my folks had done to give him a better life. But even more than the drugs, my father mistrusted the other things Danny had craved: fancy clothes, fast friends, the glamorous life in Manhattan. I couldn't blame my father for his resentments.

My mother had grown up taking fireside piano lessons surrounded by fawning doctors and their wives. To her, fresh cigars and old scotch, pretty wives, extra money, and leisure time came as the natural blessings of doing good, of making sick people well again.

My father came of age in the rough company of truck drivers, beat cops, and dockworkers. While Eileen O'Malley played the piano, Robert Curran hauled kegs, swept floors, and scrubbed beer puke off the toilets in his father's corner tavern. In that world, only the people without sore backs and calloused hands had fast cars, fast friends, and money to burn. Men of easy wealth were untrustworthy at best and dangerous at worst.

The adults of my parents' childhood lives only met when an ambulance unloaded a patron of Curran's Sligo Tavern at the emergency room of Methodist Hospital.

Danny's owning a business would get him some traction into my father's good graces.

It was something *his* father had done. But to my father, Danny had always shown the same colors as the corner hustlers outside the tavern, the same colors as his brother Johnny. Flashing a fat wallet, no matter how he claimed he earned the money, wouldn't help Danny's cause. I hoped the temptation to please and impress didn't get the better of his common sense.

"My apartment," Danny said, "isn't too far from Grandpa O'Malley's old brownstone. The couple that owns it will be selling it soon." He spread his arms like a benevolent prince. "How'd you like to move back to Brooklyn?"

My mother turned openmouthed to my father. My father shook his head.

"Daniel, how're you gonna afford a brownstone a block and a half from Prospect Park?" he asked.

"It's a special case," Danny said. "This couple, they're headed for a nasty divorce. They'll be unloading it cheap."

My father leaned forward in his chair, staring Danny down. "And how do you know this?"

I knew the answer. I thought of the naked Superman and his bi-curious wife. I let Danny play it.

"I live in the neighborhood," he said with

a shrug. "Everyone knows; you'd know about the same situation on this block. Look, Dad, it's not like I'm footing the bill or buying it outright. I would if I could. This is something I thought we could all do together. That's the beauty of it."

"With some help from this Bavasi character," my father said. "Shit, he was a crook when your grandfather was alive."

"Not financial help," Danny said. "But, you know, his place is a neighborhood institution like the Sligo used to be. He has some influence."

"I'll bet," my father said. He turned to my mother. "Don't say it."

"Robert," Mom said. "Mr. Bavasi's helped this family before. At great risk to himself. He was never anything but good to us."

Danny and I traded glances. So there it was. Had Grandpa done it himself or just set it up? Frontier justice on the streets of Brooklyn. I recalled Danny's pinched fingers, the sunlight beaming through the tiny gap between them. It seemed the distance was smaller than even he had guessed.

"Listen," Danny said. "I've done everything possible to divide this family; I know that. I came back now because I have something to offer that can bring us back together."

"*We've* been together," my father said, "the three of us that you left behind to go out gallivanting with your cool, dangerous friends. It's *you* that's been gone. Being family doesn't mean you get to come and go as you please, Daniel." He glanced at me, then back at Danny. "No matter how forgiving your brother is about your escapades, Kevin doesn't speak for all of us."

"Bobby, please," Mom said. "Danny knows all this. A lot of the time he was gone, it wasn't his choice. He was hardly out 'gallivanting.' What's done is done. We have to think about the future."

My father turned to me. "You're in on this, of course."

"From the beginning," I said. I had heard Danny mention it. I let that qualify as aiding and abetting. Let my father think me a sucker. "I think it's a great idea. C'mon, Dad. You've missed Brooklyn since the day you left. What is there for you here?"

My father raised his hands. "What's for me there? We left over twenty-five years ago."

"That house is there," Mom said, reaching out for my father's hands. She turned him to her. "My house, Bobby; it could be *our* house. Can't we at least consider the idea? Think about it. The fireplace, the pocket doors, the high ceilings. Those old trees and sidewalks. The park. Bobby, you could find a nice pub like the Sligo for yourself, meet the boys for drinks while I cook us dinner. Think about it." Mom sighed, gazing up at the ceiling. "This place, it's had its time. We raised our boys and it was good for that. But they won't live here when we're gone. There's no history here. Before us and after us there's nothing but blank spaces."

"We'd be together, Pop," Danny said. "Free and easy in the old neighborhood. Kevin could live downstairs in the old office. Teach at King's or wherever. My apartment would be practically around the corner. Ma could just about holler out the window for me. There's a great Irish joint catty-corner to Bavasi's place."

My mother held her hand out to Danny, as if saying *See?* to my father. I thought they might high-five.

My poor dad didn't have a chance. Not against the light burning in his wife's eyes. If she decided she wanted this, he'd give it to her. Like he always did, Dad would complain about us browbeating him into our way of thinking and we'd all play along like we always had. But it was an act. Nothing in this world made my father happier or made him feel more like a man than giving his wife something she truly, deeply wanted. He knew it and *she* knew it.

Dad unleashed a long sigh and stood, grabbing his glass for a top-off though it hardly needed one. He glanced at my mother. She shook him off. She couldn't stop smiling.

"Boys, give your mother and me a few moments alone," Dad said. And so it began, the negotiation of his surrender. Danny and I respected his need to do it in private.

We grabbed our drinks and bolted to the backyard, giggling. We lit up as soon as we got outside. My father about scared us out of our shoes when he threw open the screen door. "No smoking out here. Your mother don't want butts in her flowers. Take it out front."

We did as we were told, stubbing our smokes out on our soles. The line about my mother and her flowers was bullshit, but the old man felt better giving orders.

Out in front of the house, Danny and I lit up and walked to the curb. We chuckled at the rippling curtains across the street. Danny spat on the asphalt and leaned on his new car.

"The old man," he said, running the fingers of his free hand through his hair.

"That's another reason I bought this lame car. I showed up in a Porsche, he'd call the FBI on me."

"Could you really afford a Porsche?"

Danny kicked at the crabgrass under his feet "Doesn't matter. I'm sinking my money into real estate, anyways."

"Go easy on Dad," I said. "Especially after you sandbagged him with the grand Curran homecoming like that. Nice work, that."

Two houses down on our side of the street, an older man in slippers and a bathrobe stepped out onto his porch. He pretended to fiddle with his porch light while staring straight at us.

"You believe this shit?" I said. "We grew up on this block."

Danny pried himself off the car and started walking down the street in Porch Light's direction, calling out to him. "Yo. Hey. Buddy."

For about two seconds, the man stood his ground before dashing back into the house. Through a crack in the door he let his dog outside, a filthy, mop-like beast that pissed on a corner of the stoop and then fell asleep in the driveway with a heavy, world-weary sigh. I heard the dead bolt slam into place and the chain guard rattle from where I stood.

"You call that toilet sponge a dog?" Danny yelled. "That's right. Get back inside and mind your fucking business. It's a free fucking country."

The dog lifted its hairy head and grumbled at Danny, who held up his hand. "My bad, I take it back about the toilet sponge."

When the curtains across the street fluttered again, Danny raised his middle finger high as he walked back to me.

"The neighborhood tomcats probably take turns ass-fuckin' that mutt. That ain't even half a dog," Danny said, standing in the center of the street, his arms open wide. "You know what these people are?" He didn't wait for an answer. "They're fucking old, is what they are. That's all there is for our folks on this block, getting old."

"Dad wasn't kidding when he said he'd kill you," I said. "This Brooklyn thing really raises the stakes."

"What's he gonna do?" Danny said. "Kill me twice?" He lit another cigarette off the first. "Been there, done that."

"We oughta get back inside," I said. "Mom's been waiting three years for this night."

"In a minute." Danny reached into his jacket. "I brought something I need to show you." He handed me a copy of a black-and-white photograph.

Seated on a metal bench set against a tile-covered wall were half a dozen shirtless, barefoot children. Their misshapen heads turned every which way, as if they'd all heard a noise but none of them knew its source. Only one of them, the smallest one, seemed aware of the camera. I looked up from the picture at Danny.

"This afternoon, after you went to teach," he said, "I went over to the college library. Hell of a research section. Quality copy machines. I was impressed."

I looked down at the paper in my hand. It was hard to figure their ages. Most looked four or five, maybe a little older; discerning their sex was impossible. The mongoloid contortions of their smiles hid a lot, but not enough to distract from the rest of their bodies. There was no hiding the timid slump of their shoulders, the long, white fingers of their clawed hands, the stark topography of their ribs, their bare, matchstick legs. The children looked like bags of broken sticks. Except for one. One boy stared right into the camera, his eyes burning with unveiled, unembarrassed hatred. That boy looked like he knew everything bad that had ever happened in the world and had decided the blame landed wherever his gaze did.

His ordinary hands, fingers spread wide, rested in his lap. He had his bony ankles crossed. He alone wore a shirt, a torn T-shirt stained so filthy that he looked like he'd puked up a Rorschach test. Clumps of sweaty, dark hair stuck to his forehead. Just as they had that night in the car three years ago. Like they had for most of his life.

"Control Group Six," I heard Danny say. "The Devil's hand-me-downs. My roommates and me. The ones I left behind."

That fierce-eyed boy in the picture was my brother. A year, maybe two before he became a Curran. It was impossible to deny. In the house my folks had a dozen old pictures where Danny had that same fury in his face. He looked cleaner and healthier, sure, but no less angry. I'd always thought he just hated having his picture taken.

My parents had lied to me, badly.

Danny took the picture by a corner between his forefinger and thumb and plucked it out of my hands.

"How many . . . ?" I stared at my empty hands.

"All of them," Danny said. "Except for me. In that graveyard. Somewhere." He folded the paper in half, closing the picture. He tapped the paper against his thigh, staring at our parents' house. "Still think I'm misremembering things?"

"Jesus Christ." I wiped my sweaty hands on my shirt. I glanced at the house, then back at my brother. The first curl of a grin tugged at one corner of his mouth. "Danny, please, I'm begging you. Don't do this." I held up my hand, pointer and thumb half an inch apart. "Please. Don't do it to her. We're *this* close. I'll take you to Whitestone's office tonight. I'm all in on the brownstone. Anything. Everything."

"Stop," Danny said. He unfolded the paper and held it up. I looked away. "I know you're in with me. I knew it all along. This is not a threat." With his free hand, Danny dug into the pocket of his jeans. "This is just proof. Let Mom and Dad believe, let them remember whatever they want. I don't care anymore. The future's gonna be hard enough for them. As long as *you* know, I can forgive them. It only takes one other person knowing to kill a secret."

He held out his hand, a lighter resting in his palm. "Say you believe and we never have to talk about this again." He tilted his head at the house. "Any of us."

"Danny, I . . ."

My brother tapped his finger on the photo. I looked.

"That puddle there?" he said. "On the floor? That's piss. We go back, that stain is probably still there. They stuck his face in it." He moved his finger to touch one of the adults. "The motherfucker that hurt that kid? I bit his leg so hard I drew blood."

"Danny, what do you want me to say? Jesus, this is gonna give *me* nightmares."

"Say you believe me."

"Of course I do," I said, one hand over my eyes. "Of course. I did when you took me to Bloodroot."

"Look at me when you say it. I need to know your heart is in it. And I'll know if it's not."

Above the paper all I saw was his eyes, the same eyes as the ones in the photo. No shame in them, only an animal fury barely restrained by bitter patience.

"They fed us each others' diseased shit to test their vaccines," Danny said. "Because it saved money on hypodermics. Shooting heroin was a step *up* for me."

"I believe you, Danny! I *believe.* Fucking Christ." I didn't want to hide my eyes again so I covered my ears. "Stop this."

"Funny, I often had the same thought." He wiggled the lighter at me until I took my hands away from my head. "Overpowering feeling, isn't it? Like hysteria, like mad-

397

ness. That *need* to make it all go away."

I grabbed the lighter from him and struck a flame. I held the fire to the bottom edge of the paper. The flame raced in both directions for the corners, acrid chemical smoke rising into my eyes. But I couldn't look away from the photo. It didn't matter. It wasn't like I'd ever forget.

"See the black kid?" Danny said. "Third from the left? Look quick, before he's gone." I found him on the page. Fire crawled up his shins. "See the bandages on his hands? Infected fingers." The flames climbed into his lap. "He wore the tips down to the bone trying to claw his way out of our room. The nurses poured alcohol on his hands. That was their idea of first aid. You wouldn't believe the screams."

The fire consumed the boy's ruined hands and scampered up his chest toward his throat. I looked up at my brother. The flames threw light and shadows across his face, racing for his fingertips. He didn't seem to notice or care.

"It's over now, right?" I asked. "We're at the end of this?"

"In my sleep I still hear that boy," Danny said, "scratching at the walls." He tossed the last of the burning photo into the gutter, spit on it. "The end? It's gonna take a lot more than one little fire. But don't you worry; we're gonna get there."

I heard the front door creak open. "Boys?" My mother. "Everything okay?"

"Outstanding," Danny said. "Sorry to make you wait. Kevin and I had some catching up to do." He smiled at me and raised a finger to his lips. "Shhhhhhhhh."

EIGHTEEN

Danny and I stood outside Whitestone's office door at half past midnight, dressed in the same clothes we'd worn to the Curran family reunion. Having spent half the night watching the history building from the trees, we knew we had almost an hour until any security guards made it back to this floor. Our only worry. Danny had seen no alarms or cameras on Whitestone's floor. Apparently, the history department of Richmond College ranked low on Al Qaeda's hit list. Everywhere else in the building, I was our excuse for being there.

With a gloved hand, Danny slipped a key into Whitestone's lock.

"Where'd you get that?" I asked.

"Remember that laser pointer? Digital technology, baby. It can do anything." Danny turned the key and opened the door. "God bless America."

"That brownstone's an expensive fucking

building," I said. "And you know I got nothing to offer, moneywise."

Danny eased the door shut behind us.
"Except for your fat payday from Santoro."

"Will that be enough?" I asked.

"Maybe," Danny said. "It's not like there's
ever a shortage of work."

"Whoa, whoa . . ." I said.

"Listen, Santoro has his own reasons for
those sex videos to hit the streets," Danny
said. "I don't particularly care what they
are. But when the dirt goes down, I know
he'll give me a line on that place, first dibs."

I bared my teeth in a grimace. "So you
haven't actually brought this up with Santoro."

"Of course not," Danny said. "You think
I'm gonna ask him for a favor without a
couple of solids already in my pocket?"

"Bavasi?"

Danny looked at me, exasperated. He sat
at Whitestone's desk, twirling a silver disc
on his finger. He turned his attention to the
PC. "Trust me."

"What choice do I have?" I said.

He tapped the mouse. The computer
awoke, washing Danny in the bluish light of
the monitor.

"He'll have a password," I said.

Danny scoffed. "So? Passwords were

obsolete ten years ago. They're an illusionary comfort that's sole purpose is to get you trusting the wrong people. Don't be fooled."

"Okay, what should I do?"

"Sit and stop waving that damn flashlight around," Danny said. "We're gonna have jets landing in the quad."

I plopped down into the same chair I'd occupied that afternoon. Danny fed the disc to the computer. He clapped his hands. "All right. This'll take about three minutes." He picked up the desk lamp, turning it over and pressing his finger into the underside of the base. "Audio? Done."

Okay, so he'd put a microphone there. That made sense. "The phone?"

"That mike'll hear both sides of any phone call in this room," Danny said, "plus every conversation. It doesn't listen as much as it *absorbs*. It's complicated."

Too complicated for my simple brain, I guessed, since Danny didn't offer any explanations. Instead he steepled his fingers, fluttering the tips against one another. He hummed some song I knew but couldn't place, bobbing his head. I tapped my flashlight against my knee in time with Danny's head. Right before I asked about the song, the computer ejected Danny's disc. Danny waggled his tongue at me. *"Lick it up/Liiiiiick it up,"* he sang. "Man, their middle period is totally underrated. That's a wrap. Drinks are on me." The head bob returned. *"It ain't a crime to be good to yourself."*

Standing, Danny dropped the disc into his jacket pocket.

"You'll tell me," I said, "if there's anything about me on there?"

In truth, it was Kelsey I wanted to know about. Was she on next semester's schedule? Was her letter of resignation already in Whitestone's files? But I didn't ask. She'd tell me her decision about Chicago when she was ready.

We left the office and Danny locked the door behind us. He held up the key. "Want this?"

"I better not. I might use it."

We headed down the stairs, Danny leading the way, augmenting the red glow of the emergency exit signs with his flashlight.

"So you'll tell me, right?" I asked again. "If those files you copied say anything about me? Anything that might come in handy the next time Whitestone's giving me shit?"

When we hit the bottom of the stairs, we hid the flashlights in my schoolbag and I unlocked the door with my faculty key. Outside, Danny tossed the key to Whitestone's office into a trash can. We headed for the parking lot, having not yet encountered a single security guard.

"I didn't copy any files," Danny said. "I planted a spy program in his computer."

"Don't tell me we have to get in there again. You threw away the key."

"Whitestone's Internet hookup is wireless, right?"

I nodded. The whole campus had gone wireless.

"With that program in there," Danny said, "I can access everything he does, every file he has now or gets or creates in the future. All from my own computer in Brooklyn. I can e-mail his shit, print it, change it if I really wanted. Basically, I made his computer an extension of mine. Think about what schedule you want for next semester."

I waited at the passenger-side door as Danny slipped into the driver's seat. He reached across the car and let me in.

"Goddamn," I said. "I didn't know that kind of shit even existed."

Danny started the car. "Dude, technology-wise, I'm on the same level as Israeli military intelligence. All it takes is cash and a certain morally casual attitude." He turned as he backed us out of the parking space. "You wanna know the best part?"

"Do I?"

"You do, you're like me, you have a deep appreciation for irony."

We headed down Campus Road, passing in and out of the glow of the streetlamps.

"All this fancy computer shit I use?" Danny said. "I order it off the Net. God bless America."

When we hit the Expressway and headed north, I figured Danny was taking me home. That was fine with me; I didn't need him to keep his promise to buy drinks. What I really wanted to do was take a quick shower and call Kelsey. I needed some company; no, if I was going to be honest, I needed *her* company. But then Danny turned the wrong way at the Bay Street exit and I knew I'd have to wait. I protested weakly, telling Danny of my plans.

"Give me another hour," he said. "Maybe less. We gotta talk to Al real quick. He called when we were in the office."

I rolled my shoulders and looked out the window. I hoped Kelsey had told me the truth when she said not to worry about the time.

"So, loverboy, you get a drawer yet?" Danny asked. "C'mon, don't pout. We're having fun."

"A what?"

405

"A drawer in her dresser for your stuff," Danny said. "That's the next logical step."

"I haven't asked and she hasn't offered," I said. "It's weird. We seem to be doing everything backward."

"Doesn't matter," Danny said. "You pass through the drawer stage no matter what direction you come at it from. You gonna give her one?"

I said nothing, keeping my gaze fixed on the passing mix of sagging, tumbledown houses and gated, graffiti-stained store-fronts.

"Has she even been to your place yet?" Danny asked. He sighed. "Of course not. That money's sitting in a shoe box under your bed, isn't it? Spend some, pretty the place up for her. Go out on a limb and buy a bed."

"And who's got a drawer set aside for you?" I asked.

"My line of work prohibits enduring romantic relationships," Danny said. "Trust issues." He slid the car into a parking space about a block and a half from the Cargo Café. "My clothes go from my back to the floor and on again before they wrinkle. No big deal. Couplehood ain't a priority for me right now." He put the car in park and turned to me. "Listen, bro. Your life is different now, live like it. Take advantage. What's the point of all this otherwise?"

"For the record, the money's not in a shoe box," I said, one hand on the door handle. "It's in a loafer in my closet. And couple-hood wasn't on my list, either."

Thankfully, a large, noisy crowd filled the Cargo. I was feeling the need to disappear. The bar was three deep. Under the plate-glass windows along the front of the building, every booth brimmed with patrons sitting jammed shoulder to shoulder or propped up on one folded knee. The tables overflowed with spent napkins, sweaty pitchers of beer, plastic taco baskets, and metal pizza trays. Shirley Manson growled through old boxy speakers suspended in the ceiling corners. The chalkboard above the pool table had a long waiting list.

A waterfront bar with a great view of Manhattan, the Cargo had been my regular haunt when I'd first moved to the neighborhood, not long after I took the job at Richmond. With its proximity to the boat, and thereby Wall Street, the Village, and midtown, its long list of designer drafts and fruit-flavored vodkas, and its early alternative-heavy jukebox, the Cargo hosted a lot of Staten Islanders for whom thirty was a memory but who still saw forty as a curve in the road yet to appear.

The main attraction for me had been the better than average menu; the bar had for months been my kitchen. I'd liked both the food and the chance to float among people my age making something of themselves and their lives. Of course, at the end of the night I took a cab back to my dark apartment while they drove home in Explorers and Pilots back to houses they owned, many of them with husbands or wives. Any survey or census would've called them my peers but I spoke to very few of them.

Talking baseball with the head bartender, a guy who had introduced himself to me as John but who answered to Junior, constituted the limit to my socializing. I could see him behind the bar as Danny and I shuffled out of the way of the entrance.

John wouldn't talk about it but I'd heard stories that he'd mixed it up pretty good with the cops and the Mob over his father's murder and lived to tell about it. And that he'd stolen some hotshot lawyer's girl in the process. I hadn't put much stock in the stories when I heard them. They were too outlandish for a moody but otherwise pretty contented, normal person.

But as I watched John pour out a brace of

martinis into chilled glasses, the stories didn't seem so unbelievable. Not because of any new information or perception I had of him, but because of what I'd done myself recently and still planned to do. I'd slipped without any real effort from a normal life into a criminal enterprise. Slipping back aboveground was going to be difficult, if not impossible. My stomach went cold when a woman seated in front of John asked for a splash more martini in her glass, holding her forefinger and thumb an inch apart.

While Danny scanned the crowd for Al, a redheaded waitress blew by, leaving us awash in a cloud of Secret, fried jalapeños, and burnt cheddar cheese. I couldn't place exactly when and why I'd stopped coming to the Cargo. The staff at least pretended to be friendly. The clientele hadn't deteriorated, nor had the prices gone up. Looking out the front windows at the Manhattan skyline, I realized my balcony did offer almost the same exact view. Maybe that had been the reason. A sad one if that was the case.

As if he'd felt Danny's eyes seeking him out, Al stood and gave a lazy wave from a corner of the bar. Danny nodded toward the courtyard entrance. I followed Danny and Al followed us. The three of us found an empty table in the far corner.

Al looked downright bad, his face pale and clammy, his eyes restless and vague. His hair sprung up in all directions. Instead of cologne, I smelled only alcohol. He'd been drinking pretty hard while he waited for us and he made no effort to disguise it. Danny ordered two Guinness from the frazzled waitress, the same redhead from inside. She hurried away.

"And another goddamn double Crown and Seven," Al yelled after her. "Ya dumb bitch. Can't you fucking count? There's three of us here." He turned to us, his mouth hanging open, his hands raised, as if he expected commiseration over the waitress's shoddy counting skills

I turned away from him, my face burning with embarrassment. I hoped no one working that night recognized me. I sank lower in my seat. Al kept staring at Danny and me, sucking on the ice from his dead cocktail.

Danny sat back in his chair, his hands in the air. "You wanted this meet, Al. What's up?"

Al rolled his eyes and pushed up out of his chair, tottering as he stood. "Didn't realize I was wasting your precious fucking time. Never fucking mind."

"Sit down," Danny said, glaring up at Al and pointing to the empty chair. His words were a quiet, firm command. Danny picked up the candle in the center of the table and lit it with his lighter. Using the candle, he lit a smoke. "You cursed at that poor girl for a drink, sit the fuck down and drink it. You're buying this round, too, and you better fucking come up with a righteous tip."

Grumbling, Al tossed his credit card on the table. "Like I give a fuck." He dropped back into his chair, nearly going over backward into the landscaping. "It ain't fair. It ain't right."

"What ain't?" Danny asked. "You can afford it."

Al shot his arm over the table, pushing his inverted palm at me. "Him. He ain't."

"What'd I do?" I asked.

John brought out our drinks. Not a good sign. The waitress, a skinny slip of a girl, glared at us from the doorway, chewing on her thumbnail. John set the three drinks down one by one. He looked at me. "Kevin, right? Been a while."

I stood to shake his hand. "Right. This here is my brother, Danny, and our friend Al." John nodded at the others but he didn't shake any more hands. "Look," I said, "I'm sorry about the bad manners."

"Don't apologize to that cunt for me," Al said from low in his chair, deep in the shadows. He wiggled his fingers at his credit card. "Put it there."

"I'm out here as a courtesy to you guys," John said, looking back and forth between Danny and me, pointedly excluding Al from the conversation. "Next time this trained ape talks to Maureen like that, she's gonna stab him in the eye with a four-inch switchblade. There's nothing I can do to prevent it. And believe me, when that happens? I'm gonna be way too busy to call nine-one-one." He picked up Al's empty glass. "This round is on me but I'm afraid it's gonna be the last one for you fellas tonight."

Danny leaned forward, folding his hands on the tabletop, his face warm with obvious admiration. "We're grateful for the hospitality." He turned to Al. "You won't have any more trouble from us, I promise. We'll make things right with Maureen."

"Appreciate it," John said. "Nice to meet you, Danny. Don't be a stranger, Kev. Shame about the Mets. We'll get 'em next year."

On his way back into the bar, John said something into Maureen's ear that pleased her. She shot us a self-satisfied grin and walked into the bar.

"Tell me when I became your bitch," Al said, staring into the space that Maureen had just vacated.

"When you started acting like one," Danny said. "What's your fucking problem?"

"I'm losing work and money," Al said. "I been, like, practically laid off. Bavasi said the word came from Santoro himself. They're in love with Mr. Smarty-Pants over here." He threw his hands in the air. "I got bills to pay, man. Debts. What if there is no next job? What if it goes to the professor over here?"

"This is a one-time thing for me," I said. "After this project, I'm out."

"Al, you're overreacting," Danny said. "I know for a fact you got another job. Shit, you're lucky you're still sucking air after that fuck-up with the bodies. And that was after that shit in Atlantic City. Which was after you got whipped by Waters."

"La-dee-fucking-da on the new job," Al whined. He spit on the deck. "I'm fucking babysitting again. Sitting on some creep from the school named Whitestone. He's almost as boring as the professor here."

"I got you that fucking job," Danny said. "And I had to work it hard." Turning away from me, Danny leaned closer to Al. "Whitestone's important work. We can probably turn this whole thing on just him. Kevin and I are working him from the inside."

"It's fucking charity baby work, is what it is," Al said.

"I'm telling you it's important," Danny said. "Whitestone knows Kevin and he's met me. You're the only one that can tail him and not get made. Tell me you've got something on him and that's why you called. We could really use some help."

Al straightened in his chair and hopped it closer to the table. Danny's bringing him back into the mix reinvigorated him. That Danny had gone to bat for him surprised and impressed him.

"He's married," Al said. "The broad's got a face like a hyena but she's got money. Couple of young kids in the house. Two boys. Also the broad's. Never takes 'em anywhere." Al stared into his hands as if they held an open notebook. "Kids go back and forth to school, that's it. Nice house by the water in Great Kills, over by the beach. Decent but nothing too fancy. He drives an old Saab convertible."

It made me queasy, the ease with which Danny manipulated Al's interest and mood. I wondered if someone else would see the same dynamic, someone like Kelsey, maybe, in the way Danny talked to me. I didn't want to know. Besides, I wasn't as dumb or as drunk as Al.

"The kids," I said. "They do anything after school? Play sports or anything?"

Al shook his head. "Don't look like it to me. Couple miserable spoiled bastards from the looks of them."

"Nieces?" I asked. "Nephews?"

"Doubt it," Al said. "I know what you're talking about. I seen him out there at Willowbrook. He doesn't talk to anyone, just wanders around. I don't know whose kids he's interested in out there, but they're not his."

I turned to Danny. His face had gone cold, become a stone mask, his eyes disappearing deep into his face. He wasn't breathing. Al noticed it, too.

"Oh, shit," Al said, half-covering his mouth with his hand, his eyes popping wide. "You don't think . . . oh, fucking gross."

"I knew that guy was wrong," Danny said. "Minute I laid eyes on him."

"No, no, no," I said, leaning closer to Danny. I needed him to focus on me. "It's nothing sick like that. Listen, I got this figured out. It's Kelsey he's out there for. He knows she doesn't want him there so he watches from a couple fields away."

415

"She does look good in them shorts," Al said.

Danny didn't move, but his eyes slid in my direction. A touch of color returned to his face. He exhaled.

"I told you, she plays soccer out at Willowbrook a couple times a week," I said. "Whitestone always seems to be out there the same nights." I hated pleading Whitestone's case, but I had to do it for Danny's sake, to haul him back from where his imagination had taken him. "I was out there with her tonight. She told me all about it. I talked to him myself."

"It's true," Al said. "I saw the three of them out there this evening." He reached for his drink. Danny got it first and poured it out in the bushes beside the table.

"You gotta keep your shit together," Danny said. "This is serious fucking business. We need to know what this guy is really about, as soon as possible. Kev and I got a lot riding on this job."

"Like I give a fuck," Al said. "Maybe I would, though, if I had real cheese coming to me like it was supposed to."

"Do your job. Think of the future," Danny said. "We'll get paid big when that property flips and those dorms go through. Stay on Whitestone. In fact, do me a favor. I gotta

416

get Kevin home. Tell Bavasi we're into Whitestone's computer. We'll know a lot more real soon. Do it tonight. In person, no phones."

"I'm your fucking errand boy, now? You want me to drive over to Brooklyn drunk like this?"

Danny wiped his hands down his face, exasperated by Al's return to petulance. "Fuck you, Al. You've driven out to Atlantic City in worse shape than this. I thought you wanted more work, to make some points with Bavasi. You're so unhappy, fucking quit. Go get a real job. Maybe you're right, maybe we don't need you after all."

Al laughed. "Quit? There's no fucking quitting Santoro's crew." He stood slowly, digging around in his pants pocket. "And A.C. was your idea." He tossed a hundred-dollar bill on the table and picked up his credit card. He chuckled to himself, raising his chin at me. "Quit. Yeah, right. Come to think of it, you need to give Mr. One and Done here a reality check, Dan. With the way he talks about getting out."

He walked away. After Al had disappeared into the bar, I turned to Danny.

"You promised me I could get out after this," I said. "I got things waiting for me on the outside."

"Relax," Danny said. "Don't listen to him. Who you gonna trust? Me or him?"

"He's not gonna fuck this up on us, is he?"

Danny bunched his lips and shook his head, staring through the doorway and into the bar. "No fucking way. I won't allow it."

I took a big swallow of Guinness. "Why do we need Al tailing Whitestone if we're in his computer?"

"We don't," Danny said. "Santoro wants Al kept busy and close to me."

"Why?"

Danny didn't answer. He lit another cigarette off the candle. Watching smoke rush from Danny's nose, I remembered John the bartender telling me that lighting cigarettes with candles brought bad luck. Every time you did it, he said, somewhere out at sea a sailor died.

Borrowing Danny's cell, I called Kelsey as we left the bar. She'd been about to give up on me and go to bed, she told me. Then she told me to come over. She'd be awake and would leave the doors to her building and to her apartment unlocked. She didn't ask where I'd been. I couldn't wait to get to her.

Though we were only blocks from my apartment, Danny cheerily agreed to drive me halfway back across the island. He drove fast, humming to himself as we sped down Victory Boulevard, passing slower cars to the left and right. His recklessness seemed to be for his own entertainment, not haste. If Danny had any worries about Whitestone or Al, they didn't show. He didn't seem concerned about the rest of his night. I didn't ask about his plans.

Like a warm blanket, a great tiredness settled on me. I didn't fight it. More and more Kelsey was the calming solace that awaited me, a place I could disappear into safe and untouchable after these long, bizarre nights with Danny.

Moving from world to world, from school to my folks to Danny to Kelsey, came easier every day. I thought little about what Danny and I did while I was with Kelsey, thought about it less while I went through the motions in the classroom. And yet the different pieces of my life, despite my best efforts to keep them distinct and discreet, had started integrating, like the convergence of historical forces that preceded an event worthy of its own chapter in a history book.

Danny had come back into the family. Kelsey and Danny had met. I thought about the dresser drawer and Danny's disappointment over Kelsey having never seen my apartment. Like my brother had said outside the Cargo, my life was different. And despite the convoluted route I'd taken toward love, liberty, and the pursuit of happiness, my life was steadily improving. What harm, really, had come to any of us? What had I been so afraid of?

For such a long time I had felt and lived so separately from others. Now I wondered if perhaps I had overestimated the distance. Maybe the things I wanted hung from branches that were more within reach than I had ever thought.

"What we did before in the office," I said, Danny again rolling us through a red light, "is really what you do for a living?"

"Most gigs are more complicated," Danny said. "Broader, more intense surveillance. And it's usually dirtier work, more like what you saw at my place. But yeah, that's about it. I spend a lot more time observing than I do acting." He shrugged. "It's a job. It's got its highs and lows, its good and bad points."

With each passing mile I felt I better understood Danny's chosen career. It depressed me but made sense in a sick, sad kind of way.

Despite his still-virile hatred of them, in what I knew was a slow, subconscious metamorphosis, Danny had become a free-roaming version of the Bloodroot doctors in his dreams. He peered through his own private windows into the lives of others, waiting to see what his subjects would do and trying to judge what it could be worth to him. He rejected any responsibility for what he saw by casting himself as a fly on the wall, a silent, multi-eyed thing that only reflected events that he had neither unleashed nor had the power to restrain.

What he watched was stomach-turning ugly in the everyday world, but compared to the depravity, destruction, and death he'd witnessed and even played a part in on the streets, the images on his computer screens probably deserved nothing beyond a bored yawn. Superman and his wife were going to wreck their lives no matter what. Stopping people from shitting all over each other was flat-out impossible. History proved it. Why not gain from what people were going to do anyway? Danny was hardly the first person in history to turn a profit on misery.

As we turned onto Kelsey's street, I waited for a pang of conscience over becoming my brother's accomplice. The ache didn't come. The doctors at Bloodroot had no such pangs, nor did the institutions chasing the final days of people like my mother and Kelsey's mother. Corporations ran those places, not charities. My mother didn't get her medical care or her drugs for free. The sicker she got, the more hands went into my parents' pockets. Danny always had to pony up the cash for his fix, no matter how pathetic his condition. Whitestone certainly didn't care about using tragedy to feed his ego as well as his bank account. Wars cost a fortune and minted rich men by the hundreds.

Human history teemed with kings and queens, with presidents and popes who had watered their coffers with the blood of poor, desperate men. Jesus Christ himself used misery — the outcast, the sick, and the lame — as teaching tools. At least He'd been willing to look misery in the eye and take it up in His hands. At least He'd tried to create something good out of it. What was noble about denying the misery that permeated life? I wasn't about to confuse Danny or Santoro with Jesus, but at least, like Him, they didn't pretend. They didn't gaze down from their balcony like one of history's kings and act as though the sad, loud, terrible lives playing out below them happened in a separate world.

Danny parked the car outside Kelsey's building. "You all right? You don't look so good. Don't worry about Al. I can handle him."

"It's not him," I said.

Danny looked up at the one apartment window with a light still shining. "It'll all be over soon. Don't worry. You should be done. From here, I can handle everything myself. You can get your life back to normal." He smiled. "The battlefield is nearly ours."

I thought about his fine clothes in a heap on his cold floor. I wondered if there was ever a light left on for him. "What're you gonna do?" I asked.

"Same thing I always do when work is over. Go home, eat something, have a glass of wine, see if I can't sleep through the night." Danny grinned. Ghosts played behind his eyes. His nightly companions, reliable as my corner boys. "I like my chances tonight. We gotta take our perks where we can. The dirt we do isn't all there is to life. You gotta pluck what grows from it."

"Deep." I reached for the door handle. "Call me tomorrow."

"Will do," Danny said. "Go see your girl." He bounced his eyebrows up and down his forehead. "And, bro? Don't do anything I wouldn't do."

■ ■ ■ ■

Kelsey sat cross-legged on her couch wearing sweats with holes in the knees and a blue silk camisole edged with black lace. She tossed her magazine on the coffee table and got up to hug me. I set down my bag by the door. She led me over to the couch but I didn't sit. Instead, I walked into the kitchen and got the bottle of Bacardi I'd stashed in her cabinet. She didn't follow. I dumped some ice in a glass, splashed orange juice over it. I brought the bottle into the living room. If helping myself to her kitchen was out of line, Kelsey didn't let on. I thought maybe I should ask for that dresser drawer.

"It went that well," she said, watching me pour as the juice went from bright orange to a pale fog.

"It went fine. Better than fine, actually," I said. "Draining, though." I hadn't brought her a glass. I started to stand.

"I'm good," Kelsey said, patting my knee. I sat back down. "Nothing sucks the life out of you like family, does it?"

"Not if you're my mother," I said. I pulled off my jacket, tossed it on the arm of the couch. "You should've seen her. When we left she looked reborn."

"So it was worth it, then?" Kelsey said. She went to work on the buttons of my shirt.

"Oh, yeah. Without a doubt."

I kicked off my shoes and peeled off my shirt but the disrobing stopped there. Even with Kelsey's participation, there'd been nothing sexual to it. I enjoyed the feeling. She raised her hand to my face. I closed my eyes and let the weight of my head lie in her palm.

"I don't want to pry," she said, "but there's something about your brother that seems to wear you out. And not in the way the job does, or staying out late." I could feel her face move close to mine. "Or the way I do. It's deeper than that."

"He's hard to keep up with," I said. "Always was. Too much of a night owl. I'm out of practice."

I opened my eyes. She hadn't bought the lie. I wanted to turn away but her hand held me in place. It was too late anyway. She'd already seen what I would've been trying to hide, the fact that she was right.

"It makes me worried," Kelsey said. "Not that your brother's a bad person or anything like that, but that maybe he takes a lot from you and doesn't give it back."

"I have you for that," I said. I lifted my head, kissed her, and leaned back into a corner of the couch. "Don't worry, I'm just going through an intense couple of days with this family shit. It'll pass. Nothing lasts forever."

"Seems like a sad thing to count on," Kelsey said.

Funny thing for a woman quite possibly on her way out of town to say, I thought. But I kept that to myself.

Kelsey's impending departure had afforded me the nerve to get involved with her in the first place. Would I stick around if she did? Of course I would. By now it wasn't a question of desire. I'd do back flips if she canceled her plans to go away. No, I wanted her to stay and she knew I did. Now, it was only a question of nerve. Had I enough of it to go after something so dangerous as love on my own, without Danny leading the way? When it came to Kelsey, I was on my own.

She took my drink, sipped it and winced. "Let me splash some more OJ in there for us." She raised my chin with her fingertip. "When was the last time you ate something? I got some olives, some cheese and crackers. Sit tight."

Sinking deeper into the soft couch, listening to Kelsey move around the kitchen, I nearly dozed off. But then something Whitestone had said at the soccer game leaped into my mind and I popped awake. It had hardly registered at the time. Teasing me, he'd said that Kelsey was leaving Staten Island in a matter of weeks.

Why had he said that?

Technically, he was correct. If you wanted, you could count the months between October and the next summer, when her teaching year was done and she would head off to Chicago, as weeks. Hell, you could use days, hours, or minutes if you felt like doing all that math. Maybe he had simply used *weeks* for dramatic effect. And had he really been talking about Staten Island, or had he just meant the college?

My brain painted a gloating smirk on Whitestone's face as he spoke those words over and over behind my eyes. I wanted to believe I just misremembered the moment, even as the memory and the questions it inspired rubbed like sandpaper against my skull. Was Kelsey hiding something?

She came back into the room, drink in one hand, a full plate in the other. The smells of red vinegar and sharp cheddar filled the warm living room. I wished I had fallen asleep.

"I gotta talk to you," I said. "Something important."

Kelsey set the glass and plate on the coffee table. She sat beside me on the couch. "You promised me some time."

"I'm sorry. These days time is something I don't have." I lit a cigarette. "At the game, Whitestone said you were leaving in a matter of weeks. As if you wouldn't be here in the spring."

Dragging hard on my smoke, I waited for her to fill in the blank. She didn't speak and she didn't look away. She tried keeping her eyes light, even cheery, but a hard swallow pulsed down her throat and the rich, warm blood fled her face as if something or maybe many things inside her were trying to run and hide. For both our sakes, I preempted the coming lie.

"You're leaving early," I said. "Were you even going to tell me?"

"It's not what you think," Kelsey said.

"How do you think I'd feel if come December you just up and disappeared on me?"

"I'm not going to disappear," she said. "I'm not your brother. It's true I told Whitestone I'm not teaching in the spring. I'm not. I can't stay at Richmond, it's not nearly enough for me." She smiled. "But Chicago in the winter? Not the best time to move."

"They have winter every year," I said.

"The weather's not what we're talking about."

"Of course not," she said. "The weather's nothing to be afraid of."

"Then what *are* you afraid of?"

Because fear was what we were talking about. Not teaching, not grad school, not long-held or suddenly fluid plans, and certainly not Chicago winters. I remembered what Danny had said about fear. That its true consequences came not through lack of action but in what it made people do. Fear made them run away, for instance. Run away from the future, from the truth. From the people who might hurt or betray them, from the people who might love them and want to be loved back.

I knew it well, Kelsey's fear. I had felt it my whole adult life every time I got somewhere that anything real — my future, my heart, my beliefs — was at stake. And so in my infinite wisdom I'd done the only logical, safe thing. I'd fallen in love with a woman just like me, who ran away from the same things I did. A woman who, as she sat there beside me, knew everything I was thinking because she was thinking the same things. Don't do anything I wouldn't do, Danny had said as I'd left the car. I had a feeling falling in love made that list. I'd decided when confronting my folks about Danny that my time to be brave had arrived. Were these strange days Kelsey's time, too? What would she decide?

Kelsey's hand moved up my arm. Her fingers glided back and forth across my shoulder blades. "I love your shoulders," she said. "You seem like at any moment you might sprout wings, like you can barely hold them inside."

"Maybe one day they'll just bust on out of my skin," I said. "Stick around, it'll be spectacular when it finally happens. They might be big enough for the both of us. You'd be surprised what love can do to people."

Her hand stopped moving. I felt her fingertips press hard against the back of my neck. "Kevin." She licked her lips. "I don't want to leave you. I don't. I want us to be together. I do love you." She looked around the apartment. "But building a nest isn't enough. I need some wings of my own. If you're up for that, then we're good." She turned to me. "Are we good?"

"We were never anything but," I said.

NINETEEN

In the dull predawn glow of Kelsey's kitchen, I washed last night's rum-reeking glass and made enough coffee for us both, her share staying warm in the pot. When she awoke in a couple of hours, I had every intention of delivering her first cup of the day to her bedside. Outside of the office, I couldn't remember the last time I'd made coffee for someone else. That's how alone I'd been. But that's all over now, I thought, as I carried my coffee to the table.

Through the window over Kelsey's kitchen sink I watched the sun spill its first feeble attempts at light through the potted sage and rosemary on the sill and then over the stainless steel and granite of the counter. I sat at the table, both hands wrapped around my mug, waiting for the coffee to cool. I'd already burned my tongue once. The sunlight crept like a pool of blood across the floor toward my bare feet. I'd only slept for a couple of hours.

My eyes fluttered closed then snapped open as I fought nodding off, my head hanging over the mug. My body begged for the bed, reminding me in a whispery voice of the cool, soft sheets and the warm, supple female body that slumbered there. Didn't my body deserve it? Just a few more minutes, it whispered. Kelsey will protect us. My brain, on the other hand, had no interest in going back to sleep and so forced me to deny my body its simple, reasonable desires.

I'd awoken startled, the pillow sweat-damp, my brain fleeing a vivid nightmare of malformed children buried chest deep in the dirt, flies crawling over their eyes and mouths. My brain, no matter what my body said, wasn't taking the slightest risk of going back there. Frightened and depressed is no way to start my first day in love, my heart said, jumping into the argument. Deal with it, my brain answered. Selfish prick, my heart said. Then I passed out.

At the bleating of Kelsey's clock radio alarm, I came to a couple hours later facedown on the table. Wiping the drool off my chin, I heard Kelsey roll over, groan, and hit the snooze button. I got up from the table and poured her coffee, added a dash of half-and-half, the color of a paper bag was how she liked it, and carried the steaming mug to her bed. Mine was cold and I left it at the table.

I sat on the edge of the bed, watching her sleep, watching her breathe. I tried not to think about anything at all as I waited for the minutes in between alarms to tick away. When the bleating began again I fought the urge to smash the clock radio to pieces. Kelsey killed the alarm and fell back on the bed, one arm draped over her eyes. She rolled over onto her stomach, her face still buried in her elbow, and reached across the bed with her other arm, searching for me.

"Goddamn," she said, grabbing a fistful of sheet. I watched the knuckles of her fist turn white.

"I'm right here," I said.

Kelsey pushed up on all fours, looking over her shoulder at me through her wild hair. I used to sleep like that, so deep that waking felt like rising from the bottom of the sea. I'd forgotten what that was like. I handed her the coffee. She scuffled around on the mattress until she sat cross-legged and leaned back against her mound of pillows. Holding the mug in both hands, she slurped and sighed.

"Thanks," she said. Life rose in her eyes

like the sunlight had moved over her kitchen. "You're up early."

"Bad dream," I said. "I've only been awake long enough to make coffee."

She sipped again. "You got it exactly right." She blinked at me, rubbed the last of the cobwebs from one eye with her fist. "Been an awful long time since someone brought me coffee in bed. It was worth waiting for." She wiggled deeper into the pillows. "Hey, let's play hooky today. We'll go into the city or something. A teachers-only field trip."

"Kind of obvious, don't you think? The two of us skipping out on the same day? Whitestone'll go berserk. I want to stay off his radar."

I crawled across the bed and sat on my knees beside her.

"Scaredy-pants," Kelsey said, pouting. She glanced at the clock. "We've still got time to enjoy our coffee."

"Mine needs a warm-up," I said, climbing out of bed. I craved a cigarette. It was the first time since I'd started again that I'd wanted one in the morning. "And I left my cigarettes in the living room. I'll be right back."

When I turned from the couch, lit cigarette between my fingers, Kelsey stood in the doorway brushing her brown hair. She looked so pretty, her eyes fully awake now, her cheeks flushed and puffy from sleep. Her camisole hung crooked, revealing the white skin atop one breast and hiding all of the other. One strap fell off her shoulder. I could see the scrapes on one knee through the hole in her pajamas.

Kelsey Reyes was a beautiful accident. A glimmering angel cast upon a dirty wall by sunlight streaming through a broken window. Standing in that doorway, Kelsey was a perfect moment that couldn't last. I could see that clear as day. None of that convinced me she was a bad idea. Hell, I'd thrown my lot in with Santoro, at least for a while. Compared to him, Kelsey didn't seem like that great a risk. And one with a payout that far eclipsed any number of stacked Ben Franklins.

Looking at her, I felt I could understand what Washington felt when he watched the sun ignite over the Virginia hills, what Jefferson felt when he read that final draft of the Constitution by the dying light of the fireplace. The perfect moment couldn't last. But hope, promise, independence, those things would remain in its place.

"Let me get my coffee," Kelsey said. "And I'll join you."

I held up my hand. "Don't. Just stay right there. Please."

Confusion crossed her face but she didn't move. She held her hairbrush at her side, tapping it against her thigh. She waited almost a full minute before she turned into the bedroom. It was enough. I wouldn't forget.

In the bedroom, the phone rang.

"Let it ring," I said. "They'll call back." I picked up my watch off the coffee table. It was after nine. If we were going to work, we needed to get moving. The phone had stopped ringing.

Kelsey appeared in the bedroom doorway. She held out the phone. "Kevin, it's your brother."

I jumped up off the couch. He'd found something good, something we could use. It was all but over. I took the receiver from Kelsey. We were gonna be free and clear and pretty close to rich. "Top o' the mornin', Dan."

"We gotta move," Danny said. "Now. Today."

"Move? Move what? I gotta go to work today."

"No," Danny said. "Not today you don't."

"C'mon, Danny," I said. "I can't just drop everything. Not today. What're you doing calling here? I said no one calls here. You said we were gonna watch and wait. You said I was done."

"Wait for what?" I heard Kelsey ask. "What's going on?"

"This," Danny said, "is the most important phone call you've ever gotten in your life."

"You know what? You sound high. That's what I think. You need a chauffeur? Is that what this is about? Find someone else this time."

I would've hung up but Danny started laughing, a crazy laugh that stopped my heart.

"Shit," Danny said. "I wish I was high. What's happening now? It's so much worse you wouldn't believe." He breathed heavy into the phone. "But you and me? We're gonna make it right. Believe that."

Kelsey grabbed my arm, her eyes wide with fear and anger. "That black car just slammed to a stop out front. I think someone got out."

I ran past her into the kitchen. Looking out the window I saw Al's Charger idling at an angle in the middle of the street, the driver's door flung open. I didn't see Al but that didn't matter. I knew where he was going.

Danny's tinny voice called to me from the phone. I put it back to my ear, rushing back into the living room.

"What the fuck is Al doing here?"

The front door buzzer sliced through the room. Kelsey yelled my name from the bedroom.

"Get in the car with him," Danny said. "I'll explain everything when you get here. Lives are at stake. Many, many lives. Trust me." He hung up.

The buzzer sounded again. I threw the phone on the couch.

From the bedroom: "Goddamn it, Kevin!" I heard Kelsey slamming drawers, rushing to get dressed.

I hopped around the living room, trying to get my pants on.

Kelsey stormed out of the bedroom, still in her camisole and pj's, a chrome .38 in her right hand. She strode to the door and leaned on the intercom button. "You better run, motherfucker! I'm calling the cops! They're not here in ninety seconds and you are, I'll shoot you myself!" She walked toward me, her free hand extended. "Gimme the phone."

I raised my hands. "Wait."

Kelsey wouldn't; she grabbed the phone off the couch. I caught her arm. The look on her face, I thought she might shoot me.

"You can't call the cops," I said.

"Oh, I'm doing better than that." She tried pulling her arm free. I wouldn't let go. "I'm calling *the* Cop. The one downstairs, Waters. He'll straighten the fucker out." A pause. She stopped fighting me. "Kevin, let go of my arm."

I didn't. The buzzer again. I'd gotten one leg into my pants.

"Go back to the intercom and tell him I'll be right down," I said. "No cops. I'll handle this."

"That's brave, Kevin, but I heard he was a drug dealer or something."

I would kill Danny for this. If he was high, I was done with him. Forever. "It's okay. I know that guy out there." I held out my hand. "Give me the gun."

Shock stole Kelsey's breath away. I waited with my hand out while she mouthed the air like a beached fish. "You *know* him?"

"Not well, we're not friends," I said. "But he's here for me."

The phone rang. Kelsey tossed it on the couch like it burned her hand. Danny. Calling to see why I was still there and not on my way to him. I didn't bother to answer.

"You knew him when he camped outside? When I told you he scared me?"

439

"And what happened after you told me that?" I asked.

Kelsey licked her lips. "He stopped coming around."

"He wasn't stalking his ex, or you," I said. "He was out there watching me."

"That doesn't make me feel *any* better. What the hell is going on?"

"Kelsey, I gotta go," I said. "I'm sorry. My brother's in trouble. He said lives are at stake; I'm afraid one of them is his. I'll explain everything later." I stuck out my hand again. "Can I have the gun? I might need it."

"Kevin, wait a minute —"

I had no idea whether she believed everything or nothing I said. I snatched the gun from her hand.

She stepped back from me, crossing her arms over her chest.

"I'll tell you everything," I said. I dropped the gun in my jacket pocket. "I will. I promise. But I gotta go help Danny first. Whatever happens today doesn't change what I said last night."

"We'll see about that." She straightened and stiffened, but the hardness didn't reach her eyes. "Go. And while you're gone I'll decide whether or not I ever want to see you again."

I stopped at the front door. "I'll be back soon. A couple of hours tops."

"I might not be here," Kelsey said.

I pulled the door open then froze in the hall when Kelsey called out to me.

"Make it worth it, Kevin," she said.

TWENTY

At high noon, outside Danny's apartment, Al unlocked the door and pushed it open. I waited for him to go through ahead of me.

"I'm supposed to wait out here," he said.

I ran up the stairs. Danny's apartment was unlocked. I didn't see him. I closed the door and locked it. I took a few hesitant steps into the room. I was about to call his name when the video stills on the screens of Danny's workstation stopped me short. My head went light at what I saw. It was all I could do not to throw up. I clutched at my stomach with both hands, twisting my flesh in my fingers.

Naked children, frozen on every screen. Some bound, some blindfolded. All suffering, all terrified, all doing things children should never do. Doing things children *would never* do. Except under the fearsome power and command of adults. Doing things to each other, to disembodied parts of faceless adults. Children's bodies writhing under the thick knuckles and pink fingers of adult hands. Large, grotesque hands alive and crawling in places that grown-up hands should never be, not parents' hands, not doctors' hands. I stared like a zombie, a thin beam of fire carving the images into my brain. The screams of the cherubs over Danny's bedroom tore at my ears. I felt struck by lightning into idiocy.

On the screens before me flickered the great evil of our species. Snapshots from the secret world of monsters who walked among us.

Above it all hovered the wild-eyed Saturn, his mouth a tortured howl, his own bloody, ravaged progeny clutched in his fist. Days ago in his eyes I had only seen the blind rage of the insane, but now? Now I saw the agony. Agony born of knowing full well the horror of his actions while at the same time knowing he lacked the strength to stay his own hand. Saturn's eyes told a horror story as old as the human race. A man at the mercy of all the darkness in the world, doomed to the execution of evil. A man who knows not only that evil is real, but that he is its agent.

Why did my brother have these pictures? I

stared up into the image of raging Saturn, too horrified to look anywhere else. Terrified to my core that I might find a young Danny in one of those stills on the screens.

I knew the black cycles of life, at least secondhand. Danny had lived a fine, normal life in our house, but only he knew what had truly happened to him before those days. Had Dr. Calvin been Danny's personal Saturn? Doing so much damage that my mother carried Danny through the doors of Bloodroot a white flower corrupt at the root.

Had even worse things gone on at Bloodroot than Danny had told me?

I walked toward the workstation, holding my hands in front of my eyes and feeling as if I was tightroping the edge of an inferno, both afraid of and unable to imagine doing anything other than destroying it all. Just to make it go away. I remembered our trip to the dump with the bodies, the heat and the fumes as they burned. A fire might not be a bad idea.

"Kevin, I'm sorry," Danny said, stepping out of the bedroom. He stood in the doorway, the seven howling cherubs arcing like a hovering crown above his head. "I'm sorry about making you walk into this but I needed those pictures to hit you hard. It

444

was the only way I thought you could understand."

My brother wore his uniform of a stylish T-shirt under a suit jacket, everything black. In his left hand he clutched his pilot glasses, in his right a leather duffel bag bulging with something heavy.

"Understand what?" I asked. "Danny, what the fuck is this?"

"You had to feel *exactly* what I felt," Danny said.

His face was smooth and calm, as cool and placid as Willowbrook pond used to be on a windless day. No sweaty forehead, no black circles under his eyes, nothing but clear blue skies in them. He did not look the least bit high. He looked nothing like he had sounded on the phone. He looked perfectly sober and sane. He terrified me.

"So you'll understand why I'm doing," Danny said, "what you now know, having seen these pictures, has to be done."

"Danny, turn that shit off," I said. "I can't concentrate with that . . . that sick garbage hanging over my shoulder."

Danny reached into his pocket and took out a tiny remote. He pointed it at the workstation and the screens went black. "Doesn't really make it go away." He walked toward me, tossing the remote on the desk and dropping the bag on the couch. Without thinking, I backed away when he approached me.

"I swear on the graves of everyone I left behind at Bloodroot," Danny said, "that those pictures are not mine. I didn't take them. I didn't buy them. I am not in them. I found those videos, Kevin, on Whitestone's computer."

He shrugged, raising his hands, knowing he didn't have to speak another word for me to know his plans. He was going to kill Whitestone.

"I followed the money he gets for that group," Danny said. "Like we planned." He turned, passing his hand through the air at the workstation like a magician at the conclusion of his greatest trick. "The money led me right to those pictures. Took me all night to work through the maze, one dummy website, one fake bank account after another." He grinned. "I traveled all over Europe in one night. And I feel like it."

"No, Danny," I said. "No, no, no. You can't do this."

"Oh, I can," Danny said. "And I will. There's no one else. No one else could've solved that maze, no one constrained by two continents' worth of silly laws, anyway."

"You've uncovered his secret," I said,

"done the work the law couldn't do. Take it to them now."

"I didn't find Whitestone's big secret, Kevin. It was *delivered* to me. Like a *revelation.* Whitestone is mine."

"Please, Danny. Let someone else take it from here."

"What if Washington had said that," Danny asked, "at Valley Forge? No. In that bag is a booklet of computer discs. The blue one tells how I pulled the pictures from Whitestone's computer and has a map of the money trail. The other *five* contain all the child abuse files on his hard drive at work. Only the one at work." He paused. "His hands, literally, are all over them."

"I understand, Danny," I said. "I do. I get it. But you can't kill this guy, you can't."

"Why not?"

"Why not? Christ, you'll go to jail, for one. What about Mom and Dad?" I saw a flicker in his eyes and I thought I might've had him there. "They'll be crushed. This would put Mom over the edge for sure."

"They've lived with what Grandpa did," he said. "More than that, they'll be proud. Like they are of him, whether they admit it or not." He checked his watch. "Now shut up. There's more you hafta do for me and I'm running out of time."

"Listen, uh, okay, let me take the discs," I said, "to the police, or the FBI or whoever deals with this shit *before* we do anything else."

Danny gave me a disapproving frown. "Kevin, really. Considering our circumstances and who we're involved with, does that make any sense as a first option?"

"You can fix the computers, right? To hide all Santoro's shit? C'mon, I know you can. They don't have to be involved at all."

"I've already destroyed everything on the computers that could hurt Bavasi or Santoro, so forget about them. You have to follow through on the discs. There's enough on there to go after a dozen people in four countries. Think of those kids if you're afraid. If I can't, someone has to protect them."

"Wait. Listen, listen," I said. I thought of Waters. "I got another idea."

"I'm losing my patience," Danny said.

"I take the discs," I said. "Tell the cops, tell Kelsey's cop, just him, that *I* found them in Whitestone's office. I was, uh, early for a meeting and snooping around in his office, you know, and I took the discs because . . . because I thought they had schedules or salaries or whatever and I wanted to hook myself up." I clapped my hands. "Perfect.

I'm a total loser, it's a totally viable story. Yeah. There you go. Whitestone gets punished, Santoro gets his land, we get paid, and everybody wins. Just jump on the computer and get rid of anything that implicates you."

"Kevin, I'm disappointed in you," Danny said. "Everybody wins, except those kids in the pictures. Without my instructions, how will the law find everyone else involved? The feebs, Interpol, they can have the others. But Whitestone is something I have to do myself."

"You can't get revenge for those kids, Danny," I said. "You can't undo what's been done to them. You know this better than anyone."

"How long do you think," Danny said, "it'll take the FBI to get their asses in gear? Nobody in those pictures is riding a camel and holding a rocket launcher. They'll watch Whitestone and the others, track him, waste weeks or maybe months building their case while those kids still get hurt. No. No way. No good. I can't take that chance with all those lives."

"You kill Whitestone," I said, "and you're killing their case, their star witness."

"With those discs, no one needs Whitestone."

"What about Santoro?" I asked. "Shouldn't you talk to Bavasi first, at least? Wouldn't they want to know? With all they have at stake here? Bodies attract cops, missing husbands and fathers attract cops."

I stopped to catch my breath and to think of more questions. Time. I needed more time. To think of a way to get Danny off this plan. I had no sympathy for Whitestone. I could give a shit if he lived or died, but Danny had just started to get his life back. I couldn't let him destroy it and our family over scum like Whitestone. We were so close to free. Danny had already found the keys.

"Think of what they did for Grandpa," Danny said. "Believe it or not, some things are sacred even to them. I tell Bavasi about this, all he'll do is ask me why I haven't killed Whitestone already. I'd be ashamed to show my face to him with Whitestone alive. Shame is something I won't do anymore." Danny stopped talking to light a cigarette. "I got the body covered." He pointed to the couch. "In that bag is also half a million dollars in cash. If you do not hear from me by dawn, then the discs go to the FBI and you take the money home.

"This is where your job gets hard. You have to explain to Mom and Dad why I'm gone again. Tell them anything as long as they believe it. I don't care what you say or what they believe about me." He glanced at his watch. "It's time. Go home and wait for me there."

He slipped his shades on and headed for the door.

I reached into my jacket for the .38. I had trouble getting it out and needed two hands. I held it out in front of me, pointed at Danny. "Wait!"

Danny stopped, looking at me over his shoulder. He slammed the door shut and turned on one heel with a heavy sigh. He took a few steps toward me. I couldn't stop my hands from shaking. Reflected in his glasses I looked small, bent, and terrified. Not at all how I had pictured myself that night in Maxie's driveway. But I held my ground. This time, I would not step off the tracks. Danny reached behind his back and produced a pistol of his own, a shiny, blue-black semiautomatic.

"This can't be how you really wanna do this," Danny said. "It can't. It's not you." He cocked his head to one side. "Wait a minute. Didn't I give you a nine? What the fuck is that?" He smiled. "I guess you got comfortable living with a gun."

"It's Kelsey's. She loaned it to me. I left

mine home." I squinted and shook my head. "What's the difference? You're not going anywhere."

"Can she shoot? She give you lessons? That's pretty sexy." Danny raised his own gun. "She tell you that you can't hit a barn shaking like that? That's what the girl who taught me to shoot said. 'Course, she was talking about my needle and my veins." Danny's finger slid over the trigger. "Now, put that down before you hurt yourself." He smiled under his glasses. "That's what I wish *she* woulda said. Such is life."

"I can't let you do it," I said. "I can't let you wreck the family. Not again."

"For you or for me?" Danny asked.

"Why do you *always* have to do this? Why do you always have to go chasing something? Always have to go where I can't follow?" I cocked the hammer back. "I swear to fucking Christ, I'll shoot. I'll hit something, a shoulder, a leg, something. The bullets'll bring Bavasi running. He'll stop you." I pressured the trigger, getting that feeling again like I was seeing myself from a distance, watching myself do things I couldn't stop doing. "Why, Danny? Why can't you just fucking *come home?*"

Danny's thumb slipped off the safety then pulled back the hammer. "Here's the difference between you and me, between history and a history book. I will pull this trigger. I will shoot you. I will not miss. Junk ain't all I learned to shoot over the years. I will not kill you. You're my brother and I love you and I know you're only trying to help, trying to do what you think is best, like always. It's what I love most about you.

"But, and this is a big but, I will shoot you right through the fucking foot if you don't lower that gun. I've got quite a gun here. You might lose that foot. You've read a thousand books but you don't know the half of what I've done to survive in this world. Shooting my brother in the foot for his own good ain't nothin' to me."

"Danny . . ." The .38 wouldn't stop shaking.

"Kevin, please." Danny turned his gun a hair to the side, to better see me over the barrel. "Don't make me do it. It doesn't have to be this way. We're brothers but you're not like me. You get props for trying, but you failed. Thank God for it."

I lowered my gun. Danny kept his raised. We both exhaled.

"Apologize to Kelsey for me," he said. "I'm sure I upset her. Do everything you can to hang on to that girl." He smiled. "That's just brotherly advice." He lowered the gun and opened the door. He turned to me. "You won't have to wait for me as long as you did last time, I promise. Don't worry about me. Whatever happens, one way or another, justice will be served. That's the American Way."

Danny ran out the door, slamming it closed behind him. I raised the gun and pulled the trigger. Nothing happened. I'd left the safety on. Story of my fucking life.

TWENTY-ONE

I showed up at the history building wearing the remnants of yesterday's work clothes and carrying a leather bag containing 499,800 dollars. Two hundred bucks and two hours. That's what it took to talk a Brooklyn cabdriver into taking me across the Verrazano and halfway across Staten Island to campus.

I'd dropped the gun when I grabbed the bag before bolting down the stairs after Danny. I promptly locked myself out of his apartment, putting out of reach any spare keys to his new car. He had taken off with Al. They and the Charger were gone when I hit the street. I beat on the door of Bavasi's restaurant, kicked at it, screamed his name, but got no answer. When a neighbor threatened to call the cops, I gave up and went looking for a cab, slipping a few hundred into my pocket so no driver would see me reaching into the bag.

The first thing I did on campus was run upstairs to Whitestone's office. His secretary, as I expected, told me there'd been an emergency and the dean had left early. She sneered when I asked who had called and where he'd gone. She asked if I was drunk when I asked for a copy of Kelsey's schedule. I knew she was teaching but had no idea where. Running frantically from room to room through six floors of classes would only draw more attention. I went down to the office to wait for her, precious time ticking away. Her class didn't let out for half an hour.

I sat at my desk, the bag on my lap, both arms draped through the handles and over the top. None of the other teachers so much as looked at me. I just watched the sweep of the second hand of the clock on the wall. After pounding down a cup of coffee, I leaped from my seat. Fuck this.

I found Kelsey on the fourth floor. I dropped the bag and rapped on the open classroom door. Kelsey was not happy to see me but she came right to the door. Her students hunched over their desks, eavesdropping so intently their ears seemed to stretch away from their heads. Kelsey stepped into the hall.

"I'll call you when I want to see you," she

said. "If I want to see you."

"I need your help," I said.

"I covered for you with Whitestone," Kelsey said. "He was none too pleased with you, as usual. You need to get up there and kiss some ass. Don't make him come looking for you. He hates that."

"Whitestone's gone," I said. "You seen my brother on campus today? Or that black car?"

"What?" Kelsey said. She closed the classroom door. "You look like death. You're sweating like crazy. Take off your sunglasses. Let me see your eyes."

"Just meet me outside," I said. "Fuck it." I held out my hand. "Can I borrow your car?"

"No way." Kelsey turned and watched her class through the window in the classroom door. She chewed the inside of her cheek.

I rubbed my bare wrist; I'd left my watch on Kelsey's coffee table. "I'm in a huge hurry. Please."

I didn't know what I'd do if she refused to help. I hadn't thought of a Plan B. I didn't know what to offer, what I had to bargain with to convince her to help me. Kelsey stared at her students. I'd have to bring her into things. Maybe I could at least control how deep.

"Danny's in trouble," I said. "He's out there somewhere about to do something that'll ruin him forever. I'm trying to catch up and he's got a big head start."

Kelsey put her hand on my chest, covering my heart. "If Danny's getting high, there's nothing you can do about it. Junkies, they have their own rules. If he's got you into it —"

"It's not drugs," I said. "It's worse. Believe it. Kelsey, please. I know where he's going. I know what he's gonna do. For once, I can stop him. Kelsey, he's my *brother.*"

Maybe she believed me, maybe she thought of her mom and the chance she never got to save her. Or maybe I was so pathetic she couldn't resist. Whatever her motivations, she spoke. Finally.

"Give me two minutes to get rid of these guys," she said. "Meet me at the car."

Gravel sprayed everywhere as Kelsey pulled a fishtailing U-turn in the parking lot. Then she slammed on the brakes.

"That Saab," she said, pointing across the lot. "That's Whitestone's car." She looked at me. "I thought you said he was gone for the day. Why do you know that?"

"I'll explain on the way," I said. "Take us to Willowbrook Park. Main entrance."

Kelsey leaned on the gas and we hurtled out of the lot into traffic. She darted past three cars on the campus road and launched us through oncoming traffic at the intersection, tires screeching. I grabbed onto the dashboard for dear life.

"What?" Kelsey said. "You said we were in a hurry."

"Jesus, we're no good to him in the back of an ambulance."

"Don't worry about that," Kelsey said. "Light me a cigarette and talk."

I did as I was told, and lit one for myself. I tossed the pack on the dash, where it slid back and forth, threatening to bounce out the window as Kelsey bobbed and weaved through traffic. I flashed on the pack of Kools that had done the same dance in Danny's Escort three years ago. I should never have left him alone that night. Never again.

"The bag in the back," I said. "There's a whole lot of money in it and some DVDs. Take the bag home after you drop me off and keep it safe until you hear from me."

"You robbed someone. A bank? One of Danny's old dealers?" She pounded her hand on the steering wheel. "I am such an asshole. I gave you my fucking gun. You motherfucker." Kelsey hit the brakes and swerved onto the shoulder.

"No, no. Keep driving," I protested. "It's Danny's money. No one is after us, I promise. It's the DVDs that matter."

"Kevin!" Kelsey shouted. She gunned the engine and threw us back out into traffic.

"If you don't hear from me," I said, "the DVDs go to the FBI." I swallowed hard. I lit another smoke off the first. "It's child porn. Danny pulled it off Whitestone's computer. Promise me you won't look at it."

"Wait, what? *Child porn?*" Kelsey started crying. "All I wanted was to see what you were like in real life, maybe in bed, before I moved to cold-ass Chicago where all I could do was wonder. I never woulda come up with this. Christ Almighty."

"Turn right up there," I said. "That's the park entrance, right around the corner."

We slammed to a stop in the parking lot and tumbled out of the car. Kelsey grabbed the bag from the backseat and tossed it in the trunk. She pulled her cell phone from her pocket. I raced around the car and squeezed it shut in her hand.

"Ow, Kevin, that hurt."

"What're you doing?"

"I'm calling the fucking cops," she said.

"Like I shoulda done this morning. This is nuts."

"No. No cops."

"Why not?" Kelsey asked. "You said you guys didn't do anything illegal."

"I said we didn't rob anyone."

She flipped the phone open. I lunged for it but she was too quick. She held the phone high above her head. But she wasn't dialing.

"Danny's got Whitestone at Bloodroot," I said. "As a hostage."

I thought about making another move for the cell. The look on Kelsey's face told me I'd be trading in my testicles for that phone. I didn't want to fight her for it. I wasn't sure I could win.

"He's gonna kill him," I said. "Over those DVDs."

"Kill him?" She blinked at me like I'd just told her I was from Jupiter. "Your brother's gonna kill Dean Whitestone? Over child porn? This is so fucked up."

"I can stop it," I said. "I don't need the cops. You and me can go back to your place later, get drunk, roll around, and forget this ever happened, that we were ever here."

Kelsey snorted. "Fat chance."

"Take the bag back home. I'll be there soon."

"It'll be safe in the trunk for now," Kelsey said. "I'll hide it in the house when we get home."

I backed away from her. "You're not coming with me. Stop fucking arguing with me. Someone's gonna get killed."

"It ain't gonna be you." Kelsey strode forward, shaking the phone at me like a weapon. "Either I go with you or I call nine-one-one. Those are your only options."

Jesus, this woman was as stubborn as my brother. I wished Danny would've just shot me at the apartment. If he were here, I thought, what would he do? Cut a deal, I heard him say. Give something to get your way.

"Okay," I said. "How's this? Give me half an hour then call that cop from your building. Tell him Al Bruno's up to his old tricks. Tell him whatever you want, just get him out here alone." I backed up a few more steps. "Deal?"

"Fifteen minutes."

I couldn't get to Bloodroot and back in fifteen. It didn't matter what time we picked. She was going to give me three minutes, maybe five once I took off.

"You wait here for Waters," I said. "You'll have to lead him in. If you hang a right at the last backstop, there's a trail. You gotta look for it. It looks like it dead-ends in the woods but if you keep going, you'll come out into the graveyard. You can see Bloodroot from there."

"What if Danny's not there?" Kelsey asked. "Then what?"

No chance. I knew in my heart he was there. "Then we go home," I said, "and wait for him to find us."

I booked it across the fields, jumping and shoving my way through parents leading their kids to their cars. I broke through one all-American family after another, separating husbands and wives, brothers and sisters, the groups re-congealing behind me as I ran. For a second I worried about one of them calling the cops, but I knew none of them would be willing to put off dinner and TV long enough to wait around for the police.

The late afternoon sky was overcast, weakening the daylight, but I had enough to find the trail and duck into the woods. Even if Kelsey had already called, by the time Waters got to the park the sun would be dipping into the tops of the trees, filling the woods with shadows. The darkness would make them cautious, slow them down. That was all I needed. Just a little more time than she was willing to give me.

I fought my way through the woods as fast as I could, sliding all over on the dead leaves. Thorns and dead branches scratched at my shirt and skin, a few drawing blood. I tried pretending I was twelve years old again and chasing my brother along this very trail, or through the snows of our long-ago camping trip. We'd been the hunters then, too. And we'd arrived too late to stop the blood from spilling.

My brain worked overtime on the past but my body betrayed me in the present. I tripped over a tree root and, stumbling off the trail and into the brush, rolled my ankle. Limping back onto the trail, I tried forcing my brain to defer the pain and file the accident away for future reference, but the future proved to be about six steps away. My chest heaved, granules of glass burning my lungs at every breath. Why had I started smoking again? When had this trail gotten so fucking long?

Finally, I spilled head over heels out of the woods and into the graveyard just like I had the last time I'd met Danny there, knocking the last of the breath from my lungs. My heart beat into the earth like it wanted to break free and burrow away and hide. Was this how it would go down? Me on my face gasping like an old man with heart failure, my brother only three hundred feet and a few flights of stairs away, shooting his life to hell?

Prone in the grass, I gathered what new air I could. I struggled to my feet and climbed over the wall. Hobbling now, I jogged across the graveyard and up the hill to Bloodroot. Heavy clouds, outlined in fire, moved over the sun. The eerie, marigold glow of a false sunset settled over the field. Shadows oozed down the walls of the asylum like spilled ink. I had no flashlight to guide me through the building. I started running again, wincing in pain every time my ankle hit the ground. If things did go to hell, it wouldn't be because I gave up.

I ducked under the boards over the front door and wandered into the lobby, calling my brother's name. No surprise, he didn't answer. I limped across the tile. The Vandals and Goths had been at it again. The place reeked of burnt things, the odor rank enough to make my eyes water and to make me wish for one of Al's cologne-soaked bandannas. I covered my mouth and nose with my hand. It didn't help much. My hand stank of old cigarettes.

I started up the stairs, leaning on the greasy railing with my free hand, keeping what weight I could off my leg.

Walking the halls, peering into the labs and shouting Danny's name, I found nothing. Frustrated, I tried to be grateful that I hadn't tripped over Whitestone's dead body. I stopped on the landing of the third floor, leaning on the wall to give my ankle a break. Moldy paint flaked off the walls everywhere I touched. I tried to catch my breath but all I did was choke. The higher I climbed through the building the worse the burning smell became. Acidic and sweet, it burned like chemical steam. Alcohol. Formaldehyde. Heroin simmering in a black spoon.

I rubbed the heels of my hands into my eyes. If I was going to find Danny, I had to stop thinking like me and start thinking like him. Danny had cracked wise about justice before running out of the apartment. That's what had brought me to Bloodroot.

In Danny's brain, this hell house was the only logical place to bring a man he'd caught victimizing children. My brother could say what he wanted about protecting those kids, but he always took something for himself. He wouldn't miss the chance to strike down some of his own phantoms, even if it had to be by proxy. Once he was here, then, what was the next step? I'd already come up empty in the labs. The room where that picture had been taken? The one he showed me at our folks' house? I had no idea where that was. I could've been through it already. No. Not there. His old room. Where he'd first heard that terrible scratching that still haunted his nights.

I began my long trek up the stairs, the awful fumes settling like fog over my throat and into my stomach.

As I neared the top floor, I wondered if what I was inhaling was getting to my head. I heard strange scratchings, bumpings, and chirpings in the walls all around me, above me in the ceiling. I ignored the noises, trying not to think about what made them. When I made the top floor, I didn't even bother calling for my brother. He was either in that room or he wasn't. And if that room was empty, I was out of ideas.

Nearing the end of the hall, I heard something else over the sounds in the walls, sounds that told me I'd picked the right place to look. A grown man was softly crying, fighting for breath and words as sobs broke apart his voice. Another voice, unintelligible, spoke in stern, definite tones. Whitestone and Danny, with Al standing silent watch.

Outside Danny's old room, I stopped, pinned myself against the wall. Should I announce myself so that Al didn't shoot me on sight? I licked my lips but my brother's name died in my throat. I couldn't imagine what I was about to see. How would I not see it again every time I closed my eyes? I turned the corner.

The room was empty.

Impossible.

I turned circles in place, balancing on my good leg. There was no place to hide, no closets, no anterooms. The room was too small, the sunlight still strong enough to reveal the corners. I hadn't hallucinated those voices. I had followed them here. I still heard them. Something low on the wall caught my eye, a wet and glistening stain.

I staggered over and crouched, reaching out before I could think to stop myself. My fingertips came away dark red and sticky. Tiny shreds of flesh stuck in the blood. Whitestone's one chance at salvation had been clawing his way out of the room. I'd made the right choice. I'd just arrived too late. With nowhere else to do it, I wiped the remains of Whitestone's fingers on my pants. From where, then, came the voices? I looked up. From above me. They came from the roof. I was hearing them through the window.

The window was barred. There was no

way up from inside the room. Nothing outside in the hall. I headed back to the stairs. At the landing, set back in the shadows was a steel staircase. It led up to a single black door.

At the top step, I tried the handle. Unlocked. Still the door wouldn't budge. I leaned into it and the door gave but didn't open. Stuck or blocked. I pushed harder and it gave some more, a few inches. A slice of dim sunlight fell through the crack onto my legs. I put my back to the door and shoved, my bum ankle screaming at me. The door opened just enough for me to squeeze out onto the roof.

I fell over something heavy, whatever it was Danny had used to block the door, landing hard on my hands and knees. I righted myself, brushing my hands on my shirt, and turned to look at what had tripped me. My breath died in my chest. I'd tripped over Al's dead body, lying facedown at my feet. I stood in the pool of blood seeping from his ruined head. I stumbled out of the puddle, staggering dangerously close to the edge of the roof. I looked over at my brother.

Whitestone, alive, lay crumpled in a fetal position at Danny's feet. Danny's gun hung at the end of his limp arm, an afterthought, as if its necessity had passed. He stared at me from behind his sunglasses. "Wow."

"Let him go," I said. "Leave him here and come with me."

"Eventually," Danny said. "But not yet. I'm not done."

I walked toward him. He watched me, his head tilted to the side, raising the gun to his shoulder, barrel pointed at the fiery ginger sky.

"Careful, careful," he said. "What'd our old Spanish teacher used to say? *Cuidado, Señor.*"

"You shoot me up here," I said, "and you either gotta carry me down all those stairs or throw me off the roof."

At the sound of my voice, Whitestone dropped his bleeding hands from his eyes. The fingertips looked chewed by rats. He turned his head toward me, searching for me by sound like a blind man, both eyes swollen nearly shut. Danny had beaten the shit out of him.

"Kevin?" Whitestone croaked. "Kevin, is that *you?* Oh, thank God."

Danny kicked him. "Shut the fuck up." For the first time that day, he sounded angry.

"Police. You brought police."

I stared at Whitestone, bile rising in my

throat. I was disgusted to even hear him speak, to have anything remind me he was human, that he was even the same species as me.

"Well, answer the man," Danny said. "I kinda need to know myself anyway."

"No," I said. Technically, it wasn't a lie. "No, I didn't bring the police. I'm not here to save *you,* Whitestone. I could give a fuck about you." I stepped closer to my brother. "Danny, leave it here. For chrissakes, stop and think. Look at what this is doing to you. Look at what you did to Al."

With a heavy sigh, Danny glanced over at Al, looking at him like he couldn't remember how the dead man got there. "Yeah, Al. I feel bad about that."

"Jesus, Danny. Why?"

"I talked to Bavasi last night after I dropped you at Kelsey's. He'd called Al off you and Kelsey before we ever got a chance to talk about it. So I got to thinking. Who else lives in Kelsey's building?"

"Waters," I said. "The cop."

Danny tapped the barrel of his gun to his temple. "Indeed. It would make sense." He shrugged, gazing sadly at Al, as if the dead man was a favorite toy broken beyond repair. "Al knew he was running out of chances with Santoro. He probably thought

Waters could save his life."

"You know this for sure?" I asked. "We've known Al half our lives. I thought you owed him."

"I did ask about Waters," Danny said, "before, well, you know. Al's an awful fucking liar, especially when he's nervous." He kicked at Whitestone, who pawed at Danny's shoes.

"They weren't mine," Whitestone said.

"So you killed him?" I said.

"Listen to me," Danny said. "I'm sure he didn't think it'd be today or that I'd be the one to do it, but Al chose his fate years ago. Al was lucky to last as long as he did. Considering his track record, he lasted longer than he should have. It's all in how you look at it."

"They're not mine," Whitestone screeched. "They're for a project."

Danny kicked him again. Whitestone puked blood and bile onto the rooftop.

"Would you give it up with that shit?" Danny said. He spat on Whitestone's back. "That's his excuse. That the pictures were research for some child abuse project. Weak, very weak."

The idea, that it might be true, perched in my brain. I wished Whitestone had never said it. "Danny, maybe he's telling the truth."

"Oh, believe me, I checked and I double-checked. All fucking night looking at that shit." He whacked Whitestone on the back of the head with the gun. "Could be why I'm so crabby today. You know what I did find in those pictures?" Danny waved me over with the gun. Blood dripped from it. "C'mere, Kevin. We can't have any more problems with your fucking conscience."

I walked over. Whitestone had started twitching, his bludgeoned nervous system shorting out. He stank like piss and shit. Shooting him might be an act of mercy.

Danny reached down and snatched up one of Whitestone's hands, badly twisting the dean's arm. "This. This is what I found," Danny yelled, waving the hand at me. "Look!"

I took Whitestone's limp, slippery right hand in my own. On the back of it was a sloppy ring of old, rubbery cigarette burns. I'd seen those scars before. So had Danny. Not just in Whitestone's office, but in those awful pictures on Danny's computer screens. I dropped Whitestone's hand, disgusted.

"They're all over him, his back, his chest," Danny said. "His other hand. Like a fucking disease. Who was it? Momma? Dad? Grandma? How're your two boys? You mark them up yet?" Crouching over Whitestone, Danny screamed, "Take it like a fucking man! That's what you always said to the boys, wasn't it, Doctor?"

Danny stepped back, rolling and spreading his shoulders, dragging the back of his hand across his mouth, not seeming to care that blood and whatever else Whitestone was leaking slicked it to the wrist. He licked his lips. Clumps of black hair fell over Danny's forehead, dripping sweat onto the lenses of his sunglasses, tripling, quadrupling the twisted images of Whitestone. He reared back and kicked Whitestone again. He raised the gun, pointed it at Whitestone's skull. "On your feet, Doctor."

Whitestone rolled around on the roof, trying to either get up or just irritate Danny into shooting him.

This was beyond me. Where the fuck was Kelsey with the cops? God, was I a fool. I'd handed a woman I hardly knew half a million dollars and *told* her to take it home. Yeah, you go ahead, I'll wait here for the cops. See ya never, sucker. Who in their right mind wouldn't disappear with that money? I just couldn't stop fucking up. I was on my own.

Like puffs of smoke, clusters of bats tumbled from the building into the evening air. Looking away from Danny and Whitestone, I realized I didn't just *smell* something burning, I felt it, waves of heat rising from the sides of the building. "Oh, shit."

"Yes indeed," Danny said, smiling, nodding. "The whole fucking shithouse is going up in flames." He took off his glasses and sailed them off the roof, spinning into the air, punching a hole in the swirling cloud of bats. Confused by the smoke and the over-abundance of sunlight, the bats cycled like a tornado over our heads, their numbers growing by the moment. Doctor. Danny kept calling him *Doctor.*

"It's not him," I said. "Danny? That's not Calvin. No matter what he's done, no matter how bad you want him to be, he's not Calvin. The family already took care of him, remember?"

"Same monster," Danny said. "Different skin."

The air around us rippled with heat. The soles of my shoes got warm.

"You feel that, Doctor?" Danny said. "You feel it?"

Whitestone whimpered. "Dear God . . . dear God . . ."

Danny raised his gun high over his head,

brought it down swift and hard into Whitestone's face. I wouldn't have thought so but there were bones left to break. I heard them crack.

Danny screamed, "God? God's gonna save you? You stupid motherfucker. Who do you think fucking *sent* me? All my life I've been coming for you." He grabbed the back of Whitestone's shirt. "Get your ass up. We finish this, I finish this now."

Whitestone, his lizard brain transmitting that obedience might still save him, staggered to his feet. Smoke pirouetted in tendrils through cracks in the roof.

"Holy shit, Danny. We gotta go. Leave him, let him burn."

"That's more like it, Kevin." Danny turned his blue eyes on mine. With one hand, he held Whitestone on his feet. "We are the choices we make under duress, big brother. Yours is always to run away, ever notice that? Don't feel bad. George Washington created this nation on strategic retreats." He smiled at me. "You taught me that. You go ahead and get out of here. I'll be right behind you."

The burning air rising through the building below us punched more holes, bigger holes, in the roof. Twisting arms of bats and smoke soared into the air. The tar under my feet was melting. Swatting at the bats, I stumbled backward, falling on my ass as the roof burst open inches from my feet, a gaping hole now yawning open between my brother and me. Rising up on my elbows, I saw Danny couldn't reach me. The gulf between us was too wide to cross. He was trapped on his half of the roof; he had no way down. My only option was to run, to save myself. I didn't move. I couldn't leave him.

Danny looked at me. A helplessness washed over his face that I had never witnessed, not even when we were kids, a surrender that maybe nobody, not even his dealers, had ever seen. All the arrogance, all the defiance, all the wit had died. Knowledge was all that remained. None of us would make it off that roof alive and Danny was utterly heartbroken I had to be part of it. It was not what he had planned.

After everything he'd put me through, not just over the past few days but all our lives, Danny had finally drawn a line and tried to protect me from the things he did. He'd called me to Brooklyn that morning not only for the money and the discs, but also to get me out of the way while he went after Whitestone. He had warned me not to follow him, even pulling a gun on me to keep me away. But I hadn't listened. After all the things I'd let him talk me into, I'd finally told him no. That choice had trapped us on the roof of a burning asylum.

I forgave Danny his part in where we'd arrived; it was his nature, in his blood. He'd never had much choice in what he did while I'd always had choices and had spent most of my adult life refusing to make them. I hoped he could forgive me my part in our end. And finally, I told myself, when the roof caved in we would do something together that could never be undone. I nodded to him, hoping the message got through. Danny nodded back, his sad eyes wide open, his mouth a thin, grim line.

One fist still full of Whitestone's shirt, Danny propped the pulpy sack of a man on the ledge. Only the bloody bubbles rupturing at his nostrils showed Whitestone was alive.

"And you?" Danny said. "You will do what none of the others ever did." He released Whitestone's shirt and grabbed his face, holding the man aloft by his jaw. "You will look me in the eyes when the shot comes."

Danny pushed Whitestone back against the ledge. Elbow high, he pressed the barrel of the gun between Whitestone's eyes and pulled the trigger. The shot was deafening.

Whitestone's whole head exploded. His body dropped to the roof. Danny blinked for a moment at his empty hand. He tossed aside the gun and with both hands wiped at the mask of wet, crimson gore on his face. "Damn."

He rubbed his hands on his jacket. His face streaked with blood, he took a step toward me then stopped at the edge of the smoking chasm between us. "Go, Kevin. Run. You might make it."

"Danny, no —"

"Don't worry about me, I've been dead before," Danny said to me. "It's not so bad. And it's not as far away as you think."

He turned and with a short running start leaped from the roof.

His black jacket blowing open, arms flung wide, he hovered a moment, a black angel in the burning sky. Then the tumult of bats yawned open and swallowed him. Danny vanished as if he had transformed into one of their anonymous multitude and shot off into the night on brand-new wings. I never saw him fall.

I lay down on my back, exhausted beyond belief, disoriented and nauseous from the smoke and fumes, sinking like a dinosaur into the softening tar. The flames were only moments away. God only knew what was burning down there, what I had breathed into my lungs and into my blood. It didn't matter. Danny would come get me, let me chase him to the other side. We would run forever, never grow old, never run out of trail, never run out of time.

I heard someone screaming my name. Kelsey. No, no, no. Hadn't enough of us died up here in hell already? Just take the money, sweetheart. Enjoy Chicago. Stay warm. Study hard. Leave me here. My brother's coming. I can wait.

I turned my head, tar pulling my hair, to see her arm and the top of her pretty head squeezing through the door. She wasn't going away. Why didn't she listen? Wasn't I talking?

I watched her search for me, stumbling, crying out, her hands reaching in front of her. Flames like fingers stretching under a door groped around the rooftop. Whose hands would reach me first? Kelsey really wasn't that far away now, was she? I rolled over on my hands and knees and crawled toward her. I might have called out Kelsey's name, because she found me. Danny was right; I couldn't resist a strategic escape.

I felt her arms slip through my armpits. She lifted, chanting in my ear as she heaved. "Getupgetupgetupgetup."

I tried. I folded my legs under me and pushed. With her help I found my feet. She dragged me toward the door. "Where's Danny?" she asked.

"He's gone," I said.

Kelsey led us in a controlled fall down the stairs. The air seared our lungs with every breath we tried not to take. Between the second and first floors we collided with someone, someone large. He grabbed us by the back of the neck and shoved us ahead of him with the power of a wave. Water, filthy, putrid water rained on us from above.

He pushed us, hacking and puking, sliding on the wet tile, through the lobby and out the front door. Then he was gone. On the steps, more arms wrapped us in blankets and carried us far away from the burning building. The arms set us down in the cool grass like swaddled babies.

I shook off the blankets, fought off the arms and stood. I collapsed in the grass, flat on my back. Helicopters pounded the air over our heads, their spotlights sweeping huge patches of white light over the burning building. Sirens flashed red, white, and blue. Shouting men in heavy boots ran past me, crackling voices shouting back at them over their radios. Kelsey had indeed brought the cavalry. She sat next to me, her knees drawn to her temples, puking into the grass at her feet.

I stood again. I wobbled some but stayed upright this time. Someone handed me a water bottle. I chugged it down then threw it up all over my shirt. Damn. An EMT put her hand on my shoulder, a plastic oxygen mask waited in her other hand. I cocked my fist and she backed up. Not yet. No one, nothing could be in my way. Danny wasn't here. I had to see it for both of us.

The roof fell first, smashing and roaring its way through floor after floor, the flaming wreckage gathering weight as it descended. An explosion of embers and black smoke burst into the night sky. The walls tumbled almost straight down, not unlike Whitestone had. Maybe like Calvin had when his time had come. Almost as fast as Whitestone, the building had collapsed into a dead, faceless heap. Flames lit the sky as firefighters circled from a distance, spraying huge arcs of water onto what was left of Bloodroot. They didn't seem to be trying very hard. I couldn't blame them. Let it burn. Eventually, when it had consumed everything within reach, the fire would burn itself out. That part I didn't need to see.

I sat back down in the grass and wept for

my brother.

Kelsey poured cool water over my head, running her fingers through my hair and whispering my name. Her voice sounded like a song. Like a song Danny used to sing when we were kids.

Twenty-Two

While I was in the hospital, the first couple of times I tried to tell my folks the truth about Danny, my mother did the same thing. She smiled, told me not to talk, and folded my hands over my stomach. My father said nothing, looking at anything else in the room but me, like he was the one with bad news. At first, I got impossibly angry with them. How could they put Danny out of their minds so quickly? So easily and completely? Practice, I figured. Then, slowly, another explanation for my parents' casual attitude about their missing son dawned on me. Maybe they knew something I didn't. But whenever I tried asking them about this, my mom would just comment on how kind it was of Detective Waters to be visiting *again.*

Once, I thought I awoke to see Bavasi at my bedside, a dark, wide-shouldered figure behind him in the doorway to my room. But

I couldn't be sure; I was loaded with Demerol at the time.

Someone had put serious work into getting the mostly brick, concrete, and tile Bloodroot building to burn like that. The FDNY found traces of a high-grade accelerant in the wreckage. Someone would need "serious connections" to get their hands on enough of that kind of chemical. There was no way anyone could carry enough in one trip. Al might've had help. Might've just taken his time. Along with the accelerant, two sets of remains had been discovered on site. Al Bruno and Dr. Whitestone.

It was what the FBI found on Whitestone's computer, everyone surmised, that had put him and Al on that roof. In addition to a history of violent crime arrests, Al Bruno also had six young nieces and nephews. No one had to think too hard to figure out what business they had gone there to settle. As far as the law was concerned, justice had been served.

It was Waters who kept us posted on all the developments in the weeks after the fire. That was all we called it: The Fire. Right after, he'd asked some questions of me, my folks, Kelsey, and the feds. He never got decent answers from any of us. He didn't seem surprised. It didn't surprise him when the feds took things out of his hands, either, in the process giving him a world of grief for letting his new informant run wild, committing kidnapping, murder, and quite possibly arson and suicide, all without giving up one good word about any kind of crime. Since the feds had everything figured out, Waters did not feel compelled to tell them Kelsey and I had been there. We didn't tell them, either.

The feds did get one thing right, though, even if it was decades too late. Bloodroot was finally declared a crime scene.

When, a few weeks later, Santoro and Sons Construction came to clear the site and prep it for the new dorms they planned to build, nobody got in their way.

The feds' computer guru eventually linked the mapping DVD to another computer with a Brooklyn Internet account, but when they got to the Park Slope apartment they found it stripped bare. Nothing but walls, floor, windows, ceiling, and a weird sculpture of seven baby angels that gave everyone the creeps. The landlord, Gino Bavasi, told the feds they'd gotten their signals crossed. No one had rented that place in over a year. One couldn't let just anybody move in, Bavasi said. Park Slope was a nice neighborhood. You could never be too careful.

Christmas Eve, stretched out on Kelsey's couch, "our" couch now, I answered a phone call from Brooklyn. I pressed the mouthpiece to my chest as I lit a cigarette.

"You're not smoking, are you?" Dad asked.

I held the cigarette at arm's length, watching the paper burn and the smoke spiral toward the ceiling. I had permanent scarring on my lungs from the fire, or so the doctors told me, but I'd developed a mistrust of doctors. I'd quit one day, to make my mother happy, but for the time being I was hooked and didn't feel like fighting it. I tapped the ashes into the spider plant on the coffee table.

"No. I told you, I quit."

"Don't let your mother find out. You coming tomorrow?"

"Yup."

"Good boy. See you tomorrow. Leave early, the Verrazano's gonna be jammed. Hang on, your mother wants to talk to you."

"Kevin, are you smoking?" Mom asked.

I sighed into the phone.

"Put Kelsey on," Mom said. "She'll tell me the truth."

Kelsey sat cross-legged in an armchair beside the Christmas tree, engrossed in a history book. Prep work for her first semester of doctoral work at NYU.

"She's busy," I said.

Mom stayed quiet for a long time, a condensed version of the silent treatment for lying to her. "Have we told you," she finally said, "about our trip to Vegas for New Year's?" She had. Twice. "We've got a special, special friend out there. Your father and I can't wait to see him."

"Ma, you don't have to talk like that," I said. "No one is spying on us."

"Oh, I know," Mom said, giggling like a schoolgirl. "It's kind of fun, though. And it annoys the hell out of your father." She cleared her throat, took a deep breath. I knew what was coming, the same offer she'd made twice before. And I knew what my answer would be. "You could come with us, Kevin," my mother said. "You and Kelsey. Our friend would be thrilled to see you."

"We already have plans," I said. "I promised Kelsey we'd go to Times Square for New Year's. I'm not going to disappoint her. I'm sure your friend understands."

"You're right," Mom said, "you should keep your promise. If you change your mind, let us know."

"Thanks, Ma. I love you. See you tomorrow."

"I love you, too, son." She hung up.

I set the phone on the coffee table and stubbed out my smoke in the ashtray. I reached down and scratched Maxie's ears. While I was in the process of moving, old Mrs. Hanson had died in her sleep. She was found when Maxie's incessant howling drove a pissed-off neighbor to call the cops. It took six officers from Animal Control to subdue him and get him away from her body. A blind dog that old had no chance in the city system. He needed a family to take care of him. I claimed him before they got him in the cage. I wasn't ready to give up on him yet. With someone looking out for him, there was no telling how long that old dog could last.

When Maxie dozed off, I reached for one of the Christmas cards Kelsey had on display. My favorite. It had come addressed to Colonel G. Washington. I'd waited a week to open it, hiding it in my sock drawer under the blank postcard from Vegas. I was afraid of what the Christmas card might say, afraid of what it might offer, but Kelsey's gentle encouragement that we would face whatever happened together finally gave me the necessary courage to read it.

On the front of the card, against an emerald background, two angels hovered above a Christmas tree, each with one hand on the golden star. The inside was blank, white as snow. Except for one sentence, written in black ink. Its author's handwriting hadn't improved since the eighth grade. I knew it well.

Not for Christmas, it said, *but soon, I hope. God Bless America.*

I closed the card and closed my eyes, warm and comfortable on the couch, drifting toward sleep. He was waiting this time. Waiting for my invitation, for my permission, and for my forgiveness. We both knew it was the least he could do. And we both knew I'd eventually give him everything he asked of me, as I always did. Not for Christmas, but soon. I couldn't see it any other way, and I didn't want to, either.

Brothers have to stick together. It's the only way the world makes any sense.

AUTHOR'S NOTE

While the Bloodroot Children's Hospital is a fictional place, its creation was partially inspired by the awful history of the Willowbrook State School on Staten Island, an institution for the mentally and physically disabled that was closed not long after the media revealed the terrible abuse and neglect of its residents. As mentioned in the novel, the exposure of Willowbrook inspired a chain reaction that led to momentous change in the care of the disabled throughout the country.

Writing this novel had a profound effect on me. In response, I am lending my support to children's aid organizations such as the Matheny Center in New Jersey (www.matheny.org) and the Roots of Music organization in New Orleans (www.theroots ofmusic.com). I encourage you to make an effort, no matter how small, on behalf of the children in your neighborhood. A little

kindness and respect goes a long way.
Danny will be proud of you.

ACKNOWLEDGMENTS

Gratitude and love to the Four Families: Lambeth, Loehfelm, McDonald, and Murphy. Love especially to my bighearted brothers: Stephen, John, and Michael McDonald, and Kevin and Kory Loehfelm.

Thank you, Jarret Lofsted, Joe Longo, Jackson Moss, and everyone at nolafugees .com, for always speaking the truth. Thank you, Joseph and Amanda Boyden, for consultation, straight talk, and love. Thanks to the owners and staff of the Rue de la Course and CC's coffeehouses, the Garden District Book Shop, and the Wild Lotus Yoga Studio. Love to Vince Booth and the rest of the Ibervillains rock 'n' roll band. Deep affection and gratitude to the UNO Creative Writing Workshop, where so many great stories begin, and to the Krewe of Parkview, where so many great stories are told.

Thanks also to Barney and the Krewe of Karpfinger, for efforts above and beyond the call of duty; to my stellar editor, Chris Pepe, for keen-eyed stewardship, inspiring conversation, and infinite patience; to Erin, Ivan, Stephanie, Summer, and everyone else at Putnam and Penguin Group (USA) for their faith and enthusiasm.

Merci beaucoup to the Tragically Hip, a great band whose powerful, inspiring music helped me write this book.

Thanks also to Syracuse University, for preserving the stunning, heartbreaking photography of Burton Blatt and for their online resources, and to Kevin Walsh and forgotten-ny.com.

All of my love to my magnificent wife, AC Lambeth. The true compass of my heart and soul, you always light my way.

ABOUT THE AUTHOR

Bill Loehfelm was born in Brooklyn and grew up on Staten Island. In 1997 he moved to New Orleans. He is the winner of an Amazon Breakthrough Novel Award, and his work has appeared in the anthologies *Year Zero, Life in the Wake,* and *Soul Is Bulletproof.* Loehfelm lives in New Orleans's Garden District with his wife, the writer AC Lambeth.

Visit the author's website at:
www.billloehfelm.com